DEATH OF A CHANCE

SHARON ROWSE

THREE CEDARS PRESS

DEATH OF A CHANCE
A Barbara O'Grady Mystery
By Sharon Rowse

Copyright © 2021 by Sharon Rowse

Book cover designed by Sharon Rowse and Three Cedars Press
Cover Photo © Sharon Rowse
Published by Three Cedars Press
www.threecedarspress.com

ISBN: 978-1-988037-4-55

ALSO BY SHARON ROWSE

The Barbara O'Grady Series: (in order)

Death of a Secret

Death of a Threat

Death of a Promise

Death of a Shadow

Death of a Lie

Death of a Dream

Death of a Chance

The John Granville & Emily Turner Historical Mystery Series: (in order)

The Silk Train Murder

The Lost Mine Murders

The Missing Heir Murders

The Terminal City Murders

The Cannery Row Murders

The Hidden City Murders

The Dockside Murders

Want to be the first to know when Sharon's next book is coming out? Sign up for her mailing list at: www.sharonrowse.com

CHAPTER ONE

On an unusually gloomy Monday morning in mid-October, I was staring out my office window, watching the clouds roll in across the harbor. The weather had turned early this year. Big dark thunderheads were forming over the ocean, and the light was flat. We were due for quite a storm. I'd smelled it in the wind when I went for a run that morning, and now I could see it building in the west.

I still wasn't used to being able to look out instead of up from my office window. In my former office, my view had been the rooftop of a permanently grimy parkade across the alley, and the sky above it. But when my assistant Marie Deslauriers and my former art school nemesis Justine Grayson got together while I was out of the country—and busy getting Justine's firm out of trouble—they'd expanded the office premises and moved my office from the adjoining suite to this one.

It was an expansion Marie had been pushing for, which, despite the benefits, I couldn't afford. Until Justine decided that with the amount of money my team's efforts had saved her firm, we deserved a bonus. Together, she and Marie delivered a surprise office expansion, designed by Justine—an internationally acclaimed designer. Her notion of a 'bonus' also included fifteen years of pre-paid rent.

I ended up with a larger, edgier office space for Barbara O'Grady Investigations. Plus a corner office that faced north and west, in a building that was on the edge of what was becoming a trendy district as the city morphed and changed around us. And with what I saved on rent, I could afford to hire the staff I needed to grow.

That was nearly a month ago, and things are just beginning to fall into a new normal. I've even started to get used to my fancy new offices. Maybe.

I still missed the feeling of working in an old-style PI office in what had once been a rundown part of town, furnished with what-ever I could afford at the time. Even if it had been tired and dated from the day I set it up, it was mine. I'd earned every inch of it, the hard way.

I drank some coffee, the dark richness of it reminding me that I didn't hate all the changes. I loved the new, top-of-the-line espresso machine—Justine again. And my streamlined, curving desk with the dark eggplant top was now a firm favorite. I reached out and stroked the top of it, wondering yet again what exactly it was made of. It was ridiculously tactile, whatever it was, and something about it deeply pleased the artist in me.

I drank a little more coffee and had just opened my computer when Marie stuck her head around the door. "Barbara? You got a minute?"

I looked at the emails I had yet to deal with. "Not really. What's up?"

"We have a new client," she said.

Her smug look told me she considered this one a real coup. Which meant trouble. "What client?" I demanded.

But Marie had already vanished, leaving me staring at the door. This wasn't the first time she'd pulled this kind of stunt.

Marie DesLauriers, my former assistant, had taken on the role of my office manager. Also known as 'the one who makes everything work'. And she was scarily capable in that role. Much to my surprise and occasional horror.

Marie's version of how my business and my office should function is very different from mine. And she's proved really good at finding creative ways to advance her vision while I'm focused on a big case. With a lot of assistance from her new mentor—none other than Justine. A relationship that made no sense at all.

Making it a typical Marie move.

In her latest transformation, Marie has abandoned the smoothly elegant short blond cap of hair that Justine had talked her into, and gone back to the spiky red hair she'd worn when I met her. It was nice to see her looking like herself again. But somehow she made that cut look elegant, too, which the Marie I'd first met could never have pulled off. Or wanted to.

I found that unsettling. Marie was changing fast as she experimented with who she wanted to become. And she was bound and determined that her job—and my company—were going to change right along with her.

That didn't bode well for my peace of mind. And the battles I could see coming were going to be epic.

I'd deal with those when they happened. For now, I needed to deal with a new client.

Who shouldn't be a client at all.

I'd never given Marie the authority to sign client contracts. Especially not big ones. No matter how much she'd proven herself capable of managing the office, I didn't trust her sometimes oddly off-center judgement when it came to new clients. Or her unexpectedly soft heart for a sob story.

Unfortunately, that hadn't stopped Marie committing us to new clients in the past. And it sounded like she was at it again.

I was still muttering to myself when the door opened again, and Marie ushered in an attractive, very well-dressed woman with a face easily recognizable to anyone in the art world. "Barbara O'Grady, I'd like to introduce Annegret Carli."

"I've heard good things," Ms. Carli said, striding forward and holding out a manicured hand. "I'm very pleased you had time to take us on."

The 'us' in question would be Annegret Carli Fine Arts, the very well-known Swiss gallery she'd grown from nothing to one of the best galleries in the world. From what I knew of the gallery's history, Ms. Carli would be perhaps a dozen and a half years older than me, though she certainly didn't look it. Both her sharply edged hairstyle and her business suit were cutting edge design, making a strong statement. Yet she carried the look with confident ease.

Justine would have been impressed, I thought sourly. In fact, they probably knew each other.

"The pleasure is mine, Ms. Carli," I said, shaking hands.

"Please, that is so formal. Call me Annegret."

"Barbara," I said, waving her to the two eye catching burnt orange bucket chairs surrounded by sweeping potted palms on the far side of my office.

"How can I help you?" I asked as I sat down at a slight angle to her, and considered her with interest. Since she was, apparently, my newest client.

Though I might have to find a creative way to break that contract. I'd done it before. Marie was getting pretty good at nego-tiating—except for the pitfalls she tended to miss. But I was better, luckily for all of us.

It all depended how this interview with my potential client went.

Everything about Annegret was professional, and expensive, if I was any judge. And I was rapidly becoming a decent judge of clothing styles, as my firm had begun to attract clients that were more high end than I'd ever dreamed of.

I still wasn't sure how I felt about that. Or what I wanted my firm to become.

Stubbornly, I'd been refusing to part with my 'boots, well-cut jacket and denims' approach to my working outfit. Though both Justine and Marie had been lecturing me about the need for my 'image' to fit my expanding business.

I already had an image I was comfortable with, thanks.

Though Marie had been giving me the once over lately in a way that had me worried. Once seemingly wedded to her neon-bright bicycle gear, my former assistant had bloomed under the mentorship of Justine into a seeming hothouse plant with a cutting edge style and an artistic edge that made everything she wore uniquely hers.

My artistic eye might appreciate what she was growing into. My knowledge of Marie's tactics made me fear for my denims. But there were limits, and those were mine.

Annegret was considering me as carefully as I was her. "Before we actually signed a contract, I wanted to meet with you. In person," she said.

So Marie hadn't actually finalized the contract with Carli Fine Arts. Good to know. I was even more skeptical about taking on this potential client now she was sitting across from me. Why had someone like Annegret Carli come all this way to seek out my much smaller firm? What was she looking for?

Unless Justine had recommended my firm? That was possible, but it didn't do anything to recommend this client to me.

I hadn't missed the harshly controlled edge in Annegret's beautifully modulated voice, either. At a guess, she was hiding something. Which wasn't unusual for people seeking out a private investigator, unfortunately, but it set off my spidey sense.

If a client is going to be a problem, I like to know right up front. My firm may be bigger and fancier than when I first started out, but I still seem to attract mostly impossible clients. With impossible cases.

At least there's good money in it now.

"Why was meeting me in person so important?" I asked her.

Annegret's dark eyes gleamed with a sudden hint of humor. I relaxed a little. Maybe this one wasn't going to be completely impossible.

"Aside from the fact that we are a large client, and it is your agency?" she asked.

"I get the feeling there's a little more to it," I said bluntly.

She nodded. "Yes. You're right. There is."

She leaned forward, met my eyes. "I wanted to meet with you because before we get into this shit storm," she said, her polished accent at odds with her blunt language. "I wanted to know exactly who I would be dealing with. I needed a sense of who you are, outside of the news stories."

Which was not what I'd expected? "Why?" I asked, equally bluntly.

"It has recently come to my attention that my firm is rumored to be dealing in multi-million dollar forgeries," she said.

And she sat back, still watching me.

CHAPTER TWO

I stared at Annegret Carli, momentarily at a loss for words.

Forgeries? It was the last thing I'd expected to hear. Annegret Carli Fine Arts's reputation was impeccable, with never a whisper of fraudulent dealings. Of any kind.

"You're kidding."

"No."

"How did you hear about these rumors?" I asked her.

"A friend—someone in the industry—told me she'd heard something that I needed to look into. But she wouldn't tell me where she'd heard it, or even how widespread the rumors were," Annegret said. "She's a very good friend, so I didn't ignore it."

She paused, twisting hands sporting long, beautifully manicured nails together on her lap. "She was right about the rumors."

"Who is spreading them?" I asked. "Do you know?"

She shook her head. "No," she said. "Whoever it is, we haven't been able to track them down. Not without causing even more rumors. And exposing ourselves further."

That had an ominous sound. And there was something in her voice… "What aren't you saying?"

"I'm afraid the rumors are true," she said. "At least partially."

I hadn't expected that one. "Annegret Carli Fine Arts is dealing in forgeries?"

"Yes, in several of our recent transactions. Or at least, that's what our internal investigations are indicating."

"What kind of forgeries?" I asked.

"Paintings," she said bluntly.

I considered the implications. There are reported to be a surprising number of forged paintings floating through the global fine art networks. Including some in a number of very well-regarded collections and museums. So this wasn't as surprising as it might have been.

But if this was true, Annegret's description of her problem might have been an understatement.

"What did you find out?" I asked her, keeping my tone neutral with an effort.

"At least some of our works apparently don't stand up to advanced technical testing," she said. "But our investigations aren't complete. We've been hampered by our need to keep this as quiet as possible. You understand."

I did. A gallery like Annegret Carli Fine Arts relied on its reputation for trustworthiness and confidentiality for most of its sales. Especially when modern testing methods seemed to be uncovering more fraudulent works by the month, around the globe.

"How many forgeries did you find?" I asked.

"Three out of the seventy recent transactions we've reviewed are forgeries," she said, her jaw muscles tightening as she spoke.

Roughly four percent, then? That could be manageable, depending on the artists involved. "Are these forgeries the work—or purported work—of any particular artist?" I asked.

"No. But all three are old masters. Which the rumors I've heard point to as well. These are lesser works, but still. As you probably know, even those works command high six or seven figures. And up."

Ouch. This case just got even more difficult. With that kind of fame and money at stake? When this was discovered, it would be front page news around the globe.

Annegret Carli Fine Arts had to get out ahead of the story. They had to be the ones to break it, too. Or they were finished.

And with all that at stake, they'd turned to my small firm? When there were so many big, well-connected investigation firms that would have jumped at the opportunity? Why?

"What about the source of these frauds?" I asked.

"The three we've found came from three different sources—a dealer, a collector and another gallery," she said. "We haven't been able to find any common link. Or the point at which each forgery could have been done. But we're hampered by the need to keep this investigation quiet."

As I made a note, she added, "So far, the provenance looks good. On all three of them."

I winced. Provenance was the documented history of each work —the records of sales ownership, starting with the original sale by the artist—that was intended to prove authenticity.

If the provenance had been faked well enough that Annegret's gallery had missed it? There might be no limits to this case. Depending, of course, on how widespread the forgeries were in her firm.

In the worst case scenario? The damages—and the hit to their reputation—would be insurmountable. Even the best case scenario would need careful handling for them to get through this, given that there were already rumors floating around.

Despite their history and solid reputation, even a gallery as strong as Annegret Carli Fine Arts might not survive.

And Annegret knew it as well as I did.

"How did your gallery end up with this many forgeries all at once?" I asked her.

"That is a very good question," she said, her eyes bleak. "We don't know."

"Do you—or does the gallery—have any enemies that would be capable of setting you up like this?"

If this was a setup, and not bad management within the gallery, that is. But this was not the time to ask that question. It was one angle we'd investigate. If we took the case. Which I was still reluctant to do.

"We have competitors," Annegret said. "And sometimes the competition can get intense enough that people are willing to shade the law. But this?"

She shook her head. "I don't believe it."

"My opinion? Someone is out to destroy you."

"I know." Her voice was heavy, and despite her expertly applied makeup, she suddenly looked beyond exhausted.

"Whoever that is knows enough of what's going on behind the scenes at Annegret Carli Fine Arts to start the rumors," I said.

Her lips tightened, but she didn't say anything. In her shoes, I'm not sure what I would have said, either.

"How loyal are your staff?"

"Before—all this, I would have said I trusted each and every one of them without question. Now? I just don't know."

"Someone must have been passing on confidential information."

"Probably," she said. "But I can't authorize an internal investigation without tipping that person off. If they even exist. Such a move risks starting even more rumors. And possibly forcing whoever is behind this to move even more quickly. We can't afford that."

She took a deep breath, met my eyes. "Which is why I came to you," she said.

Well, at least I had my answer. But while a forgery case in a high end art gallery seemed pretty white-collar, I'd run into armed gangs the last time my team and I tangled with forgers. And that one had started out as a local case.

I wouldn't be taking on this case lightly.

"Why my firm? Why not contact Interpol?" I asked her. "International art forgery is their specialty."

She nodded. "And you're the one that broke a case that perplexed them for a dozen years."

I couldn't argue, since it was true. And explaining that it had been more accidental than deliberate wouldn't help.

She didn't wait for my response, in any case.

"Besides, when it comes to high end fine art, everyone knows everyone. A hint dropped at a cocktail party here, a slip of the tongue at a liquid lunch there…" She gave a slight shrug, as if to say 'what can you do?'

I didn't believe that hint of helplessness for a second. So far, every move I'd seen her make was calculated for effect. And just like that I was back to wondering why she really wanted to hire us.

"It's nearly impossible to keep anything quiet," she added. "And if my firm is to have any hope of surviving this disaster, we need to keep the whole matter as quiet as possible. Until it's sorted out."

That part was true, at least.

"Let me get this straight. You think we can sort it out for you?"

"Yes." She nodded, gave me a worried look. "Will you take the case?"

Good question. I hadn't been expecting another forgery case when I came in this morning. But given the reputation my firm has begun to develop, perhaps I should have been.

I fought back an inappropriate desire to laugh at the direction my day had taken, and focused on the matter at hand. What was her real agenda?

Annegret didn't wait for my response.

"All work will be at your usual fees, of course," she said, leaning forward. "Including expenses. And we will pay a bonus of fifty percent of your bill if you successfully solve this case."

She was trying to buy me. She must be desperate. Which explained the careful manipulation she'd been doing.

But I found I couldn't turn this case down. It had nothing to do with the money. And everything to do with her desperation, and the complexity of the case.

My team were up to the challenge. And she needed help. Annegret Carli Fine Arts was a good operation. She didn't deserve this.

Probably didn't deserve this, my pragmatic side whispered in my ear.

But Annegret had just made it impossible for me to turn down this case. Which, judging by her relieved expression, she knew. Well, two could play at that game.

I nodded. "Yes, I'll take your case," I said, and held up a hand to stop her next words. "If you tell me exactly what's going on. Starting at the beginning, and leaving nothing out."

I gave her a hard look. "And I do mean nothing. Especially if it's embarrassing. If you try to whitewash anything, or forget a few details? Trust me. I will know."

Her lips tightened just a bit, but she nodded and held out her hand. We shook. And to her credit, she started in on her story, including even the smallest detail.

And she didn't leave anything out.

Nothing apparent, anyway.

But my spidey sense was still tingling when she finished.

I made a last note, looked up and met her eyes. "What else aren't you telling me?"

———

AFTER ANNEGRET LEFT, I spent some time reviewing and fleshing out the brief notes I'd taken, coffee in hand. Nothing like a good cup of dark organic coffee to get the old brain cells firing.

Annegret had sworn up and down that she hadn't held anything back.

I didn't believe her.

Yes, I'm that cynical. You don't spend as much time as I have in this business and keep believing that even the most desperate of clients tells you everything. In fact, in my experience, the desperate ones are the worst. Probably because they really do have something to hide.

Hence the desperation.

I'm fairly sure Annegret gave me all the facts of the case. The ones she knew, anyway. Even on review, her story seemed consistent.

Didn't mean I believed everything she'd said. Or that she hadn't left something out.

Like the fact she was afraid of something. It was just a feeling at first, but one that had got stronger the longer I talked with her. And I couldn't get a sense of exactly what she was afraid of.

I signed the contract anyway. She needed help, probably even more than she was willing to admit to herself.

And I wanted to know what was really going on here. And who was spreading those ugly rumors. Whoever it was, I intended to stop them.

I spent some time pondering the revised version of my notes. Then I duplicated the file. In that second file I added my impressions of Annegret and what she'd told me. As well as my initial reactions to the case and the beginnings of a theory or two.

I played this game with every case. Oh, I'd always created a file based on my intuitive reactions. But now I had a team, I created the detailed first file, based strictly on facts and observations. That one was for sharing with the team.

Then I added the intuitive leaps to the second file, which no-one saw but me.

It wasn't that I didn't trust my team with my intuitive leaps. Quite the opposite, in fact. I preferred to leave them free to form their own first impressions from the data. Make their own leaps. Which would likely be radically different from mine. And from each other's.

That's what made working together so interesting.

I sent copies of the first file to everyone, asked them to do some initial digging, and join me in the meeting room in fifteen minutes. Then I strolled out to the front office to get another coffee and have a brief word with Amber Mellis, the receptionist I'd recently hired on a recommendation from Marie and my nephew, Cory.

Amber was a key part of the team, and so I made sure she was more fully briefed on our current cases than was the norm in our business. I also paid her better than was usual. The way I saw it, if she didn't know what the team was working on, how was she supposed to effectively handle clients and potential clients? Let alone direct or re-direct calls, texts and emails.

Between them, Amber and Marie now ran the office like a well-oiled machine. And they never seemed to discuss it, either. I had no idea how that worked—I just knew I wasn't asking. Some things I was better off not knowing.

CHAPTER THREE

With the rich odor of freshly brewed coffee recharging me, I joined Marie in the meeting room. Despite the cloudy day, the meeting room was bright. Large windows on one end helped, as well as giving a feeling of space. Pot lights overhead kept the light even, and directed where we needed it.

The end walls were covered with whiteboards, and wipe off markers in a variety of colors were set ready for use. Marie teases me that this office runs on whiteboards. She's not far wrong.

Marie was sitting near one end of the long meeting table, looking out the window. She had a tablet in front of her and a cup of coffee steaming gently beside it. I automatically took the seat at the head of the table, facing one of the whiteboards.

I smiled a greeting as Badger joined us, her laptop in one hand, coffee in the other. A computer genius—and former hacker—Badger has proven herself invaluable to my small team. I'm still not sure why she agreed to join us full-time, but I'm not about to ask.

Badger actually does have more than one name, as I'd discovered when I officially hired her. But since she'd threatened to leave immediately if I so much as breathed that name to anyone—and I'd believed her, making it a very effective threat indeed—I promptly erased that name from my memory banks. And continued to think of her only as Badger.

Anything else seemed superfluous, anyway. Plus it diminished the risk of losing her.

Cory wouldn't be joining us—he was still in high school, and he didn't have a spare period that day, or I'd have re-scheduled the meeting. But I knew my nephew—he'd be digging deep into the case tonight. He'd eat dinner at his computer if my sister, Susanna, would let him. Probably annoying her even further.

Cory was nearly as obsessed on solving cases as I was, and Susanna, for some reason, blamed me for that, too. My nephew's version of finding solutions couldn't have been more different than mine, though. Not only did he look at things from a completely different angle, he could make a computer sing. When it came to digging out information, he left both Marie and me in the dust.

Just another reason Badger was invaluable. She was Cory's mentor, a former white hat hacker—or maybe grey. I'd never dared ask exactly where she drew her boundaries, but she was careful to respect mine, especially when it came to Cory.

And I knew the value of that.

Badger and Cory together were an unstoppable force. And I credited her influence in his determination to build his own career as a good guy hacker.

My sister should be thanking me, not criticizing me at every turn. But she'd never see it that way. I blamed Godfrey, her husband, for that. Probably quite unfairly. But it was less painful than admitting that the old tension between Susanna and I had just found a new outlet.

"So was I right, or was I right?" Marie demanded as Badger pulled out the chair beside her. "I knew you couldn't resist Annegret. Or her case."

I rolled my eyes at Marie's exuberant glee that I'd actually signed the contract. Behind Marie's back, Badger shot me a wry grin and rolled her own eyes.

She and Marie couldn't have been more different—I still couldn't figure out how they managed to work together. I'd been half-afraid Badger would refuse to join any team that included Marie. But the very non-social computer genius had condescended to work full-time with all of us—on the condition Cory remained part of the team.

A condition I still suspected he'd put her up to.

I wasn't entirely sure why Badger had gone along with it, though the three of them mostly seemed to enjoy working together —and with me—to a degree I'd never anticipated. Some days it made me nervous, it worked so well. It especially made me nervous because, based on what I'd seen so far, I suspected this team worked best in crisis mode.

It was clear I needed to keep a supply of really challenging cases coming in, or I'd be dealing with either anarchy or mutiny. Or maybe the mother of all staff feuds.

I hid the cold shiver that ran down my spine at the thought of what that might look like—especially given Badger's skills and unknown morals—and prepared to brief them on the case that was probably going to devolve into our latest crisis.

Badger surprised me. "Can you start by giving us your perspective on the kind of art fraud Annegret Carli Fine Arts are accused of?"

Which wasn't like her. Badger's usual approach is to do a mountain of research, digging deep into databases and other online sources that I'm amazed even exist. And some of them don't. Or not officially, anyway. Since none of that data will ever see a courtroom, I don't ask too many questions.

Until she's done that digging, she usually doesn't say much. Or ask questions. But in the fifteen minutes since I'd called this meeting, she hadn't had time for that kind of research.

"Why do you want my perspective?" I asked, curious to hear her thinking.

I should have known better. Badger is even worse at explaining than I am. And that's saying something.

She gave me a smile that was no more than a quirk of the lips. "Humor me," she said.

Okay, then.

"Art fraud, at least when it comes to the old master paintings—which is the kind of fraud Annegret Carli Fine Arts has apparently run into—is generally about oil paintings that have been created to look like the work of some of the most celebrated artists in history. Renoir. Vermeer. Raphael. Van Gogh. Monet. The list goes on."

"Why them?" Badger asked.

"Mostly because of the money those works command in today's market," I said. "Their better-known works are worth multiple millions."

"So forgers just create copies of the best works and sell them to anyone who will pay?" Badger again.

Marie and I exchanged glances. She rolled her eyes. I wasn't sure exactly how much Marie knew about this particular corner of the art world, but it had to be more than what Badger was professing to know.

Though neither of us believed her.

Badger would have done at least the basic research. Probably in less than five minutes. And she'd already have answers to the questions she was asking me.

I'd have been irritated by the waste of time, except I knew Badger well enough to know she'd never waste her own time like that. She had a reason. And it would be more than making sure we all had the same information at the start of a complex case. I just couldn't see what she was up to. Yet.

"Not exactly," I said. "Anyone willing to spend that kind of money would have the expertise available to verify a painting for sale. If someone tried to sell the Mona Lisa, for instance, the buyer would immediately be in touch with the Louvre, who have owned it for centuries.

If it was a lesser painting, or being sold by the known owner, they'd run other tests. The technology has evolved to the point that forensic analysts can date the age of the paint or the canvas. The various aging techniques that forgers have used for generations to deceive buyers aren't working any more."

"Then why is there a market for these frauds at all?" Badger asked.

I smiled. "Because the forgers keep getting smarter. And people will always be greedy to own something rare and beautiful. Art collectors especially."

"How?" Badger asked. Challenging me.

"They copy a lesser known work. Or recreate a 'lost' work," I said. "One that was documented in some fashion around the time of its creation, but has since vanished from the records, and has no known ownership. Sometimes it's a painting that vanished during one of history's upheavals. Sometimes it's a work the artist mentioned and described in their journal, or that a contemporary did, but one that hasn't been seen in decades. Or even centuries.

Sometimes the forgery is of a work that actually exists, but is owned by a collector that obtained the original illegally, and can't ever admit to owning it."

"I've never got that one," Marie said. "Why put all the money into something you can't even display?"

"For some collectors, it's the love of the painting itself. Or sometimes, knowing you have something the whole world values and considers lost," I said.

Badger snorted.

Marie grinned at her. "Yeah, but then the collector dies. How come the work doesn't get 'found' then? With all that money tied up in it?"

"It's the same thing we ran into on the Courtland case, but on a far larger scale. Valuable art has become a kind of alternate currency in the criminal world. One that never loses its value, and apparently, can sometimes convey status at the same time."

"There are auction sites on the Dark Web," Badger said. "If you know where to look, and are willing to spend time deciphering exactly what's on offer."

That figured. And of course she'd already looked into that.

"Too bad we're not looking for a lost painting, then," Marie said flippantly. "Then that information might have some value."

Badger glared at her.

I still can't figure out the relationship between those two, and how they manage to work together. And as long as it works, I don't want to know.

"So with all the testing that's possible now, how come there are still frauds being sold?" Badger asked.

Why did I feel like she was testing me? I answered anyway. "There have been forgers for centuries, because for some artists, who have both the skills and a gift for imitation, it was an easy way to make money."

"For some, it was the only way they could keep painting. The frauds supported their own work," Marie said.

I wondered if she knew anyone like that personally. Or if she'd run into it in relation to her late, unlamented aunt's work. Marie had inherited a large chunk of that complicated estate.

And Anthea Swann's work—and her sister Eleanor's—had increased exponentially in value over the last few years. Enough to attract forgers? Probably.

"New techniques that became available in the industrial age caused a boom in forgery," I explained. "Some of those forgers were so successful, we're only now discovering the frauds. Thanks to new technology, quite a number of the 'lost' works supposedly rediscovered during the Victorian era are being proven to actually be successful forgeries. And some of these works have been in well-known museums for more than a hundred years by the time they're finally uncovered."

Badger frowned at me. "Go on."

"In addition to lost works, there's the problem of 'newly discovered' works," I said. "Paintings 'found' at the back of an attic in somebody's family home, or 'spotted' at a yard sale or an antique auction. Sometimes those paintings have been attributed to one of an old master's students. Sometimes they are so darkened with age they aren't recognized at all. Often there is no historical record for those paintings, leading to a great deal of controversy."

"Some of them really are lesser, unknown works by one of the masters," Marie said.

"True. In very rare cases," I said. "Some of them are recent forgeries. And some of them are forgeries done decades, or even centuries before."

"So why isn't every painting being tested before it's sold?" Badger asked.

Trust her to cut straight to the heart of the issue.

"Because it's expensive. And a lot of this is still controversial," I said. "Even the most advanced testing methods have a margin of error. Some of them, like some of the paint tests, are slightly destructive to the painting. Even if it's only to the margins, which are typically covered by the frame. And while technology can give us specific answers in some cases, some decisions are being made by evaluating things like whether the brush strokes are consistent with an artist's known works, and if the materials, including the paint colors, are consistent with ones the artist typically used in earlier works."

"Except sometimes a careless forger uses a paint color that wasn't even invented at the time the painting was supposedly done," Marie added.

"Exactly," I said. "It's a complicated business. And there's so much money at stake, not all collectors or museums want to know if they own a forged work. Let alone how many frauds their prized collections might actually contain."

"I get that," Badger said. "But, say Renoir had decided to paint something *avant garde* and changed all his methods and materials, it could now be declared a forgery?" Badger asked.

"Possibly. It would more likely be attributed to one of his students," I said. "'In the style of Renoir', something like that," I said.

Now Badger was nodding. "That's what I thought," she said. "You'd have to be an idiot to collect art."

Now Marie was scowling at her. "I could say the same about the value of a computer game. Pretty easy to hack, right? So why would anyone buy it?"

"Because it doesn't cost millions?" Badger said.

"Tell that to Xtreme Gaming. Some of their best games are insured for way more than that," Marie said heatedly, referring to a former, and very successful, client.

"Yeah, because they sell so many copies of each game. We're talking one painting here."

"Let's focus on our current client," I said.

"Why does she need us?" Badger asked.

The answer was already in the briefing I'd sent. If it hadn't been Badger asking the question, I might have been annoyed. But it was Badger, so I just wondered why she wanted to hear it again.

What was she up to?

"If the rumors about Carli Fine Arts keep spreading, the damage to their reputation could ruin them," I said. "And they can't investigate this themselves."

"Really? Why not?" Badger asked.

Had I missed something? Or had she already uncovered something, but wasn't ready to mention it? Sometimes it takes a leap of faith on my part to trust Badger's sense of timing.

"They need the distance," I said. "If a rumor that they're looking into this gets out, their reputation? Gone. They could lose everything. They're already going to have to test a ton of paintings—and if the number of forgeries is high enough, they could still lose everything. Either way, they're in deep trouble."

"Won't insurance cover them?" Marie asked.

"The insurers will make the case that they should never have bought those works, or sold them, in the first place without due diligence. We've never seen this tested before. Not on this scale."

"Better get their payment up front, then," Badger said.

"Already done," I said.

I'd learned that one the hard way. But just how bad were the odds against the company's survival—the ones Badger had obviously already calculated—for her to make that remark.

This case might be worse than I'd thought.

CHAPTER FOUR

When I got home, exhausted, Cat was waiting for me at the door. With that 'feed me tuna, now' look on his furry face. A very large orange tabby with an independent spirit, his previous owner had called him Butterscotch. He'd apparently been a very sweet kitten. But it sure didn't fit him now.

I'd called him Cat since the day he'd shown up in the middle of my living room. I never did figure out how he got there. But now he lived here full time, since his former owner had to move to a senior's home that didn't allow pets. And I'd somehow found myself offering to take the annoying beast. So here we were.

He stared at me expectantly. I got a dish with his tuna and his dry food and he pranced after me like the kitten he hadn't been in at least five years. There was no point in trying to make my own meal until he'd been fed. I'd never hear the end of it.

I shook my head at his antics, fighting back a smile. Then poured a glass of red wine and grabbed some cheese and crackers, taking them out on the balcony to contemplate the view of the trees on my block and the busy shopping district beyond. The leaves of the cherry trees had turned scarlet and yellow, and the Japanese maples in front of the condominium complex next door to mine had turned a rich burgundy. The wind was crisp, but not yet really cold, and the rain from earlier had departed, leaving the air smelling fresh and invigorating.

I contemplated going for a run later. It would be a terrific evening to head down to the inlet, and the fresh air and exercise might even help me figure out what was going on with Annegret Carli's case. I took a sip of wine, and spread a little herbed goat cheese on a whole grain cracker. The constant rush of traffic headed downtown on the major streets that bookended my block faded into a familiar background sound as I savored a moment of peace.

Then my landline buzzed, and I jumped. Yes, I still have a landline. The building entry system is outdated, to say the least, and the connection is hardwired into the building. I tried to get it set it up to work with my cell phone, once.

It was an exercise I'm not planning to repeat. It was easier to keep the landline, and the phone company actually gave me a great deal. For a change.

Putting the wine aside with a muttered curse, I hurried in to find the handset. Which had been abandoned beside the couch, I thought. This time I was right.

I wasn't expecting anyone, was I?

I knew I didn't have plans with Nick Markham, my significant other—and besides, he has a key now. Probably a wrong number. Or a salesperson.

"Yes?" I said.

"Barbara? Can I come up?" came Andrea's voice, barely identifiable over the crackling of the line. Did I mention it was old?

"Come on up," I said, confused, but buzzing her in. Surely, I hadn't made plans with my best friend and forgotten them, had I? Things had been busy lately, but surely not that bad.

Still, Andrea just doesn't show up at my door unannounced. I might show up at hers on occasion, but my efficient friend is too organized for that.

I'm only four floors up, but our elevator is the same generation as the phone system, so it's slow. By the time Andrea reached my door, I had it open and a glass of wine in my hand.

"Oh, you have no idea how much I need this," she said, accepting it and stepping in. "You were out on the balcony?"

"I was. You want to sit in or out?"

"In please," she said with a shiver. "I don't love fall weather as much as you do. And the balcony isn't private enough."

That didn't sound good. I wondered what was coming. Andrea didn't have any crises happening in her life right now, not that I was aware of, anyway. But I haven't seen as much of her as usual, lately. As I said, things have been busy.

Had she been having problems and I didn't even know about them? Now I felt guilty.

As my petite blonde friend sank into the oversize sofa, I went out to the balcony to fetch the wine and the plate of crackers and cheese. It was looking a little meager, so I detoured to my narrow kitchen and added a couple of kinds of olives and a bit of the blue cheese that Andrea and Nick both love. I keep it in for them.

Plunking everything on a tray, I added the half full bottle of wine, and carried it through.

"You're a lifesaver," Andrea said with a smile, eyeing the tray. "I didn't interrupt anything, did I?"

I guess that meant we didn't have plans.

"Just some research for a new case. It can wait till tomorrow," I said, sinking into my favorite wing chair opposite her. "What's up?"

"Nothing good," she said, and her eyes teared up. Angrily she brushed the tears away with one hand, and took a gulp of her wine. "Mostly I just need food. And company."

"Luckily we have both," I said. Knowing she hates to let emotion get the better of her. "And we can always order in."

That earned me an only slightly watery grin. "Good plan," she said. "But the cheese and crackers will do, for now. You even got out the blue cheese."

She knew I wasn't fond of the aroma. Though I will confess that with the right chef, there is the occasional dish with blue cheese I love. In my opinion, you can't go wrong with a really good pear and blue cheese salad.

"So what's going on, Andrea?" I asked.

But she wasn't looking at me. She and Cat seemed to be engaged in a staring contest. "He hasn't done this with me before. Is he hungry?" she asked.

I sighed. "No. He likes blue cheese even better than you do."

"That can't be possible," Andrea said. Then she looked from Cat to me and back again, and grinned. "Are you telling me that you feed your cat blue cheese? I knew you were a wimp when it came to this cat, but…"

"I am not," I said. "Well, at least not this time. It wasn't me. It was Nick, while I was in Vegas on that last case."

"Nick? Your Nick? The RCMP cop who thrives on investigating gangs and murders? Fed blue cheese to your cat?" Andrea asked, with a giggle that reminded me of the pigtailed little girl she'd been when we first met. "I don't believe it."

"Believe it," I said resignedly. "Nick's a big fan of blue cheese too. According to him, Cat was so lonely with me gone…"

"How is that possible?" Andrea said. "You're never here, even when you're in town."

"Exactly," I said. "It's an excuse. He was here one night, watching TV. To keep Cat company he said…"

"Aha," Andrea said. "Now the truth comes out. It wasn't Cat that was missing you. It was Nick. You really should move in with him like he wants, you know."

"He wants to buy a house together," I said. "It's an enormous commitment. And have you seen real estate prices lately? It's too much."

"I know compromise isn't your thing," she said, giving me that eagle eye. "But that sounds like a classic Barbara excuse to me. You and Nick are great together."

"Sure, but it's too much pressure, too soon. I don't know if our relationship can handle it."

You do know you don't actually have to buy a place in order to live together," she said. "Haven't you ever heard of rentals?"

Of course I had. That just complicated things. "Too many options," I said.

Andrea looked ready to argue when Cat chose that moment to place one huge paw delicately against her knee. She looked over at that wide-eyed gaze and started to laugh.

"He's adorable."

I grinned. "Apparently Cat was staring at Nick just like that while he was eating blue cheese. So he gave him a bit, to show Cat he wouldn't actually like it."

"Just like you're doing," I added, as Andrea extended her index finger, with a crumble of blue cheese balanced on the end, towards Cat.

Who purred, and licked the entire chunk delicately from her finger. His purring got even louder, turning to a deep rumble as Andrea repeated the exercise.

"Stupid cat," I muttered. And refrained from sharing my thoughts about boyfriends and best friends and spoiling my cat. Wait till the next time they tried to give me a hard time for feeding him tuna.

At least these days it was cat tuna, the kind that was sort of good for him.

"Don't get blue cheese on the rug. It's a royal pain to get out," I told her. "You came here to talk. So talk."

She fed Cat a third bit of the cheese, then sat back with her wineglass and grinned at me. "You're annoying, you know," she said. "Probably why you're good for me."

"Ditto," I said, grinning back. "Now, spill. What's got you all twisted up?"

She blinked hard, and belted back a little more wine. Then refilled both our glasses, and settled back again. Finally, she was ready to talk.

"I met a guy," she said.

That wasn't unusual. She met a lot of them. Or they met her.

Andrea's love life was never dull, but it tended to be varied. Very few of the guys she dated made it past the first few months. Even fewer made it past six months. Don't ask.

I give her grief about her standards being too high now and then, but the problem is older and deeper than that. And both of us know it. When she's ready to talk, she will.

But Andrea didn't usually get wrought up over her dates, no matter how long they lasted. Or didn't.

"Oh?" I said.

"I met him a couple months ago. When you were finishing off your show."

I'd realized a long held dream in September, when I'd had a one-woman show of my paintings at the Courtland Gallery. And yeah, I'd been a little distracted getting ready for it. So shoot me.

But Andrea and I had been friends for decades. How had I missed this?

"Why didn't you tell me?"

"It—he—didn't seem important at the time." And I could swear she blushed a little.

Andrea? Blushing? "What changed?"

She glanced down, and drank some more wine. "Well, nothing at first. I kept seeing him. He's a nice guy, and we had fun together. But I kept expecting it to end, you know."

Like all the others had. I knew. "This nice guy have a name?"

She nodded. "Greg. Greg Younger."

The name didn't ring any bells. "Go on."

"Well, I started to realize this might be more, but it was so low key that I wasn't really sure, you know?"

"And that's why you didn't tell me?" I wasn't sure how I felt about that.

"Sort of. You were all caught up in Justine's case by then, you know? And we weren't seeing each other as much as usual."

She was right. I hadn't really thought about how little I'd seen of Andrea lately. But to have missed this? I felt awful.

"I meant to tell you," she said, giving me a sideways glance, then swallowing a bit more wine.

Apparently she felt as guilty as I did about letting our friendship get lost in the pressure of everything else. Didn't help me feel any better, though.

"And it didn't seem like a big deal, dating him, I mean," she added. "Because it was so easy. Except that he kinda slipped into my life, and just seemed to fit there. You know."

I did. Nick and I had started just like that. Except that he'd slipped into one of my cases, and by the time it ended, he was part of my life. A fact I was still trying to figure out. How this all worked. And what came next.

Other than buying a place together. Which was not a logical next step, in anyone's book.

But this was about Andrea.

"You still haven't told me what's upset you so much," I said.

She grimaced. "This is hard to say."

"Yeah. It always is, when it matters," I said. Then wondered where that little pearl of wisdom came from. And how come I'm not so clear when it's my own problems, instead of Andrea's. "Have some more wine."

"Thanks. Good idea." She refilled her glass, drank a little, then seemed to be contemplating the deep richness. The silence stretched between us.

When silence turned into tension, I figured she might need a little help. "How did you meet this guy?"

"He was a client," she said. "He runs the local branch of a hi-tech security firm, and they needed a temporary receptionist they could trust."

That figures. Andrea owns the best temporary help firm in town, and she vets her employees carefully. And cares about them, too, so they tend to be loyal. Over the years, she's attracted and kept some of the best people, and that's only helped her build her firm's reputation. It didn't surprise me she'd met this guy through work.

In fact, she'd known Nick before I even met him for exactly that reason. He was undercover for a white collar fraud operation, and needed a discreet receptionist. Which Andrea was happy to provide.

"How long have you known him as a client?"

"It was about six months. Which is as long as that temp assignment lasted. Then he asked me out."

"He waited?"

"Oh, yeah. He thinks about things like conflict of interest."

Interesting. He obviously had a mind for risk management.

"That's the problem," she said, putting down her wineglass and leaning forward. "He needs more staffing help, and he wants to go to another firm."

"That's understandable, isn't it?"

She nodded. "It would be. Except he plans on using Cushings. And he won't listen to me when I try to warn him."

Oh, that was a bad move on his part. Cushings was a local employment agency that also specializes in temporary placements. And Andrea's pet nemesis. "So he's being obstinate?"

"I wish. No, he doesn't trust me to be objective. Or honest," she burst out.

Oh, boy. Andrea is a great judge of people, which is why she does so well in her field of choice. And she's honest to a fault. To have someone she's starting to care about not trust her integrity? That would be a blow.

"Are you sure that's his thinking?" I asked cautiously.

"How can you ask me that?" she said.

Okay, then. A different approach was called for.

"You're right," I said. "We hate him. You should drop him immediately, and never see him again. Or talk to him. In fact, you should ghost him on every service that exists or will ever be invented."

She glared at me. "You're mocking my pain? What kind of a friend…" Then my words sunk in, and she started to grin. Reluctantly, but it was a grin.

"I am *not* overreacting."

I took a sip of my wine. "Are too."

"No, I am not." She couldn't sustain the glare she threw my way. "And tell your cat to stop staring at me. He's not getting more cheese."

I'd bet he was. Just like I'd bet that Greg hadn't actually said what Andrea thought he'd said. But I was going to run a background check on him anyway.

It's what a best friend does. Especially when they realize how out of touch they've been with their oldest friend.

"Fine. So I need to talk to him again. See what's really going on," she said. "And stop gloating."

I wasn't touching that one. But Andrea could probably use more wine. And more food, too. "Feel like a pizza?"

"There's nothing wrong with my blood sugar."

"Touchy, touchy," I said with a grin. "Bacon and mushroom or the works? And when the pizza comes, I'll open more wine."

"Fine," she said. "Make it the works. The extra-large."

"Forget to eat lunch again?"

She stuck her tongue out at me, and I started to laugh. Seconds later, she joined me.

CHAPTER FIVE

The following morning, we had a regular team meeting scheduled at eleven. I prefer to meet first thing, but Cory has a free period on Tuesday mornings just before lunch, so we set meetings then. He only has two hours before he has to be back in class, though, including nine minutes of cycling time each way. Which actually works out fine, as it tends to keep our meetings pretty focused.

The late start came in handy that morning, because it gave me extra time to do the rest of my research into Annegret Carli Fine Arts and their problems. Andrea and I had talked until midnight the night before, so I'd only managed another hour of digging into the firm before falling exhausted into bed. And no way was I cutting short my morning run.

Then I'd spent a few minutes looking into Andrea's Greg. What are best friends for, after all? Greg Younger ran the local branch of BladeSecure Canada, and both he and the firm had a stellar record. I couldn't find anything negative on him, anywhere. At least I didn't have to break bad news to Andrea.

Out of curiosity, I also ran Cushings Agency. Whoa. Andrea was right about them. Not only did they have a ton of client complaints, according to GlassWindow, their own staff didn't have much nice to say about them, either. Hadn't Greg Younger done his own research before he hired a temp through them?

With a glance at the clock, I turned back to my case. I had less than two hours before the meeting. And too much digging left to do.

When I made it to the meeting room, I was the last one there. Amber had ordered in sodas and sandwiches with a variety of breads and fillings, and Badger, Marie and Cory had already served themselves. I grabbed and filled a small plate with a selection of sandwiches, and sat down.

With only four of us in the room, we still had plenty of space around the long table. By seemingly unspoken agreement, Marie was the first to report.

"I dug into reports of forgery at well-known art galleries," she said. "I sort of knew there had been some major incidents, but I wasn't paying much attention to that side of the art world then. The one that really worried me was easy to find—a major New York gallery that had been around for more than a century and a half."

I wasn't surprised she'd found that one—the collapse of the Montaugh Gallery had been a big story—though I was a little surprised she hadn't already known about it. Marie was an art student, after all, as well as the daughter of one artist and niece of another. Still, at the time this all came to light, Marie would have still been in school. Her mother had died years before, and her aunt had been—well, reclusive was a kind description.

"They'd been selling paintings and drawings by the big names in American Expressionism from a previously unknown collection," Marie explained to Cory and Badger. "And they'd done so for more than twenty years. Until all of those paintings were finally exposed as forgeries."

"You're kidding me," Cory said. "What happened to them?"

I wondered what Cory had been researching. It hadn't been art gallery frauds, clearly. Which was just as well. We needed as many different perspectives as possible.

Marie was grinning at him. "Nothing good," she said. "Which is why I'm kinda wishing we hadn't taken on this client."

"That bad?" Badger asked.

"Yeah. They went out of business."

"After more than a hundred and fifty years?" Cory said. "Were they guilty?"

Marie shook her head. "Dunno. Opinion is still divided on what the gallery itself—or at least the manager and the owner—knew about the forgeries, and when they knew it…"

"So what happened?"

"The FBI investigated. In the end, no-one from the gallery was ever charged. But there were a number of civil suits, mostly settled out of court, and the gallery had to reimburse all the purchasers. They'd already closed by then. The official story was the business had been declining, and they'd been considering closing for good even before the scandal broke."

Badger snorted, but didn't say anything. I wondered what she'd run across in her research.

"Why is that the report that worried you the most?" I prompted Marie. I shared her opinion, which she probably guessed, but I wanted to hear her thinking.

I had a strong feeling this new case of ours wasn't going to be solved by thinking in straight lines.

"I found a bunch of museums that have had fakes exposed in their collections. And famous collectors with multi-million dollar forgeries hanging on their walls," Marie said. "But this one? A famous, long-standing art gallery got taken down."

"So?" Cory said.

"So what does that say about our client? Her gallery's only been around for thirty years, not a hundred and sixty, but their reputation is stellar. And one thing everyone who got involved in this particular fraud agreed on? They trusted the gallery's reputation and their manager. They didn't think they needed to worry about forgeries for the works they bought from her."

"Fools," Badger muttered as she made a note.

"Annegret's gallery is in the same boat," Marie said. "How're we supposed to help them?"

"To be fair," Cory said. "You're only looking at half the story."

Marie frowned at him. "And what do you think I'm missing?"

"That big gallery scandal broke over a decade ago. Things have changed."

"What things?" Marie asked.

"One thing that hit me in my searches," Cory said. "There seems to be general agreement now among experts and a lot of high-end collectors that there's a scary number of forgeries around."

"That isn't new," Marie said.

Cory grinned. "Maybe not. But that knowledge is much more wide spread than it used to be. Everything is online and discover-able, for one thing. And besides that, the technology for recog-nizing and proving forgeries has improved by leaps and bounds."

"So?" she said. Digging at him.

He grinned. "So, these days there are also lots of experts of various stripes making their living doing highly technical authenti-cations of multi-million dollar paintings." He looked at me. "Did you know people will pay tens of thousands to have their paintings examined?"

I did know that. But Badger answered before I could.

"Makes sense," she said. "Get the purchase authenticated before they shell out multi-millions on a painting."

"A little like buying a house?" I said.

Then wished I hadn't let my worries over Nick and his plan for buying a house together intrude, as I got a confused look back from all three of them. I guess they're all too young to be thinking about buying a place, especially now.

Our housing market is more than a little over-inflated. Which is part of why I'm dragging my heels on Nick's plan. Well, that and the fact we haven't even lived together yet.

"You wouldn't spend a few million on a house without paying a qualified house inspector, would you?" I said with a grin.

"Why not?" Marie asked, seeming genuinely curious.

Just how much money was her aunt's estate worth these days, anyway? I knew Marie didn't share an apartment with her sister any more, having moved to a downtown loft a few months ago, which I'd assumed she was renting. Maybe I'd been wrong.

"To check if the impressive renovation the owners did before putting it on the market covered up potentially expensive problems like the foundation and the wiring," I explained. "As a concept, it's the same with artwork."

Marie looked thoughtful, and Badger had an odd expression on her face.

Come to think of it, Badger had moved recently too. And I knew she sometimes took consulting projects on the side. It had been part of the terms of her contract when I'd hired her. Those side projects were probably pretty lucrative, given that she was genius with computers.

Maybe both of them would understand my real estate issue more than I'd thought they would. Cory was too young to care, though.

I glanced over at my nephew's intent expression. Or was he? He'd taken Badger as a mentor. If at twenty-four she was considering buying a place to live—or maybe had bought her current place? Then Cory would probably see that as an achievable goal for himself. At sixteen. I was in my late twenties before that possibility occurred to me.

And wouldn't my sister love that one?

While I was struggling with the realization of just how outdated my assumptions about my team might have been, Badger was thinking about the case.

"Maybe it's similar when people are buying a new piece of art," Badger said. "But from the digging I did, no-one is in any hurry to expose just how much fraud is actually hanging on their walls. Ignorance is…"

"Bliss?" Cory said, giving Badger a sideways look. She made a face at him.

"Hardly. In this case, ignorance preserves an investment worth multiple millions of dollars."

"Ouch," Cory said.

Watching his expressive face change, I wondered exactly what he was thinking about. I didn't wonder for long.

"If that's the case, then why is someone pointing the finger at our new client?" he asked.

"A good question," I said.

He grinned, and looked over at Badger. "Are you sure about your facts?"

Cory, questioning Badger? I hadn't seen that before. In fact, I'd thought him several years away from gaining that kind of confidence. What was going on here?

I felt my shoulders hunch involuntarily, just a little, in anticipation of the coming fireworks. And it would be up to me to protect Cory against Badger. Oh joy.

"Why do you ask?" Badger asked. Nothing in her voice to indicate she was annoyed with him. Nothing to suggest she wasn't, either.

She'd make a killer poker player, I thought as I watched Cory's reaction. The question didn't seem to faze him.

"One of those industry-leading technical experts is a company in Switzerland. XTC Tech."

I found it interesting that the company's name made no reference to their specialty in art forensics. That had to be deliberate. Were their clients trying to maintain deniability?

Which didn't say anything good about the state of the art world.

"Apparently there's a big storage facility for really expensive paintings there, too," Cory was saying. "If this is something everyone's ignoring, how come there are so many expensive experts around?"

"Maybe the buyers are using experts. And the owners and the sellers are the ones who don't want to know?" Marie suggested.

Cory nodded. "Maybe. But then shouldn't the galleries be doing their due diligence before they sell something? Since they're making money as the intermediary?"

As the word rolled off his tongue my eyes widened. This was Cory? My skipping school, mad at the world nephew? I'd known he was changing, but when had this happened?

No wonder Susanna was mad at me. She'd think I'd fixed something broken in her son when she hadn't been able to. And if I told her I had nothing to do with it—and I didn't, short of hiring him to do something he was unbelievably good at—she wouldn't hear me, no matter what I said.

"Carli Fine Arts suddenly has a four percent fraud rate, when the industry rate can run as high as thirty percent," Badger said. "Along with a lot of new rumors. Maybe the problem isn't with Annegret and her team."

"Thirty percent?" I repeated. It wasn't a number I'd heard before, and it flabbergasted me to hear it now. "Are you sure?"

Badger just looked at me. Of course she was sure. Stupid question. She gave a slight inclination of her head, as if to confirm my realization. Good enough.

"Did our new client happen to mention if she'd talked to XTC Tech about this problem? At all?" Cory asked.

Interesting. And a very good question. "I didn't ask who was responsible for finding the three forgeries. So she may well have used them."

"It's a good sign if she has," Badger said. "I get that she's probably trying to keep this thing quiet, but…"

"She knows we'll need to bring in the experts," I said. "But we need to get a handle on what she's dealing with here before I go back to her," I said. "Let's take a mental break, get some coffee. We can talk over dessert before Cory has to go back to school."

And I wanted to be sure we'd diffused any lingering tensions. The last thing we needed was dissension this early in a case.

———

IN LESS THAN TEN MINUTES, the room smelled of good coffee and the plate of donuts in the middle of the table was half empty. I wasn't quite sure how Cory planned to get the powdered sugar off his t-shirt before he went back to class.

I could live with that. There was no sign of the tension that had worried me earlier. In fact, I still wasn't sure exactly what I'd been seeing.

I pointed to the whiteboards behind me. I'd used the time while everyone was sorting out coffee to put up quick notes on what we'd discussed so far. "Anyone got a different piece of this puzzle?"

Again, Marie spoke up first. "I found cases of art dealers buying legitimate works, then having five or six copies made overseas, that they then sell as the original to collectors," she said. "All while keeping the actual original for themselves. Having access to factories full of what we'd consider forgeries..." she shook her head.

"That's what supposedly happened to the *Mona Lisa*," Cory said excitedly. "Minus the overseas factories. A crook had copies made by an expert forger, stole the original from the Louvre and replaced it with a copy. Then he kept the original for himself and sold off the other copies into the collecting underground. While representing each copy as being the original work. The original wasn't found—or the theft discovered—until decades later."

"Yeah, I found that one, too," Marie said. "I've even run into versions of that story at my art college, where groups will debate forever on whether the work hanging in the Louvre is actually the original. Or a copy. And if it's a copy, is it one the museum displays while keeping the original in the vault to protect it? Or do they think it's the real thing, when it isn't?"

"Regarding this case," Badger said pointedly. "I found several factories in China that mass produce 'copies' of the better known old master paintings, complete with fake signatures. Ostensibly for home display."

"Weren't those sites in Chinese? How did you translate them?" Marie asked.

Badger rolled her eyes and said something rude that had Cory sniggering. Then she proceeded as if there had been no interruption.

"Mostly I concentrated on the Dark Web," Badger said. "And found two sites offering to create copies of existing works. One was blatantly offering forgeries on demand. They advertised *"Any work. Any artist."* The other was more coy about their offerings, but before they took on a new client, they required payment up front."

The meetings in dingy bars and secret code words of history's best art forgers had apparently gone online. I suppose it made sense—good forgers have always been all but invisible. The more money they make, the harder they are to find. The internet just makes that simpler for the forger. And for their customer.

And the Dark Web was the darkest alley going.

"Then I looked for auction sites for high end art," Badger continued. "There were a few sites I could get into. And several more that are members only, and require a substantial deposit to create an account. A kind of buy-in fee, if you will. Those will take me longer to crack."

There were art auctions on the Deep Web? Of course there were. It was inevitable. I shouldn't have needed Badger to tell me that.

But the knowledge worried me for the outcome of this case. And Badger's report only made things worse. Those auction sites had to be well-funded ones. I couldn't imagine the level of security it would take to keep Badger out of an online site for this long.

"Did you find old masters for sale?" Marie asked.

"No."

"Good," I said. But my relief was cut short.

"I suspect those will be limited to the member sites," Badger added.

"So what was on the non-member sites?" Marie asked.

"All kinds of more recent art for sale," Badger said. "Starting in the thousands, and moving up. I did find a few sellers offering Anthea and Eleanor Swann paintings. I made copies for you. If you like, I'll show you the sites later."

"Thanks," said Marie, who had gone pale.

"What about trends?" Cory asked. "Anything obvious?"

"I ran a comparison of paintings in the Carli Fine Arts online gallery against what I was able to find on the Dark Web. Only one match," she said.

"So does that mean the Carli Fine Arts painting is a copy?" Marie asked. "Or is the one you found a copy of the Carli Fine Arts original?"

"Another good question," Badger said. "Could be either."

"So where does that leave us?" Marie asked.

Badger gave her a look, then looked over at me. "Is it too late to turn down this case? This whole thing is a nest of stinging beetles, that people are pretending are gems. I see nothing but headaches ahead. For all of us."

I knew Badger was right. Between us, we'd already uncovered enough to confirm that the case was going to be nothing but trouble. And I clearly needed to talk to Annegret Carli again. It wasn't a conversation I was looking forward to.

But it was one I was going to be prepared for. As well prepared as was possible at this stage of a new case, anyway.

I grinned at my very high-end hacker. "I'm glad you share my perspective on the case. And yes, I've signed the contract. It's cases like this that pay your salary, remember?"

"And the attention we'll get when we solve it? That'll bring in the next big case," Marie said.

"First we have to solve this one," I said, and looked around the table at my team. "I already have a few questions for our client tomorrow. What else do we need to know?"

And we dug in, covering the whiteboards around us with the little we knew. And everything we didn't.

CHAPTER SIX

The following morning, I met with our new client again. Annegret had told me she'd be in town for several days, and that she'd be expecting to discuss our plan of action after we'd had a chance to evaluate the situation.

I'd thought it arrogant of her, but it was a good strategy from her perspective.

Good from mine as well, as it turned out. She strode into my office precisely at ten, wearing a subtle cinnamon suit with a darker shade blouse in a rich silk. She looked confident, polished and expensive. Someone collectors would trust.

If she was worried about our coming discussion, no trace of it showed on her face or in her body language as she smiled a greeting. I was behind my desk, but she ignored the chair opposite me, and walked straight to the burnt orange chairs on the far side of the room. The ones we'd occupied at our previous meeting. Which forced me to walk around my desk and take the chair opposite her.

It was a smooth way to ensure I couldn't keep the power position by staying behind my desk. Not that I'd intended to, but the maneuver told me a lot about her, and why she'd reached the level of success she had.

For this meeting, though, I needed her a little off-balance. I'd decided on my strategy after the team meeting yesterday, but as I took my seat opposite her, I rapidly rethought it.

"The three forgeries you found. How did you test them?" I fired the words at her, launching straight into a challenge. And watching her carefully for any reaction.

Not that there was one.

She smiled as if she was pleased at the question. It's possible she was. This was as much her testing me as it was me testing her. I don't often get that feeling from clients—on most of my previous big cases, the clients were too distraught to play games.

Annegret had seemed genuinely devastated in our last meeting. Was that only to get me to sign the contract? There was no sign of that emotion today. She seemed calm and confident.

"We reviewed every painting we've bought or sold over the last year, as I told you yesterday," she answered. "Then we tested the ones we had even the slightest concern about, in light of our current situation."

Interesting. It wasn't quite the picture she'd painted on Monday. "And how many did you test?"

"Seven."

Three forgeries out of seven wasn't nearly as reassuring a number as three out of seventy. "How did you explain that process to the owners of the works? And have you told any of them the results?"

"We had to be exceptionally careful not to feed the rumors until we knew exactly what the problem is," she said.

"Of course," I said. And waited.

"We have a restorer we've worked with for many years, who is on retainer with the firm. I trust her, but told her only that we needed an additional level of scrutiny on the attribution of the paintings for insurance purposes, before sending her to review all the paintings. We told owners that we needed additional documentation on their painting's condition, again for insurance purposes," she said, twining her fingers together in her lap.

She was more affected than she was letting on.

I noticed that today Annegret's manicure perfectly matched the color of her suit, and wondered if she'd had to have the polish custom blended. She took her presentation—her brand, Justine would call it—seriously.

Or maybe it was a thing, if you had the money. And cared about such things. Who knew?

I wondered again if Annegret knew Justine. Customized nail polish seemed like something Justine would do. And Marie, too, probably—if she'd noticed. Which was an unnerving thought. And hardly what I needed to be focusing on.

"The reviews our restorer performed did allow us to add another level to our descriptions for our insurance documents. So we didn't lie about it." Annegret added. She seemed pleased about that.

But this all seemed too easy, especially in a situation that could destroy everything she'd worked decades to build. "And how did you test the seven paintings that she identified potential issues with?"

"We sent them to XTC Tech. To the technical experts there."

It was the same company Cory had mentioned. So far so good. But something was still off. What?

She was watching me. Waiting. For what?

"And what did you tell the owners of the seven paintings you sent off for this testing?"

If I hadn't been watching her so closely, I'd never have noticed the little jerk in one of her hands, or the way her fingers tightened around each other. No wonder she kept her hands twined in her lap like that. It was to hide that tell-tale movement.

I suddenly wondered if the perfectly matched nail polish was a deliberate distraction. It had almost worked, too.

"As it happened, the works we sent out for testing are all in our current inventory," she said.

"Sent out. You mean to XTC Tech?" I asked, just to be sure.

"Yes."

"So none of the seven you tested had been sold yet?" I asked.

"No."

Oh boy. I'd sensed there was something wrong with what she'd been telling me. And not telling me. This was it.

"And none of the paintings you'd already sold were available for testing?" I asked, just to be sure.

"They were all examined closely by my restorer, and none of them raised red flags. But they were not sent out for a deeper review. That is correct," she said. Clenching her fingers more tightly together, the movement almost invisible if I hadn't been watching for it.

She was still attempting to shade the truth.

"Look, Annegret," I said, leaning forward into her space just enough for her to notice subliminally. "When I took this case, it was on the condition you were completely honest with me."

"As I have been," she said.

"Including not leaving anything out." She started to protest and I held up a hand. "Just how many paintings did you actually test?"

"Seven."

"All of them from your unsold stock?"

"As I just told you," she said. "Yes," she added, at a look from me.

"And of the seventy paintings you had examined by your restorer, how many of them are still in your unsold stock?" I asked.

"Fifteen," she said, and her voice had lost most of its certainty.

"So nearly half of the unsold paintings had enough concerns to send for further testing?"

"Yes."

"And of the other fifty-five paintings, the ones you'd already sold? Not a single one under this review showed any red flags at all? Not one?"

"No," she said. She couldn't meet my eyes.

"Annegret?"

She said nothing.

"Perhaps this is the time for us to end our association," I said, standing.

She stood as well. "I'll double your fees," she said.

"I'm afraid that isn't the issue," I said. "You can't buy us."

"I apologize," she said. "We—I need your help. We couldn't test the sold paintings, not without triggering further rumors. The testing we did do was enough to tell me that we—that I have a problem. And I need an unaffiliated firm—yours—to investigate what is really going on. It's why I'm here."

"Did you actually do the visual review you described on all seventy paintings?"

She nodded. "We did."

"And you used the same review format, with the same degree of depth and the same expert, that you used to review the fifteen unsold paintings?"

"Yes. Everything was exactly the same."

"And you have the documentation on all seventy reviews?"

"I do."

"And full documentation on the seven works you sent to XTC Tech?"

"Yes," she said. "And before you ask, I'm willing to provide you with all of that documentation. And anything else you require."

"I'll need the full files you did on all seventy works," I said. "Including the names of the original owners, all of the documented provenance, the names of your gallery associates involved with the acquisition or sale of those works, how much they sold for, and under what circumstances. I also require the full names of the current registered owner—even if it's a numbered company. I'll need to know who really bought those works, as well as any intermediaries who were involved in the sale."

She went pale, but nodded. "You'll need to sign a confidentiality agreement."

"Of course."

She met my eyes, her gaze firm. "It will take some time to provide everything on that many paintings."

"Start with the documentation that you have now. I'll need that as soon as possible, especially the testing data and the provenance.

Have someone you trust compile the data on the gallery associates involved in each acquisition or sale and anything else that isn't immediately available, and get it to us as quickly as possible."

I paused, took in her strained expression. "You do have someone you trust with that?"

She nodded. "Yes. My manager, Amara Duvant. She's my right hand, runs the gallery any time I'm away."

Which was probably often, given the number of buying trips Annegret likely made each year. "Good. Will that work?" I asked her.

"Yes. Amara can take care of allocating this work, as well. She'll make sure it gets done as quickly as possible," Annegret said. "You should have most of what you need by tomorrow morning."

The time difference was working in our favor. While we slept, they had a full day to get the reports we needed. I nodded. "I'll be expecting it."

We both knew the consequences if she didn't follow through. In this case, she needed my help more than I needed her business.

No matter how much it might, or might not, help build our reputation.

———

AFTER ANNEGRET LEFT, I pushed my chair back and stared out the window for a few moments collecting my thoughts. Something was still bothering me about the conversation.

What was it?

I pictured our meeting, and my elegant client as she sat in the deep chair opposite me. The gallery owner had seemed increasingly tense today. Much more so than she had in our previous meeting. And she was holding herself with a stiffness in her spine and shoulders I hadn't noted the previous day. The restless movement of her hands—and her distracting nail polish—were both new, too.

It felt as if she'd been braced for a confrontation.

Towards the end of our conversation, she'd gradually relaxed. Whatever she'd prepared for hadn't happened. Or maybe she'd expected a question I hadn't asked.

What had I missed?

I ran through the questions I asked, the information I needed from her. I'd covered everything that the team and I had questions about. And yet she'd relaxed.

She was still holding back, I decided. But why? She'd hired us because she needed us. Or so she said.

I'd need to go through everything again.

Starting from the first meeting.

Annegret had seemed slow to share the information we'd need to find out what was behind the rumors about her company. Which didn't match her stated reasons for hiring us.

Had she some other reason for doing so? Granted we had a growing reputation in the art world. But we'd only dealt with fraud on a few cases. One of which was a highly visible case, but the potential impact of this case on Annegret's gallery was much more drastic. A wrong move could destroy everything she'd worked so hard to build.

Annegret's gallery had a much higher visibility in the art world than my firm did. She could have hired any firm she wanted, anywhere in the world. So why would she fly all the way from Switzerland to the west coast of Canada to hire us?

Was she using us as some kind of cover for something else?

I didn't like that thought at all, but it resonated for me. I might not have the reason yet, but I had the strong sense she was using us for something.

I hated to be so cautious, but politics in the art world can be cutthroat. And galleries live and die by their reputation. Someone who had risen as high and as fast in the business as Annegret Carli was no dummy. She was a player, and a good one. She wouldn't hesitate to use any tool at her disposal to save her gallery.

And she'd be ruthless about it.

I'd have to make sure I was, too.

At that moment the phone rang. It was another client, wanting an update on a case we'd been working for a week or so. I rapidly brought up the case notes on the team's shared database. Badger had unearthed a few interesting facts, and things were progressing nicely. I reassured my client that everything was in hand and I hoped to see the case wrapped up by the end of the week. That seemed to satisfy her, and we rang off.

I glanced at the time on the screen, and realized if I didn't leave now, I'd be late meeting Nick for lunch. Not happening. Lunch together isn't something we often manage. Today he was testifying on a case at the downtown courthouse, and for a change, both our schedules were free from twelve to one-thirty. Quickly refreshing my lipstick, I grabbed my bag and headed out.

CHAPTER SEVEN

That afternoon I signed off on several smaller cases Marie and Badger had finalized, one of them with Cory's help. And tried not to think about the house listings Nick had shown me over lunch. He's been so patient on the subject lately, I thought maybe he'd given up. But apparently not.

I made non-committal noises that had him giving me a sharp look, but he didn't ask the questions he had to be thinking. Just as well. I can't even explain to myself what's still holding me back, let alone to him.

I glanced at the doodles I'd just drawn on my calendar blotter and winced. This wasn't helping.

So I went back to my case, and worrying at the problem of my meeting with Annegret. At least I could solve that one. Eventually.

And whatever she wasn't telling me, the sooner I knew about it, the better.

I picked up the phone, and called Adrien Keller, Interpol's top expert in international art theft and fraud. I didn't expect him to be in his office, not when it was nearly eleven in the evening there. But he surprised me.

"Keller here."

"It's Barbara O'Grady. We worked together on the Mexican museum case."

His voice warmed immediately. "Nice to hear from you, Barbara O'Grady. Don't worry, I remember you very well indeed. How are things out there in lotus land?"

I glanced at the rain sliding down the window, and laughed. "Soggy, as it happens. You're thinking of LA, not Vancouver."

I could hear the shrug in his voice. "It was sunny, and we drove by beaches thronged with suntanned bodies. On a weekday," he said.

He had a point. "You'll have to come and visit in the winter. It'll adjust your perspective in a hurry," I told him.

"Happy to," he said. "Why, do you have a case that might require me to travel there?"

"Not exactly," I said. I wasn't going to tell him who my client was, or even that I'd be more likely to be visiting him in Lyon than he would be coming here. "I just need a bit of information. And since it falls in your bailiwick as well as in your backyard, I immediately thought of you."

"That's fair enough. What can I do for you?"

"I'd be grateful for anything you can tell me about the Annegret Carli Fine Arts Gallery."

There was a small silence on the other end of the line. If I hadn't worked with him in the past, I'd have missed it.

He knew something, obviously.

"Since the gallery has been around for decades and their reputation is well-known, I gather you are interested in something more current," he said. "Perhaps even the rumors?"

"Exactly," I told him.

"There is little I can tell you," he said, an odd tone in his voice. "They are a pillar of the art establishment here, and as such, are often very boring."

And here was someone else who wasn't telling me everything. Which meant more than the words he was actually saying.

Keller and I had worked together successfully on that last fraud case. And he was brilliant, a quick thinker who spoke as fast as he thought. Those little pauses, the very precise language? Those weren't like him at all.

He knew something about Annegret's gallery. Either they were involved somehow in a case he was actively investigating. Or he was investigating them directly.

Either way, it wasn't good news for my new client.

Or for my need for more information on her and her gallery.

"Is there someone I could talk to that finds that gallery less boring than you do?" I asked him.

He chuckled. "I do appreciate working with you, Barbara. You must involve me in your next case."

Or the current one, perhaps? Now I really wanted to know what was up with my client. "I'll see what I can do," I said, deadpan.

"In the meantime, you might find it worth your while to talk with Birgitte Jessup," he said. "I think you'll find her interesting."

And he gave me her number, but without identifying who Jessup was or what organization she was with. Which was more unusual behavior for him, and clearly deliberate.

I thanked him and rang off. Then spent the next half hour googling Jessup. Who turned out to be absolutely fascinating. Including the fact I could find no reference to her current employers.

I called the number Adrian had given me.

"Jessup here," said a crisp female voice.

"My name is Barbara O'Grady," I said.

"Of Barbara O'Grady Investigations," she said immediately. "Yes, I know of your work. Perhaps Adrien Keller suggested you call me?"

Which surprised me again. Though after what Google had told me about her past employers and her various skills, it shouldn't have. If she had any interest in Carli Fine Arts, she probably already knew Annegret had hired me.

"Yes to all of it," I said. "Do you have a few minutes to talk?"

"About?" she asked.

"I'm looking for some background information on the Annegret Carli Fine Arts Gallery," I said.

There was a click on the line. Had she been recording me, and stopped? Or was she recording me now? It may be illegal, but it can be hard to prove.

"I'll come to you," she said. I noted that she didn't ask for the address. "Does four o'clock work for you?"

"This afternoon?" I asked, surprised again. Birgitte Jessup currently seemed to be based in lower Manhattan, when she wasn't working out of Geneva. If she could be here by four, she had to be in town. Why?

Before the silence got too noticeable, or so I hoped, I regained my mental balance. "Yes, four is fine."

"I'll look forward to seeing you then," she said, and disconnected.

I sent a quick text to Amber, letting her know to expect my guest. It was odd to know that my formerly rundown office would now stack up against an internationally focused Manhattanite's expectations—Jessup would be offered excellent coffee with fresh cream, and a comfortable seat in our cutting edge waiting room.

Not that any of that mattered—our new high end tech systems were far more relevant for our actual work—but the transition still made my head spin some days.

A quick rap on my door distracted me. Before I had a chance to respond, Badger walked in and dropped into the leather chair opposite the desk.

"We need to talk," she said.

Which isn't her usual style.

"What's gone wrong now?" I asked, half-expecting a complaint about Marie, or about the limited hours Cory has available.

But it isn't only the physical office that has changed in the last month.

"I don't like what I'm seeing on this case," Badger said. "There's too much attention on our client and her gallery."

"What do you mean?" I asked, with a sinking feeling I already knew.

She gave me a sharp look. "Who'd you just talk to?" she asked.

It's a good thing I'd let go of all my expectations of hierarchy within the office the day after I hired Badger as a consultant. Not that they were very high to start with—rigid office structures make my nauseous. I'd been at the mercy of enough of them in my days as an office temp to cure me of that kind of thinking forever.

"Adrien Keller of Interpol," I said. "And Birgitte Jessup. He…."

"Recommended her," Badger said, nodding as if to herself. "Which explains why a ghost firm like I^2 is suddenly checking into us."

I made a mental note to ask her later why she'd called I^2—which is pronounced Eye Squared—a ghost firm. "Us? You mean they're checking out the firm?" I said. "When did this happen?"

"Probably seconds after you called Jessup," she said. "What number did you call her on?"

"So Brigitte Jessup works for I^2? The plot thickens," I said, passing the notepad I'd jotted the number in across to her. "So that's how she knew Keller had sent me."

"It would figure."

"Are I^2 set up to automatically track all new calls, then? Or just ones from specific numbers?" I asked.

"Yes," Badger said, with a wry look.

In her terms, I was asking idiotic questions again. No matter. It worked for me. Hopefully for her too—she hadn't quit yet.

And the few people who knew anything about Badger's real talents were still slightly stunned that she'd ever accepted a job at all, let alone with a company as small as mine. But for some reason, she liked being part of the team.

"Great." I thought about being tracked by I^2 for a minute. "Jessup is coming here at four. What can you find out about her by then?"

"She's in town?" Badger asked. "Why?"

"That's one of the things I need to know. But at a guess, I'd say it's because Annegret Carli is here."

Badger was nodding, as if that made sense to her, too. "Just how big a mess is our new client in, anyway?"

"And that would be the other thing I need to know. Can you do it?"

Badger just gave me a look and did her own ghost imitation out the door.

———

BY FOUR O'CLOCK I felt much more prepared to meet with Birgitte Jessup. Until she walked into my office and gave me an assessing stare. This was not at all how I'd pictured her, based on the business-like tone I'd heard over the phone.

Jessup was tall, over six feet if I was any judge, with an athletic build—currently confined in a custom tailored black trouser suit that I suspected minimized some solid muscles—and a direct gray gaze. Long blond hair was scraped back in a tight braid ending halfway down her back, and she wore minimal makeup.

I went forward to shake hands, and felt small by comparison. Not a feeling I'm used to—I'm nearly five foot ten and a runner. But Jessup had a physical presence that was immediately notice-able. No custom nail polish here, I thought, then immediately glanced at her hands to be sure. Nope, short cut, well-polished nails with a clear varnish. Okay then.

"Nice to meet you," I said, waving her to a seat. I deliberately took the power position behind the desk to offset a little of her physical presence. "Though I'm surprised you're here in town."

She smiled, and it was genuine enough to touch her eyes, if not warm them. She was assessing me as carefully as I was assessing her. I wondered rowhat she saw. Or thought she saw.

"I had a little business here," she said. "And it's a beautiful city, even in the rain."

So she wasn't about to share any more information than she had to. This was going to be fun.

"There's a magic that happens at night, when the city lights gleam through the rain," I said.

"I've seen that," she said. Then leaned forward in her chair. "But I'm not here to talk about the city. You called about Annegret Carli Fine Arts. Why?"

"As I said, I'm looking for some background, since it impacts on a case we're working on," I said.

"And I don't suppose you'd tell me who your client on that case that might be?" she said.

"I don't suppose I would."

"Or whether it has anything to do with the fact that Annegret Carli herself is in town at the moment?"

"Oh?" I said, deliberately keeping my face and tone neutral.

"Mmmm," she said. "She had an appointment with you on Monday."

"And you're keeping track of her, why?" I asked.

"Are you sure I'm not keeping track of you?" she asked, with no hint of the humor I suspected lurked behind the question.

"Your people are good, I'm told," I said. Badger had been very clear on that. "But so are mine."

"So I've heard," she said, tipping her head a little to one side, the blond braid shifting along her arm with the movement. "It's why I wanted to meet with you."

"Go on."

"I'd like to share information," she said. "Discreetly, of course."

"Anonymously, perhaps?" I suggested.

"Exactly," she said, still with no expression on her face. "I am so glad we understand each other." And she winked at me. She had her body language so under control that for a moment I couldn't believe I'd actually seen that hint of levity. But it had been there.

I'd been right. This was definitely going to be fun.

CHAPTER EIGHT

Half an hour later I watched Jessup leave, still shaking my head over the complex dance of deniability the two of us had engaged in. Then I grabbed a coffee and headed into the bullpen, as I'd come to think of the main office where most of the time Marie, Badger and Cory—when he wasn't at school—hung out. It was time for another team meeting.

Which made the third in as many days. A record for us, and not one I was impressed with. But as much as I needed time to process and make sense of the information Annegret and Jessup had each thrown at me, I needed to get the team involved in clarifying the details as they unfolded even more.

As I walked into the bullpen, Cory's eyes widened. "Aunt B? What's wrong?"

I hadn't expected him to be there. "Why aren't you in school?"

"Technical training," he said, as if that explained anything. "Teacher's half-day," he added, apparently reading my blank look.

I nodded. "Make sure you get your homework done," I said, mindful of my most recent promise to his mother.

He gave that the eye-roll it deserved. "Yeah, yeah. You can't distract me that easily. What's wrong?"

"What makes you think something's wrong?" I said.

You'd think I'd know better.

"You're pale," Marie said. "And you've got those little frown lines."

Always good to hear.

"And you just met with Birgitte Jessup," Badger added. "Who has a reputation as a barracuda, one who is very comfortable working in the shadows. And never misses a trick."

Yeah, she'd told me that before the meeting. She'd called it right, too.

"You come up with any more on I^2 while I was meeting with Jessup?" I asked her.

She gave me a look and didn't answer.

Why me? I wondered, as I looked from one concerned face to another.

Cory grinned. "You're wishing we'd at least pretend to believe what you tell us again, aren't you?"

When did he learn to read me so well, anyway?

"We need a meeting," I told them, giving up. "This case is getting crazier by the minute, and I think we're going to have to work hard just to stay on top of it."

"I've got stuff, too," Badger said, and had already turned back to her laptop, her fingers flying, before I could answer.

My nephew grinned. "I'll make the coffee," he said.

Marie nodded. "Good idea," she told him. "I'll call downstairs, and see what they have."

The bakery that had opened downstairs had figured out there was a market for fresh pastries all day long, and they were going intent on cornering it. They were going to be responsible for me lengthening my morning run every day, not just once in a while. But it was worth it. "See if they have bear claws," I said.

After surviving half an hour with a barracuda, I deserved one. Maybe two.

———

THE BEAR CLAWS were every bit as soft and fresh as I'd hoped, and the chocolate they pour over them every bit as richly decadent as I'd remembered.

"What happened with our new client?" Marie demanded as I savored the first bite.

Impatient as ever, I thought with an inward grin. I took my time finishing that bite of my bear claw. Badger had probably already filled Marie in on Jessup, anyway.

"And who is this mystery woman you just met with?" she continued.

Or maybe not.

"The most recent meeting was with Birgitte Jessup," Badger said. "She works for a very private company called I Squared. Only they got cute and use the symbol."

Marie squinted at her. "I^2? What exactly is that?"

This should be interesting. I took another bite of my bear claw.

"I^2 is a private company that was set up in the 70s. Back then, they were known as Information Squared," Badger said.

Cory was frowning a little, like that meant something to him. Which surprised me.

Marie shook her head. "Okay, so I gather they deal in information. But what kind of company are they?"

"A multifaceted one, that deals in secrets," Badger said. "I^2 is like an iceberg. What they show is only a tiny bit of what they're really up to. And they've got tentacles everywhere."

"Icebergs don't have tentacles," Cory said. Probably to irritate her.

"This one does," she told him.

"They're investigators?" Marie asked.

"Very private ones, who deal in secrets. They can also handle any high level security evaluations a client might want. Including technical security. The list goes on," Badger said.

"Would they provide security monitoring and guards?" Marie asked.

"No. They'd design the security architecture, suggest firms that could handle the day-to-day. Even evaluate their work, should the client require it," Badger said.

"So who do they work for?" Marie asked.

"Law enforcement. Big companies. Countries. Anyone who will pay their going rate. Which is high. Really high."

Most of which I already knew, but only in general terms. I'd never dealt with them myself, or had a client who did so, either. Not that I knew of, anyway. "Are their operations legal?" I asked.

"On the surface, anyway," she said.

That's what I'd thought. "So what's under the surface?"

"Stuff that's mostly on the Dark Web," she said.

"They sell their services there?" Cory wanted to know.

"Not that I've found so far," Badger said. "It seems to be mostly about information. They'll pay, and well, for what they want."

"So how do they advertise?" Marie wanted to know.

"They don't have to," I said. "If you're big enough, and deep-pocketed enough to need them, you'll know about them."

"Oh. One of those," she said. "If you have to ask, you can't afford us anyway?"

Badger nodded. "Exactly that," she told Marie.

She turned to me. "So why did their most valuable operative want to meet with you?"

Jessup was I^2's most valuable operative? That certainly wasn't public information. It did explain a few things about the meeting I'd just had with her, though. I wondered how Badger had dug that up. And knew I'd never ask.

"She was taking my measure, I think," I said slowly, thinking it through even as I answered her. "She either guessed Annegret had hired us..."

"Or she'd seen the money transfer," Badger said.

"Or that," I agreed. "She wanted to confirm it."

"You told her?" Marie asked, looking a little green.

I'd caught her reading a book on business law the other day, which she'd promptly hidden. I guess she'd got to the chapter on client confidentiality and legal implications.

"Of course not," Cory said. "Don't you know Aunt B. better than that yet?"

At which Marie turned a little red, and I tried to keep a poker face.

"I^2 has access to very good data, and Birgitte Jessup is very, very good at reading people. She had my number within the first minute," I told them. "And once she did, she wanted to share information, while retaining deniability on both sides." I paused to let that sink in. "More coffee anyone?"

"You aren't going to just leave it there," Marie said, leaping up from her chair and standing over me. "We're a team, you said. You can't just decide what information gets shared."

Oh, yes I could. But I hid a grin, because for a change I was way out ahead of her.

"And this is information you all need to know," I said. "Which is why we're meeting, remember?"

"Oh," she said, and glanced from Cory's grin to Badger's sardonic smile. "How about I get the coffees."

Which enabled her to make a graceful exit. Or what was probably meant to be a graceful exit. It put me in mind of a glossy beetle scuttling for cover, its little legs flying. That she was wearing all black only enhanced the image.

Not that I planned to tell her so. She was already having a bad day. And she was smart. She'd figure it out.

———

WITH FRESH COFFEE steaming in front of me, I started at the top. "We need to revisit this case, and rethink whether we're going to take it on."

"What? Why?" Marie said, staring at me. Her posture was defensive. She still felt sorry for Annegret. Which didn't surprise me, but it was good to have that confirmed now, instead of being blindsided by it later.

"That's why," I said. As she bristled, I added, "This case has us all on edge in different ways. I suspect that's only going to get worse."

"But…" Marie began.

Clearly, I needed to have another chat with her about trusting clients too far. She needed to recognize it as the professional weakness it was. One that can be particularly lethal early in a case, because it can color our interpretation of the facts.

No matter how much I valued Marie's unexpected soft side—particularly since it was such a complete contradiction to her usually prickly personality—she needed to develop a bit more discrimination when it came to evaluating potential clients and their stories.

"I've been digging," Badger said, breaking the tension that was simmering in the air. "We've only seen a tiny portion of what this case is about. What I've found so far makes *me* nervous."

That distracted Marie, and she and Cory both stared at Badger.

"You? I've never seen you nervous about anything," Cory said.

"It can happen," Badger said. "Just not often."

"What did you find?" I asked her. Certain that things were about to get much worse.

"Someone on the Dark Web is using Annegret Carli Fine Arts as a conduit for washing dirty art," Badger said.

"Like laundering cash?" Cory said.

"Exactly like that," Badger said. "Only much more lucrative."

"How do you wash dirty art?" Marie asked.

I had a mental image of a woman dressed all in black hanging out canvases on an old fashioned clothesline, complete with wooden spring-loaded clothespins, in someone's grassy backyard. Despite how bleak I felt about this case, the image had me hiding a grin at the ridiculousness of my imagination.

"Just like you'd expect," Badger said. "You hire a talented forger to create the art, and probably the documentation, work up a cover story that explains where the paintings originated, and find a gallery gullible enough, or crooked enough, to sell the works. It also helps if the gallery you choose has a sterling reputation."

"That's what happened with the Montaugh Gallery," Marie said. "They went under."

"You told us. And they'd been in business a hundred and fifty years, too," Cory helpfully reminded her.

She glared at him.

"Can you tell where the forgeries are coming from?" I asked Badger before Cory could make things worse. "Or whether Carli Fine Arts is the only place being used to launder art?"

Badger shook her head. "Not yet. Whoever this is, they know how to use technology to their advantage and stay hidden."

"What about the gallery itself? Any sign anyone there is involved?" I asked.

"There are a few too many trails leading to the gallery," Badger said. "And all of them are easy to find—unlike the rest of this scam. Which suggests to me that this could be a set-up."

Marie perked up a little. "So Carli Fine Arts might be a victim?" she said.

"Possibly," Badger said. "Or someone there is very guilty and is using a complex double bluff."

"Which wouldn't fool Interpol for a moment," I said. "Let alone my new buddy Jessup. Could it be an inside job, but with only one or two key people involved?"

"Again, it's possible," Badger said. "I have more digging to do."

"When you followed those trails to the gallery?" Marie asked. "Where do they lead?"

"Most of them point to Annegret Carli directly," Badger said. "It could mean she's guilty, and being set up to take the fall by her partners, the forgers. Or that she's innocent of all of this, and one of her employees is setting her up. Or even that Carli Fine Arts is the victim in all of this."

Badger's tone said she didn't believe the last possibility, and Marie's face fell. But our tech genius had nicely summed up our current situation. Unfortunately, that didn't move us forward.

"Based on what we know now, those seem like the logical options," I said. "But if it's this messy now, I think we have to assume that we're missing quite a bit. And it's only going to get worse."

"So what now?" Marie asked.

"We start over. From the beginning," I said. "We are going to verify every fact. Starting with the frauds Carli Fine Arts found."

"Your meeting this morning," Cory said, nodding sagely.

I hid a grin at his tone, but he had it right.

"Exactly. But before I get into what we know so far, it looks like we'll be dealing with some pretty sensitive information," I said. I was pretty sure they could hear just how seriously I was taking this resonating in my voice. "Everything we learn, everything we discuss has to stay confidential. You can't even tell your dog."

Knowing full well none of them owned dogs. Which served to make the point without saying anything that could be construed as finger pointing.

Badger nodded.

"We already signed a confidentiality agreement," Cory said. "I know what it means." He sounded proud, which amused me.

"Marie?" I asked.

She looked up, seemingly startled.

"Is something wrong?" I asked her.

"No. I was just thinking…"

"About?"

"How much I love being part of this team," she said.

I blinked at her, wondering where that had come from. "I'm glad," I said. "About the confidentiality?"

"Of course," she said. Dismissing it with a wave of her hand. "You know I won't talk."

I'd been ninety percent sure of that, but it was good to know she took it as a given. And confidentiality was now top of mind for all of them. I had a feeling that could be important in the not too distant future.

"Good," I said. "So those three frauds that our client said her gallery found when they reviewed their most recent purchases and sales? They did use the well-known testing facility that Cory found, which is good. But they only sent seven paintings to XTC Tech."

"And found three frauds?" Cory said. "That's… bad."

"Wait. A gallery that famous only sold seven paintings last year?" Marie asked. Either the fraud rumors have already spread everywhere, or they're in bigger trouble than they've told us."

"No. They handled—bought or sold—seventy paintings in the last year. They had an internal expert review all of them," I said. "And they only found questions worth getting checked further in their unsold inventory."

"So asked XTC Tech to test seven paintings out of seventy?" Badger said. "How did they review the others?"

"According to Annegret, their internal expert did the same technical review on all seventy works, checking for anything questionable. And out of those seventy reviews, only half of the fifteen they hadn't yet sold raised any concerns," I told her.

"That's impossible," Marie said. "It sounds like they used a visual checklist. And not a very thorough one"

I nodded. "Exactly. And it gets worse. After I talked to Annegret, I called Adrien Keller of Interpol, and asked if he'd heard anything about Carli Fine Arts."

Which drew nods from all three of them. They all knew Keller from his involvement in that previous case.

"He mentioned rumors, but said he couldn't talk about it," I finished.

Marie frowned. "But…that means he's heard about the fraud rumors. And that Carli Fine Arts are somehow involved in one of Interpol's active cases."

"Exactly. Even if it only turns out to be a peripheral connection, they are on Interpol's radar. And then Keller referred me to Birgitte Jessup."

"Of I^2," Marie said. Her mouth had tightened. "And what did she tell you?"

"It was mostly by implication," I said. "Someone—presumably a client—must have brought I^2 into Keller's investigation. And they aren't bound by the same confidentiality rules that Keller is. It seems Interpol and I² are looking into a swath of recent art forgeries that they suspect may be connected, which stretch across Europe and into the Middle East. And Carli Fine Arts is definitely a major focus for both of them, though Jessup wouldn't—or couldn't—tell me why. Or what exactly they suspect."

"Annegret must know something is seriously wrong," Marie said. "Or she wouldn't be hiring a private investigative firm."

"Especially not one this small and from so far away," Cory said.

Impressing me again. I hadn't expected him to make that connection.

"Then she lied to us," Marie said flatly.

"It gets worse," Badger said.

We all turned to look at her, and she gave us a tight smile.

"In addition to the forgery rumors, it looks like someone on the Dark Web might be using Annegret Carli Fine Arts to launder money," she said.

She'd been right. That was worse.

"How would that work?" Marie asked.

"Switzerland used to be a haven for playing money games with tax laws," I said. "Until they changed the game in '16. I'll have to dig into the relevant laws to be sure, but I think the seller—in this case the gallery—is responsible for verifying the source of the buyer's money."

"So if they were laundering money, then those proofs would be forged, too," Cory said.

Sometimes it worries me how quickly my nephew understands criminal behavior.

"And someone at the gallery has to be making the bad guys look like outstanding citizens," Badger said. "It doesn't look good for our client."

"Can you tell where the money is coming from? Or if there are other art galleries involved?" I asked her.

"So far all I've got are the equivalent of rumors," Badger said.

"But they point to the gallery?" Marie asked.

"Yes." There was no doubt in Badger's tone.

Marie looked really upset. She'd liked Annegret, might even have seen her as a possible mentor? After the example her late, unlamented aunt had set for her, she would need to know that her artistic dreams were possible.

And that she was allowed to dream.

If I was right, that explained a lot.

"But when you followed those trails to the gallery?" Marie asked Badger. "Where do they lead?"

"Most of them point to Annegret Carli directly," Badger said. "It could mean she's guilty, and being set up to take the fall by her partners, the forgers. Or that she's innocent of all of this, and one of her employees is setting her up. Or even that Carli Fine Arts is the victim in all of this."

Badger's tone said she didn't believe the last possibility, and Marie's face fell. But our tech genius had nicely summed up our current situation. Unfortunately, that didn't move us forward.

"Based on what we know now, those seem like the logical options," I said. "But if it's this messy on the third day of our investigation, I think we have to assume that we're missing quite a bit. And it's only going to get worse."

Marie drew in a deep breath, and I could see her focus that drive of hers. "So we'll find those missing pieces, until we really know what we're dealing with," she said, giving me a wry smile. "Which means we can't trust anything our client tells us."

I nodded. There was no point in telling her that was my usual starting point on any case. She didn't need to develop my brand of cynicism, not after a horrible childhood with an embittered aunt who mostly ignored her. She was just beginning to explore the possibilities the world might offer her.

Same went for Cory. Though some days, I'd swear that kid had been born cynical. But his sense of humor made up for a lot.

Badger? We shared a look. Whatever her background was, at twenty-four she was a more hardened cynic than I was.

I appreciated that about her. And the fact that we both knew neither of us was about to burst Marie's optimism.

"Marie is right," I said. "We need to keep digging. Annegret is sending as much information as she and her manager can gather relating to those seventy paintings. The provenance, how and when the gallery acquired them, anything they have on who the works were bought from and sold to. We should have some of it in the morning."

"Good," Marie said. "That should give us the answers we need."

I didn't have quite as much faith in either the documentation or the people gathering it for us. I exchanged a glance with Badger, then answered Marie.

"It will give us a starting point in getting those answers," I cautioned her. "No more. We need to dig, and hard, to uncover which of those 'facts' are true, and which are clever frauds."

"Then we'll need to start with the three frauds XTC Tech identified," Marie said. "Those will show us where and how the frauds were hidden. We should be able to work backwards from there with the other works."

There was hope for her yet. I didn't let my grin hit my face, but I felt like hugging her. Except she'd hate it.

"Good plan," was all I said. "If I can leave that to the three of you, I want to dig into what Annegret is doing in Vancouver."

"Didn't she come here to see you?" Cory asked.

"It's a long way to come," I said. "And even if she'll only hire people face to face, we've already signed the contract. She has a business to run. Yet she's still here. Why?"

"Oh. That make sense," he said.

I grinned. "I thought so."

He looked a little sheepish. Then grinned back.

"Badger and I will work together on that data," Marie said with a firm nod. "We each have half the equation. I understand the art side, she'll catch how the truth was rewritten in a nanosecond."

I glanced at Badger, who raised an eyebrow. But didn't argue.

Alright, then. We had a plan.

Cory cleared his throat very deliberately. And looked to Badger. "You're with me on this," she said. "Running errands."

He looked pleased.

Which left my worrying about exactly what errands she had in mind. And how upset my sister would be if she knew about it.

CHAPTER NINE

As Annegret had promised, by nine am the following morning I had the first installment of the data on the paintings Carli Fine Arts handled over the past year. I took my time going through it. Nothing jumped out at me, though I was impressed by how much her team had managed to pull together in a single day. Not only was it three-quarters complete, it was extremely well organized. They'd worked hard.

Clearly Annegret's confidence in her gallery manager was justified. Now maybe we could get somewhere on this case.

I skimmed the data again. Still nothing grabbed my attention. It was going to take a lot of work and expertise to pull the patterns out of this much data. Which I'd expected. If the source of their problems had been obvious, Annegret wouldn't have needed to hire us. I sent the data to the team, along with an additional request to Marie, and set off to engage in my own personal brand of digging.

Twenty minutes later I sat in Margaret's suddenly Zen-like office, wondering if I was in the right place. I almost didn't recognize it.

Somehow Margaret had corralled the mountains of paper that used to climb over every surface. I'd always loved studying whatever art she had on her office walls at any given time—and the Courtland Gallery always had an amazing selection of current artists to choose from—but the room itself had always been best described as chaotic. In a creative kind of way.

Now, the feeling was very calm. Serene, even. I blinked, and stared.

Margaret's large maple desk was clear of paper except for a few neatly labeled files on one corner. The top of the matching filing cabinet—which I'd never before noticed was maple, was also clear, except for a streamlined document scanner. There was even a pristine white orchid blooming on the small table in the corner.

From behind her desk, Margaret was watching me with a little smile. I was relieved to see she hadn't been subject to the same treatment her office had received. The wiry gray curls were still springing up here and there, and she wore blue jeans with low-heeled black boots and a blue sweater that matched her eyes, with a white smock over top. Slightly dusty white gloves lay on the desk in front of her.

I wondered what kind of collection she'd been examining, and where it had been stored to be so dusty. I'd never known Margaret and her husband Len to show anything but the best of the new art. Most of it from the West Coast, drawing on the urban environment as much as the rainforests, mountains and oceans that Emily Carr and artists after her are known for. Last year, she'd been the one to give me my first solo show as an artist, after pestering me about not giving up for a few years before that. Now she wanted to talk about a second show, and when I might have enough paintings ready.

I really didn't want to talk about it—there have been so many changes in my life recently, each with their own demands on my time, that my painting has taken a step back.

Painting is too important to me to lose, so I always manage to carve out a little time for it. But the pressure of committing to another show, with a scheduled date, and an advertising plan? No. Just no. I don't need the pressure right now.

Because of that, I'd been avoiding Margaret. And she knew it. I wasn't sure if that smile was because she'd finally got me in her office, where I couldn't avoid the discussion she'd been wanting to have. Or if it had to do with the utterly unrecognizable state of that office. Probably both.

I knew I was in for an uncomfortable conversation.

But it was a price I was willing to pay. As it became clear just how much of a mess the Annegret Carli case was, Margaret was the first person I wanted to talk to. And she'd immediately agreed to see me this afternoon. Which had probably meant rescheduling her entire day.

That told me that I was unlikely to get out of here without making some kind of commitment on my next show. I just hoped the information she could give me would be worth it.

"I'm glad you called, Barbara," Margaret said before I could speak. "What do you think about the changes I've made to my office?"

"It's amazing," I said honestly.

I still wasn't sure if it was amazing in a good way, or a bad one. I'm not entirely convinced that all this minimalism is good for creativity. But the new version of her office struck me as a good place to hold a difficult conversation, so there was that. Since we were about to have exactly that kind of conversation.

Margaret seemed pleased, but I had the feeling she'd read me like a book. "So. Annegret Carli is in town," she said.

I nodded. On the phone I'd only asked if she knew Annegret, and when she said yes, I'd asked if she'd be willing to talk about her. Margaret had agreed without asking a single question. Which was unusual enough to raise all my suspicions.

"You didn't by any chance refer Annegret to me, did you?" I said.

She laughed. "Of course I did. She called me a week or so ago, said she was planning to be in town, and after we arranged for a visit, she asked for the name of a reputable P. I. who knows something about the art world. I gave her your name, naturally."

"Thanks, I appreciate it," I said automatically. I still wasn't sure if we'd be keeping Annegret as a client. "Did she happen to mention why she was coming here?"

"She does a lot of buying trips, looking for artists."

It wasn't quite an answer. But I knew Margaret well enough not to push her on it. Not too far, anyway. I'd have to find out why Annegret was here some other way.

"A buying trip on the West Coast? It's a little out of her usual range, isn't it?" I said, trying to think of anyone here that would fit with her gallery's mandate.

"You might be surprised," Margaret said with a small smile that had me quickly running through the list of newer artists I knew. No-one fit.

Still, Annegret Carli had founded her gallery and built a stellar reputation. Who was I to question where she looked for artists? And yet.

"How do you know Annegret?" I asked.

"The art world is a small one," Margaret said. "We all know who handles certain types of art. I've been ConnectLine friends with her for years now. And Len and I stayed with her in Geneva when we took that trip to Europe a couple of years ago."

Margaret had ConnectLine friends? Somehow I hadn't expected her to be that comfortable with social media. Which was ridiculous, because the Courtland Gallery is very active and well represented on social media. I'd just assumed she hired that out.

Making me feel a bit of a Luddite. What time I spend on social media is usually research for a case. It's amazing how much information is lightly shared. It can be invaluable for a P. I., but it makes me wary of doing much posting personally.

"Then you're the right one to talk to," I said. "What can you tell me about Annegret and her gallery?"

"I'm assuming you're looking for an overview?" she said.

"Actually, I'm looking for anything that isn't common knowledge," I said.

"If you're looking for dirt, I wouldn't share it with you, even if I knew any," she said bluntly.

"And I wouldn't ask," I told her equally bluntly. "They've had an impeccable reputation for decades. Has that changed?"

She looked shocked. "Their reputation? No."

I'd had my answer just from her expression. "Have you heard anything about business troubles?"

"With Carli Fine Arts? Absolutely not," she said without waiting for a reply. "They are rock solid, and always have been. But why are you asking this? Is Annegret in trouble?"

"I'm sorry…" I began.

But she interrupted me. "I know, I know. You can't tell me. Because she's a client. That's why you're here. Isn't that why she's really in town?"

The flow of words told me how genuinely shocked she still was. "Margaret…"

She held up a hand. "Never mind. I know. I'll call her, see if I can help. Don't worry, I won't mention you."

"Thank you." Though I suspected Annegret wouldn't be surprised that I'd talked to Margaret. Or that she'd figured it out.

"Now, since you're here, let's talk about your next show," Margaret said, leaning forward a little.

And just like that, the in-control business woman was back. I stifled a groan. I'd hoped to avoid this discussion. "It can wait, Margaret," I said. "I'm a little busy at the moment."

She gave me that shark's look. "All we need is to set a date. Once it's on your calendar, you'll get the paintings done."

She knew me too well.

"But at what cost?" I said. "There are people that need my help. Urgently." Like your friend Annegret, I thought but didn't say.

She nodded, not missing the inference. It didn't sway her at all.

"You're a very good investigator," she said. "But you're an artist first. It's why you're doing so well in the field you've chosen—you bring a unique perspective that others miss."

She paused, gave me that eagle eye. "You told me after your last show that you were never going to let your business take over from your art. That's why you have staff, remember?"

This was so not going to go well.

———

BACK IN MY OWN OFFICE, I added the May date for my second solo art show to next year's calendar with a grimace. I was committed now. I turned back to Annegret's file with a sense of relief. Which lasted all of thirty seconds. I was still getting nowhere on this one, and so far, with every fact or rumor the team dug out, the situation seemed to get worse.

Hopefully there were answers in the data sets the team was digging into now.

As if in answer, the phone rang. I glanced at the number. Nick. And to my shame, I almost didn't answer.

Avoidance wasn't going to solve anything. Except maybe make the problem of moving in with him go away. Permanently. Which I didn't want. That much I was clear on.

"Hey, you," I said.

"Hey, yourself," came Nick's deep voice. "You free for dinner tonight?"

I glanced at my schedule. "I can make it work."

"Great. I'll pick you up at your place around seven?"

"Make it seven-thirty, and you've got a deal" I said. "Guido's?"

"Done. Gotta run," he said, and disconnected.

Except for the house listings he'd brought to lunch yesterday, Nick had been pretty quiet about moving in together since all the disruption in my office after my last big case. He'd been working on something he couldn't talk about, too, so maybe that was it.

But he was a patient man, especially when he wanted something. I had the feeling he was just waiting for things to settle down in my business life before he proposed any more changes in my personal world. Smart man.

Not that my business life ever really settled down. Or his did either. But the recent expansion of my office, and the kind of cases coming my way now...? That was different.

Nick's patience made me a little nervous, though. What happened when it ran out? Would it run out?

Still, for now it meant I could look forward to seeing him tonight, and just enjoy an evening without more decisions or problems. I'd just started to look forward to that when the door burst open and Marie bounced in. I hadn't seen her bounce like that since she'd adopted her Justine-mentored, sophisticated persona. Now what?

"You scheduled your next show!" she said.

Oh. I'd forgotten they'd linked the calendars on all the office computers. So the minute I added the new show to my laptop, everyone had seen it. Including Marie.

"We'll have to talk about adjustments to your schedule," she said, plopping down in the chair across from me. "So you have time to get your painting done for your second show, even when we're in the middle of big cases. You know how important it is to follow the success of the first show with another success."

Here we go. This was not a conversation I wanted to have now. Maybe not ever. But especially not now.

Then it hit me.

A few years ago, if you'd told me I'd be having a second solo show at the Courtland Gallery, I'd never have believed you. Now I was avoiding even thinking about it?

I couldn't ignore my non-work life forever. Not if I actually wanted to have a life outside the office, anyway.

Another dream that had once seemed impossible.

None of which I was going to discuss with Marie. Who was watching me with a knowing look in her eyes. What was that about?

"I thought you were looking into how much of what our new client's told us is true. And how much is lies?" I said.

Marie made a face. "I did. But I didn't get very far online before

I ran into dead ends. So I passed what I did find to Badger. She and Cory are looking for recurring patterns."

Of course they were. "And Annegret?"

"I tracked her recent travel, and she's been here as long as she said she has. And she's staying where she said she was, where she is booked for another three days. The front desk was happy to leave a message for her," Marie said.

"Well done," I told her.

"It's a start," she said. "But I'm not getting anywhere. At least not till Badger hands me the next piece to work on. And it gets kinda depressing, not believing the clients you like. Your upcoming show is way more interesting," she added with a grin.

"But it doesn't pay your salary," I said. "And the frustrating digging for information bit comes with the job."

"Yeah," Marie said with her old scowl. Then her face smoothed into the perfect employee look that hid too much. "And between us, we'll get this one solved fast. So you can start planning your show."

She was up and out of my office before I could think of a suitable retort. But she paused at the doorway, and winked at me over her shoulder.

Nice to know my life was providing distraction and amusement for her, I thought as I turned back to the issue of our current difficult client.

I still didn't know what Annegret Carli was doing here in the middle of October. And staying for a week? It made no sense.

There was no big art-related event happening. I didn't believe Annegret was here looking to sign a local artist—I'd have heard. A show at Annegret Carli Fine Arts was big news. So why *was* she here?

It couldn't have been just to hire us—we could have video conferenced. And a week was too long for her to stay, even if she had needed to meet me in person before deciding to hire us.

I drummed my fingers on the desk while I thought back through my meeting with Margaret. She'd been evasive about why her friend was in town. Professional courtesy? Or was Margaret worried about something and not wanting to talk about it? Maybe something Annegret had said or done that didn't ring true?

If there was something, Margaret clearly wasn't going to tell me. But if Margaret had noticed something off, then others would have too. I just had to find them. And get them to talk to me.

I messaged Marie, asking her to find out as much as she could about what Annegret had been up to while she was here, and send it to me. Then I grabbed my new favorite purse, the one Andrea had introduced me to a few months before. It was black, of course, and very well made. Also expensive. But as far as I was concerned, it was worth every penny.

It was one of a line of capacious bags that would hold practically anything I needed on a case and keep it organized, while still looking professional. Mine had a few extra pockets that I appreciated, but still managed to keep that sleek profile. It even felt appropriate for a business dinner. To me, anyway. I'd probably get a few arguments on that one. I grinned at the thought, and after a glance at the lowering clouds outside, grabbed my waterproof coat. I let Amber know I was gone for the rest of the day except for emergencies, and headed out.

Leaving the car behind, I headed out into the biting wind of a late October afternoon. There was no snow on the mountains above the city yet, but I could smell it in the wind. It wouldn't be long now. That should make the skiers—and the resorts—happy. We were overdue for an early skiing season.

I walked along Water Street, heading towards the downtown core and the very upscale hotel where Annegret was staying, which wasn't far. I had a few ideas to follow up, but I was hoping Marie would dig out some concrete contacts before I got there. Either way, I needed the walk in the brisk air to clear my head.

Marie came through. My watch buzzed to alert me that she'd emailed me. She must have had help from Badger to get this much detail so fast, I thought as I scanned the list of Annegret's appointments over the last few days.

I quickly glanced around me, realized I'd just passed one of my favorite coffee shops, and slipped inside, shaking off the light rain that had begun to fall.

Over a cappuccino, I reviewed Annegret's appointments, looking for a pattern and trying to get into her head. She'd met with the Director of the Vancouver Art Gallery, and also with the owners of several private galleries, including Margaret. She'd also had meetings with several banks, which I found odd. Switzerland was the gold standard—literally—for private banking around the world. Why would she be meeting with Canadian banks? Yet she was.

And why here? The head offices for most of these banks are back East. Except one. HSBC, which has branches around the world, including in Switzerland. And the Canadian head office was three blocks away from where I sat. And just around the corner from Annegret's hotel.

A pattern? Or was I reaching, because so far I was missing the connections that might make sense of this case?

I still had no idea. Which annoyed the hell out of me.

CHAPTER TEN

By the time I got to Guido's that evening, I really needed the glass of red wine he already had ready for me. It's like he has a sixth sense or something—he always has my wine ready when I get there. No matter that I seldom make reservations.

My eyes swept the cozy, familiar restaurant, automatically cataloguing the faces at the bar, a few of whom I half recognized, the fact that the place was still half-empty. Otherwise, everything was the same, the colors and textures evoking the Umbrian countryside that was Guido's proud heritage. What did it say about me that I found the sameness reassuring?

Yes, this case was a tricky one. But there was a reason Guido's was my favorite neighborhood haunt on a street with any number of delicious alternatives to suit every style and cuisine. I hate to think of myself as boring, but in this case, I guess I am.

My gaze stopped on a booth in the back corner, as Nick caught my eye and smiled. No wonder Guido had known to have my wine ready, I thought as my knees melted a little at that smile. Both men thought I needed to relax more, and were rarely subtle about it. I suspected a conspiracy.

Which the militantly independent part of me found annoying.

On a day like today, though, that care felt like a warm blanket on a cold night. Though I'd never admit it to either of them. They'd just ramp up their efforts.

I smiled back, and wound my way towards the back. Sliding into the thickly upholstered booth, I took in the dark gold liquid in the squat glass he was holding. "Whiskey?" I asked. Which he rarely drank during the week, though we both enjoyed a good Scotch on occasion. And judging by the color, this wasn't the good stuff. "Your day must have been even worse than mine. And mine was a lulu."

He grinned, and lifted his glass in a toast. "To you."

I clinked glasses with him. "And to you."

When had we developed traditions, I wondered as we both drank. And why didn't the idea scare me more?

"Tell me," I said as I put down my wine.

"It'll take too long," he said. "You start. Then we'll order."

Oh boy. This wasn't good.

"Mine is short, but hardly sweet," I said. "My latest case is on track for being one of the worst ones I've ever taken on."

He grinned. "Let me guess. Client isn't telling you everything. The facts you do have aren't adding up. There are no leads. And it involves art, in some way. Oh, and the money is too good to turn down. In other words, the early stages of any big case."

"Not bad," I said, sipping my wine. "The first three are no surprise. But where do you get the art involvement from?"

He looked at me. Shook his head. "Really, Barbara? Think about your last big cases."

"This isn't about the money," I said. "It isn't why I took this case."

"No, it was probably one of the reasons you nearly turned it down," he said. "And when I say your big cases, I'm not talking about the money."

"Then what are you talking about?" I asked. Trying not to sound grumpy. He was right, and I didn't want to admit it. "And how did you know that bit about my nearly turning the case down when the client offered to double the fee?"

He laughed. "I hope you took the higher fee."

"Of course I did. If it's this annoying already, I'm going to earn every cent of that fee before this case is done. Which doesn't mean I won't cancel the contract if the client won't start working with me. Instead of against me."

"Uh huh. Sure you will," he said.

"You don't believe me?"

"I think you won't be able to resist the case itself," he said. "Client or no client. Especially with the art connection. What is it this time, by the way?"

"Fine art fraud. Forged paintings," I said.

Chuckling, he raised his glass to me again. "What did I say? No way you're leaving a case like that to some other firm to solve. Where?"

And he drained the rest of his glass. Which worried me. Something was really getting to him. What?

"Switzerland," I said. "I might have to spend a few days there."

"I won't be here to notice," he said.

There was a bleak note in his voice I didn't like at all. For an instant I worried that I'd finally worn out his patience, and he was ending us.

But even in that instant I knew better. Knew *him* better.

Just like he seemed to know me.

Whatever was going on with him, it was tied to this thing that was taking him out of town. And the odds were it was a case.

I could have kept pushing for answers, but he looked suddenly drained. He's only a couple of years older than I am, but even in the warm lighting, he looked as if he'd aged at least a decade.

"Why don't we order?" I said instead. Food almost always helped. Especially for the two of us.

It worked this time too. We ordered pasta, and lots of it—bolognese for him, four cheese for me—with lashings of red wine for both of us. By the time Guido brought out the huge serving of tiramisu, his specialty, Nick looked a lot better. And I'd forgotten to worry about my new client. Or the perils of moving in with Nick.

Walking back to my place, both of us wrapped tight against the wind that blew off the mountains on the north shore, the world felt right side up again. Nick hadn't said much about his case—just that it was drug-related and nasty. And that he was one of the experts that had been seconded from other detachments to help out a community that needed them. He didn't know how long he'd be gone, or how often he'd be able to call me. If at all. He wouldn't tell me exactly where he was going, either.

"North of here," he'd said briefly. Something in his tone told me it was probably quite a ways north. And to a place small enough I'd know too many details if he told me. Which meant it had been in the news lately.

And that calling it "nasty" was probably an understatement.

So I asked the only question I could. "Can you stay?"

He nodded, and we spent the next few hours making each other happy.

After feeding Cat, who alternated between being miffed I'd left him alone so long, and purring madly at Nick. All was right with my world again.

Until two a.m., when the incessant ring of my phone woke both of us from a sound sleep. I sat bolt upright, every nerve alert. Nick muttered something and rolled over, then opened one eye, watching me. If needed, I knew he'd be up and dressed in the time it took me to find my hairbrush.

Meanwhile Cat went flying and hid under a chair, staring at me with huge eyes. It took me a moment to find my phone as adrenaline surged, and my mind cycled through worst case scenarios.

"Yes?" I said abruptly once I found the phone on the carpet beside the nightstand. I grinned. Nick and I had really enjoyed ourselves.

"Barbara? Is that you?" came a frantic voice.

Annegret?

"It's me," I said. "What's wrong?"

Whatever it was, at this hour it couldn't be good.

"I need to see you," she said.

"What's wrong?" I said again.

"Amara is dead. My gallery manager. They… they just found her body. Behind the gallery. In Switzerland," Annegret added unnecessarily, her voice shaky.

"I'm so sorry," I said automatically, while I scrambled to catch up.

Her gallery manager was dead? The one she trusted. The one she'd asked to compile potentially sensitive data on the fraud investigation?

Oh no.

"You think it's related to the fraud?" I asked her.

"It has to be," she said. "Don't you see? I have to fly home immediately, but I need to meet with you. Can you come here?"

"Your hotel?"

"Room 417," she said. "Please hurry."

"I'll be there in forty-five minutes," I said.

It ended up being thirty-five. I didn't waste any time. But I did take the extra minutes to say a proper good morning to Nick, and to wish him safe journeys.

Neither of us were sure when we'd see the other again. It wasn't a good feeling.

CHAPTER ELEVEN

On Monday morning, I landed in Geneva's bustling airport, still uneasy about my decision to honor Annegret's request and follow her back to Switzerland. But when she'd called on Saturday to confirm that Amara Duvant's death had officially been declared a homicide, I saw little choice. Given the circumstances, trying to investigate even this early phase of the problems at Carli Fine Arts from Vancouver no longer made any sense.

I hadn't been sure from the first that it made sense anyway. Which was part of my problem in taking on the case. Even though I'd anticipated at least one trip to Geneva as part of the investigation, the distance involved put my firm at a disadvantage.

But I'd never anticipated murder.

The earliest flight I'd been able to get was the one-fifteen flight on Sunday afternoon. With the time difference, it meant I was arriving on Monday morning, three days after the murder, since the poor woman had been killed in the early hours of Friday morning, Geneva time.

The waters of Lake Geneva were dark and wind tossed in the glimpses I had through the downpour as the cab sped towards my hotel. In the flat morning light, the rain made it impossible to see much of the city sprawl as we passed through it. As we got closer, I could just make out the Jet d'Eau fountain, the huge plume of spray being flung in a flattened arc away from the city. I wondered how often the quays and the streets closest to the shore got drenched.

I was booked into the Hotel L'Étoile along a picturesque street in one of the older—and pricier—sections of Old Town, a few blocks from Annegret Carli Fine Arts. I just wished I was more confident that I'd actually be able to do something now I'd arrived. English may be the language of business, but in this part of Switzerland, French is the common language.

It's never easy to investigate when you don't speak the native tongue. Especially in a case this complex. And even more especially when it comes to murder. I did study French in school—it's Canada's official second language, after all, though you don't hear it often on the West Coast—and I can read it fairly well. But it's a stretch to say I speak it.

At least I'd been able to leave things in something resembling order at home. In fact, it had been surprisingly easy. Which always makes me nervous. This time Marie had volunteered to look after Cat, since Nick was now out of town on the assignment he couldn't talk about. And I still didn't know where he was, which I found more unsettling than I'd expected.

On the work side, Marie and Badger between them would handle the current caseload, since most of our focus at the moment was on this case. Which all three of them would keep digging into.

And Marie has proved herself a past master at delaying potential clients while making them feel the delay was for their benefit. Of course, she also had a tendency to think she knew what was best for them. And for the office. And then act on it.

On this worrying thought, the taxi pulled up in front of the gallery. Other than a cheerful red awning and white window boxes that held something bright red, I couldn't see much, as the rain had suddenly begun dumping down.

Luckily I'm used to that. With a quick *"Merci"*, I paid the driver, grabbed my travel umbrella and carry on bag, and swung myself out of the cab, opening the umbrella above me as I did so. I'd considered checking in at the hotel, taking a quick shower and ditching my suitcase first, but I didn't want to waste any more time than I already had. A decision I'd probably regret, but as long as they had strong coffee, I figured it would be worth it.

The sidewalks were empty, so I bee-lined for the door, painted a cheery red that matched the awning. An inset frosted multi-paned window spilled out the light within.

The gallery was clearly open, which was a good thing, since in the dash to the airport, I'd forgotten to check their hours. I'd have felt like an idiot for not going straight to the hotel if I'd found myself stranded outside in the pouring rain.

There was a neat doorbell off to one side, but I didn't need it. The door swung open just as I reached for the polished brass handle. They'd been expecting me.

"*Bienvenue*. Welcome. Come in, come in," a cheery voice said from inside. "Annegret said you would probably come straight from the airport, so there's fresh coffee and croissants in the back, if you'd like some?"

As I stepped into the warm, brightly lit interior of the gallery, I took a grateful sniff. Behind me I heard the click of a lock. Which explained the doorbell. Good for them. At least their basic security procedures were in place.

The coffee smelled wonderful, dark and rich, and the croissants were fresh enough to fill the air with the aroma of baking. I've always loved France for the coffee and the baking—well, all the food, really. Not to mention the art, and the atmosphere, and...

"Focus, Barbara," I told myself. Lack of sleep was no excuse for mental fogginess. And I'd slept on the plane. Sort of.

It seemed I was going to develop a similar love for Geneva, I thought, as a tall slim young woman with her long brunette hair pulled back and wearing a chicly fitting black skirt and light grey blouse led me towards the back of the gallery. Those enticing smells grew stronger as we grew closer.

As we passed down the generous hallway, I caught glimpses into several of the rooms. Enough to absorb the feel of the place. While the gallery itself wasn't huge, a good layout and a clever arrangement of moveable walls made it feel spacious and yet intimate in a way that invited patrons to browse. Everything was elegant, and from the flow of the layout to the perfect level of lighting in each area, it was designed for its effect on the customer's comfort level. But nothing was ostentatious, or overwhelming.

Except the art. I caught only flashes of color from the hallway, but the little I did see had my mouth watering in another kind of hunger.

All of this took a great deal of taste to accomplish. And an even greater amount of money.

Before I got too far in this case, I needed to spend some time in those rooms, let myself be drawn into my own exploration of the displays, and the individual pieces hanging on those walls. And my own impressions of the gallery itself.

Somehow this gallery was at the heart of a massive fraud, and was possibly being framed for it. Ironic though that sounded. Or, worse, the gallery might be the center of an even more massive cover-up.

Part of my job was going to be figuring out which. No matter what my client thought. But first I needed coffee.

Lots of coffee.

For now it wasn't the beauty of the gallery or the art that was important. It was the ugliness of fraud. And death. And lies.

That's what had brought me here.

And I needed to get past that impression, and get to the truth. Only then could I do the job I'd come here to do.

———

LOTS OF COFFEE was indeed what I was offered. And the reality lived up to my hopes. Surpassed them, even.

"Annegret sends her apologies, and hopes you will enjoy this small breakfast," the young woman said, waving me towards a brightly lit white room with framed art prints on the walls. "She is meeting with the *surete*—the police investigators, and will be with you shortly. If you need anything in the meantime, please, let me know. I am Giselle," she said with a lovely smile.

And she was one of Annegret's assistant managers here. Marie's thorough research had told me that much. She seemed pleasant, and to genuinely like people. Which was a helpful trait in her profession, if not necessarily relevant when it came to murder.

I glanced around me. The exceptional design I'd noticed passing through the gallery extended here, though this room was obviously designed for the comfort of the staff. It was small, but boasted an efficient kitchenette and a white marble topped bistro table with four elegant wrought iron chairs. There was a red geranium in a black pot blooming on the table, and a breakfast setting for one in pristine white china. A plate of croissants, both plain and filled, awaited me. Beside them sat a large French press wrapped in a white linen napkin, a small pot of cream and a covered sugar bowl, again in white china. It smelled heavenly.

"This is perfect," I assured Giselle. "Exactly what I needed. Especially the coffee, after a long flight."

"I understand the jet lag," she said. "The croissants are plain, chocolate filled, and almond filled."

I glanced at the pastries, the drizzle of chocolate on two, the thinly sliced almonds on another two, and smiled. "Even more perfect," I told her.

She smiled again, lighting up her face, but as she turned to go, I noted that despite the dark honey tone of her complexion, lines of strain were evident around her mouth and in the dark shadows under her eyes. Grief? Or something more?

It was my job to find out.

I'd need to talk to her, but that could wait. At least until I'd had my first cup of coffee. Then if there was still no-one else here, I'd ask if she could join me. Unless Annegret returned first.

Stacking my carry-on and my purse in a corner, I draped my damp coat over the back of one chair, and seated myself at another.

My umbrella had been left in an elegant umbrella stand by the front door. Year-round, Geneva gets close to the same rainfall that Vancouver does in late spring and early fall. It showed.

Inhaling deeply, I poured a dark stream of coffee, and reached for the cream. The first sip was heaven. Rich, smooth. I could feel the caffeine jolting through my still foggy brain, jolting every tired cell. My stomach growled. At least it had waited until Giselle left, I thought as I reached for a chocolate croissant. Taking a bite, I savored the flaky goodness.

And it finally hit me that Giselle had said that Annegret was with the *surete*.

Why?

I straightened from my exhausted slouch, and swallowed another mouthful of coffee. If there was something going on, I needed to be there, not here.

But since Annegret had left word with Giselle that she was delayed—and told her why? Then surely she would have asked that I join her there, if she'd needed me.

I took another bite of my croissant as I considered that. As the sweet pastry melted in my mouth, I decided that my time would be better spent getting a feel for the gallery and the art they dealt in. Rather than tearing off to a police station where I didn't speak the language.

I'd confront my client when she got here. And for that, I needed to be as sharp as possible. Which meant finishing my breakfast. And probably most of the coffee.

Maybe all of it, given how long it had taken me to register where Annegret was.

———

AFTER FOUR CUPS of coffee and two croissants, I was focusing again. And my urgent feeling that I needed to spend time in the gallery showrooms had resurfaced. Even without the demands of the case, I'd have been doing this. Show me an artist who doesn't love to spend time with great art, and I'll show you someone destined for a very short career.

Whether because of the weather or for some other reason, I had the showrooms to myself. I started with the room nearest the front door, which was mostly abstracts, with strong colors and design. These were were mid-century European works. Those displayed nearest the doorway were works on paper, with the oil paintings dominating as you went deeper into the room. All were for sale, though several had discreet 'sold' tags.

A framed poster near the entrance told me this particular exhibit had another month to run. Another framed poster hanging beneath the first informed me that the next exhibit would be 21st Century realism.

I let myself flow through the room, from one work to another. Not lingering anywhere, but getting a feel for the strengths of the exhibit and the gallery. Each artist had a strong vision and style that ran through each of their works. Though very different in style and approach, all these works reflected their era, while maintaining a modern sensibility.

It was so well done. No wonder Carli Fine Arts enjoyed such a stellar reputation. Or had done so, until recently. The reminder of my case moved me on to the next room.

Which took my breath. Impressionists. And those who followed them. And not second-rate artists, either.

These were the greats, the originators.

Monet. Renoir. Van Gogh. Degas. Manet. Cassatt. Cezanne. Morisot. Pissarro. Picasso. Dali. All of them were represented here, each work a separate jewel against the neutral tones of the walls. I had to remind myself to breathe.

Many of these were works on paper—I had to stop to take in the exquisite shading of a Degas drawing, the clarity of line in a Picasso. The oils were lesser known works, often smaller—but brilliantly chosen. I knew—had studied—every one of them. Though I'd never before seen the actual paintings. And each work stopped me in my tracks, leaving me without words.

So did the discreetly listed prices. I'd always wondered what it took to own an Impressionist painting. Now I knew. It took the kind of money I'd never see.

That was okay. Just to stand in the same room as these works, to be able to see the artist's actual brushstrokes, their choice and placement of color on a canvas—it was a gift.

With difficulty I forced myself to move on. I wanted to gain that first impression of the entire gallery before Annegret returned.

The next exhibit was so beautifully lit and hung, it felt more like a museum than a commercial establishment. The room was laid out so that you viewed each work in the isolated splendor it deserved. Until you physically moved on to the next. And every painting or drawing stopped my heart.

These were the old masters.

Da Vinci. Michelangelo. Raphael. Dürer. Vermeer. Rembrandt. Botticelli. Bruegel. El Greco. Rubens. Goya. Delacroix. They were all here.

In this amazing room, the paintings came first. Then the works on paper, nearer the exit. Like the Impressionists, these were mostly smaller, or lesser known paintings. But they were no less impressive for that.

There was a small Rembrandt with such amazing lighting that I had to stop and stare, and an exquisite Dürer miniature engraving. I could happily have spent the entire day looking at any one of these works. If I wasn't here on a case.

I quickly noticed that none of the paintings in this room had prices listed, which didn't surprise me. If you were able to afford any one of these, you wouldn't need to ask about price.

How could they could have paintings like these displayed without an armed security guard standing next to them?

When I finally tore myself away, I was surprised to find myself back in the hallway near the reception desk. I hadn't even noticed that I'd been led in almost a circle through the gallery. Whoever had designed the layout had done a masterful job. And lessened their security issues in the process. Supposedly, anyway.

As I exited the old masters room, Giselle looked up and smiled. "How was your tour?" she asked easily. No doubt she was used to the effect the exhibits had on those who hadn't seen it before.

"Stunning."

"Isn't it though?" she said. "It's my favorite thing about working here. Every time I tour the gallery, I see it differently."

"I can only imagine," I said. And meant it. To see those paintings, that kind of art, every day? In different lights, in different moods. It would be like being able to visit a major art museum every day for months.

And I'd just found a new item for my bucket list. Though it would take me forever to decide which museum belonged on that list. The Louvre? The Met?

"I can put on more coffee, if you'd like some," she said, interrupting my wishful thinking. "And there are fresh pastries, too. Help yourself."

"Have you heard from Annegret?"

"No. She should return soon, I would think."

I had considered asking her to show me through the working and storage rooms of the gallery, but that would have to wait. My tour had shown me how key her presence was at this exit from the showrooms.

"I will have more coffee, then. Thanks."

CHAPTER TWELVE

I had just finished eating my third croissant, and was savoring the last swallow of coffee, when a soft tone alerted me to the opening of the gallery. A customer? Or Annegret?

Moments later my client swept into the small, cheerful room on a wave of cool damp air and Chanel No. 5. "Barbara, you arrived safely. I am glad. And Giselle has welcomed you?"

"She did. And splendidly," I said, waving to the somewhat denuded table. "After the flight, it was exactly what I needed."

"Do not worry about hunger. I will take you out for lunch," she said. "Something special, to make up for not being here to greet you. But for now, why don't we talk in my office."

I hoped her office was sound proof. We had a lot to talk about. And Annegret wasn't going to want Giselle—or any patrons that might brave this rain—to overhear any of it.

It probably was, given the size of the deals that flowed through that office. Fraudulent paintings or not, they dealt with an amazing amount of money. And yes, Badger had dug that up, too. Or at least the amounts Carli Fine Arts reported annually.

I gave Annegret a speculative look, wondering how honest she was prepared to be. Under these difficult circumstances, faced with the murder of one of her own? She didn't have much choice, not really. Though she might not see it that way.

———

ANNEGRET'S OFFICE carried through the elegant theme of the gallery, but married it with a cold efficiency that surprised me. I wasn't sure why, so I paid attention to that feeling. There was something I'd missed about my enigmatic client, and given the complexities of this case, I couldn't afford to miss anything.

I glanced around me, seeing none of the standard, heavy—and rather masculine, come to think of it—office furniture I'd half expected. Nor did I see the cutting edge modernity my newly renovated premises now sported. Instead I saw a very feminine setup.

Everything from the walls to the heavy drapery to the furniture was in tones of white and cream. The exquisitely carved off-white desk with one shallow drawer had elegant Louis XIV style legs, as did the chair and the side table behind her desk. Slim, antiqued silver glass table lamps gleamed against the smooth finish, and gave off a warm light.

Yet the office felt ruthlessly efficient, though I couldn't have said why. Perhaps it was because every surface was clear, though I saw no other drawers or cupboards anywhere. Which reminded me a little of Margaret Courtland's new office look. And they were friends on ConnectLine. Maybe it was a thing. Could private art galleries be going entirely paperless?

But aside from Annegret's streamlined computer and her cellphone, I didn't see any technology, either. Well, aside from the security cameras on the ceiling. I dismissed the matter as interesting but not relevant, and focused on my reason for flying halfway around the world.

As soon as we were seated, I took out my notebook and pen. They weren't strictly necessary, but they helped set a tone. With Annegret, I suspected I'd need it.

"Why did the *surete* want to see you?" I asked her.

The words seemed to grate against all that elegance. Maybe they'd be enough to finally shake loose some truth from my challenging client.

Though I wasn't holding my breath.

Annegret drew the flat of her hand across the clear, smooth top of her desk, as if seeking reassurance. It struck me as an oddly revealing movement for her to make.

Was this delayed shock? Grief? Guilt? I couldn't tell. But it was in stark contrast to any emotion I'd seen from her before.

When I'd reached her hotel room in Vancouver, just over half an hour after she got the call about her employee's death, she'd been clearly upset, but very focused. Even as we talked, she didn't stop moving, as she efficiently returned her belongings to her suitcase.

She was determined to take the next flight out. And to take me with her.

Now, several days later, she looked distracted, not quite focused. It was a complete contrast to the mindset her office revealed.

I couldn't tell how much of Annegret's current reaction was shock over the murder of someone she'd known well, how much was grief for a valued employee. And how much might be—something else.

Had the interview with the *surete* unsettled her that badly?

Or was there something more I needed to know about?

"The *surete* had some questions for me," Annegret said. She straightened her spine until her back didn't touch the chair as her eyes sharpened on me. "About things that the autopsy report revealed."

"What things?" I asked.

"She was shot. Once. Through the heart," Annegret said. "Amara... My manager."

"She must have died instantly?" I asked.

She nodded and swallowed hard.

That sounded like a professional hit. Which must have been hard news to hear. No wonder she didn't seem herself.

"The *surete* are still certain this was murder?"

"Yes, they are," she said. "Even more so."

"What did the *surete* ask you?"

"They asked if I knew anyone who might have done this thing. Who might have had a reason to do such a thing. To her."

"And do you know who it could have been?"

Again her throat worked. "No. I couldn't think of a single person. Not to Amara."

"And then?"

"They wanted to know why she was there, at the gallery—and alone—so late at night."

"What did you tell them?"

"That I had no idea why she might have been there. The assignment she was taking care of for me—for you, actually—she'd sent the data to me before seven that evening. It wasn't her habit to stay at the gallery later than that. And she had no reason to be there, afterwards," she said, the words coming hard.

No legitimate reason, perhaps.

"Are they sure she was coming from the gallery?"

"They seemed certain."

"Sometime after midnight?"

"Yes."

I made a note. "Did they say how they know?"

"No. I assumed she was caught on camera. But they said very little. Just kept asking questions."

Which could be telling. "Where are the cameras at the gallery?"

"There are several in every room, as well as those covering the front and back doors. They are motion activated, of course, but there is also infrared."

Reminding me yet again of exactly how much money passes through her gallery. "And who handles your security for you?"

"SaltonSecure International. I've been with them for years."

I recognized the name immediately. SaltonSecure was top of the line. "Have the *surete* taken copies of those recordings?"

"Yes. They got warrants the next day."

"So they would know if she'd been inside that night? And when?"

"I suppose so."

"Have you seen the footage yourself?"

"I… no. I didn't think."

Again she seemed unusually vulnerable, and I had a sudden mental picture of a former client who had been through hours of a police interrogation before finally asking for a lawyer. Surely not.

"Was your lawyer with you this morning?" I asked.

"No," she said.

Which was also out of character, at least for the woman I'd met in Vancouver. Was no-one advising her?

"I'm not under suspicion," she added. "I wasn't even in the country, as you know."

Which didn't necessarily clear her, as she presumably knew. She needed to protect her rights. "Have you spoken with your lawyer about this at all?"

"Of course," she said. "And with my security people. And with my insurance agents. There are potential liability issues."

There were even bigger issues than that—like murder—but if her lawyer hadn't warned her of them, I wasn't bringing it up. This wasn't the time.

A thought struck me. "Does your lawyer know about the fraud rumors against the gallery?"

She looked away. "I haven't told him."

That might explain the seeming lack of concern on her lawyer's part. Especially since she'd been out of the country at the time of the murder. But still.

"Do the *surete* know about the fraud rumors?"

"No. How could they?" she said instantly. "That is… why would they? They are only rumors. There are no charges being made."

No point asking if she'd told them. Not with her focus on protecting the gallery's reputation. And her own.

But what if she was wrong about the rumors, and what the police knew?

I still didn't know why Interpol was so interested in Carli Fine Arts. Not to mention Birgitte Jessup. Neither of whom I'd mentioned to my client. Yet.

"So the *surete* haven't asked you any questions that might connect to those fraud rumors?" I asked her.

"No."

"Did Mme. Duvant know about those rumors?"

"I didn't tell her. I didn't tell anyone connected with the gallery."

Including her lawyer. That made no sense.

"I wanted to investigate the rumors myself, first," she continued. "Before I confused the issue with other people's beliefs."

And she'd decided to investigate by hiring a P. I. from thousands of miles away? Even if that decision had been a good one—and that remained to be seen—it wasn't the obvious choice for her to have made. Leaving another key question.

"Could your manager be connected to the frauds you uncovered at the gallery?" I asked.

"Amara?" She gave a bitter laugh. "Before last week, I would have said it was impossible that Amara was involved. That *any* of my employees were involved. Now?"

She gave that elegant shrug that I was learning was a signature for her. "I just don't know. It seems I don't know anything any more."

"That's why you hired me," I said. "To uncover the truth."

"I am no longer sure I want to know the truth," she said bitterly.

Which was understandable. But this wasn't the time for coddling. Not with murder added to fraud.

"You have no choice. Especially now. The price for choosing not to know could be your business at best, your freedom at worst."

She went pale, her eyes wide. "I... I..."

"You know this," I said, watching her as she gave a tiny nod.

"Yes. And no. I don't want to know it."

Maybe not. But willful ignorance wasn't one of her options. Not anymore.

"Call your lawyer," I said decisively. "You need to tell him or her about the fraud rumors. And he or she needs to hire me to investigate some of the details around this murder."

She stared at me. "But why?"

"Worst case scenario? So that I can't be forced to testify against you in a murder trial," I said bluntly. "Best case, you and your gallery need all the help you can get."

The fine lines around Annegret's mouth deepened, but she didn't argue. She called her lawyer.

CHAPTER THIRTEEN

While Annegret brought her lawyer up to speed, I fetched us both coffees, and the rest of the croissants. When I returned to her office, she was staring out the window.

"Well?" I asked as I passed her coffee to her, then sat down with my own cup.

"He'll be here at three. And he tells me the work you do for him as an investigative consultant will be covered under lawyer/client privilege for the duration of this investigation."

Leaving me wondering exactly what she'd told him that he'd agreed to rearrange his schedule so quickly. And agreed to my role, when he hadn't even met me yet.

"Good," I said. "Before that meeting, we need to review everything you know about the situation you now find yourself in. Starting with everything the *surete* have told you. Or asked you."

She turned paler yet, if that was possible.

"Wouldn't it make sense to wait for this afternoon...?" she began.

I felt sorry for her. But not dealing with this wouldn't be doing her any favors. "We can't afford to wait. Not in a murder investigation," I said bluntly.

She nodded, looking resigned, and sipped her coffee. Her color came back a bit. She'd obviously had a tough morning.

"Very well. It might help to get this over with. And you need to hear it. Then we shall go for lunch, and I plan on having a martini. Or perhaps two."

Fair enough. "What exactly happened at the police station this morning?"

"After the part I already told you, they asked me about Amara. What she does for me, how long she had been with the company, whether I was aware of any problems in her life..." she choked a little on the words.

I waited until she'd regained her composure, then said. "And you told them...?"

"That she's my right hand, that she runs the business day to day, and handles everything when I am traveling on business. Which is often. Amara has been with me for more than ten years, and I trust her implicitly." She glanced at me. "Trusted her, I suppose I should say."

"You no longer do so?"

"With everything that is happening? I don't know who to trust," she said.

Not surprising, given what was going on. "And the issues in Mme. Duvant's life?" I asked.

"Oh, like all of us she had money issues from time to time. She is married, and the marriage is difficult, I suspect. Her husband is one who values appearances. Here in Geneva? That can be expensive."

"And Mme. Duvant? Did she also value appearances?"

"Hmmm. Perhaps. But she had a Frenchwoman's sense of style —with much achieved from very little. She had an exquisite wardrobe, but a limited one. Only key pieces. A few well-chosen accessories gave life to those pieces."

"She knew how to live on a budget?" I interpreted.

"Yes. And the importance of maintaining the gallery on one, also. I paid her well, so for her money should not have been an ongoing issue. It was not one she talked about. But one gets a sense…" Again that shrug. "There was a tension in her, at times, when her husband Gregoire was mentioned."

"And yet you have no idea at all what she was doing at the gallery at that time of night?"

"No. I really don't. And any guessing I might do… No. It would not help."

I considered her for a moment, then decided to come back to that question.

Annegret glanced at her watch. Looked up with a little smile. "Besides, if we are to be back in time to meet with my lawyer, perhaps we should leave now for an early lunch."

She still wasn't facing her situation. "What is the latest we could leave for lunch and still get back in time?" I asked her.

"We have at most an hour and a half," she said flatly.

"Then let's make it count. Before we leave, you need to finish telling me what the *surete* asked you," I said. "And show me exactly where Mme. Duvant was found that night. We'll also check out the security recordings from that night. All right?"

Annegret swallowed hard, and nodded. "They—the *surete*—really didn't ask me much more. They verified when I'd left Geneva and when I returned. And where I had stayed. But they'd contacted me at my hotel in Vancouver just a few hours after the murder, after all. Surely I can't be a serious suspect."

She glanced at me, then away. It seemed to me then that she'd correctly interpreted my skeptical look, and wasn't yet ready to face the implications.

Time was to prove me wrong on that one, unfortunately.

"Then the *surete* wanted me to go back over a copy of Amara's calendar for the days before the murder," she said. "And also the calendar for the gallery itself from those same days. There seemed to be nothing there that helped them, though. At that point the meeting ended."

"We'll need to review those calendars, as well," I said.

"And then lunch," Annegret said. "I will need that martini, very much."

I suspected she was right. And that we would both need one. Too bad mixing jet lag with martinis was such a bad idea.

Especially when I was anticipating a difficult meeting with her lawyer.

————

WE STARTED WITH THE ALLEY, which ran behind the gallery, and for several blocks in each direction. Annegret led me back along the hallway, past their coffee room and out through a white painted door. It opened out about half-way along a narrow, cobblestoned alley.

The alley itself struck me as very Swiss—neat, and very clean. There were no street lamps, just elegant wrought iron fixtures on several buildings. No reeking dumpsters. And no cars parked in the alley, either.

The bistro on the corner had a patio that extended into the alley, with pots of flowers and a few tables set out. Further down the alley, I even spotted several window boxes full of geraniums, undaunted by the weather. The air smelled of the recent rain.

I glanced around, spotted the camera over the gallery door, and similar cameras above several other establishments, both across the alley and on either side of the gallery. Undoubtedly the police had reviewed whatever had been caught on camera. I needed to see that footage.

"Where was Mme. Duvant found?" I asked.

Annegret swallowed hard. "Over here," she said, and turning to her right, she led the way further along the alley. She stopped several doors down, pointed.

"They found her here," she said, pointing just to one side of a blue painted door. "Up against the wall. They tell me the man who found her saw only a pile of dark fabric, at first. She was wearing her raincoat, and the hood had been pulled up."

Why here? I glanced around, tried to imagine it at night. Even in darkness, there was nowhere to hide. "She was right beside the door?"

"Yes."

"As if she'd been trying to get in?"

She nodded. "The *surete* did not say so, but yes, that is what I think too."

"Which shop is this?"

"The jewelers," she said.

"Do you know the owners?"

"Yes, we all know each other, on this block. The ones we share the street with, and the ones we share the alley with also."

"So Mme. Duvant would know them, too?"

"Of course."

"Well enough to come here for help?"

She nodded. "Yes, but it was very late."

"Do any of your neighbors work late, sometimes?"

She stared at me. "Yes, of course. Though not often as late as when Amara died."

"And this neighbor?"

"He creates his own gold pieces. He often works here, after the shop is closed. When inspiration strikes, he works sometimes long into the night."

There was a small barred window with a blue awning on the other side of the blue door. Just past where Mme. Duvant's body had been found. I pictured the alley as it must have been that night. It had been a clear night—I'd checked—with no moon. In the darkness, any light from the jeweler's would have been very clear.

"If he'd been working late, could Mme. Duvant have seen the light from this window as she exited into the alley?"

She frowned. "Yes, I suppose so. This is his workroom."

"Have you talked to this neighbor since you got back?"

"No, why would I?"

I needed more coffee. It might be my jet lag, but this seemed painfully slow. As if Annegret was too shocked by what had happened to think clearly or put anything together. I felt sorry for her.

Unless she was trying to hide something? The thought wouldn't be kept out.

"What about your other neighbors? Have you talked to any of them about that night?"

She shook her head. "No, I… I couldn't."

"The *surete* must have talked to the jeweler? To some of the others?"

"Oh," she said, and looked around her as if she'd never seen the alley before. "Yes, of course. Of course they must have. Probably before my plane even landed."

Most likely. And the disconnect I was seeing in her could be a combination of shock, grief and jet lag.

"Did the *surete* give you any information on what they've found so far? Are there suspects?"

"It is an ongoing investigation," she said heavily, obviously quoting someone.

Yeah, I knew that response. They weren't telling her anything. Likely she was still a person of interest, even if they weren't looking hard at her.

"Should I be talking to my neighbors? I mean, would it help you if I did?" she asked.

"Let's wait until we talk to your lawyer this afternoon," I said. "For now, let's take a look at your security footage."

"And the calendar," she said, as if she thought I'd forgotten.

This was not the woman who'd hired me.

CHAPTER FOURTEEN

Back in Annegret's office, she got on the phone with SaltonSecure. They were quick to send the camera feeds she'd requested to her computer.

"Ask them if these are identical to the information the *surete* requested," I said just as she was about to hang up. She nodded and did so.

At the response, a surprised look crossed her face.

"What?" I asked. "What is it?"

She held up a finger for silence, listening to whatever the person on the other end of the line was saying, with a small frown of concentration between her finely shaped brows. After a moment she shook her head.

"I don't understand. Why not?" she asked.

I wished I'd suggested she put me on speaker phone for this one. Though she might well have refused. I'd keep it in mind in future, though.

Meanwhile, Annegret was nodding, and making quick notes on her computer, her fingers flying. The screen was turned so I couldn't see it, so that didn't help, either. Then she paused, and frowned deeply.

"Just send it all," she said curtly, clearly in answer to something that had displeased her.

"What was that about?" I asked her as soon as she disconnected and turned off the phone.

"They sent the *surete* everything from that week," she said. "Even though the warrant only covered the hours after the gallery closed."

Now I was frowning too. "Why would they do that?"

"I don't know."

"Clearly you asked them."

She nodded. "He didn't have an answer for me," she said. "Not one that made sense, anyway."

"What exactly did he say?" I asked.

"Just that it is their policy to cooperate with the *surete*," she said.

"Which where I'm from doesn't extend to providing a client's information if the *surete* haven't obtained a warrant for that information," I said. "I assume that's also true here?"

She nodded, her mind obviously elsewhere.

"Whom did you talk to?" I asked.

"What? Oh, the day supervisor for this account," she said. "Who appears to be unforgivably ill informed. There's no excuse for this. I need to talk to the account manager. But I'm wondering whether to wait until I… we've talked with my lawyer."

"You might as well wait. The damage is already done," I said. "Better to spend that time reviewing the footage. See exactly what information the *surete* have, and what it tells us."

She nodded, still deep in thought. After a moment she focused on me. "Yes, you're right."

She adjusted her large screen so that we could both see it equally well. Then stood up and adjusted the window blinds so there was no glare on the screen.

When she opened the download the security supervisor had sent her, I looked at the list of video files it contained. There were quite a few of them, and they were large ones. This was going to take forever.

"Hang on. Before you open those, why don't we have a look at the calendars for the day. Then we'll know who was scheduled to be here. Anyone who wasn't on the calendar is worth taking a second look at."

"That makes sense," she said, and with a few quick clicks brought up two calendars, which she displayed side by side. "The one on the left is Amara's calendar for that day. The one on the right is for the gallery."

"So the gallery appointments could be handled by… whom?"

"Anyone who was available. Usually one of our assistant managers, like Giselle, would take them. But sometimes Amara would meet with a valued client if she was free."

"And if you're in the office?"

"I am always the one who meets with certain of our clients."

I nodded. "Is there a list somewhere of all the appointments from that day?"

This was one of the times when a whiteboard would have come in handy.

Annegret clicked her mouse a few times. "Giselle will bring in copies of the printouts," she said.

They must have a networked printer at the reception station, I realized. That would work.

———

HALF AN HOUR LATER, my eyes burned from watching the video recordings, switching between fast forward and pause. It hadn't been quite as bad as I'd expected, though. If there was more than one camera in a particular room, we saw the room on a split screen, from multiple viewpoints. Which took a little getting used to, and was the reason for so many pauses, to be sure we knew what we were seeing.

But we quickly hit a rhythm, finding it worked best to follow each visitor from room to room for the length of their visit, then cut back to the front door cameras to pick up the next person. And we now had a verified list of everyone who had been inside the gallery on the day of the murder.

Annegret had recognized every one of them, too. Which was helpful.

I stood and stretched out my aching shoulders. Computer eyestrain can play havoc with those muscles.

"So what do you think?" I asked her. "We've seen everyone who came into your gallery that day. Anyone you didn't expect to see? Or whose actions seemed off?"

Annegret frowned at the list in front of her. "No," she said slowly. "It seems a perfectly normal workday."

"Then let's have a look at that night," I said, and she leaned forward to press the play button.

We'd stopped the recording just as Giselle had walked the last customer to the front door, and locked it after them. This screen was split into quadrants, with two cameras on the interior wall showing her back, and a partial view of the street through the door. Two exterior cameras showed the sidewalk and street just outside the door.

The angles were good enough to see the last client walking away, and disappearing from view. And we watched in normal time as Giselle double-locked the door, then stood for a few moments, looking out through the paned glass of the door.

I wondered what she was seeing. A late customer, perhaps? Or was she checking the weather? The recording didn't tell us, not even the street view from outside the door. Even though we paused it several times to check the faces of people walking past.

We watched Giselle give a slight shake of her head, as if amused at herself, though none of the cameras caught her expression. She pulled down the blind over the door, then clicked a switch.

I glanced at Annegret.

"That switch closes the blinds behind the display window. No one can see into the gallery itself once those are down," she said, as we watched Giselle on the recording head for the back of the gallery.

Giselle rapped lightly on the door of Annegret's office, waited a moment, then opened it and entered.

We paused that recording, and switched to the two cameras inside Annegret's office. I still found it odd that Annegret and her manager had shared the one office, depending who was scheduled to work on a given day. It was a good use of space, though, and made traveling on gallery business or working from home simple. Maybe that explained the oddly impersonal feel of the office?

Annegret had showed me how their individual accounts were stored in the cloud, so only documents they both accessed were on the computer. I made a mental note to check with Badger about how secure that practice was.

On the recording, as Giselle walked into the office, Mme. Duvant was sitting behind the desk, looking towards the door, and smiling. I still found it hard to see her alive and seemingly happy, knowing what had happened to her later that night. I couldn't tell how Annegret was coping. It had to be painful for her, but she didn't let on.

On the screen, Giselle walked a few steps towards Mme. Duvant, and said something. Mme. Duvant gestured her towards one of the chairs opposite the desk, and Giselle shook her head, saying something. If the angle had been better, I might have been able to lip read, but it was a little off on one side.

So where was it focusing? I squinted, then reached across to pause the recording, and glanced around for the camera.

Which was unobtrusively placed near the ceiling in one corner of the room. If I hadn't known where it had to be, I'd never have spotted it. The design of the camera made it hard to recognize as a camera, and it was almost impossible to tell where it was focused. But from the little I could see, and from the recordings we'd already seen, it seemed to be focused on the guest chairs. Which made sense.

I glanced back at the paused recording. This time I was looking at the other side of the split screen, the one showing Mme. Duvant's face. The focus on that one was a bit odd too, meaning I couldn't quite read her lips, either. I glanced at the wall behind me, found the camera, and looked back and forth.

Annegret watched me in silence.

"Do you know where this camera is focused?" I asked her.

She looked past me at the camera, then glanced at the screen.

"I'd thought it was focused on the desk, for when contracts are signed."

We both looked at the screen.

"But it isn't angled right for that, is it?" she asked.

"No, it isn't. And I'd like to know why." I made a note. "Let's keep going."

She nodded, and pressed play.

The interaction between Mme. Duvant and Giselle didn't last long, and thanks to the odd video angles, didn't tell us much. It seemed amicable enough, and at the door, Giselle turned and said something to Mme. Duvant. I glanced at the time display. Just after six in the evening.

She'd probably wished her manager a good evening, since we followed the assistant manager to the back room, where Giselle collected her coat and purse from a small locker, then exited out by way of the door into the alley.

Annegret stopped the recording, and switched back to the one that showed Mme. Duvant in the shared office. She rewound it to when the last client had left, and pressed play. Mme. Duvant was at the desk, working on something on the computer screen, which we couldn't see. Presumably the data I'd asked for. She seemed very focused. We watched for about five minutes in real time, then Annegret sped up the video. Nothing changed at all until the scene we'd already viewed when Giselle came in.

Annegret pressed pause and glanced at me. "Continue here?"

"Do you have any idea what she might have been working on?" I asked.

"No." She clicked the mouse, moved and clicked for a moment until she was looking at the shared directory. "I'd thought this must be the data you needed. But that should have been in our shared folder. And there's nothing here that was worked on that day at all," she said. "Whatever it was, it must have been in the cloud."

"Let's see how long she keeps it up," I said.

We watched the video in fast forward until Mme. Duvant stretched, finished off the last of her coffee—which must have gone cold—then opened a small, sleek container sitting beside the computer. It looked a bit like an undersized glasses case. She took out a small flash drive, about the length between the joints on her middle finger—and she had small hands. Inserting it into the back of the computer, she pressed a few keys.

"Did she just save whatever she was working to the flash drive?" I asked.

"What is a flash drive?"

"Portable data storage," I said.

"Then yes. For some reason she either wanted to take a copy of whatever she was working on with her..." Annegret said.

"Or she didn't want it saved to your system," I finished for her.

"That can't be good."

"Probably not."

"And the *surete* would have seen this?"

"Oh, yeah. They've seen it." I glanced at her stricken expression. "They didn't ask you about this?"

"They did not."

That couldn't be good, either. "And you have no idea what she might have copied?"

"None."

"Do you recognize the container she took the flash drive from?"

She just shook her head and pressed play. We both watched as Mme. Duvant finished whatever she was doing, removed the flash drive from the computer and replaced it in the container. Then she opened her email, added an attachment from the computer drive, and sent it off.

"That's the document she sent me," Annegret said. "See, the time sent is right. Just before seven. But the document she sent was finished sometime earlier."

While we stared at the screen, Mme. Duvant, still alive, powered down the computer. Turning off the desk lamp, she picked up the container, and left the room.

We switched to the recording that followed her down the hallway. She retrieved her purse and a navy coat from a locker, paused to set the alarm and left by the alley door, locking up behind herself.

As Annegret pressed pause, I noted the time. Almost exactly seven p.m. Mme. Duvant had less than seven hours to live.

What could have happened in those seven hours?

———

THE VIDEOS DIDN'T TELL us much. Mme. Duvant returned to the office just after ten. She'd come alone, dressed the same as in the earlier recordings. Which suggested she hadn't gone home, wherever else she might have been.

We watched as she came in the back door, carrying a flashlight and her purse. She paused in the hallway just inside the door, and seemed to be listening.

Whatever she'd heard—or not heard—seemed to satisfy her, because she turned and locked the outer door behind her. Then after a quick glance down the hall towards the darkened office, she turned to her left, pressed a button, and vanished into what I'd thought was a solid wall.

"Where did she go?" I asked.

Annegret was looking worried. Very worried. "There's a kind of hidden door, just there. It goes down to the cellar."

"The cellar? What's down there?"

"Storage, mostly. Framing and packing materials. Shipping containers. Extra office supplies."

"Art?"

"Oh, heavens no," she said. "We'd never be able to insure anything down there. Though we do a bit of framing there."

"So I'm guessing there are no cameras down there?"

"I'm afraid not."

"Where are the infrared cameras in the hallway?"

"One by the back door, one by the front."

"Does their range extend far enough to reach into the cellar?"

"I have no idea."

"We'll check that," I said. I made a note and turned back to Annegret. "Why would Mme. Duvant come back at that hour, and go down to the cellar?"

"I have no idea."

"You must have some thoughts?" I said.

She shook her head.

"Guesses?"

"I can't begin to imagine a good reason for her being there."

Nor could I. "What about a bad reason?" I said.

Annegret's lips seemed to disappear as she pressed them tightly together, but she said nothing.

"If the fraud rumors are at least partially real, and if Mme. Duvant was somehow involved…" I began.

She started to protest, and I held up a hand to stop her.

"This is worst case," I said. "But you know the runnings of the gallery better than anyone. If your manager *was* betraying you, what could she possibly have put on that flash drive? What might she be up to in that cellar in the middle of the night?"

Annegret started to shake her head.

"Whatever it was, it got your Mme. Duvant murdered, Annegret," I said.

She looked away.

When she looked back, she met my eyes. "If the fraud is real, there are places in that cellar no-one ever looks. Things could be stored there, undiscovered, for as long as needed."

"Things?" I said. Just to be clear. And to force her to face it.

No matter how hard such a betrayal from a trusted employee might be, not facing it would only compound the catastrophe looming over her and her gallery.

Annegret swallowed hard. "Paintings."

"Forgeries?"

"Yes. Or even originals for someone to copy," she said.

"You're thinking this gallery could have been a kind of central distribution point?"

"I don't want to think it," she said. "But it might fit the few facts we have."

"When you say originals?" I said. "Do you mean original works from the gallery? Could paintings have been moved in and out of this gallery without alerting any of your security systems?"

"It shouldn't be possible," she said. "And I hadn't been thinking of them being our originals."

"But?" I prompted her.

"But at this point, I'm not prepared to assume anything. I need to do a complete security check. And I won't be involving Salton-Secure in that process," she added, her eyes bleak.

"You suspect they might be involved?" I asked.

"I have no reason to suspect them," she said.

"Other than the probably actionable amount of access they granted to the police force," I said, watching her.

Her face showed nothing of her feelings, but her voice did. "Yes," she said flatly. "Other than that."

"It will be interesting to see what your lawyer has to say about that."

She grimaced.

"He won't be happy. But for this worst case scenario, the one involving my gallery," and her face hardened on those words. "As a distribution network for high end art fraud? That would take a team. And my security would need to have been breached, somewhere."

"An internal betrayal would be the most effective way," I finished for her.

She nodded. "If I'm forced to accept that my trusted employee betrayed me, I'm willing to suspect everyone this gallery deals with. At least until we get to the bottom of this."

I was beginning to understand why she'd looked to hire an

investigative firm—mine—from so far away. It suggested she'd had at least an inkling of what might be an enormous conspiracy before she flew to Vancouver.

It would also explain the interest Interpol and I^2 had in her and her gallery.

"Let's finish watching these recordings," I said. "And I want to see if the infrared will tell us anything, before we go for lunch."

"Which will include three martinis," she said, with a sideways grin that suddenly had me liking my difficult client.

Despite the major details she'd neglected to tell me about this case.

CHAPTER FIFTEEN

The restaurant Annegret took me to for lunch was in a beautiful old stone building that had probably seen at least two centuries come and go. Inside it was all clean lines and green plants hanging from glass shelves above the windows. The furniture was clean lined and modern in light woods and some high tech material Justine would probably have loved. We'd barely sat down when Annegret ordered a martini, extra dry. I ordered white wine, also dry.

Much as I'd have liked a martini right then, I had a job to do. So did Annegret, but she was having a really bad day. And it wasn't my gallery facing all the trouble.

We'd gone through the last of the videos, including the ones recorded in infrared light—which were limited to the entrances, exits and the display galleries themselves. The infrared didn't tell us much—it hadn't extended to the cellar unfortunately. But the rest of the videos had yielded more shocks for poor Annegret.

And not much information that was going to help me.

Amara Duvant had stayed in the cellar for several hours, reappearing on video at a few minutes before midnight. She'd gone into the little kitchen, where we caught glimpses of her as she made a pot of coffee, setting out a tray with two mugs she'd found somewhere.

She hadn't poured the coffee yet when she paused, cocked her head as if listening, then put the sugar bowl down and went to the alley door. She cracked it open, looked through, and then opened it wider. A person several inches taller than her and slightly bulkier, wearing dark jeans and a dark hoody of some matte fabric came in. He, or she—it was impossible to tell, though I was leaning towards he because of the way he stood, at least in the brief glimpse we'd had—had a brief exchange with Mme. Duvant, then headed down the cellar stairs.

Annegret and I had exchanged glances as she reversed the recording, then played it back again in slow motion. It was clear he —I still thought the figure was male—had been to the gallery before. He knew where the cameras were, and kept his face turned away. He also knew where the cellar door was, and opened what Annegret told me was a tricky catch with the ease of familiarity.

"Who is that?" I asked her.

"I have no idea," she said. "Again. I don't seem to know anything, do I?"

It was a bitter comment on the situation she found herself in.

Or appeared to be one. I was mostly on her side now, but I was still waiting for proof that the situation was as she now presented it to be.

"What do you think? Male? Or female?" I asked her.

"Male," she said decidedly.

I agreed. "Does he remind you of anyone you've ever seen before? Possibly in company with Mme. Duvant?"

She'd thought for a moment, then shook her head. "No. There's something distinctive about the way he holds himself, even in the brief glimpses he allowed the camera. I think I'd have remembered if I'd seen him before."

I thought she was right. And was reluctantly impressed by it.

She'd make a better ally than a suspect. And I was hoping that's what she'd prove to be.

But until I knew more, I was trusting my own judgement.

Mme. Duvant returned to the kitchen, poured and doctored the two cups of coffee, and followed her midnight visitor through the door leading to the cellar. Neither of them reappeared for nearly an hour. Just after one Annegret came back upstairs with the tray, washed each item she'd used and replaced everything.

Then she called down to her visitor, who joined her in the hall. Mme. Duvant still had her purse, but otherwise neither of them was carrying anything. The camera timer read a few minutes before one. The two of them quickly left via the alley door.

Wordlessly Annegret switched to the alley cameras. Again, Mme. Duvant's visitor did a good job of hiding his face—we saw no more than shadowed glimpses as the two of them set off along the alley, towards the place where Mme. Duvant would die. As they passed out of our view, there was no sign of anyone else in the alley.

Had her visitor killed Mme. Duvant? Why? And what had they been doing down in the cellar?

Annegret backed up the recording and I expected her to replay the scene we'd just watched, but she didn't stop until the timer read ten p.m. Again we watched Mme. Duvant return to the office from wherever she'd gone. Instead of following her inside, Annegret let the video play, fast-forwarding it when there was no movement. Slowing it if anything moved in the alley.

There was nothing but a stray cat that apparently called the alley home between ten and midnight. At least we knew the security cameras were sensitive enough to catch what we needed.

Just after midnight, Mme. Duvant's visitor appeared, coming from the west. His hood was raised, and he clearly knew exactly where the cameras were, either avoiding them or making sure the angle was poor.

"I'm hoping he doesn't know as much about the neighbor's cameras," I said. Though it was a long shot. Especially since the police had had this footage for days now. And there had been no sign of an arrest, or even a person of interest. Unless you counted my client.

Annegret had glanced at me, then returned her gaze to the screen, saying nothing. Until half an hour after Mme. Duvant and her visitor had gone inside, Annegret inhaled sharply. I saw it too. On the screen, a dark figure ghosted down the alley, keeping to the shadows of the buildings opposite.

He or she—it was impossible to tell which—was dressed much the same as Mme. Duvant's visitor. And didn't slow as they passed the gallery. Nothing indicated they were aware of it being there. Not even a flash of eyes in the darkness.

Whoever it was kept going on past, heading east. Towards the barely perceptible glow that was the jeweler's shop? I strained, but the shadows were too thick. And the figure in black never stepped into that glow. I couldn't tell if they stopped there, or kept going.

Was this Mme. Duvant's killer? Her co-conspirator? Her visitor's accomplice? Or someone unrelated to whatever we were dealing with? It was impossible to know.

Annegret re-ran the segment from midnight, slowing it to a crawl as Mme. Duvant's visitor appeared. Then sped up until the dark figure appeared—12:32 a.m., I noted—and slowed again.

She repeated that twice. Yet even with both of us watching for the slightest clue, there was nothing to see.

"*Merde*," she'd said at last, bashing the keys that shut down the recording.

"There's a truth," I said. "I think it's time for that martini."

"Finally," was all she said.

Until, martini in front of her, she passed the elegant menu to me. "Anything with fish is delicious," she said. "But I highly recommend the steamed perch with white wine and shallots. It will be fresh from the lake, and though perch can be disappointing, the chef has a delicate touch with it. You might as well enjoy something that isn't a disaster today."

And she lifted her glass in a wry toast.

———

WE DIDN'T TALK about the case through lunch—which was even more delicious than Annegret had promised—or during the walk back to her office. In the twenty minutes we had until her lawyer arrived, I asked to see the cellar.

She nodded, and led the way downstairs, flicking on the light from the switch at the top of the stairs.

Following her down, I was relieved to see the expansive room was well-lit, though the lack of windows meant it would be utterly dark when those lights were turned off. From the look of it, the cellar ran under the entire gallery upstairs. It was also full height. That helped. Crouching over is no way to investigate anything.

"Can we be overheard down here?" I asked.

"Probably," she said. "I have no idea where the venting runs, but you know old buildings. Sound carries in odd ways."

"We'll talk when we get back to your office, then," I said. "How is this area organized?"

"Packing materials to the left, along with a packing station," she said. "Office supplies and such are straight ahead. There are framing materials to the right, and a framing station there, too. We do some of our own framing, mostly for the newer pieces, though occasionally we'll handle a special order."

I nodded and headed left. She followed me.

"Just ask if you have questions," she said.

Most of it was fairly self-evident. The cellar was well laid out, with the packing area closest to the stairs. The table was a large, sturdy one, with scissors, string, measuring tapes, and a variety of pre-printed labels close at hand. Behind it were wooden shelving units stretching back to the far wall. Someone had labeled the shelving units.

"Who organized this so well?" I asked.

"Amara," Annegret said. "She was very organized."

She certainly had been. And it meant she likely knew this space better than anyone else who worked here.

Without comment, I walked back into the rows of shelves, scanning both sides as I did. Well-organized or not, there was a ton of stuff back here. And at both ends of the aisles, where the shelving ended in a wall on one side, the half-enclosed stairwell on the other, it was full of shadows despite the decent lighting in the central areas. I walked down to the end of the closest aisle, finding shelf after shelf of folded boxes of various sizes and depths, big rolls of wrapping paper, boxes full of tissue paper. It went on and on.

I quickly walked every aisle from beginning to end, looking for anything out of place, anything that might have been recently moved and not put back quite straight. Anything that might give us a clue as to what Mme. Duvant and her visitor had been doing down here.

I found nothing. Which wasn't surprising, given that I didn't know what I was looking for.

"Does anything seem out of place to you?" I asked Annegret, who had been silently following me. "Or recently disturbed?"

"Nothing," she said. "Though I don't come down here all that often."

Of course she didn't. That would have been much too helpful.

"Do you know if the *surete* came down here?"

She looked startled. "I don't know. I can ask Giselle?"

"Hold off for now." I didn't want to telegraph our sudden interest in the cellar. Just in case.

In case of what I wasn't sure. But it felt right, and over the years and the cases, I've learned to trust that feeling.

Finished with the wrapping area, I did the same walk through of the office supplies area, which was built on a much smaller scale. Only two aisles deep, the various items were smaller and easier to identify. Printer paper. Toner cartridges. Pre-printed envelopes of various sizes. Boxes of pens, staples, tape. You couldn't hide a painting in these shelves. Unlike in the packing area.

Where I was afraid I was going to have to do a box by box search. If it wasn't already too late.

Having determined that there was little helpful in this section, I checked with my client. Who had seen nothing to alarm her, either.

We turned to the framing section, which was nearly a mirror image of the packing section. The same kind of large, sturdy work-table, this one of battered oak rather than metal. I briefly wondered how they'd even got the thing down here, it was so big.

Beyond this table was a similar well-stocked area with all the tools needed to frame any kind of artwork. In addition to an industrial-sized paper-cutter, there were several large cutting mats, and every size of precision knives. The shelving held a variety of frames, both assembled and unassembled, in various sizes, colors and finishes, as well as mat-boards in every color and texture.

I stared for a moment, mesmerized by the choices and possibilities. Suddenly I was wishing I had a proper framing area for my own work, or at least access to one half as well-stocked as this one.

I forced myself to keep going, to examine the shelving units on this side as closely as I had the ones on the other side. It was more challenging, as I kept getting distracted by the sheer volume of items there, so many of them things I'd love to have for my own work.

But the volume of possible opportunity for fraud, and for hiding places for fraudulent work, kept me focused. Again, I saw nothing disturbed, nothing that looked wrong. On the surface, at least.

One thing I was sure—they hadn't been creating fraudulent works here. There were no paints or brushes, no empty canvases just waiting for that pseudo-masterpiece. But there were pliers for stretching canvas, wooden frames to stretch them onto, staple guns and staples for attaching them. A work on display upstairs could be brought down here in the dead of night, the original canvas removed from its frame and stretcher, replaced with a fake version. The original canvas could be carried away in a mailing tube, perhaps rolled with an inexpensive print as camouflage.

I could see it, feel the texture of the paint, the effort it took to stretch a canvas, the satisfying look of a properly stretched painting against just the right frame. It played in my head, each motion so familiar, each action unrolling after the last.

Mme. Duvant had been down here for two hours before her visitor arrived. Giving her plenty of time to trade a fake painting for an original, and tidy up after herself, leaving everything exactly in its place.

But she hadn't carried anything downstairs with her. Except her purse. And neither she nor her visitor had carried anything out with them. If she'd been switching a painting, where was the opportunity? I couldn't see it.

Which didn't mean it hadn't happened.

Didn't mean it had, either.

But if it had happened, the original work must still be hidden in this cellar. Somewhere. I stifled my groan at the thought of going through every single box in this place.

But what if someone else had a key, and knew the passcode for the security system? There would have been time to remove any evidence after Mme. Duvant's murder.

But the passcode would have shown up on the security report as being Mme. Duvant's, after Mme. Duvant's death. Had anyone checked?

Or was that something else SaltonSecure had failed to follow procedures on?

That thought was replaced by an even worse one. What if Mme. Duvant hadn't been the only employee of the gallery involved in whatever this was?

The odds of any evidence of fraud still being down here were shrinking by the minute. But we'd still have to search.

Make that I'd have to search. At this stage, who else could I trust? How far could I even trust my client?

Though why would Annegret have hired me, if not to clear her name?

Or to appear to clear it. Which, unfortunately, might be another reason for hiring a small firm like mine. One from so far away, one that presumably wouldn't know the ins and outs of Swiss and international law. Or any of the players in the art world at her level.

"We need to get back upstairs," Annegret said, breaking into my bleak thoughts. "It's time."

Time to talk to the lawyer. And I still had too many questions and too few answers. I wasn't looking forward to this.

CHAPTER SIXTEEN

Dominic Marbach was tall, dark and confident, with a charming French accent that made me glad I was committed to Nick. Even if we weren't living together. Annegret gracefully performed the introductions, and Dominic, as he invited me to call him, welcomed me to the team. Which I thought was a nice touch, since he'd officially be paying me.

Then the three of us seated ourselves around the small table at one end of her office, and Dominic glanced from me to Annegret. And focused on her. "So tell me what this is all about," he said. "And why I am just hearing about it now?"

"I wasn't sure what I was dealing with," Annegret said. "If anything. I hired Barbara because of her work on a previous fraud case. And since she isn't one of the known players here in Switzerland, she could investigate quietly until we learned what we were dealing with here."

"I see," he said. "And this dreadful murder of your charming gallery manager? How does that connect to the fraud?"

"I wish I knew," she said. "I'm still hoping it doesn't, but..." And she explained to him what we'd seen on the surveillance videos.

I was watching him closely. As she talked, he made rapid notes on a legal pad. His shock at the news was evident, but I was impressed to see he was using a mind mapping technique to lay out the information randomly and then connecting it. Rather than just doing the usual laundry list of 'this happened and then that happened.'

This was an intelligent and creative mind, one unafraid of doing the unexpected. Annegret was lucky to have him on her team. With a more traditional lawyer, this meeting would likely have gone from bad to worse. With him on board, we might just have a shot at saving both her and the gallery.

And I thought more highly of my client for hiring him. Despite what so far seemed to have been an unfortunate decision in hiring her security firm. Though given the firm's international reputation, I couldn't exactly blame her for that one.

When Annegret finished her summary, Dominic nodded, drawing a last line on his mind map. "What have the *surete* told you so far? Have they identified a suspect? Or suspects?"

"I don't think they have. And so far, they've told me very little."

"You mentioned you'd had a session with them this morning. Tell me about it."

This time the notes he made were that laundry list. What was asked, what was said, and the exact order of each. I was even more impressed.

He didn't say a word while she spoke, the silence between her words broken only by the skritch of his fountain pen.

When she was done, he set the pen down and looked at her. "And you didn't think to take me there with you?"

His voice was calm, and there was no accusation in his gaze or his tone. But I'd never seen my client so flustered.

"I… well, I. No. I didn't see the need," she said. Which was what she'd said to me earlier.

He didn't like it any better than I had, that was obvious. "I'm glad you finally decided to involve me now," was all he said.

"Actually, that was Barbara," Annegret said. "She insisted."

I gave her points for that one.

Dominic nodded to me. "Thank you," he said. Then turned back to Annegret. "And now the three of us need to develop a strategy. Have the *surete* said anything to you about this fraud you have brought Barbara here to look into?"

"No. Nothing."

Again, it was the same conversation I'd had with her earlier. Her lawyer just nodded, and didn't ask further. Clearly, he knew her better than I did. Which wasn't surprising, given I'd only known her a few days. But again it gave me a flicker of hope.

"I was wrong not to involve you as soon as I heard about the rumors," Annegret said. "I'm sorry. There's something else you should know, too."

And she told him what we'd learned today about SaltonSecure. "I plan to change firms as quickly as it makes sense to do so," she finished.

"I'm glad to hear it," he said. "Their actions are completely unacceptable. Do you wish me to review their contract with an eye to suing them?"

"No, not in the middle of all this," she said.

"I do have one question about your security," I said. "And the answer might affect your decision about suing them."

Both of them turned to look at me.

"Your security system," I said. "Is there one passcode for the entire system, or do you each have your own?"

"We each have our own. Why?"

Well, that was something, anyway. And should make it easier.

"I was thinking about our speculation that this gallery could have been used as a hub for smuggling frauds," I said to Annegret. Dominic immediately looked up from his notes, his eyes on her.

"Mme. Duvant and her visitor weren't carrying anything when they left that night," I added. "And I was wondering if that visitor— or someone else—might have returned to the gallery later. To retrieve something that was left here."

Annegret's face looked strained, and her lips tightened.

"When you asked for the video recordings from the day Mme.

Duvant was murdered. Did they send you a list of which passcodes were used as well? And when?" I asked.

She blinked, then scowled. "No. They didn't."

Dominic leaned forward. "Do you get a regular report from them showing the usage of all the passcodes?"

"No," she said slowly. "I don't. And I should be getting one."

"Yes, you should," he said. "And you shouldn't have to ask for it. It should be automatic."

"What do you get from them?" I asked.

"I get a report each week that says they have reviewed all of our records, and flagging anything that I need to look at," she said. "Usually there is nothing flagged. Which is remarkably paternalistic, now I think about it. And leaves me far too dependent on the honesty of their employees."

She turned to her lawyer. "I think I may want to sue after all. Especially given SaltonSecure's excellent reputation. Which is clearly undeserved. But not until I've got everything I need from them. And have their replacement in place. Can you recommend several security firms?"

He nodded. "I'll have a list to you by the end of the day."

And I'd have a quick chat with Keller at Interpol about the matter.

"Good," Annegret said. "And I'll get in touch with my SaltonSecure account manager and get a copy of that report on the passcodes. It sounds like we need to review it. Now."

She walked over to her desk, pressed a couple of keys on her computer, and made the call. I felt sorry for the person on the other end, who appeared to have told her he'd have the report to her by the following day. By the time she'd finished with him, the requested report was open on her screen.

"Idiots," she muttered as she turned back to us. "Dominic, do you have a copy of my contract with SaltonSecure?"

"I believe so," he said.

"Can you review it and let me know exactly what they are contractually required to do for me?" she said.

He smiled. A shark's smile. "I would be happy to do so. This promises to be entertaining."

"Only if I'm not trying to pursue it from behind bars," she said.

"You are that concerned about your situation?" he asked, looking startled.

"Let me put it this way. Normally I'd send this report to our shared printer. But in this case, I'm going to ask both of you to view it over my shoulder."

He frowned. "You are so concerned about the honesty of your employees?"

"I am that concerned about how large this conspiracy might be. So far, it seems to extend from my trusted manager—who may have been murdered over it—to my security firm. I have no idea how much further it might go. But I'm beginning to suspect a deliberate effort to pin any suspicion caused by their actions on me."

Clearly he hadn't yet made the connection to SaltonSecure. And given that he'd only been told about the fraud rumors a half hour ago, that wasn't surprising. But I thought Annegret was right. About all of it.

Dominic glanced at me. I nodded.

"Then let us have a look at this report," he said grimly.

———

IT WASN'T ideal viewing circumstances by any means, but none of us were complaining. The large screen made up for a lot, and the circumstances demanded we review it immediately. And it was easier than it sounded, at least to start with.

"Since we have nearly two months worth of data here, we should be able to start with any access outside of normal hours," Annegret said. "If there is a pattern, it should show up quickly."

"Makes sense," Dominic said.

It would make more sense to have my team analyze the data, but I recognized my client's need to dig into this herself, immediately. It also seemed a good way to bring her lawyer up to speed quickly. And that could be critical, if she was being framed.

The police were looking for a murderer, and as far as we knew, had no obvious suspects. Annegret would be an all too easy target.

I'd grabbed my notebook, and as Annegret scrolled through the data, I made quick notes.

"The gallery closes at six most nights, and Amara seems to work until seven or eight," she said, scrolling through September's data.

"Is that usual?" I asked, jotting down the times.

"An extra hour is reasonable, and two some of the time. This seems a little high, but I'd have to look at older data to be sure," she said. "I don't see her leaving the office and returning, though."

"And none of the other employees seem to be here outside of regular hours," Dominic said, looking over her shoulder.

"Until October," Annegret said. "Look here. Several times this month, Amara left at what would seem a normal time. Then came back several hours later, and stayed for several more hours. Just like she did on the night..." her voice broke. "Last Thursday."

The night she'd been murdered. I made quick notes of the pattern.

"Is it always late at night?" Dominic asked.

"It seems so... no, wait. She was in early two Saturdays in a row. And Jana was here with her."

"Who is Jana?" Dominic asked.

Thanks to Badger's investigation of the gallery's employees, I could have told him. But I wanted to hear my client's assessment of her newest employee.

"She's one of our associate managers. She started with us at the beginning of the year," she said. "Jana Bertrand has a degree in fine arts, and has worked with several reputable galleries abroad. She only moved to Geneva from Cannes at the end of last year. She's personable, quick to learn, and very passionate about art. We were lucky to hire her."

She stared bleakly at the screen. "Or so I thought."

Annegret's assessment of Bertrand matched what Badger had

found. The only thing missing was that Badger had flagged the relatively short time she'd stayed at previous galleries, and that she'd moved around quite a bit within Europe. Badger hadn't found any hint of criminal behavior or affiliations, though.

"Was there some reason they would have been in early?" I asked. Just to be sure.

Annegret switched to the online calendar. "Let me check."

She toggled back and forth between various screens, then pulled out her smartphone. Glanced at us. Taking the hint, we politely looked away as she checked something. Presumably her personal calendar.

"Nothing," she said. "It still doesn't mean anything… Let me check one more thing."

We watched as she flipped a few more files on the big screen. "Jana didn't put in for overtime. Which doesn't make sense."

Or it made too much sense. Depending which way you looked at it.

I didn't say anything, and nor did Dominic, though we exchanged glances. Annegret wasn't fooling anyone. Including herself, judging by her bleak expression.

"What about the rest of this month? Were there more unexplained hours?"

"Not for Jana," she said. "Or at least, not ones she coded in for. But if Amara let her in…"

Then we had no way of knowing about the extra hours. Or who else might have been there, too. Short of going through all the recordings. Which might not be a bad idea. "How long are your videos kept for?"

"Six months," Annegret said, following my thinking with no effort. "And we could take a look at every occasion where she is recorded as being here outside her usual hours."

Then her face fell. "Unless that's another area they're not following through on." She glanced at Dominic. "Should I call and request all of them?"

He shook his head, at the same time as I said, "No, don't."

"Why not?"

I answered for him. "If someone at SaltonSecure is working with the bad guys? Suddenly asking for that much data sends a signal that we're on to them. And we don't want to do that. Not until we have more information."

"Especially not if you're right that whoever is behind this is working to frame you," Dominic said to her.

"Without that information I can't prove a thing," she said. "So what am I supposed to do?"

"Leave it to me," I said.

Which earned me surprised looks from both of them, followed by a slow grin from Dominic. That was one appealing man. And he knew it, too.

"My team is excellent at… analyzing computer data," I said, choosing my words carefully. "Much faster than the three of us could ever be. Let me put them on it, see what they come up with before we go any further."

"That's smart," Dominic said to Annegret. "And there's one more thing I'd like you to consider. If you seriously think the *surete* are looking at you? And that you may be framed for both murder and fraud? I think you need a criminal lawyer even more than you need me."

She nodded slowly. "I suppose that makes sense. Your firm handles criminal law as well, doesn't it? Can you recommend someone very, very good?"

He gave her that slow smile. "As it happens, I do know such a person."

"Can you work with him or her? And he with you?" she asked. "Whoever it is needs to be willing to work with all three of us, because you have the business side. I want you to stay involved."

"I don't think that would be an issue," he said with a slow smile. "Our best criminal lawyer just happens to be my twin sister, Elise. If you're in agreement, I'd suggest the four of us meet here tomorrow morning at nine. In the meantime, I will undertake to sort out where you stand with your security firm.

And perhaps Barbara's team might have some analysis for us by then."

"I'll see what I can do," I said.

Knowing my team was up to it. Especially with the time difference working in our favor.

CHAPTER SEVENTEEN

After Dominic left, Annegret and I went over a few things. Then I grabbed my suitcase and a cab and headed for my hotel. Jet lag was hitting hard, and if I needed to be up and coherent to talk to my team, I needed a power nap before dinner. Or two.

Annegret had suggested meeting for dinner, but I wanted some alone time to process the direction the case had taken. And I had some work to do before I talked to Badger and Cory, in particular. Which probably meant room service.

Though I might venture out later for a nightcap. I needed the fresh air and a chance to stretch my legs. And maybe to scout out a running route for the morning. The way this case was unfolding, I'd be swamped all day tomorrow. And I was going to need my exercise routine more than ever.

My hotel—L'Étoile—was utterly gorgeous. Warm old stone and a huge lobby glowing with intricate painted wrought iron chandeliers and tapestry in rich shades of red and russet and gold. Even the air smelled luxurious. I couldn't decide if it was a really good potpourri or essential oils. Possibly both.

By the time I'd checked in and got settled in my spacious, well-appointed room—thanks to Annegret's generosity—it was a little past four-thirty in the afternoon.

Nine hours earlier in Vancouver. Seven-thirty on a Monday morning. Right. E-mail time.

I hauled out my laptop, began to type. Given the security issues around this case, I was wary about what I put in the email, even though Badger had assured me no-one was breaking the levels of encryption she'd put on my devices.

At this stage of the investigation, though, I wanted to discuss where we were at, and where we were going. The email itself boiled down to, 'I have information. Need research. Call me.'

I sent the email to Marie, with a copy to Badger and Cory.

It was probably at least an hour before I could expect a response. Which would give me time to unpack, and review my notes. I'd only got as far as putting my toiletries in the expansive grey-streaked white marble and chrome bathroom when my cell dinged. I glanced at the call display. Which was blank.

Probably Badger, I thought with a wry grin. It surprised me she was up so early on a Monday. And I wouldn't have expected her to be working. At least security wasn't going to be an issue for this call. She probably had it routed all over the world, and encrypted about six ways.

"Barbara O'Grady," I said.

"What do you need?" Badger asked.

I gave her a quick rundown of what I'd learned that day, and the questions it had raised for me. "Since we don't seem able to trust SaltonSecure,"—she snorted at that—"I'm hoping you can get hold of what we need."

"Which is?"

"Copies of the security video from the gallery, going back six months. Same for the passcode log for the doors. Anything you can pull out of the infrared cameras—including can the range for the one by the rear door be extended to show any part of the cellar? Plus I'll need all of it analyzed for anything that's outside the normal patterns. With a particular focus on the actions of Amara Duvant and Jana Bertrand. Can you do it?"

She didn't dignify that with an answer. "I may be able to clean up the videos enough to identify Duvant's 'visitor', as well as whoever you spotted in the alley a half hour later."

"That would be amazing," I said. "We're meeting again at nine tomorrow morning…"

"Cory and I will have it for you in a couple of hours. It'll be in your inbox," she said, and disconnected.

Cory? Why would he be available to work with Badger at this hour on a Monday morning? Didn't he have school today?

I decided I was better off not knowing.

I glanced at my watch. Given Badger's timeline, I probably had a couple of hours, which brought it to nine or ten in the morning, their time. Most likely ten, given the tasks I'd set them. So, around seven p.m. here. Now what?

Time differences made my head hurt. And the jet lag wasn't helping any. I needed that power nap. I also needed to review the case, get my thoughts straight.

I debated whether my current mental fog would benefit most from dinner? Or the nap?

I glanced at my watch again. On the other hand, it was nearly eight a.m. back home. Which, given he was on assignment, ought to be the perfect time to call Nick before his official day began. The thought put a smile on my face.

Given his travel, my travel and our conflicting schedules, I'd barely talked to him since our dinner at Guido's on Thursday. That had been a good evening. I missed him.

Being thousands of miles away didn't help.

Though when it came down to it—there was no real difference between being hundreds of miles apart and thousands of miles apart. As long as there was a functioning internet connection.

Except in an emergency.

Like murder. Which brought me back to Annegret, and her relationship with Amara Duvant. Now that I was away from her, there was something off there. Something in the way Annegret spoke of her murdered colleague. Not so much in what she said. It was in what she didn't say.

I still didn't have a clear sense of their relationship, or how she'd felt about her key employee. For people who had worked together as long as they had, that seemed odd. What was I missing?

As I pondered that, I clicked on Nick's cell number.

"Barbara," he said when he answered.

There was something neutral in his tone. Not exactly the welcome I'd expected. Either I'd done something to royally piss him off—and I couldn't think of anything, this time. Or he wasn't alone.

"There's someone there?"

"Mmm-hmmm."

"Should I call back?"

"Later would be better. Tell you what. I'll call you."

This was so out of character I knew he had to be in the middle of a dicey situation. At eight in the morning?

"Sure. I'm in Geneva, so don't forget we're nine hours ahead."

There was an odd little pause.

I had told him I was off to Switzerland, hadn't I? Of course I had. Had he forgotten?

Just what was this assignment, anyway?

But I couldn't ask now. And he probably couldn't tell me anyway.

"Of course. I'll call you tomorrow then," he said in his most professional tone.

"I miss you," I said.

"Thanks for calling," he said. And disconnected.

I stared at my phone for a moment, my mind turning over too many possibilities. None of them good.

For the first time I wondered if I'd dragged my feet too long on moving in together. What if he'd moved on?

Shaking it off, I called down to room service for a burger and fries, and coffee. I needed comfort food. And caffeine. Lots of it.

A power nap was off the table now. So I might as well get my mind back on my own case. Whatever Nick was mixed up in, he knew what he was doing. And we'd be fine. If anything was wrong between us, I trusted his blunt honesty to just tell me.

Eventually, a little voice added.

I ignored it. Stupid jet lag.

But maybe I'd take another look at house rentals that could work for the two of us. Just because the commitment of buying a place together scared the bejeebers out of me? That didn't mean we couldn't live together.

As Andrea had annoyingly pointed out to me.

I hadn't been ready to hear it. There were too many other changes in my life. But life tends not to wait until we are 'ready' for things.

There's a reason people are still saying 'Carpe Diem'. One, it was a great movie. But two, it resonates, even in a dead language. Sometimes you really do just have to seize the moment.

And that was quite enough philosophizing for one day. Andrea would be laughing her head off at me. This is why I hate flying across time zones.

I needed coffee, and I needed it now. They'd said half an hour. I glanced at the clock. Taking a fresh look at my notes would go better with coffee. And it was just after eight a.m. back home.

Which meant Andrea would be up, and mostly coherent. And I hadn't followed through on how it was going with her and that new guy. What was his name? Greg Younger, that was it.

A few clicks, and it was ringing.

"Hello?" Andrea said in a distracted voice.

"It's me," I said.

"Barbara? But you're in Switzerland."

She'd got that right, anyway. "I know. I had a few minutes, wondered how things were going for you."

"Nick couldn't talk, then?" she said. Now her voice was clear and focused.

"Nope. Blew me off," I said with a grin I knew she'd hear. "You free to talk?"

It had finally occurred to me that her new love interest might be there. Even though Andrea wasn't big on letting them stay overnight when she had to work the next day, this guy had sounded different when she talked about him.

But if he was there, that meant this new relationship was big. And I hadn't known.

"Andrea?" I repeated as the silence dragged. I heard low murmurs in the background. He was there.

"I'm sorry, Barbara. I hate to do this to you, when you've taken the time to call like this…"

"Andrea, it's me. What's with the formality?" I said. "Is he there? Greg?"

"Yes, that's it," she said. Still sounding stilted. "I'll call you?"

"Email is better, with my case and the time difference."

"Right. Okay. Well, I'll email you. When I'm free."

And the line went dead.

Okay, that didn't sound good. But it was hard to be sure, from this far away.

We'd go for dinner, when I got back, just the two of us. Or maybe the four of us? I wanted to meet this new guy of Andrea's, the one who had her breaking long-standing rules.

That had to be a good thing. Didn't it?

———

BEFORE I COULD WORK myself into a jet lag inspired funk, the phone rang again. Badger. "That was fast," I said.

"For a security firm, they're ridiculously easy to break into," she said. "Or at least, our client's account with them is."

Wait a minute. Badger wasn't one to waste words. "You mean her account, in particular?"

"Uh huh. Somebody's set it up with a back door. And they haven't done a particularly good job of it."

"So there is an inside player," I said. And probably someone with some tech ability, but no real expertise.That explained a lot of what I'd seen earlier. "What did the data tell you?"

"Cory is still running that algorithm of his on the recordings. He's done some tweaking. It's pretty good," she said.

Coming from her, that was high praise. "But it's legal?"

"Since the video belongs to our client, sure."

Close enough. "And the passcode log-ins?"

"I took a look at those," she said. "Looks like whatever this is has been going on for at least six months. So I went back a full year."

Hadn't Annegret said the firm only kept six months worth of data? Had they lied to her about that, too?

Then again, this was Badger. Supposedly deleted data wasn't safe around her. "And?"

"And Duvant has been coming in at odd hours, then coming back late at night, for most of a year." Before I could ask, she added, "Cross checking those dates, she's spent most of that time down in the cellar."

"What about the others?"

"No real pattern until Bertrand started there in January. Then Bertrand is coming in early or staying late at least once a week. Video shows her in Duvant's office or the cellar."

So Jana Bertrand and Amara Duvant were both involved. "Assuming there's an insider at the security firm…"

"There is," Badger said.

"Have they doctored any of the data before they sent it to our client?"

"It doesn't look like it," she said. "They just held some of it back, and didn't send other stuff that the contract committed them to."

Of course she'd checked into that.

"If they weren't sending everything to their own client, why in the world would they give the *surete* more than the warrant covered?" I asked her. I had my own suspicions, but I wanted to hear a hacker's take on it.

"Three options. One, it wasn't the insider that sent it, probably someone green. Two, they were trying to bury the incriminating stuff in too much data. Or three, they were setting up a frame for the client."

"And you think it's the third option," I said.

"Don't you?"

I grinned, but kept it out of my voice. "It makes the most sense."

"Then why ask?"

"Because you look at data from a perspective that would never occur to me."

She laughed. "True that. And a good thing, too."

"There's a reason everyone in the investigative world is jealous you're working with me."

"Yeah, yeah. You want Cory to send you the analysis as soon as he's done?"

She sounded uncomfortable. Had I managed to embarrass her? I'd have to remember that.

"Sounds good. He can call if he wants."

"I'll tell him."

"How are you making out with the frauds?"

"Too soon to say. I'll be in touch when I have something." And she disconnected.

I had embarrassed her. Oops.

The knock on my door was a welcome distraction. Room service? I glanced at my watch. I was hungry, but checked the peephole before opening the door. The black slacks and vest with white shirt looked right, as did the trolley in front of him. I couldn't make out what was on it, but I swear I smelled fresh coffee, rich and dark.

I flung open the door. Yup, a carafe of coffee, a cola, one mug, and two covered dishes. I'd weakened at the last minute and ordered *sachertorte*. I could never resist the rich, heavy chocolate. And I was planning on running an extra mile tomorrow to make up for it.

The room service guy waited while I moved my computer, then carefully set the tray on the desk and adjusted the chair as I sat. As if I'd ever mistake a hotel room, even one as swanky as this one, for a real restaurant. But I appreciated the effort. He even lifted each silver dome-shaped cover, as if to make sure everything was to my satisfaction. It was.

And I suddenly realized I was starving.

Once I'd signed for the meal, including a healthy tip, and locked the door behind him, I settled down to enjoy my piping hot burger and fries. The first bite was sheer nirvana. They'd got the beef just rare enough, and everything else tasted fresh picked or fresh baked. Except the ketchup, and they'd gone with the real thing. Of course, hunger might have something to do with how wonderful it tasted.

I reached for a fry, and my phone rang. I glanced at the number. Cory. Of course. With a sigh I re-covered my plate and poured myself a coffee.

"Cory? What did you find?"

"You'll never guess," came his eager voice.

"I'm jet lagged, Cory."

"Oh. Right. Sorry."

I hadn't meant to deflate him. "So what did you find?"

"These guys are good. But they're idiots at the same time." He was grinning now, I could hear it. "How do smart people end up doing such stupid things?"

"It's a mystery," I said dryly. And waited.

At this rate, I could have been eating my burger while I waited for him to get to the point. At least the coffee was good.

"Sorry," he said again. But he was too focused on whatever he was so anxious to tell me to really mean it. "But they doctored the recordings."

They what? "How?"

"I don't know how. Badger's looking into it now."

"What did they change? And how did you find it?"

"Same answer to both questions." He was grinning again, I could tell. And far too pleased with himself.

This was one of those times it would have been useful to video conference, the three of us. At least Badger would just answer the question. I'd have to ask her whether there were really secure video conferencing options out there, for situations like this.

"So?" I said.

It took an effort to keep my tone neutral. I could have blamed jet lag again, but I could see how Susanna had begun to say 'teenagers', and roll her eyes a lot when it came to anything regarding Cory. Sometimes he seemed so mature. Other times? Not so much.

No wonder my sister got irritated when the only thing Cory seemed enthusiastic about was working for me. Or rather, with Badger.

I wondered for a moment if it would help if I told Susanna that it wasn't me who was the attraction. It was his shiny new computer. And his slightly less shiny new mentor.

Probably it would make things worse. Likely much worse, I decided, as Cory finally said, "They'd erased stuff from some of the recordings. Or maybe hidden it somehow, I'm not sure. But they left tiny gaps in the videos, not even a second, but too often. My algorithm caught it."

"Well done," I said. Wishing I could see his face.

So I'm a doting aunt. Sue me.

"What were they hiding?" I asked.

"That's what Badger's trying to figure out. If anyone can replace the missing bits, it's her." Something approaching awe in his voice.

Which Badger deserved. I didn't even understand most of what she could do. And I liked it that way.

Cory, on the other hand? I'd have to keep an eye on him. I mostly trusted Badger, but... Well, who knew what the two of them were really working on. And what she was teaching him.

I certainly didn't.

"But from the context," Cory was saying. "I think they were carrying stuff into and out of the cellar. Only they're good at hiding what they were doing, and some stuff was only visible for microseconds."

If that was true, it began to explain why Amara and her

midnight visitor had spent so much time in the cellar. Maybe something had been worked on, then they were delivering it. To a buyer, perhaps. Or an employer?

We had too little information for me to even guess.

"Whatever this is, it's complex," I said. "And it's been in the works for a while, for them to have this many insiders working on it. And that's just the ones we know about."

"Yeah," he said.

I started to roll my eyes, caught myself. "Did Badger say how long it might take her?"

"No. But she got that look on her face. It's a challenge, but a kinda half-baked one. And she's even more irritated with their stupidity than I am."

Okay, then. Sounded like I could expect another call from Badger tonight. I gave up the idea of going out for a glass of wine. But I needed to finish my meal and grab a shower before the next call.

"Anything else?" I asked him.

"Nah," my nephew said. "I gotta head for school now. But I'm going to work with Badger over lunch, and I have a spare first thing in the afternoon, so we'll have time to get some real work done."

"That's great," I said, doing a quick mental calculation. Looked like I wasn't going to get an early night, after all. Still, I had some research of my own to do. And I might have a few more answers before tomorrow's meeting.

"We'll get 'em," he said.

"I know we will," I said. "Thanks, Cory."

CHAPTER EIGHTEEN

The following morning four of us met in Annegret's light filled office: me, my client, and her two lawyers. At my recommendation, she'd switched off the security cameras in her office for the duration of the meeting, though I had to remind her twice. She'd also provided the coffee, which again was excellent, and Dominic had brought pastries. Which were beyond excellent. I decided I might just survive this meeting, after all.

Dominic's sister, Elise Marbach—Annegret's second lawyer—was a surprise. From her name, I'd expected long blond locks, pouty lips and floaty white dresses—the result of viewing too many perfume ads, I suspect. This Elise had the same dark hair as her twin, cut in a short, sharp-edged modern style. Her suit, every bit as well-tailored as his, was also edgy and modern, in a deep gray that looked sleekly professional, yet suited her honey-cream complexion. And her expression was all business.

"Dominic has filled me in, and this situation is serious," she said to Annegret as soon as all of us were seated. "If you don't take legal advice now, you could well end up in jail for many years for fraud. If not murder, judging what I'm hearing from my sources within the police force."

Annegret paused with her coffee cup halfway to her mouth and eyed Elise. I still couldn't read her that well, but I'd have sworn she was about to say something scathing.

Dominic must have thought the same, for he held up one hand to his sister. "A little slower please, Elise. Annegret is aware of the dangers. That is why you're here, after all."

Elise's lips tightened a bit, but she didn't back down. She was either very arrogant, or very good. Maybe both. I sat back a little. This wasn't my fight, though I hope it would give me a few of the answers I needed.

"I don't need defending," Annegret said, her hard eyes shifting from Elise to Dominic and back again. "I need a little honesty. And for all of you to work together to help me get to the bottom of whatever is going on."

She looked at me. "Preferably before I find myself in jail."

And she turned that gimlet gaze on Elise.

Well, weren't we off to a good start?

"I have some information on the security tapes," I said into the telling little silence that had fallen around the table. "My team were able to find copies going back over a year."

Annegret's expression hardened even further. "But they told me..." she began.

"You had no idea?" I asked. Just to be clear.

"None. How would I know?"

How could she not know? This was her gallery. If she didn't care, who would? But if Annegret hadn't figured that out yet, I had a feeling this case was about to provide her with a hard lesson.

"But if that's true...?" she went on. "It is—was—part of Amara's job to read the reports and verify the tapes. I trusted her to make sure everything was as it should be."

"Despite the rumors of fraud?" I asked.

"Yes. I trusted her," she repeated, as if trying to convince herself. "But my security firm. They *lied* to me?" Her face didn't seem to know whether to be stunned or furious.

"It's too early in the investigation to know exactly where that lie originated," was all I said. "But one of my team was able to dig out some of the information we need. Amara Duvant has been making a habit of spending time in the cellar for more than a year. And when Jana Bertrand joined the gallery staff in January, she met with her manager in the cellar on a regular basis."

"What were they doing down there?" Annegret said, half to herself.

"That isn't clear. Not yet. But what we do know is that there are micro-seconds missing from those videos."

"What? Which ones?" Annegret asked.

"Most of the ones showing them going to or from the cellar. The missing sections go by too fast for us even to notice them."

"How did you find them, then?" Elise demanded.

I hope that bulldog approach worked well for her in court. With her looks, the contrast to her manner was probably effective at unsettling the other side. But here, it was alienating everyone except her brother. And maybe him too, given his tightening lips.

"Thanks to a very sophisticated algorithm my team developed," I told her. Which shut her up for the moment.

"Any idea what the missing—did you say micro-seconds—show?" Dominic asked.

I nodded. "As of early this morning, we have the missing pieces."

"How did you manage that?" Elise asked, her tone hostile.

I glanced at her, wondering where this borderline rudeness was coming from. "Sorry. Proprietary information," I said.

Dominic glared at his sister. "I hope you have whatever technology allowed that properly patented," he said to me.

Of course. His legal specialty was international business, with a focus on patents and copyrights. I'd checked that out last night.

The idea of patenting my team's work amused me for a moment, as I pictured him asking Badger that question. On the other hand, the algorithms might well be patentable. As long as no-one ever explained exactly why they'd developed them. Or how they'd tested them.

I made a mental note to talk to Badger about it.

"Well? What were they hiding?" Annegret asked.

"Let me show you," I said. "Can I use your computer?"

She unlocked it for me and I inserted a flash drive I'd down-loaded from my laptop, then turned the screen so everyone could see it. At my nod, she partially closed the blinds and turned down the overhead lights to the setting we'd found worked best the previous day.

"These are broken into segments, which were taken from a number of different original recordings," I said. "Each segment had several micro-second clips taken from it. What you'll see is three versions of each segment. The first is the doctored version, without the micro-second clips. The second is a restored version of the same clip. The third is the same as the second, but in slow motion, so it's possible to see exactly what is happening.

You'll see a two-second orange screen between each of the versions of each segment, and a four-second green screen—showing the date and time the segment was filmed—between each of the segments, to make it easier to follow what's happening.

For maximum efficiency, I'll be running the entire series through before we pause or discuss any of it. This takes about fifteen minutes. Then we can review each segment. And discuss any questions you have."

Elise looked like she wanted to argue, but a look from her brother silenced her. Perhaps he was reminding her the client paid the bills.

And Annegret was clearly in agreement with my suggestions, even though I'd sprang it on her, too.

Either she'd started to trust me. Or she had too much to hide. At this point, I could still go either way.

Though I was reluctantly starting to like her.

———

ALL FOUR OF us watched in silence as the videos ran. This was maybe the fifth time I'd seen it, and I was looking for any details that I'd missed on earlier viewings. And finding them.

Badger and Cory had done a masterful job making sense of the recovered information. And they'd done so in a way that made it impossible to miss what the bad guys were trying so hard to hide.

When the last video stopped on a black screen, the other three in the room looked at each other.

"Can you run it again?" Annegret said. "I want to be sure I saw what I thought I saw."

Dominic nodded, and his sister didn't say a word.

I restarted the program. And again noted an additional detail here, another there.

This time when the black screen came up, Annegret stood up, and began to pace from her chair to the desk and back.

"They're taking things into the cellar. And out again. And some of them are going back into the gallery. And others are going out the rear door."

"And by things, you mean paintings," Elise said cooly. "I assume you had no idea this was happening."

"I mean works of art," Annegret said. "And no, I didn't even suspect such a thing. And when I inspected the security videos, all I saw was the doctored version. The lies, showing all was well. When it very much was not."

"The recordings are well done," Elise said. "But hardly provide enough proof that you weren't involved to help you in front of a judge."

I don't know how Annegret felt, but I wanted to kick the lawyer. I just hoped she was this belligerent in court.

Annegret was going to need all the help she could get.

"Good thing we have more," I said, breaking the tense silence.

"What?" Annegret said. Her active vocabulary seemed to have shrunk as her stress increased.

"Mme's Duvant's passcode was used again the night—or rather the morning after—she died," I said.

"When?"

"By whom?"

"Is there video?"

Annegret, Dominic and Elise spoke at nearly the same time. I held up my hand. "It was just after 2 a.m., and there's no video. So the only thing we're sure of is that it was not Amara Duvant."

"How did they kill the recording?" Elise asked.

"That's a very good question," I said. "We're looking into it, but the most likely answer is SaltonSecure again."

"Which doesn't help Annegret at all," Elise said.

"It speaks to pattern," I said. "And our client," and I emphasized the word just enough that Elise got my message and glared at me. "Doesn't have either the access or the technical expertise to control the security cameras from so far away."

The two lawyers exchanged glances. I suspect the female half of the team had overlooked the impact of Annegret being out of town at the time. That, or she'd been talking to the *surete*, and was already marshaling arguments against their point of view. A little too soon, in my opinion.

Before I could say anything, Dominic spoke. "Since we have no new information on the murder, I suggest that for now we focus on what we do have. The fraud."

His sister glared at him this time. "That's easy for you to say. Fraud is within your area of expertise. Which won't help our client." And she too emphasized those words. "Not when she's about to be arrested for murder."

And there it was.

"And just how do you know that?" Dominic asked.

She looked smug. "I have my sources. If you'd called me in on this earlier," and she glanced from him to Annegret and back, "I might have been able to prevent it."

"But I wasn't even in the country," Annegret protested.

Both of them ignored her.

I looked back and forth between them, wondering if Annegret

was going to have to hire a new lawyer before this was over. Or two of them? I felt even more sorry for her.

But Dominic knew his sister better than any of us. "So, that's it? You are just giving in?" he asked her. "Without even a fight?"

"Hardly," she said.

"No? It certainly seems that way."

"Our client," she said—again emphasizing the words. She really was a bulldog. No matter what she looked like. "Seems unable to admit just how high her risk is. The *surete* are not just pretending she's their main suspect. She is their only suspect. And until she accepts that, and acts accordingly, I can't even begin to do my job."

Annegret's indrawn breath teetered on the edge of a sob, but she quickly mastered herself.

Raising her chin, she matched the bulldog stare for stare. "Given that I am innocent of this murder, what—in your expert opinion—constitutes an appropriate reaction?" she asked icily. "I trust you do not expect me to cower before this misguided threat from the *surete?*"

I felt like cheering. Though I couldn't help noticing that Annegret's declaration of innocence was very specifically related to the murder. And hoping her phrasing was just words chosen in the heat of the moment, and not a careful maneuvering around inconvenient facts about the frauds.

"Sometimes you're too suspicious," I told myself. Which was true. But sometimes I wasn't.

"Of course she doesn't," Dominic said, glancing at his sister as he spoke. "Not when you had the intelligence to hire the only lawyer in the city capable of resolving this confusion and ensuring that you walk free."

Oh, he was good. He'd left both women with no option but to cooperate. I sat back to watch this one play out. And the image of a tub of popcorn popped into my head. I could almost smell the butter.

"Now, shall we see what this new information tells us about the rumors of art fraud directed against this gallery?" Dominic continued smoothly.

Annegret gave him a smile that was only slightly less icy than the one she'd bestowed on his sister.

"Given the recording we just watched," she said. "I think we can all agree that the rumors are, indeed, fact. And that whoever is behind the fraudulent art being run through this gallery is likely responsible for Amara's murder."

Neither lawyer so much as blinked.

Dominic nodded, as if he'd expected this exact response. Perhaps he had. And his sister had an excellent poker face.

I considered breaking this up now, and telling them the rest of it.

Badger had somehow got her hands on copies of the surveillance video for the night of the murder from several of the neighboring establishments. She and Cory were working to pull together enough to get a clear image of Mme. Duvant's 'visitor' as well as whoever had ghosted down the alley less than an hour before she'd died. I expected to have answers anytime now.

Trouble is, I had no idea how useful the result would prove. And given Elise's belligerent attitude, the last thing we needed was more doubt. I decided not to mention it.

False hope wouldn't help my client. Nor would another attack from her legal team.

I waited to see where Dominic would go with this.

"You're right," he told Annegret. "There is now no denying your gallery's involvement in fraud."

The lines around her lips deepened at hearing it, but she nodded.

"There are clues in that recording we didn't have before," he continued. "So, how is this fraud being done?"

I was reluctantly impressed. He was trying to diplomatically lead Annegret through what we now knew, looking for patterns and new pieces she could speculate on.

"I don't know," she said forcefully. "I wish I did."

"You'll have to do better than that," Elise put in. "Or you'll be convicted of the fraud as well as murder. You said it yourself—your manager's murder is clearly tied to the fraud she was involved in perpetrating."

And it went off the rails again.

Watching the increasingly tense exchange that followed, I was beginning to wonder if Dominic knew his sister as well as he thought he did when he recommended her to Annegret. This was getting us nowhere.

Finally, I suggested we all meet again the following day. "My team may have some new information for us by then."

Annegret nodded, white lipped.

"I should hope so," Elise shot at me as she and her brother stood up.

Annegret and I watched them leave in silence, then she excused herself for a moment.

I had a few questions of my own for Annegret. And when she returned with coffee for both of us, I started asking them.

I didn't get the answers I'd expected.

CHAPTER NINETEEN

For the next hour Annegret and I reviewed the video clips, trying to piece together which works had been taken down into the cellar. And when. And what that meant for her clients, her suppliers and her gallery. Not to mention the leads it might give us to track down the forgers.

I found it beyond frustrating, even compared to the earlier part of the meeting, with her two lawyers present. Once it was just the two of us, I couldn't seem to keep my client on track.

Every time we zeroed in on a date from one of the restored video clips, and I tried to get her to review what had been going on at the time; new clients, new suppliers, paintings taken in on commission, paintings bought, paintings sold—she veered off on an attempt to determine exactly which work had been taken down into the cellar on that date. And whether it was the same work that had then vanished out the back door. Or if that work had gone back into the gallery. And what it might mean if it had.

All of which were legitimate questions that needed answering. The issue was, the amount of detail visible on even the restored clips was so tiny as to be useless. We were slowing the clips down, and going frame by frame, and still getting nowhere.

Usually it was either Amara Duvant or Jana Bertrand who was taking the paintings into the cellar. Sometimes they were the ones bringing them out again, either alone or together. And sometimes it was someone with their hood up, whom we both agreed looked like Duvant's midnight 'visitor'. He—or she, because neither of us was completely certain it was the same figure—was always accompanied by one or both of the staff.

And all three of them were careful. When they carried a framed painting, it was always the back side of the work that the camera caught, and they held the framed works low enough that it only caught glimpses of blank canvas or a bit of the frame.

Those glimpses were usually not enough to recognize the size of the work, let alone anything about the painting itself. Or even the frame. Which was unfortunate, since some of the older frames are very distinctive.

Once Annegret thought she recognized a bit of a frame, and we paused and reran that section of video often enough that I was glad we were dealing with digital recordings, and not the old-style tape. Which would have been worn and stretched beyond recognition by the time we were done with it.

Finally Annegret stared at an enlarged segment of carved and gilded frame as Duvant carried it into the cellar. "I know that frame," she said, and stood up.

I expected her to head for the old master's section of the gallery, because I recognized enough to know that style of frame had to be three or four hundred years old. But no. She reached to an over-head cabinet, and used her thumbprint to unlock a digital lock so close to invisible I hadn't spotted it.

Reaching into the cabinet, she withdrew two ledgers covered in dark navy cloth. I caught a glimpse of other navy covered ledgers, along with several grey covered ones before she swung the door closed. It locked without making a sound.

Placing the two ledgers she'd removed on her desk, she sat down and began to flip the pages. They seemed to be in order by date, and I wondered how she ever found anything. But she did.

She only had to flip a few pages in the first binder she opened before she ran her finger down one of the pages, stopping about halfway down. And tapping her finger on the line, she nodded to herself.

"I was right. It was the Rembrandt," she said.

Picturing the painting that had stopped me cold yesterday, my heart sank. "The one in the gallery now?" I said. "It's a fraud?"

"Probably," she said.

"Wasn't this video taken before you had the paintings checked?"

"It was."

"Then... how could that painting be a fake?" I asked. "If it was one of the seven that XTC Tech cleared as being genuine?"

Which was worrying, if I was right. But I was surprised to realize that the urgency behind my question was because I hated to think of that amazing little jewel of a painting being stolen.

"We didn't test this one," she said calmly.

Caught off guard, I stared at her. "What? Why not?"

"Our restorer didn't flag it for us as being in any way problematic."

"Then your restorer must be working for the forgers," I said. "I haven't met her. Who is she?"

Oddly, it was one detail Badger hadn't given me when she dug into the gallery employees. Suddenly I wondered if that restorer even existed.

"She is on vacation at the moment. In Italy."

"In the middle of a crisis?" I said sharply. And still no name.

"She had planned this trip for months," Annegret said calmly. "I couldn't ask her to cancel it. Not when her skills are so valuable."

Really? After the restorer had missed something this big? "When is she due back?" I asked.

"End of the week."

It was only Monday. "The timing couldn't be worse. Can you ask her to come back early?" I said.

"Technically she is a contractor, though she works only for us.

In-house," Annegret explained carefully. "Unfortunately, that means she takes time away when she chooses."

"But…" I began.

"I rely on her knowledge and expertise, and have done so for over a decade now," Annegret said, rolling right over my protest.

Oh, this wasn't good.

"So what is on the wall of your gallery?" I asked. "A fraudulent copy? Or an original Rembrandt painting?"

She looked away. Then back, and met my eyes.

"A copy, of course," she said firmly. "But it isn't fraudulent."

I stared at her, speechless.

Then it clicked.

"That's why the security in your showroom seemed unusually lax," I said. "You have the originals copied, and only hang the copies."

"You are good," she said. "I was told you were."

By whom? Margaret? I put that aside for now. It could wait.

"And I only have some of the originals copied," she said.

"The ones it would cost a small fortune to insure," I guessed.

She nodded.

"Why has no-one noticed?"

"I work with a number of insurers, and have them all sign draconian non-disclosures on everything I insure with them."

Of course she did. She'd built a business from nothing. Though her methods… Unorthodox came to mind, but that wasn't it. I couldn't think of a word strong enough.

"That's why you were cagey about the testing," I said. "You couldn't have some of those works tested without giving the game away."

"Yes," she said. "And it's why I couldn't hire a local firm when the rumors of fraud at the gallery surfaced."

I gritted my teeth. "Then why not just tell me everything from the beginning?"

"I didn't think I'd have to. And there are so few people I can trust with this. Can you imagine if any of it got out?"

Only too well. And I couldn't imagine a more perfect set-up than the current one to make sure it did, either. Surely she knew that?

"Who else knows?" I asked.

"Just me. And the copyist."

"Who is your 'restorer', I take it?"

"Of course," she said matter-of-factly.

Of course she was. That explained the rest of it.

And her 'restorer' was beyond good, too. I remembered vividly the feeling that had gone through me as I stood in front of that Rembrandt.

"No wonder you have her on an exclusive contract," I said. "And she must have been working for you for longer than a decade, too."

She nodded. "Almost since I opened. She's one of my best friends. I trust her like I trust few others in my life."

I'll bet she did. She'd have to. Handled wrong, news of this could destroy her. Destroy both of them. Even if there had been no intent to defraud.

"But if the copyist can paint like that, why is she working as a restorer, and making copies instead of painting her own works?" I asked. Unsure as I did so if it was the artist in me or the investigator wanting to know. Probably both.

Annegret sighed. "The art world can be a cruel place, as you undoubtedly know. And technical skills, which she has in abundance, are not enough. Not if your eyes are set on a career in the fine arts."

Annegret was right. I did know, only too well. It took creativity and originality and drive and determination—along with a healthy dose of timing and luck. And even then... More artists chose another path or died broke than ended up with a major career.

"And your friend...?" I asked carefully.

Annegret nodded. "Has her heart set on a Career, with a capital C. She is a brilliant technical artist, but she lacks an original vision. Which I could never tell her—it would break her heart. But I couldn't bear to see her starve, either. So I hired her. And she does her own work when she feels inspired."

Hence the trip to Italy, presumably. I wondered which had come first, Annegret's need to help her friend, or her need for an alternative form of "insurance" for her gallery?

Wait a minute.

"What happens to those copies after you sell a work?" I asked.

"They are stored in a vault offsite," she said.

"You don't destroy them?"

"I used to, early on. Then I found I often handle a work multiple times, as the value increases or an owner decides they must have a better known work by the artist."

"Who else has access to that vault?"

"Only I do," she said.

"Not even your manager?" I asked.

"Not even my friend who makes the copies," she said firmly. "No-one but me."

I had a bad feeling about this. "What about the originals? The ones that haven't been sold yet? Where are they stored? In the same vault?"

"Of course not." Now she sounded offended. "I'd never allow that kind of overlap. That's how mistakes are made."

It was one way. And at least she'd been smart about it. Mostly.

"Who has access to that vault?" I asked.

"The answer is the same. Only I have access."

"No backup at all?"

"No. I couldn't risk it."

And what if something happened to her? She didn't look as if the thought had ever crossed her mind.

For a successful businesswoman, she had a very skewed perspective on risk. Despite that, somewhere along the way, she'd trusted the wrong person. She must have, for her secrets to be leaking out now.

Although the insiders who worked here didn't seem to know

any of those secrets. Or they wouldn't be stealing the copies, and replacing them with other copies. Unless…

"You do have some originals hanging on the walls of your gallery, though?"

She nodded.

"Do you have any way of telling if any of those have been stolen?"

"Yes. Those are the ones my restorer examined very carefully," Annegret said. "She had suspicions about seven of them, and we sent them to XTC Tech."

"Three of those seven were frauds."

She nodded.

"Which three?"

"I sent you all of that, already."

Or Amara had, before she was murdered. Could there be a connection?

I set that aside for later consideration.

"Humor me," I said. "Were the three stolen works similar?"

"Yes. All three were small oils, all three were mid-century modern. And all three by newly hot artists."

"Which meant their prices were rising fast," I guessed.

"Yes."

That gave me another insight into the strategy the forgers were following. I made another note.

"I'll need to talk to XTC Tech about those three works," I said.

She nodded. "Fine, I'll authorize it with them. They'll be expecting your call."

"And I'll also need the name of your restorer."

She looked upset. "I've told you. She's a friend."

"And I'm the person you hired to help you solve this. I'll be discreet."

"Fine. Her name is Jacinta Roark," she said, and jotted down her contact information.

"Thank you," I said as I accepted it. "Are there any other little secrets you've been keeping?"

"You know everything, now," she said, head held high.

If I did, I'd know who was behind the rumors of fraud. And behind the theft of the three paintings she'd had tested that had since been declared frauds.

I knew I needed to ask her more questions, but my head was spinning. I needed a break. And food. Mostly I needed time to assimilate the bombshells she'd just dropped on me.

And to get my team digging into her statements. Maybe touch base with Keller. And Jessup, too.

I wanted to be sure my client had finally told me everything.

And that her previous omissions hadn't caused me to miss something critical.

I still couldn't shake the feeling I was missing something.

I just wasn't sure what, and it was the most annoying feeling. It wouldn't let me alone.

CHAPTER TWENTY

Two hours later, I was sitting in my hotel room trying to focus on my breathing while I waited for someone to call me back. So far, my phone calls had been a bust. The team was still digging. Keller wasn't answering. And I wanted to talk to him before I called Jessup. If I did.

It had been a crazily intense day so far and I was still short of sleep. Stupid jet lag. The artist in me occasionally reminds the slightly obsessed detective that I make better intuitive leaps if I'm rested.

So I was meditating. Kind of.

The room was certainly restful enough. All shades of cream and white, with touches of cool grey and a soft blue here and there. Somebody had an eye for the impact of color. I'd have added a little green, but that was my west coast sensibilities kicking in.

The deeply upholstered armchairs were utterly comfortable. The bed was huge and soft, with indulgently plump pillows. I eyed that luxurious comfort for a moment. Why not lie down? Just for five minutes.

Meditation is supposed to be restful, after all. And it would surely help with jet lag.

Between the time difference and the team's night owl tendencies, I needed all the help I could get, just to keep up with them. Then add in this infuriating case.

My client's recent confession to her scheme for reducing her insurance and security costs didn't help either.

I was still feeling shell-shocked.

And wishing I'd never met Annegret Carli.

I wasn't sure if her actions were actually illegal, or just a gray area. I wasn't sure I wanted to know, either. But I was going to have to find out. For my own peace of mind, if nothing else.

I couldn't decide if she was an incredible businesswoman. Or if she needed a good psychiatrist for the kind of risks she'd taken. Maybe both.

Only one thing was clear to me. Annegret's big secret was not such a secret.

Someone knew.

But who? And how?

It couldn't be the forgers. And likely not the insiders, either.

This particular theft ring only worked if the forgers—and especially the gallery insiders—had no idea about Annegret's interesting method for protecting the gallery's high ticket originals. They had to be stealing what they believed to be originals. Then swapping them out for forgeries of their own.

Which Annegret unknowingly swapped out for the real original before delivering it to her buyer.

In that scenario, the only ones ending up with a fake painting were the forgers. Who were presumably passing that stolen forgery on to their less-than-honest customers for a large payout. Since both parties believed they had the original masterpiece.

But surely at least one of those back-door customers had their new acquisition tested by a lab equally willing to work off the books? That supposed masterpiece would then have been exposed as a brilliantly done copy, which Annegret's restorer had probably painted using older techniques but modern oil paints. That would have come back on the fraudster.

Costing them money and maybe more.

Unless the rumors were coming from the forgers, attempting to get even with Annegret for the double switch that had left them selling excellent forgeries to some undoubtedly lethal bad guys. Ones with big purses. And bigger guns.

Which is where my theories broke down. Under either of those scenarios, why would the forgers have continued to use Carli Fine Arts as both a base and a source for their fraud ring?

They wouldn't. None of the forgers, including the insiders who worked for Annegret, could know what her 'restorer' really did. Which brought me back full circle.

If the rumors weren't leaking from somewhere in Annegret's gallery, or from the fraudster's network? Then where were they coming from?

Either could have been bad news for Annegret, but for different reasons. Neither was… infuriating. It left me with no suspects. And my client with a rumor she couldn't disprove.

That was when it hit me.

I couldn't risk telling anyone about my client's little in-house forgeries. It was too big a secret to keep, as this whole case proved.

I didn't like keeping my team out of the loop, but what choice did I have? With SaltonSecure's involvement and so many unknown players, the information Annegret had just dumped on me was too explosive to share.

A headache was building behind my eyes, and thinking about the case was not helping. I knew the signs. I needed to stop and clear my mind before I ended up with a full-blown migraine.

Determinedly unclenching my teeth, I resumed my attempts to meditate. Lying flat on the bed while I did so probably undermined them, though.

———

MARIE'S CALL woke me from a sound sleep. Feeling disoriented, I grabbed the phone, and wished I'd thought to set the coffee machine's timer before I lay down.

"Barbara," Marie said before I could get out more than 'hello'. "I'm so glad I caught you."

"What's up?" I asked, half my attention on the coffee machine. I needed to shake off this muzziness. Maybe I could make coffee one handed?

"We have a problem," she said. Which wasn't like her.

Now she had my attention.

These days, Marie handled most things impressively well, which still occassionally surprised me. I'd learned caution after my initial experiences with her, though, which had ended up with me being shot.

"That shot just winged you," she now tended to point out if the subject came up.

Which used to be my line, back when she was trying to make it up to me for the entire situation, and I was trying to convince her my bill already included danger pay. But this Marie—the one who was Justine's protege—was a cool professional, not afraid of much. And no problem was too big.

Which could be a problem in itself.

Marie had grown a lot since we first met—maybe too fast. She still threw herself wholeheartedly into things. And she had developed the confidence in herself to take on anything. I was proud of her.

And sometimes scared for her.

She didn't always have the experience to back up that confidence. And that could get her—which meant both of us—into real trouble.

My heart rate accelerated and my head cleared like magic. "What kind of problem?"

"Badger says someone's traced one of Cory's algorithms."

They'd what?

"How is that possible?" I said sharply.

"Hang on a sec," she said, and I heard the muffled sound of voices in the background.

Then she was back. "Something about he needed more detail, and he couldn't download the older stuff easily, so it was faster just to run the analysis on their machines. He didn't think they'd notice."

I closed my eyes and took a deep breath. Susanna was going to kill me. And I had a few harsh words for my nephew. And harsher ones for my expert hacker.

Even if Badger hadn't known what he was up to, she should have anticipated something. He was a teenager, after all.

"Put Badger on," I said.

"Can't. She's doing… something. It's time-sensitive, anyway."

Okay. Maybe she could fix this. Whatever it was. "And Cory?"

"He went home hours ago."

And it had taken them this long to call me?

I glanced at my watch, which I'd set for both time zones. It was 7 am back home. Had they been working all night?

"We didn't find out there was a problem until half an hour ago," Marie said. "Badger called me in."

Had she started reading my mind, now? But that was the jet lag talking. Marie had figured out at least some of how my mind worked a while back.

Which was almost as unsettling as mind reading.

"How did you figure it out?" I asked.

"Badger was checking out something on the Carli Fine Arts account, and she noticed the silent alert."

"Can they trace it to Cory? Is he in danger?"

There was a telling pause. "Badger doesn't think so," Marie said, her tone just a little too tentative.

"She's not sure?"

"She's pretty sure." Marie sounded like she was trying to convince herself as much as me.

So not good.

And it meant Badger was the one I needed to talk to. "Have her call me asap," I said. "And thanks for letting me know."

It was like having teeth pulled to thank her for this news, but Marie was clearly as worried as I was. I wasn't taking my own fears out on her.

I put the coffee on, and tried not to count the seconds as they ticked by. I'd figured out early that in Badger's world, things happened fast. And had to be resolved equally fast.

She could think her way through a problem, and solve it, fingers flying, faster than anyone I'd ever seen. The longer she was trying to fix this, the deeper the shit we were in.

When the phone rang ten minutes later, I pounced on it. "Badger?" I said.

"Sorry," came a voice I belatedly recognized as Adrien's. "Something wrong, Barbara?"

I hadn't even glanced at the call display. I'd never been that careless in the middle of a case. And I couldn't afford to be now.

It wasn't as if Cory was under fire. Not like on the first case I'd worked with Adrien. I immediately tried to banish the thought. I remembered all too clearly how I'd felt in those moments when I thought I'd lost him.

I never wanted to relive that.

"We have a situation, but it's being resolved," I said, forcing myself to stay calm. From my lips to God's ear.

"Well, let me know if I can help with that one," Adrien said. "You called?"

It took a second too long to remember why I'd called him. And what I could—and couldn't—tell him. I had to snap out of this.

"I did," I said. "I had a question come up in the context of one of my current cases. They work with SaltonSecure, and some of the data I've been seeing looks odd. I wondered if you'd ever run into issues with that firm in the context of your investigations."

There was a little silence on his end. "Salton?" he repeated.

"Yes," I said, without elaborating.

A pause. Choosing his words? He knew something.

"Of course I'm familiar with them," he said. "Given our respective lines of work. I can't say I've interacted with them much lately."

His choice of words was telling. He hadn't answered my questions, or denied that there were issues with the firm. Or actually said he hadn't had recent dealings with them. In fact he'd used the phrase 'I can't say' instead.

From most people, that would be a colloquialism that you didn't even notice. From Keller—after that hesitation? No. He was sending a message.

Whatever he knew, he couldn't tell me about it.

"I wonder if I^2 has dealt with them lately?" I said.

"It would be interesting to know," he said. "You should give Jessup a call."

Another coded answer.

"I think I'll do that. Thanks, Adrien."

"Don't mention it. Stay safe, Barbara."

I hoped that last line wasn't a warning. But I had a nasty feeling it might be.

Whatever this case was, it was growing bigger. And turning nastier by the minute.

Now I was really worried about whatever Cory had triggered. How had that even happened? I needed some answers. Now.

I put in a call to Jessup at I^2. And got voicemail. I left her a carefully coded message of my own. One designed to get her attention.

It was time to get to the bottom of this mess.

CHAPTER TWENTY-ONE

Half an hour later, Jessup called me back. In the meantime I'd tried meditating again and given up. I couldn't fool even myself this time.

I still hadn't heard from Badger. Or Marie. Or Cory, who was presumably asleep by now.

I hoped he was, anyway. And not digging himself in deeper.

I'd downed two cups of coffee, which hadn't helped. Now I was pacing the room. And I was staring at the mini-bar.

Which wouldn't have helped anything.

My phone buzzed, and I grabbed it. Jessup.

"What can I do for you, O'Grady?" she asked.

"What do you know about about SaltonSecure International? And any issues or rumors that relate to them?" I asked point-blank.

It didn't seem to faze her. And she wasn't nearly as cryptic as Keller had been. Though she didn't actually answer my question either.

"I see why Keller likes you," she said. "You no sooner start on a case, than you identify our 'friends'"—And I could hear the quotes in her emphasis on the word—"by name."

Apparently on this case SaltonSecure International had become 'They-Who-Must-Not-Be-Named'. And wasn't that interesting?

"I take it they do have issues," I said dryly. "And that these are issues you're concerned about?"

"You take it right," she said. I could hear the grin in her voice. "Though I think calling them issues when talking about our 'friends' might be an understatement. If we're right about what they're up to."

"Which is?" I asked.

"Why don't I buy you a drink, and we can talk about it."

"You're in Geneva?" I hadn't expected that.

"Of course," she said.

There was no of course about it. Unless she'd followed Annegret from Vancouver back to Geneva? The thought worried me.

"I'll need a couple of hours, first," I told her. I'd have heard back from Badger by then. I hoped.

"Then we'll make it dinner," Jessup was saying. "I know a place you'll love."

And if I hadn't heard from Badger? I'd be on the next flight home. Meeting or no meeting.

"Fine," I said. Plan for the best, right? "When and where?"

She named a time and the restaurant, gave me directions. It was walking distance from L'Étoile, so I'd get to do a little exploring, after all. "I know you'll love it," she said. "And with luck, Adrien can join us there."

Of course, Adrien was here too.

Did that mean Annegret was in even bigger trouble than I'd believed? Probably.

It only needed that.

———

AS SOON AS JESSUP DISCONNECTED, my phone rang. No caller display. I grabbed it.

It was Badger. Finally.

"So?" I demanded.

"It's fine," Badger said calmly.

"Really fine?" I asked.

"Yes."

"Cory's safe?"

"He was always safe," she said. "It was a minor dustup, that's all."

Maybe in her world. But not in Marie's, judging by her barely restrained panic. Not in mine, either.

And whatever she said now, Badger had been concerned enough to call Marie in early.

"I need details," I said. "And your word that whatever this is hasn't compromised this case."

"You have it," Badger said. "But I can't give you details now."

At that moment, it was the worst thing she could have said to me. "Oh?" I said.

I don't know what she heard in my voice, but Badger actually explained herself.

"Thanks to what Cory was working on, I found a vulnerability," she said. "Something that could give us some real answers. If I don't follow it now, somebody's going to spot it, and that chance will be gone. As soon as I'm done, you'll get details. All of them. You have my word."

"Thanks," I told her. "And be careful where you step. From what I've gathered so far, I^2 and Interpol are both having a look at the same company you are. I'm meeting with them later, so I may have more information then."

Despite what I knew was a secure line, I was now reluctant to mention SaltonSecure over the phone. And what did that tell me?

If Badger noticed—and she probably had—she didn't mention it. "Good to know," was all she said.

"Good luck," I told her. "Yeah. I may need it."

So I wasn't the only one worried about exactly what this case was getting us into. Which didn't make me feel any better.

———

I CHECKED MY WATCH. I had an hour and a half before I met Jessup and Keller for dinner. I needed to bring the big guns to that meeting.

And right now, I had nothing. Especially since I didn't dare drop even a hint of what my client had been up to with her 'restorer'—a forger, by any other name. Though according to Annegret, the intent to commit fraud hadn't been there. For either of them.

That and a wizard of a lawyer might keep one or both of them out of jail. Or it might not.

With so many problems in this case, I needed to be extra sharp in dealing with Jessup. Which wasn't going to be easy, because at the moment my mind felt like overcooked spaghetti and my nerves the way overstretched bubblegum looks.

My biggest concern right now was my client's revelations about her ongoing fraud—which, technically, probably wasn't fraud at all, but which set her up for every allegation and rumor going. On top of the recent panic over Cory and what he'd got himself into. All of it compounded by my increasing uneasiness about what role SaltonSecure might be playing here.

Meditation wasn't going to help. I couldn't slow down my thoughts enough for that, and my brain was starting to run in circles. A hot shower might help, but not enough. I glanced at the mini bar, and forced myself to look away. I could have wine with dinner.

There was only one solution. I needed a run. I glanced at my watch again. If I timed it right, and managed not to get lost. I put in a call to the concierge, who proved very helpful, changed into my running gear and headed out.

———

AS MY FEET pounded the paths that unfurled along the picturesque promenade running along the shore of Lake Geneva, my mind gradually began to clear. It wasn't raining, but the wind was up and it was overcast and threatening, so I had the path largely to myself.

I drew in great lungfuls of crisp air and sped up, feeling the muscles in my thighs start to burn. It felt wonderful. Even if there was no familiar hint of salt from sea air, the lake water and the wind off the distant mountains gave the air an unexpected sweetness. Which went with the sharp cold of it, cutting down the back of my neck and finding every vulnerability. It felt just like home.

Along my route, trees were blazing red and orange against a thundercloud-dark sky. A few had lost their leaves, standing stripped and bleak against the darkened water, but it was a beautiful place to run. One day I'd come back and see it in the spring. For now, it gave me the room I'd needed to stretch out and really run.

Into my second kilometer, a few random thoughts began to slip back in. By the third, I was ready to think about SaltonSecure, and what their place in all of this might be.

At first, when we were just dealing with incomplete reports, I'd thought their involvement no more than an employee on the take, one who might be in the payment of whoever it was we were really after. The doctored videos had me rethinking that. Those were more sophisticated, and while one person could do it, it wasn't the lower level employee that the missing reports had suggested. I was guessing at least two of their employees had to be involved, and maybe more.

But this latest episode with Cory and his algorithms? Sure, it was a stupid move on his part to take what had clearly been a risk, but knowing him, I doubted even a mid-level tech would have spotted that anything was going on. Let alone give Badger the kind of trouble she must have had fixing it, given how long it had taken her to call me back.

This had to be someone more senior. Which had all kinds of implications for this case.

It was just a feeling at this point, based more on Marie's panic and Badger's cryptic comments than anything. Except then there was Jessup's comment. And her immediate agreement to meet. Even Adrien's silence. There was something there, something big.

I needed to know more about SaltonSecure. And to take a hard look at the relationship between them and the gallery.

If anyone was likely to uncover Annegret's habit of copying her major works—and take advantage of it—the employees of her security company might be very well placed to do so. If that was happening, it was going to be extremely difficult to address without exposing my client's questionable dealings in the process. Depending on how careful Annegret had been regarding what her security cameras might be recording, and when.

As I made it to the kilometer six marker and began the run back along the shore, I realized what had been bugging me. That little, niggling question sitting in the back of my head all day unheard—until the kilometers underfoot had finally cleared out the mental noise. If someone senior at a firm like SaltonSecure International was involved, just how far did this thing go? And where?

I told myself I was making huge leaps on very little evidence. But that small voice was not going to be ignored again.

I slowed down as I ran across the footbridge back to the south shore, and then slowed again to a fast walk to cool down on the way back to the hotel and a shower. Then I headed for my dinner with Interpol and I^2.

I was ready for them now.

CHAPTER TWENTY-TWO

I spotted Birgitte Jessup from the doorway of the very upscale restaurant she had directed me to, though she looked very different from the forthright woman that I'd met in Vancouver. From the elegant upsweep of her hair to the expertly applied makeup to the flattering drape of her very well cut burgundy dress, she fit in here. She was seated at a table along the far wall, in an alcove that gave her an excellent view of the entrance and exits while protecting her back and one side.

I held back a smile. Despite the dramatic change in her style, there was no question this woman was in security. No-one could sneak up on her from any direction, and it was the perfect location to take note of what was happening at most of the intimate tables in the restaurant.

The restaurant itself was fairly large, but designed to provide a feeling of intimacy for the diners. Low, intimate lighting only enhanced the feeling, while pristine white linens and gleaming cutlery provided a sense of luxury.

The walls were covered with a textured fabric wallpaper in shades of taupe and rich cream, which I suspected absorbed sound rather well, given the muffled sound of the voices rising and falling in conversation around the room. Which provided a level of privacy that was probably one of the reasons we were meeting here.

Most of the tables were small, intended for two to four diners. I wondered for a moment if they had private rooms available for larger parties, or if they had a very select clientele. I'd be interested to know, though it wasn't exactly relevant.

I gave Jessup a slight nod, and told the hostess who'd come to greet me that I was joining her party. She led the way to the table across highly polished sprung bamboo floors. More luxury.

And more sound absorption, too.

Until I was a few feet away, I couldn't tell whether Adrien Keller was there or not. He was screened from my view by the angle of the alcove. Which meant that while his back was protected, he had to rely on Jessup to tell him if someone was coming up behind him.

I assumed Jessup had arrived first, and chosen both the table and the power position at that table. Which could be a power play on her part. Or maybe she and Keller had worked closely enough in the past that he trusted her to watch his back. And vice versa.

This meal was going to prove interesting, on a number of levels.

Jessup smiled a welcome, and Keller rose at once, and remained standing until I was seated and provided with a large, leather-bound menu and my water glass filled. I appreciated the old-fash-ioned courtesy—and it somehow fit the ambience, which was old world, though the decor was streamlined and modern.

Whoever had decorated the place was a genius with fabrics and lighting.

Once we were all sitting down, and Keller had poured me a glass of the red Burgundy they were drinking, Jessup looked at Keller, who was seated on her right. I was on her left, directly across from Keller. Who winked at me as she asked him if he wanted to start.

"Why don't you begin," he suggested to her. "Since you're the one who brought this to me in the first place."

She nodded, took a thoughtful sip of her wine, then angled her body slightly so she fully faced me.

"It started with a case I was working on last year," she said. "The details are confidential, but in the course of that investigation, I ran across a whisper of a hint about something illegal 'our friends' might be involved in."

I glanced at Keller and he gave me a slight nod. So we were talking about SaltonSecure. And they weren't about to mention names, even in this relatively private spot. Confirming my own fears about this case.

"And did this illegal something also involve my client?" I asked.

She smiled. "Not then."

"But…?"

She glanced at Keller, who nodded.

"I—hmmm—sounded out, shall we say?—Keller here about this not-even rumor I'd heard," Jessup said. "To see if he'd run across anything similar. Our investigations often have overlapping edges, and we've found in the past that there are benefits in sharing information. Always maintaining client confidentiality, of course."

I nodded. Always that.

Of course, the last time I'd worked with Adrien, we'd been after the same bad guys. This time, one of the bad guys might be my client. Which added a few complexities to my own position. And to my, shall we say, ability to share data with these two. Oh yes, let's say it.

I had to hide a grin at the thought.

I trusted Adrien way more than I trusted Jessup at this point. I was impressed by her, I thought she'd make a great ally, and that we could work well together. As long as our interests aligned. Which I wasn't sure they did.

Especially since I didn't know how deeply my client and her gallery were caught up in this. Whatever it was.

Especially after Annegret's latest revelation.

"And?" I prompted Jessup.

"And he had," she said. "Keller's 'not-rumor' was dissimilar enough to my 'not-rumor' that I doubt we'd have made the connection at all under normal circumstances."

"Except that we'd worked together in the past on even less substantial information," he said. "And in this case, there was one point of overlap."

I bit out a curse. "Not the gallery?"

I didn't name it. I didn't have to. I had never actually confirmed who I was working for. Not to either of them. But it had been clear all along that they knew exactly who my client was.

"Sadly, yes," he said.

Jessup wagged a burgundy-nailed finger at him. The color distracted me for a second.

That was new. And her finger-nails were noticeably longer, too. She'd had them done. What was up with that?

I couldn't help wondering if the perfect manicure was intended to match her undoubtedly expensive silk dress? Or the wine. Maybe that was the point? She looked stunning. And if the low-cut dress wasn't enough to distract whoever she was talking to, then the matching manicure would do it.

My approach was more practical. Given the weather, I'd chosen straight black pants tucked into low boots, dressing it up with a topaz blouse and a black Chanel-style jacket. But I admired her style. And her moxie.

"Not nice," she said. "The only real overlap between the two not-rumors is they shared 'a business interest.'" And she made air quotes that again showed off those glossy nails.

Which had to be a deliberate strategy. I could see where that momentary distraction could be useful in our business. I wasn't about to start matching my nails to my outfits, though.

"Let me guess," I said, keeping my focus on the real threat. "It gets worse."

"Perhaps," she said, throwing an admonitory look at Keller.

I wasn't sure what game the two of them were playing. It didn't seem sexual. And I was pretty sure Adrien had a husband, in any case. It felt more like an edgy rivalry, mixed in with a certain amount of trust. And I wasn't sure what the prize was.

I didn't care, either. As long as it didn't impact my client or her business.

But I wasn't yet sure that it didn't.

"I have been looking hard at recent cases of forged paintings," Adrien said. "Especially the work of the big names. And there have been too many of them. None of which seemed to be related."

He paused, exchanged glances with Jessup, then looked at me. "Until quite recently."

My heart sank. "The gallery?"

"Again, not right away," he said. "But yes. As I began to hear little hints of connections. I started to hear, very faintly, rumors about your client."

"The line I was pursuing was related to the investment value of these works," Jessup clarified for me. "My client has a certain interest in high end forgeries. Paintings in particular."

"And these cases both intersected with our 'friends'?" I asked. Thinking rapidly through everything I'd learned since Annegret Carli had walked into my office last week. "What's the connection?"

"At first we couldn't find one. Nothing seemed related," Keller said. "Then as we dug into the various hints of rumors, focusing on ones that seemed to have the most involvement with our 'friends'…"

"In any way," Jessup added.

Keller nodded. "When we cast a really wide net, we started to see patterns."

"Let me guess," I said. "The pattern is too many forgeries are being uncovered, with no apparent connections to each other. And only vague rumors as to the source of the forgeries. And where you've been able to follow up these rumors—to a gallery or a dealer, let's say—their security system, no matter how sophisticated, shows no issues there. Which means that there is no proof of any illegal dealings. And the company that has provided those security systems—in every case?—is our 'friends'."

Jessup smiled, and this time it met her eyes. "I knew I liked you," she said to me.

"Good call, sending her my way," she told Keller. Who grinned at her and winked at me.

"I know talent when I see it," he said. "And talent squared is what it's going to take to solve this one."

"Cubed," I said, returning the compliment.

Jessup rolled her eyes. "Fine. Can we get on with it now?" she asked, meeting my eyes directly as she said it.

Apparently she was pretty good at reading people, too.

And she was right. From what they'd told me so far, we each had a piece of a complicated puzzle. One that I couldn't solve on my own.

"Let's do it," I said. But I still didn't trust her.

Keller looked back and forth between us. "So where do we take it from here?" he asked. Seemingly addressing the question to both of us.

He was good.

I looked at Jessup. She looked at me. And grinned.

"Since I called this little meeting," she said. "Why don't I take it?"

"Works for me," I said.

———

THE INOPPORTUNE ARRIVAL of our waiter left me hanging, but once we'd ordered—steak and mushrooms with roasted butternut squash, the house specialty, all around—she didn't waste any time.

"We have no proof," she said. "Our 'friends' are far too careful. And far too good at what they do. We either need them to make an error…"

"Which they haven't done so far," Keller added.

She nodded. "Or we need a way in."

Both of them looked at me.

"And you're hoping the gallery will give you that in," I said. "Or rather, that my client will do so. It's why Jessup was in Vancouver. And why you're both here."

Keller smiled. "Your call the other day seemed very timely," he said. "A possible gift neither of us was foolish enough to overlook."

Great. More code. Well, I could play that game too.

"You understand I have to protect my client in all of this," I said.

"Of course," Jessup said, clearly speaking for both of them.

"As long as your client isn't guilty of something," Keller added.

Of course Interpol would care more about legality than I^2 would. I wondered for a moment how I^2's client would stand up under the same scrutiny. And quickly decided it wasn't my problem.

My mind went straight to my own biggest problem—Annegret's recent admission about the copied masterpieces that she routinely hung on her gallery walls. And then kept in a vault in case they were needed again.

I didn't want to know how Interpol might view that—especially with Keller already obsessing on the number of forgeries showing up on the international scene. Some of which might well be traceable back to Annegret Carli Fine Arts. And attributable to Annegret's pet 'copyist'.

Had my client even worked out yet that it was likely those fake paintings had been stolen and sold on by the bad guys as originals? While their replacement fakes hung on the walls of Annegret Carli Fine Arts.

Until a sale was made. And then Annegret's lucky buyer would own an original as she swapped the original painting out of her vault for what she believed to be her own expert's copy. While the crooks resold the gallery display copy, which was also a fake, to their own unlucky—and probably less than honest—clients.

It made my head hurt. And if I'd read her right, my very bright client was currently in denial of the implications of what was going on. Making her a dead weight on my investigation.

And almost incapable of protecting herself. Not good.

"Of course," I said to him, deliberately echoing Jessup's words.

"If a client is guilty of breaking the law, then my responsibility to them is at an end. I make that clear to any potential client."

Once I was sure they were actually breaking the law. Which in Annegret's case, I wasn't. As best I could tell, it was a gray area.

I wasn't sure Keller would see it that way, though.

I needed to have a long talk with a good lawyer. One with expertise in copyright and intellectual property. Good thing I knew one.

I paused, and took a sip of wine. "But what if the client has been taken advantage of? If, perhaps, their premises and even their name have been used in commission of a fraud?"

"Then they would be protected," he said.

That's what I'd needed to hear from him. I turned to Jessup. "And your client? Where do they stand in all of this?"

Because of course I^2 would operate in their client's best interests, just as I would. Especially a client big enough to afford I^2's exorbitant fees. Badger had dug those out for me, and suggested with a sly grin that maybe we weren't charging enough.

Once I got over my shock, I'd thought that she might be right. Though I hadn't shared the thought. Even mentioning an increase to our fees would have Marie ordering new fee schedules the next day. I wasn't ready to go there. Maybe I never would be.

Still, whoever Jessup's client might be, I didn't know what they had at stake in this investigation. That hadn't been clear in her explanation. Probably by design.

I needed to know what her commitments were to them before this conversation went any further.

She didn't waste time in arguing. "My clients—and there are several of them—are victims of this fraud. They need to be made whole," she said.

More than one client, then. No wonder I^2 had put their best investigator on the case. It must be worth a lot of money to them. "I see. And does being made whole include appropriate punishments for the perpetrators?"

She tapped a burgundy fingertip against the stem of her wineglass, then took a sip.

"Of course," she said as she replaced the glass in exactly the same spot. "Though I have a degree of flexibility as to what 'appropriate punishment' might look like. And exactly who is considered a 'perpetrator', and who is not."

She gave me a little smile. It did not look friendly. "That's in my contract," she added, emphasizing the words.

I nodded, unsurprised. In fact, it was what I'd been hoping for. "And if my client is helpful in this investigation? And in recognition Interpol declines to charge my client, or make an example of their business?"

I glanced at Keller as I said it, and he gave me the slight nod I'd expected. Good.

Jessup met my eyes. "Keller and I have worked together many times. I might have more flexibility, shall we say, than he does. But if Interpol declines to press charges, for whatever reason, my clients are certainly not going to do so. You have my word on that."

So far so good. But her answer still left a great gaping hole in my case.

"And your clients' need to be made whole?" I said. "If no charges are brought against my client, then your clients are surely not looking to them for reparation?"

Her face expressionless, she gave me a slight nod, which I had trouble interpreting. Was she agreeing? Or just accepting the question?

"Unless your client is actually guilty of perpetrating the fraud, then no. My clients will not pursue them further," she said deliberately. "But any information you or your client might have or might learn about these frauds against my clients? I would expect that information to be shared."

I had what I needed. I wasn't yet completely sure how Annegret and her copyist might be caught up in the art fraud. But unless she was a far better actor than she had any right to be, I'd say the chances of Annegret being directly involved in the forgery ring were slim to none.

It was probably the best I was going to get, in any case. I'd just have to be better. Piece of cake.

Yeah, right. Good thing I had a team behind me.

"I can work with that," I said, and reached for my wine.

And the real conversation of the night began.

CHAPTER TWENTY-THREE

It was full dark when I left the restaurant, overstuffed with delicious food—and too much information. And the storm had finally broken. I put up the black travel umbrella I always carry at home this time of year. I'd just brought the habit with me to Geneva, and it kept paying off.

As I walked deeper into Old Town, the rain wasn't as heavy, but it was steady, dancing off the cobblestones and falling in a slanting stream under the street lights. The sidewalks were wet, but puddle free, which made walking easier. My flat-heeled black leather boots took care of the splashes.

The air smelled fresh, rain-cleaned. I breathed deeply, enjoying the walk back to L'Étoile, but wishing I had time for another run. It was probably just as well that I didn't. The combination of traffic, rain-wet pavement and a deserted lakefront, especially in a city I didn't know well? Could be deadly for a runner. Early morning might provide a better opportunity. If I was awake.

My jet lag was finally wearing off, and at some point my body would insist on making up the sleep deficit. I just hoped it would hold off long enough for me to get a better handle on this case.

I could always sleep on the flight home. I had too much to do now.

On that thought, I mentally ran through and re-arranged the information I'd been given over dinner. Keller and Jessup had shared more with me than I'd expected. And both had promised to email me the timeline they'd put together, as well as some of the documentation. I suspected I'd be up half the night trying to make sense of it all.

Though the first thing I planned on doing was to send copies to the team. Four minds were always better than one. I glanced at my watch, did the calculations. It was nearly ten-thirty here. So early afternoon in Vancouver. Marie and Badger would be able to get right on it. And Cory too, once school was out.

Whatever this was, it was bigger than I'd expected. The core of it I'd already known—art fraud. Forgery, to be specific. With a lot of dollars attached. But the involvement of SaltonSecure International potentially took this to a whole new level. Just how big was this thing?

I needed more data on SaltonSecure. Who ran it? Who owned it? How far did the corruption spread?

Was someone at SaltonSecure the mastermind behind all of this? Or just a piece in a larger web?

There had been no mention tonight of anyone else. But it just didn't make sense to me that a security firm, of all things, would be the ones to set up an international forgery scheme on this scale. It wasn't just Annegret's gallery. Which I'd already guessed. But the connections between companies and countries world-wide that Keller and Jessup thought could be involved in this?

It was mind-boggling.

I could see that someone from SaltonSecure would be essential in executing the plan, sure. But that would make them the how of it all. Not the why. Before I focused my own investigation on Salton-Secure, I wanted to know the why.

Glancing up, I realized I'd walked further than I'd realized. I was nearly back to the hotel. I turned down a side street.

None of the shops on this block were open, but the brightly lit windows were a visual feast on a night like this. The next block was all boutique shops. In this weather, they receded into anonymous dark blocks broken with the occasional dimly lit window.

It was an eerie feeling, especially after the conversations I'd been having over the last few hours. Suddenly I felt like a target. And an umbrella is no kind of weapon. I quickened my stride.

———

I COULDN'T SHAKE the feeling of being watched, but I didn't see so much as a shadow moving. And I made it back to the hotel just fine.

Shaking off my umbrella in the well-lit lobby—and making sure I was out of the line of sight from the windows—I wondered if I was imagining things. But it had felt all too real. The small muscles in my back were still tense.

And I wasn't about to make any assumptions. Not on this case.

Back in my now-familiar room, I triple locked the heavy door. Then headed straight for the safe to retrieve my laptop. I truly appreciated that L'Étoile had built their in-room safes big enough to hold one. I'd stayed in too many hotels where the safe was too narrow to accommodate a thirteen inch laptop, and my only choice had been to leave it with the desk downstairs.

Hello? In this day and age? That was so not happening.

Of course, that always left the option of carting my laptop everywhere I went. Which was inconvenient at best.

Cory had been trying to talk me into traveling with a smaller touchpad, and the convenience was tempting. But when I travelled, I usually needed to do real work, under a deadline. And the smaller screen just added one more strain, which I could do without.

Why add stress if I didn't have to?

On the other hand, I did keep an eye on the available options. At some point, a more portable technology would end up being irresistible. Even for me.

It isn't that I hate change, no matter what Marie says. In fact, I love new technology. I hate that I temporarily lose efficiency every time I have to adapt to new tech and update my work processes. There's never enough time to do the updates I need to do, never mind making time for the ones I don't have to take on.

As I opened my laptop, I could practically see Cory rolling his eyes the way he does every time I say something like that. What does he know? This stuff is in his wheelhouse.

An email from Badger drove everything else out of my head.

"Urgent. Call now."

Uh oh. Was it Cory again? Or…?

As I waited for the call to connect, I was rapidly running through every worst case scenario I could think of, and how I'd handle them.

Luckily for my sanity, Badger answered on the first ring.

"Barbara. You need to see this," she said before I said a word. "I've just sent a document to your laptop."

"But everyone is fine?" I asked.

"I'd have texted you immediately if they weren't," she said.

She hadn't before. It had been Marie who'd called. I nearly told her that, then stopped myself. It had been Badger who had fixed that issue, I reminded myself.

This was no time to start passing Marie's panic to her. Or my own.

Instead I opened what Cory called 'the vault' on my laptop. I had no idea how it worked, but Badger had installed one on each of our laptops after the last case. They didn't link anywhere, but using the app and a series of personalized passwords Badger had set up, we could send documents to each other's vaults. Apparently it was entirely secure.

And when Badger says something is 'entirely' secure, she means it.

She'd attempted to explain it to me once, using what she laughably considered 'laywoman's terms'. Cory had been hanging on every word, his eyes getting bigger and bigger. I'd had to hold up a hand and ask her to stop after the first two minutes.

"Some things it's better I don't know," I'd told her.

The truth was, I had no hope of even beginning to understand what she'd done without at least a decade of computer studies. Probably not even then. I could handle the basics, and any kind of research. But when it came to algorithms or programming? My brain just wasn't wired that way. It comforted me occasionally to see Badger's eyes get that same glazed look when Marie and I got into one of our occasional esoteric discussions about art.

I'd memorized the protocols as well as the passwords for my vault, because I'd feel like a prime idiot if I'd written any of it down and someone had stolen both the laptop and the protocols. And when I was traveling? No matter how careful I was, stuff happens.

There are people a lot smarter than me committed to stealing the information off my laptop. Especially since we'd begun taking cases with the scope of this one.

I meticulously followed the sequence to open the vault, then opened the document Badger had just sent me. Skimmed the list of names and numbers and dates. And everything I knew about this case re-arranged itself in my head.

And here I thought I'd begun to get a handle on this one. Clearly I'd been wrong. And I didn't like what I was seeing now. Not at all.

Just wait till I got my hands on my client.

I read through the list again. Slowly this time. "Where did you get this?" I asked.

"You don't want to know."

I probably didn't. But I had to ask. "This is the same company?"

"Yeah."

SaltonSecure. I read through the list for the third time, and my skin crawled. And I thought about the feeling I'd had on the way back from the restaurant.

"This may sound odd," I said. "But can you remotely scan my laptop?"

Badger didn't ask. "Hang on," was all she said.

In the silence that followed, I read the list through again. At the same time, I watched for any signs that she'd got in. There was nothing.

What seemed like only seconds later, she was back.

"You're clean," she said.

And I let out a breath I hadn't realized I was holding.

"But there have been a couple of attempts to hack in."

"What?" I asked, feeling far more unnerved than I should have. I'd begun to get some sense of what we were dealing with, after all. Even if it made my skin crawl.

"Don't worry," she said matter-of-factly. "I added a few extra tricks to all our computers when I put the vaults in. They'd have to be way better than these guys to get into any of our stuff."

"What if they had access to the actual laptop?" I asked her.

There was a pause. "Did they?" she asked.

"I don't know," I said, scanning the room. Nothing looked different, or out of place. It didn't feel different. I drew in a deep breath, concentrating. It didn't smell different, either.

But my skin still crawled.

And the people SaltonSecure International hired were at the top of their game. These weren't amateurs. They weren't going to leave any hint of their presence.

I explained about the in-room safe.

"Hang on," she said, and I could hear her fingers flying over the keyboard.

"They may have tried," she said after a moment. "I can't tell for sure, not without seeing the actual laptop. Your hotel is one of their clients, which would make it easier for them to get in. But they didn't get anywhere, if they did."

"Good." I said, ignoring how fast she'd managed to break into my laptop and run what had to be some incredibly sophisticated scans. I wouldn't be using the hotel in-room safe again. And I'd just got over my resistance to change.

"Want me to look into a smaller replacement computer?" she asked.

Sometimes I wonder if Badger actually reads minds. It's a little creepy, but most of the time it's been too useful for me to care. "Please. I'd like to look at a few options when I get back, if possible."

"You won't need to," she said, and I could hear the smirk in her voice. "I know just the thing."

She would too.

"You'll like it," she said. "It's just out, and this baby sings."

And would probably cost an arm and a leg. Never mind. This case was making us a ton of money. Though probably not enough, not if I was being followed and my hotel room broken into. At least they hadn't taken my laptop.

If a case like this one meant my tech needed upgrading, so be it. We'd start charging more. Sometimes a P. I. is only as good as her tools.

And her people.

"Thanks, Badger," I said. "And have a look at the rest of our tech, too. See if anything else needs an upgrade, now that we know what we're up against."

"Done," she said.

And that was going to cost me the other arm and a leg, and probably more. But it was worth it.

I nearly told her that too. But I restrained myself.

"I need a little time to digest all this," I said. "Then I'll have an update. Can you work with Marie to set up something in an hour or so? I'd like to talk to both of you, if you can make it secure enough."

"No problem," she said. "What about Cory?"

"Him too," I said, then glanced at my watch. "Except he'll be in class now. So, no. But does that mean you can link Amber in, too?"

"Sure. For this meeting?"

"That's good to know. Not this time, though," I said.

"We'll take care of it," she said. And disconnected.

I guess there was nothing more to be said. I turned my attention to the document she'd sent me. And to figuring out how it fit with what Jessup and Keller had told me.

I looked at the list again. Or not told me.

And how much trouble we were actually in. This time, I didn't automatically include my client in that 'we'.

CHAPTER TWENTY-FOUR

Just over an hour later, I was ready for the team meeting. The document I'd just put together was ready to go. My laptop was waiting on the desk, with my notes beside it for easy reference. And I'd swapped out the generic desk chair for the more comfortable guest chair I'd dragged over from beside the window.

My focus was going to be on what the team was telling me, both verbally and non-verbally. I wasn't going to be keyboarding. And it had been a long day. I could use a little comfort.

Just then my phone chirped. Incoming. I glanced at the text message. Nick.

I'd been hoping he'd call all day, though I knew he'd probably have to wait until the end of his day. I skimmed the words, then read them again more slowly.

"Hoped to call, but am being sent out. Don't worry. I'll be in touch when I can," he'd written.

The terse words, with no personal touch or even a hint of humor, told me more than he'd probably intended. 'Sent out' probably meant undercover. A difficult assignment just got dangerous.

And telling me not to worry? Wasn't like him. Making the danger even clearer. Also guaranteeing I'd worry.

And there wasn't a thing I could do about it. Not even contact him—another thing those few terse words made clear.

This sucked.

And I really wished I hadn't let that tension over moving in together get between us. At least we'd spent the night before he left together. Well, at least until Annegret's 2 a.m. call.

I drew in a deep breath, gritted my teeth.

I couldn't do anything about Nick or his case. At least I could do something about mine. Grabbing a cup of coffee from the fresh pot I'd put on, I drew in another deep breath. And sent Marie a request to set up the team meeting.

"Badger will send link. Accept it," she texted back.

What else was I going to do with it?

Seconds later an email came through from Badger with the link. I clicked. A program I'd never seen before loaded on the screen.

Suddenly I was looking at six squares on the screen. The two in the middle were blank. The other four held images, one in each quadrant of the screen. My own, and the three members of the team. Smiling at me.

How had she done that?

"Is this secure?" I asked Badger.

"Entirely," she said.

Of course it was. Why do I even ask?

"And why aren't you at school?" I asked Cory.

"I am," he said.

What? I looked more closely at the background behind him. "You're in… the band room?" I guessed.

He'd recently taken up the trombone. I had no idea why.

"I booked a practice room," he said. "It's soundproof."

But apparently not electronics proof. I glanced at Badger, who gave me a slight nod. His connection to our meeting was secure too. Good to know.

I could see Cory's trombone case beside him. Were those soundproof rooms the reason he'd developed a sudden interest in playing an instrument? I mean, the trombone? Really? Not that I'd ever mention that opinion to him.

"But I only have half an hour," he added.

Good. I hate long meetings anyway, and one where I had to stare at my computer screen the whole time? No. Just no.

On the other hand… I stared at the faces looking back at me. This felt a little like magic. And it sure beat trying to discuss a case by phone or exchanging email. Or relaying everything through Marie, as we'd been doing when a case took me out of town.

"Then let's make this brief," I said. "Badger, can you share the list you found? I'd prefer no-one makes copies. At least for now. This case is potential dynamite. Literally. I don't want any of us caught in the blast."

Before I finished speaking, the list appeared in one of the blank squares.

"Click on the image to make it full screen," Badger said. "Hit escape to see the divided screen."

I tried it. It worked like a charm.

"Okay, that's great," I said. "Have a look while I put up another document."

"Click on the empty square, and use the 'View' command to open the document from your computer," Badger said.

I did. That worked too. The woman was a magician.

I could see all three of them, though Cory and Marie were clearly reading the documents on their screens. Badger was looking at me.

I nodded my thanks. She gave me a brief nod back.

Marie looked up, clicked something, and was looking at me too. She smirked.

What was up with that?

Seconds later Cory was looking up too.

I glanced at my watch. We had twenty-four minutes left. And a digital timer immediately appeared in one corner of our shared screen, counting down the seconds. Of course it did.

I didn't bother to hide my grin, and Cory winked back.

"Okay, let's see how much we can uncover in our remaining minutes. This first list seems to be clients of the firm we've been discussing," I said, referring to SaltonSecure.

All three nodded. Good. They'd been sharing information. "Start by focusing on the references to our client. One of those dates is the day Duvant was murdered."

"And the numbers?" Cory asked.

"I'm guessing they're related to the forgery scam that firm seems to be running," I said. Wondering as I did so how on earth Badger had got her hands on this. "In our client's case, paintings."

"Three?" Marie said. "She stole three paintings the night she was killed?"

"Someone stole three paintings," Cory said. "But we have a two a.m. access that showed up under Mme. Duvant's ID that same night. And we have no recordings for that time frame at all. Whoever it was could have taken three works from the cellar. We just don't know."

"He's right," Badger said. "The alley would have been quiet then, since the police weren't called until after six a.m. The thief could easily have slipped back into the gallery and taken whatever Duvant and her 'guest' had been working on."

"Getting stuff ready for later collection?" Marie said, looking intrigued. "If these three were original old masters, they'd have been very careful in how they packaged them. Making triply sure they were protected. The packages would also need to be easily identifiable by the thieves, but completely ordinary looking to anyone else.

"Which could explain why Mme. Duvant was down there so long," I said. "That gives us another piece of the puzzle. It doesn't seem to get us any closer to who killed her. And presumably then stole her keys and passcode and used them to get into the cellar to retrieve the paintings."

Cory flinched, and I felt badly for him. Murder is ugly. And it's different when you know it's real than in movies or even the most violent games.

"The composites I pulled from the other cameras on that alley aren't great," Badger said. "Too much shadow, and both of the unknowns in the alley that night knew where the cameras were and avoided them."

"I'll try to clean that up some," Cory put in. "No promises, though."

Too bad. I'd been hoping for a break on at least one of them. "Which suggests that second figure is probably connected to Duvant's death, if not her killer," I said.

"Too bad we have no way to find him," Cory said.

"Well, I didn't say that," Badger said.

She had everyone's attention.

"How?" Cory demanded before anyone else could say a word.

"Something I stumbled across in the firm's files. While I was working on…"

"Fixing the mess I made," Cory said, shamefaced.

She waved a hand. "It's done."

"So what did you find?" Marie asked.

"I think they have an undoctored backup of the surveillance videos from Carli Fine Arts."

"How would that be different from what my algorithms already found?" Cory asked. He sounded disappointed. Because he'd missed something and she hadn't?

He really did think Badger could do anything. Which could be setting both of them up for difficulties ahead. I'd have to keep an eye on that.

"I only had time for a glimpse," Badger said, ignoring his reaction. "But the gallery's contract calls for different schedules for the different cameras. Even for the different passcodes. But if I'm right, someone at the security firm may secretly have been running all of the cameras twenty-four/seven, and saving all of it exactly as recorded."

"Which would include whoever returned to the gallery after Amara Duvant's murder. And used her passcode?" I asked.

"It should."

"Which is decidedly not in their contract," I said.

Badger grinned. "And you're surprised?"

"At this point? Hardly. In fact, I'm grateful. If you're right, that is. And if we can get our hands on it—safely," I added, with a glance at Cory, who looked embarrassed.

As well he should. I still didn't know exactly what he'd nearly got himself, and us, into. And I'd be getting to the bottom of his little fiasco when I got home.

"I'll start working on it as soon as we're done here," Badger said.

"Can I help?" Cory said. "I can't believe I missed it in the first place."

"Come by after school," Badger said. "It'll go faster if we both work on it. However they rigged the video, they did a good job of hiding this. I didn't spot it until today, either."

He nodded, looking marginally happier.

"While you're looking at that, we may have another problem," I said. "Look at the first dates for the gallery on that list."

"These go back two years," Cory said. "We didn't look far enough back on the surveillance videos."

"The fraud has been going on that long? Without our client noticing?" Marie said.

"Apparently. Which is bad enough," I said. I paused, then hit them with the kicker. "But have a look at the two most recent dates. Those ones worry me more. Amara Duvant is already dead by this time, and Jana Bertrand, who seemed to be her accomplice, has left town."

"There's someone else involved," Marie said. "Inside the gallery, I mean."

"I think so," I said. "And our client doesn't seem be aware of that. Or to have any feel for who might be involved in this thing."

"So who is it?" Cory asked.

"Given the information we have so far? No idea," I said.

Though I had this nagging feeling I was missing something. But it was still too nebulous to bring up.

"We'll run the videos. What else do you need?" Badger asked.

"Deep background on everyone involved with the gallery over the last two years who would also have access to the basement. Start with the video records for these dates, and work out from there. And we need to find Jana Bertrand."

"We're on it," she said, and Cory nodded.

"So what's with the rest of this list?" Marie asked, looking up. She'd been looking from the list to my notes, back and forth. "Some of these organizations have no obvious connection with art. What are they doing on this list? And how do I^2 fit in?"

"I suspect some of these are I^2 clients, the ones Jessup is working for. She let it slip, probably deliberately, that she'd been hired by more than one client for this one. I'm guessing these organizations handle investments, including art, for people and organizations with a great deal of cash flow."

"Legitimate ones?" Badger was quick to ask.

"And that would be the question," I said. "I'm betting at least some of the investors are not completely legitimate."

"But… how would that kind of firm be involved? And what have they hired Jessup to retrieve?" Marie asked.

"Presumably it would be the original works of art that the collector or investor thought they were paying for. Before they ended up with a forgery. Jessup didn't confirm that, but it's the logical deduction."

Marie just stared at me.

"Jessup did tell me that each of her clients on this case seems to have discovered at least one of their own staff is working for the other side," I said.

"Just like with the gallery," Marie said.

"Exactly," I said. "Which makes it easier for the firm…"

"Oh, just say SaltonSecure," Cory said. "Badger's told you this conversation is secure."

WE ALL STARED at Cory for a long moment. He looked embarrassed, but defiant.

Before I could say a word, Badger scowled at him. "You know how fast tech changes. Never assume that your hack can't be hacked by someone better."

"But…" he began.

"And just who is the expert on investigations here?" she continued, ignoring his attempted interruption.

"Aunt B," he said. A little sheepishly.

"Exactly. And if she is being this careful, that should tell you how dangerous this case is. Unless you think you know more about this kind of case than either of us?"

He turned beet red, and shook his head. I felt bad for him. But I felt like cheering for Badger.

The kind of careless arrogance Cory was showing? It's dangerous. Especially in someone with his skills, combined with his lack of life experience. Add in teenage hormones and you had a recipe for disaster.

I might have gone a little easier on him. But he'd needed to hear it. And coming from Badger, the message would stay with him. He idolized her.

She knew it, too. And she was usually subtler in getting her messages across.

Which had me wondering just how close Cory had really been to exposing himself as well as the rest of us to SaltonSecure. Or worse.

And what she'd had to do to avert that.

Maybe there was another reason she'd so quickly offered to help him take another look at the videos.

I looked at my nephew's still immature features on the screen and felt my heart stop. He was beginning to show signs of the man he'd become. If working for me didn't get him killed first.

Was it too late to fire him? Probably.

It might make my sister happy, but Cory would hate it. And most likely head straight back down that path that led to jail time.

He needed to learn his limits. Now.

"Aunt B., I'm sorry," Cory said, to his credit.

"Don't do it again," I said with my fiercest look.

What I wanted to do was hug him. But even if I weren't so far away, I couldn't afford to undermine Badger's words. Or Cory's dignity, frayed though it might be.

"I won't."

No, he'd think of something else the next time. But he was a good kid. And smart enough to only make a mistake once.

If we were going to play in these leagues, though, I'd have to talk to Badger about how we were going to keep Cory safer. So he had a chance to grow up.

Keep him off the risky projects, maybe? He'd hate that, too. But if it was that or be fired?

He'd probably never forgive me.

How was I supposed to know how a sixteen-year-old would-be hacker thought? Maybe Badger would have a better idea.

"So Jessup said each of her clients suspected an insider?" Marie asked me. Getting us back on track. And this time, her timing was dead on. Which I appreciated.

"She did," I said.

"What else did she tell you?" Marie asked.

"Not much. And she was deliberately vague about what kind of clients she was representing. Without Badger's list, her explanations sounded plausible enough. She's a smooth one. But she's clearly holding back everything she can."

For a moment I wondered what she'd told Keller. There seemed to be trust between them. There must be some way I could pry the information out of him.

In the two minutes we had left in our meeting, I gave my team their assignments, with the usual caveats. E-mails only, unless it's urgent, then text or call me immediately. Trust your gut if something feels off. If it's security related, run it by Badger.

"Go. Stay safe. And let's take these guys down. Whoever they are," I finished. I could see Badger's hand move, and suddenly I was looking at a blank screen.

Really?

Shaking my head, I turned back to my own list. Badger wasn't subtle, but she was right. We all had a lot to do.

I needed to talk to Annegret again, and soon. Without either of her lawyers present. After I got my head around her business practices. And how I felt about them.

Then I needed to talk to XTC Tech. And set the team going on what we could learn from those paintings that had failed XTC Tech evaluations.

Even with Duvant murdered and Bertrand fled, there was still a traitor at Carli Fine Arts. And the list of possible suspects was dwindling fast. One thing was now clear. Whatever had gone wrong at Carli Fine Arts that resulted in Annegret hiring me, it had been going on for much longer than the six months she was admitting to.

Did she really not know? Or was she trying to hide the knowledge from me?

And just like that, we were back to the question of exactly why she'd hired me. It still made no sense, based on the facts I now had.

And until it did, I was sticking to my decision not to burden the team with Annegret's confession of 'copying'. Not yet, at least.

Meanwhile, I had a lot of digging to do. It was going to be a long night.

CHAPTER TWENTY-FIVE

The following morning, I woke early, feeling disoriented. I let my eyes sweep the darkened room. Which didn't tell me much, since I'd drawn the curtains the night before, and they had a blackout backing. Only the slivers of bright light creeping under the bottom edge told me it really was morning.

I'd slept really well, and for the first time, it felt like I'd woken in the morning, instead of the middle of the night. I'd acclimatized. Go me.

I was going to need all the help I could get on this case, so it was good to know my body was cooperating. Finally.

As the memories of yesterday re-surfaced, I tensed. And reached for the touch-sensor on the bedside lamp, squinting my eyes against the sudden brightness. At the same time as checking every inch of the room for signs of... I wasn't quite sure what. Anything out of place.

I glanced at the door. Still triple locked. And I'd insisted on a room without a door—locked or not—opening into the adjacent suite. I don't know whose brilliant idea that design was, though it probably made economic sense for the hotels. But it was a security hole you could drive a truck through.

And I couldn't shake the feeling I was being followed. And that moment when I'd realized someone had probably been in my room last night. And not just to turn down the covers and put a chocolate on the pillow.

I glanced at the door again. Even a master key wasn't getting through a couple of those deadbolts.

"Get over it, Barbara," I told myself. I sat up and swung my legs to the floor. Good thing I was up early—I needed a run in the worst way.

Putting the coffee on, I skimmed through my emails. Stopping on the one from Badger. She and Cory had gone through all the video they had for each of the dozens of dates shown on the SaltonSecure list. She'd sent me an updated version, one where she'd added a couple of columns on the far right.

I glanced through them. Good thing I had coffee. All I saw was a forest of question marks. How long had they spent on this?

I checked my watch, decided it was worth a try, and sent Badger a text. Five minutes later I was on the phone with her.

"Don't you ever sleep?" I asked.

"Same goes. You got my email?"

"I did. Please tell me that question marks isn't the best you two could come up with."

She actually laughed. "I told Cory you wouldn't appreciate it," she said. "But he was adamant that it was funny, and that right now you needed a good laugh."

He was right about the last bit, anyway. "I don't think teenage humor translates," I said in my driest tone.

"You mean the kid was funnier when he was younger?" she asked.

Okay, maybe not. "His mother thought so."

"Well, luckily he's got real skills with computers. He'd never make it as a stand-up comedian," she said.

"Tell me that's not a career ambition."

"I'm afraid so."

I couldn't picture it. Though Susanna had made a couple of

remarks I'd ignored, so maybe. "Just teach him well," I said. "About the video?"

"The most challenging part is that there's no video coverage of the basement," she said. "Which seems to have been their center of operations for the gallery."

"You must have found something," I said.

"Oh, we did. I was right about that firm"—she meant SaltonSecure—"keeping a full backup of their original surveillance videos. Luckily for us, stupidity on their part. It was only by comparing the uncut footage to the doctored version they sent our client that we found it."

Badger usually didn't draw things out. That was Cory's trick. She wasn't supposed to be learning his bad habits.

"Found what?"

"In addition to the missing microseconds we found before, some of the camera angles change," she said.

"They what? How is that possible?"

"It's a more sophisticated setup than it seems. On the dates in question, the angles of the cameras showing the door to the basement as well as the ones showing the hallway and the back door into the alley are set slightly higher. You can't actually see if they have anything in their hands."

"And on the other days?"

"You can see what they're carrying. We didn't see it before because it's such a slight discrepancy. You only notice it when you can compare against the uncut footage."

I glanced at the list. "That must have taken some digging. None of the dates on the list are back to back."

"Exactly," she said. "Cory did a great job of rejigging his algorithm on the fly."

"Wait. On the day Duvant was killed, she was carrying her purse," I said. "I remember distinctly."

"She was. And she was holding it at an angle that the camera could see clearly. But her other arm—she was holding that just a touch too low for the camera to catch if she was carrying anything."

"Are you saying that anyone who was involved in this trained themselves how to carry stuff they were taking out of the gallery, so that it was invisible to the camera when they doctored the film?"

"That's what it looks like."

"Wow." I thought about that for a moment. "And you found the same thing on each of those dates on the list?"

"Yup."

"And all the camera angles are normal on the dates on either side of those listed days."

"They are."

"That leaves us with no way of knowing exactly what was taken. Or when. Or by whom."

I slugged back some coffee, thought about that. "I take it there's nothing more you can do with the digital footage?"

"We can't manipulate what was never filmed."

"Which leaves us still with no idea what was actually taken," I said. "Presumably on that first date you looked at, it was three paintings, either original old masters, or fraudulent copies. But."

"But. Exactly," she agreed. "I'll send you what we did find."

"I wonder if they've used similar techniques for all of the listings on that list," I said, as my inbox chimed.

"Probably. Though they'll have adapted their approach to each individual client. That is their business, after all."

"What, ripping off the clients?" I asked bitterly.

"Seems like it," she said.

Badger really was even more cynical that I am. She didn't even bother getting angry about any of it. She just expected it.

It struck me as a very bleak way to live. No matter how cynical I might think I am.

"What about our third conspirator?"

"We were able to clarify that everyone who worked at the gallery had access to the basement," Badger added. "Which widens our suspect pool quite a bit. Cory's been digging into the background of all of them, going back two years."

"But?" I said.

"So far, there's no clear suspect. And none of the other staff are present at odd times, or taking meetings with either Amara Duvant or Jana Bertrand."

"Even on the master recordings?"

"Not even there."

"How is that even possible?"

"At a guess? They either knew exactly how the cameras were set up and how to avoid them. Or they were never at the gallery."

Neither of which made any sense. We were definitely missing something. The more we uncovered, the less it seemed to help. And what did that mean?

"How is Marie making out?" I asked.

"Still muttering away in her corner."

Surely she wasn't still working on the SaltonSecure client list. That didn't sound good. "She's having trouble finding information on our friends' other clients?"

"Nope. She's finding too much information. But she said to tell you she'll have something headed your way soon."

I glanced at my watch, calculated the time difference. Winced. It was nearly midnight there. Badger was a night owl and kept her own schedule anyway. And if Marie wasn't complaining yet…

I needed that data.

"Thank her for me. And tell her what I need to start with is a high level overview. Who they are, what they do. Anything that might point to what role our friends—and their clients—play in this thing."

"I thought you said the clients were an intermediary? Like a bank, only with tangible investments, instead of money or stock."

"That's Birgitte Jessup's explanation. We can't afford to assume that what she shared with me was either accurate or complete."

"Assumptions take cheap shortcuts," she said.

"Exactly," I said. "I'm not making any assumptions on how big this thing is. Which reminds me. If Marie can get anything more on our friend's corporate structure…"

"I'll take that one on," Badger said. "I presume you're interested in their connections, as well as any vulnerabilities?"

"Yes, particularly anything that connects back to art fraud or forgery."

"We'll get back to you," Badger said. And hung up on me.

Right. Time for a run.

———

AFTER A HARD RUN along the lakefront in the misty quiet of early morning and a long, very hot shower, I felt ready to face the day. And whatever this case threw at me. Belting on one of the hotel's luxuriously thick white toweling robes, I set more coffee brewing. Then my phone began to ring, the sound loud in the muffled silence of a high-end hotel room. Now what?

Wrapping my dripping hair in an equally luxurious towel, I strode back into the room and glanced at the display. No number.

Probably Badger.

For some reason I didn't want to use her name, even on a secure line. This case was inspiring an excess of caution. "O'Grady," I said.

"BladeSecure is linked to our friends. I thought you should know," Badger said.

What?

Andrea's new—well, newish—flame, Greg Younger, was running the local chapter of BladeSecure. I wondered how Badger had known. Andrea's name must have come up in one of her searches, and she'd know we were friends.

Still, it was probably nothing. Just a coincidence.

We knew that SaltonSecure International was involved in this forgery ring, or whatever it was. And at what seemed so far to be a fairly senior level, and affecting some pretty large customers, reading between the lines of what Jessup had told me. But the odds that forgery ring stretched to Vancouver? Marginal, at best.

Then I thought about the forgery ring I'd uncovered in Vancouver on a previous case. Okay, maybe the odds were slim.

The odds that Andrea's new relationship had anything to do with the case I was caught up in—those were marginal. Andrea had been seeing this guy for six months or so, and I'd only taken on the case a week and a half ago. Six months ago, no-one would have ever expected Annegret Carli to hire me and my small firm.

To see a connection at this point was just paranoid. Or maybe the sign of an inflated ego. Trust me, I know I'm not that important.

But I really don't like coincidences.

"Linked how?" I asked Badger.

"Not clear yet. On the surface, it looks like a loose affiliation, at most."

"But?"

"I'm digging through a maze of financial connections to numbered companies that all link back to our friends," she said. "BladeSecure is somewhere in that maze. But if I had to guess?"

"You do," I told her.

"Then I'd say they're a subsidiary."

"One they've gone a long way to disguise."

"Oh yeah."

"Makes you wonder what they're hiding," I said.

"Makes me want to swat them. Hard."

Okay then. "Keep digging. As far and as deep as you can. And have a look at Younger too, will you. I have a meeting with Annegret in a few hours, but I'll call a meeting and brief everyone tomorrow morning, your time. And Badger?"

"Yeah?"

"Thanks for letting me know."

"Sure," she said, and was gone.

I stared into space while I thought through the implications. They weren't good. If BladeSecure was part of whatever this was— and that was a big if—then surely Younger must be involved. But I still had too many unknowns to even begin to guess if that was true.

So did I call Andrea, or not? If I told her I suspected her new beau was a crook, and probably just using her? And it turned out to be nothing? She'd be royally pissed at me.

I could live with that. But just the suspicion that he was up to something could damage her first real relationship in a long time. Andrea was too wary as it was. She might never get over it.

And I'd carry the guilt of that.

If he was one of the bad guys, though, and I *didn't* tell her? And then something happened to her…

It didn't bear thinking about.

But all I had was a corporate connection, which probably meant nothing. And Badger's suspicions. Yes, she had good instincts. Yes, my gut said there was something there. But this case was playing havoc with my intuition.

Despite what Jessup had finally told me, it felt like I was still only seeing half the picture. And that I was mis-reading what I did know because of it.

I couldn't tell Andrea. Not yet. But uncovering the exact relationship between BladeSecure and SaltonSecure—and the role Younger played in that—had just moved to the top of my list.

CHAPTER TWENTY-SIX

Annegret and I met in her office at eleven. I ignored the by-now familiar surroundings, and focused on my client. Her suit was a flattering cherry color, very stylish, and tailored to fit her perfectly. Her hair had been recently trimmed, and the asymmetrical sides swung gently to frame her high cheekbones. Her makeup was subtle and flawless, her lips a bright cherry red that exactly matched her nails.

But despite the bright color, the perfect makeup, she was noticeably drawn, with lines around her mouth that hadn't been there yesterday. She looked as if her jet lag had grown worse, instead of better. Or as if this case—which was her life—was slowly dragging her under.

My mind supplied the image I'd seen on some nature show somewhere of a crocodile grabbing it's victim with sharp, serrated teeth, rolling them over, then slowly dragging them down into the deep water where they drowned. I swallowed hard. Pushed the image away. And reminded myself that I still wasn't sure who the victim was, here.

So far, the only murder victim seemed to be implicated in the scheme itself.

Annegret? Her I still wasn't sure of.

According to the document Badger had dug out, this sophisticated fraud had been going on at her gallery for at least two years. And was still going on. Could she really not have known?

I couldn't afford to be compassionate. Not yet.

No matter how bad she looked.

That wasn't what she'd hired me for.

Which meant this wasn't going to be—couldn't be—easy for either of us.

I leaned forward. Put both hands flat on the desk between us. The desk, a sudden instinct told me, she was hiding behind.

"This stops now," I told her. "If I'm to do the job you hired me to do, you need to be honest with me."

"But…" she began.

I held up an impatient hand. "Stop. I have a few more details now than I had the last time we met. And you don't get to lie any more."

Her eyes narrowed. "I…"

"Not if you want your gallery to survive. Or your reputation, either," I said bluntly.

For a moment her mask slipped and I saw the terror under it. I forced back the compassion I felt. That wouldn't help either of us.

"I'm here to help," I told her.

Which was true. As long as she wasn't trying to use me to cover up her own misdeeds.

She didn't respond.

I'm not sure I'd expected a response. Though I waited a few moments, just in case.

The sooner she started talking, the easier this would be. On both of us.

She just stared at me. Shock? Anger? Confusion? I had no idea. I couldn't read her at all.

No matter. We were going to have this discussion, one way or another.

I opened my capacious black bag, drew out a printout showing only the segment of Badger's list that applied to the Annegret Carli Fine Arts Gallery. Put one copy in front of her, and the other in front of me.

"What's this?" she asked. Still no expression on her face, and none in her voice, either.

"Highly confidential information on the criminal activity being run through this gallery," I said.

"How did you get this?"

"That's confidential. Read it," I said.

"With an anonymous source, how do I even know this is genuine?" she asked.

"It's real. My team verified it," I told her.

I watched her read through the list, her eyes stopping at the same dates that I'd focused on. Still no expression.

What was she thinking?

She read through it again. Finally looked up.

"This dates back more than two years," she said.

"Yes. It does," I said.

"I don't understand."

"Don't you?"

She looked down, as if compelled, and I watched her eyes move from line to line. Her lips tightened with each line she read, until her mouth was nothing but a thin cherry-colored line.

"I don't want to understand. Or believe it," she finally said. Expelling the words as if trying to get them out and away from her.

I didn't say a word.

She looked at the list again.

"This means they've been using this gallery as part of their forgery ring for that long," she said. Then one cherry red nail traced the last date on the list. "And it hasn't stopped. Even after I hired you. And Amara's death. And the police investigations."

Her voice cracked. So did her face.

I was, finally, seeing the real Annegret. The one who'd fled to Vancouver in search of my firm.

Not, as I'd feared, to find someone unaware of the local situation and gullible enough that she could trick and use them—me—to cover up her own misdeeds. But in hope of finding someone far enough away to be free of the contamination that was eating her gallery alive.

"Which we needed to know. If we're going to put an end to this," I said. "And we are. Between us we're going to put an end to this situation. With a little help from our various friends,"

She didn't look like she believed me. "Where did this even come from?" she asked, a sharp note in her voice.

At this point, I'd have been amazed if she believed anyone.

"SaltonSecure," I said.

She leaned back in her chair as if absorbing a blow. "My security firm?"

"Yes."

"They're the ones behind all of this? Behind Amara's death? And whatever she'd become involved in?"

"They're part of it, yes. Or at least someone with that firm is," I said, not yet ready to commit to exactly how widespread their involvement might be. And curious to get her reaction.

"And you're sure they're involved? It would be far too easy for whoever is behind all this to scapegoat a security firm," she said. Still not wanting to believe.

"We've verified the information trail. This is genuine," I said.

"Oh." She looked lost again. With her smart suit and sophisticated haircut, she looked for a moment like a small girl caught playing dress-up in someone else's clothes.

"But you're going to need to work with me," I said to snap her out of that mindset. I needed the confident, capable gallery owner if I was going to get Annegret and her gallery out of this disaster of a case. "No excuses. And no assumptions, either."

She gave a slight nod. "What can I do?"

"Two things. To start with, anyway." I told her. "Beginning with the forgeries themselves. Based on what you told me yesterday about the display copies your 'restorer' created, it seems unlikely anything you sold was a forgery. Unless it was forged before the gallery bought it."

She bristled. "I know my business. We're very careful…"

I held up my hand to stop her in mid-flight. "No assumptions, remember."

She glared at me, but nodded.

"We'll need to test one of the old masters the gallery sold in the last two years, as a way of proving our theory," I said. "I need you to speculate. If you assume that statistically, one of those sales is likely to be a forgery…"

"But…"

I talked right over top of her. "Which one springs to mind?"

"I…"

"You know one of them did," I said. It was the nature of the art world, when dealing with works that had been around for a long time. Some of them were going to have shaky histories. "Or maybe more than one."

It took an effort of will to avoid shaking my head over the irony of that statement, but I managed.

"I…" She stopped, swallowed hard. "Yes. You're right. I thought of two works immediately. I'll make arrangements to get them tested immediately."

"What will you tell the current owners?"

"I'll think of something," she said. "If it triggers rumors, it can't be worse than what's out there now."

I nodded. She was right. And at least it seemed she was finally facing reality.

"Send me the details," I said.

She nodded, and made a note. "What's the second thing? You said there were two?" she asked.

"We need to talk about who your third insider could be."

And her cherry lipstick stood out like fresh blood on a face that had instantly lost all its color.

CHAPTER TWENTY-SEVEN

Two hours later I was back in my hotel suite. I'd left Annegret still digging for the information I'd asked for. And we had a meeting set up tomorrow with both her lawyers. I wasn't looking forward to it. Especially if the female half of the team was still in attack mode.

She'd proved to be every bit the bulldog her brother had promised. But turning that aggression against her own client wasn't going to help. Hopefully her brother could get her to see reason.

But not too much. If we were going to save Annegret, it was the bulldog we needed now.

And I needed to be prepared with answers for every objection Elise Marbach raised.

I glanced around me, thought about what I needed to accomplish with the rest of the day. I put the coffee on, and, since I'd forgotten to eat lunch, ordered sandwiches and something with chocolate from room service. This was Switzerland, after all. Chocolate was a must. And L'Étoile's room service had lived up to their reputation for remarkably excellent food. And then some.

I set up my laptop and dragged the straight-backed desk chair back in front of the desk where it belonged—since this was actual work, not a meeting—then emailed Marie for an update. Meanwhile, I poured a cup of coffee, and went back to untangling the snarl that was the current version of my case notes.

———

I'D FINISHED my lunch and was deep in reviewing the footage Badger had sent when Marie finally called me back.

"I think I finally have some background and some answers on the I^2 clients," she said. "Sending it now."

"Great, thanks. And I've got enough for another briefing for all of you. Can you set it up with Badger?"

"Sure," she said, and disconnected. I got up and poured another cup of coffee.

Less than five minutes later, I was staring at the now-familiar segmented screen. Even Cory was there. I recognized the band practice room again.

"You're at school at seven a.m.?" I asked him.

He grinned. "I had an early practice."

Sure he did. "Then I'll keep this brief, for all our sakes."

I filled them in on what Annegret and I had discussed, still avoiding any mention of her copying scheme. "While she and I are digging into those angles, I'd like the three of you to focus on the paintings in our client's current stock that XTC Tech tests uncovered as frauds. We need to know everything about them."

Cory frowned. "Like what?"

"First off, how old is the work supposed to be—when was the original actually painted. And how old does XTC Tech say this copy is?"

"Why does that matter?" he wanted to know.

"That's a good question," I said. "It matters because if the fraud was painted *after* the gallery acquired it, then we assume the fraud happened in the gallery. If it was before, then the gallery bought a forged painting. And if it's the latter, we need to dig into the provenance and everything related to when and how that forgery was created and accredited."

Marie was nodding. Good.

"Marie, I need you to take the lead with this. Presumably that fake had every document in order, or the gallery wouldn't have purchased it. But we can't afford to make any assumptions. Check everything."

"Got it," she said.

"What happens if she finds something that looks wrong?" Cory asked.

"Then we dig. Go even deeper, and check everything. Assume papers can be forged as easily as paintings."

"We know all that, Aunt B.," he said. "We all talked about it, remember?"

I nodded at all of them. "I know you do. But some of these forgeries have been fooling experts for hundreds of years. What we bring to this is a fresh eye, and fresh tools. My competitors have begun trying to steal all three of you for a reason."

He looked surprised.

I laughed. "Oh, you thought I didn't know that, did you?"

Badger grinned. "We knew. We just weren't sure what it would take to get you to admit it."

They'd been betting on me again. I wished they'd quit that. It was embarrassing.

And saying something wouldn't help. In fact, one of them would probably win a bet the minute I did that. Best just to ignore them.

Yeah, like that would work.

"While Marie is doing that," I said. "I'll be working with Annegret on uncovering her third traitor. The footage Badger and Cory have dug out should help. Meanwhile, I need the two of you to work with taking the information Marie's dug out on that firm…

"You mean 'The-One-Who-Must-Not-Be-Named'" Cory said with a grin.

"Oh, that's good," Marie said.

I rolled my eyes. "Yes, them. We need to know a lot more about the Carlie Fine Arts account with them. And how exactly they are profiting from whatever this scam is."

"What are we looking for?" Cory asked.

"Something that shouldn't be there," I said. "Specifically, any signs of someone other than the people we already know about. Probably working behind the scenes."

Cory was nodding. "If there's someone bigger involved at that firm," he said. "They have to be subtle, right? I mean, none of us have caught even a glimpse of anyone."

Badger nodded.

"Masters of subtle. I like it," Marie said, casting a sideways look at Badger. Judging by the background behind them, they were both in our soundproofed conference room. And sitting side by side. Again.

At least she seemed to be teasing Badger, rather than challenging me. For a change.

That didn't last long.

"That's exactly the issue," I said. "And I'm also wondering who's really behind all this. It feels too big to be just the firm we've been looking at."

"The One Who…" Cory began, then subsided at a glare from Marie.

I was impressed that she'd managed that over a video screen.

"They're international," Marie said as if nothing had happened. "With a wide-ranging expertise, in everything from art fraud to corporate espionage. Who better to be behind something like this?"

She'd been doing her research. Good. "You're right, too," I said. "And I don't have answers for you. It's a gut feeling at the moment, and I'm not ready to make decisions—or even assumptions—based on it. But nor am I prepared to ignore it."

"So where does that leave us?" Marie asked, sounding irritated. She was frowning, too.

Despite her upbringing and her formerly wild choices and attire, she was far more conventional than I'd ever have suspected. Given the rest of the team, that was probably a good thing.

"Digging for information, questioning everything. And not assuming that what's in front of us is all there is to this case. What else is hiding behind the obvious?"

"Like a mastermind," Marie said.

It was my turn to scowl. "Too melodramatic."

"You mean accurate, don't you?" she said smugly.

"I mean we can't afford to make assumptions on this case. And labels come with assumptions."

"But…," Marie said.

"She's right," Badger said. "Labels can be useful, but they're often a shortcut. Fine if you know that, but make that leap too early, you miss anything subtle."

"Fine," Marie said. "Have fun digging, guys."

And I was looking at a blank screen.

No matter. They'd get the job done.

I went back to my own digging as the light through my window faded slowly.

Well over an hour later, I stood up, stretched and stood for a moment by the window watching the light change on the carved stonework of the buildings across the street as the autumn day slipped into evening. As my eyes feasted on the play of light and shadow, my brain was busily considering what I'd uncovered. And what it might mean.

That was when my cell buzzed. I glanced at the screen. No number. Now what?

"Barbara O'Grady," I said.

"We've got another body. And you've got a problem," Jessup said.

With her words, all my theories shattered. There was only one thing that mattered.

"Who? Where?" I demanded.

"Behind Carli Fine Arts," she said. "I'll meet you there."

And she hung up.

Not my client! It couldn't be Annegret. Could it?

As my mind raced with possibilities, I went on autopilot. I poured the rest of the coffee into my over-sized travel mug. Shut down my computer, stuffed it in my bag. Already regretting toting the weight of it, but unwilling to leave it behind again.

At least it all fit. Good thing I'd listened to Andrea and bought this purse. So far this trip, the bag had held everything I needed. Which now included a thirteen inch laptop.

As I grabbed my coat, I released the locks and yanked open the hall door, I couldn't keep the thought at bay.

What if it was Annegret?

CHAPTER TWENTY-EIGHT

When I arrived at the gallery, the street around it was in chaos. It wasn't full dark yet, but the clouds were moving in, and against the buildings shadows thickened and stretched. Police cars with their flashing blue lights were parked everywhere, and crime scene tapes were already up, closing off the door to the gallery.

With the bit of information Jessup had given me, I knew to go around the building towards the alley, rather than waste time trying to argue my way inside. But I was too late. The crime scene tape was up there, too.

That wasn't going to stop me. I considered trying to duck under the tape, but there were too many people standing around, and three bright spotlights on tripods were already in place. There were no shadows left to hide in, and I had no official status here.

Not that I had that much at home, either. Depending on whom I was dealing with. But I had relationships that stood me in good stead when I needed information. Which wasn't true here.

I walked briskly around the block, and worked my way down from the other end of the alley that ran behind the gallery. Deep with shadows, it hadn't yet been blocked off. I wondered who had been responsible for that oversight. Not that it mattered. I just hoped they didn't end up paying for me getting access to the site.

But I needed to be here. I needed to know who was dead. And how they had died.

Annegret? I wondered again, picturing her defeated expression as I told her exactly how deeply involved her gallery was in this mess. And for how long.

Hoping it wasn't her. Afraid that it was.

I walked faster. Just over half-way along the alley—and directly behind Carli Fine Arts—stood a cluster of people at the edge of the zone of brightness created by the spotlights. I spotted Jessup's tall frame and beside her, Keller's lanky one. I strode confidently towards them, like a woman on a mission. Which I was. With a little luck, no-one would realize I didn't belong there.

As I grew nearer, I wondered how and when the two of them had found out about this latest murder. If it was murder.

I wasn't going to get an answer to that question anytime soon. But what I did get was a glimpse of the victim. Who wasn't Annegret.

It was an elderly man. Someone I didn't recognize.

I might have hoped he was unrelated to the case, if it weren't for Jessup's call. The only way this unknown man's death could be a problem for me is if he was connected in some way to my client. And therefore to my case.

I knew there was no way I'd get answers from the locals, so I didn't even try. Luckily in the confusion they hadn't noticed me yet, or I'm sure I'd have been escorted from the site. Instead I made a beeline for Jessup and Keller.

Who were standing to one side, quietly talking while they watched every move the police made. I doubted Jessup had official standing here, but Keller probably did. Had he brought her in?

And which one had decided that she should call me?

Keller caught sight of me just then, and his sudden start answered that question. He hadn't expected to see me. And he didn't look too happy I was there. What was that about?

Maybe it was just as well I hadn't had a chance to ask him about Jessup after all.

Though I still needed to know more about her involvement in all of this. And exactly how she thought her clients' issues with SaltonSecure related to the problems Annegret's gallery was having.

I'd just have to be more subtle about it.

Not one of my usual strong points. No matter. I could adapt.

I moved to stand at Jessup's shoulder. With a clear line of sight to the body, lying on its—his—back, sightless eyes staring up at the now dark sky. In the light from the spotlights, there was no mistaking the corpse for anything else.

I wondered who had found the body, and scanned the small crowd of people standing in a rough semi-circle around him. Almost in line with the back door of my client's gallery.

I was looking for shock and fear. On a face that didn't belong here. Whoever owned that face, that was who I wanted to talk to.

But it seemed luck was in short supply today. For whoever it was lying on the pavement. And for those whose job it was to find justice for him. And if he was involved in my case, that included me.

No matter what the official force thought of my role here, I was clear why I did the job I did.

There was no sign of anyone out of place. On my right, at the end of the alley they'd cordoned off, an ambulance stood waiting, lights off and sirens silent. Waiting to take the body away? It must be, though it wasn't clear to me why the delay. He was beyond all saving.

I couldn't see any blood on or near the body. No signs of violence at all, in fact. Just the open, staring eyes. For some reason, he'd been wrapped in a rough-woven blue blanket, the kind an ambulance would carry, yet they'd left his head uncovered. Someone really needed to throw a sheet over him.

I glanced around again, looking for an ambulance attendant, a doctor, someone with responsibility for this poor soul. Whoever he'd been. I couldn't see anyone who seemed to be filling that role.

"Why are we just standing here?" I whispered to Jessup.

Who jumped a little.

Hadn't she noticed me come up beside her? My estimation of her investigative skills dropped a little. But rebounded fast when she cut her eyes at me and shook her head very slightly. Just enough to caution me.

Then she was again watching closely as exactly nothing happened in front of us.

I got the message. I joined her in that activity. While trying to make sense of the scene that wasn't unravelling in front of me.

What were we waiting for?

———

IT SEEMED to take forever before the door of the gallery banged open and a large, irate man strode out into the alley. Descending the steps as if they weren't even there, he stood glaring at the corpse. Then he looked up, and his glare extended to those of us standing around. He looked from one face to the next, and I'd have sworn he was memorizing them in the fraction of a second he took for each.

My eyes took in an unruly mop of dark hair and a mustache that would have done credit to a walrus. All of which contrasted with the well cut black suit, the immaculate white shirt, a small gold pin on his lapel. *Surete*, then. An Inspector, most likely, and in charge of this case. And not at all happy about it.

If this was the man Annegret had been meeting with the morning I'd arrived in Geneva, I wasn't surprised she'd seemed worn out afterwards. I was surprised she'd been functional at all.

The walrus's eyes swung back to me, and I fought the irrational urge to make myself smaller. But they didn't stop there, to my relief. It was Jessup he was interested in.

I felt suddenly sorry for her. In my peripheral vision I could see her standing taller. No cringing for her. They obviously knew each other. I wondered who he was, and what their history was.

And why he was so angry.

I was about to find out.

He came striding forward, and all of the uniforms in the way melted backwards. Until he was standing directly in front of Jessup, confronting her eyeball to eyeball.

"What are you doing here?"

"She's with me," Keller said quietly. I could feel his tension from where I stood. What was going on here?

"This is my crime scene," the walrus said. "I'll accept your presence—under protest—but not your *guests.*"

That last word was laden with sarcasm, and this time his eyes flickered from Jessup's to mine before returning to hers. "And particularly not *this* guest."

She said nothing, and my respect for her escalated.

"Who is the victim?" I asked clearly, breaking that staring contest.

The walrus turned his head and considered me. "Ms. O'Grady, I assume?" he said. "The *private eye,*"—more sarcasm—"that Ms. Carli saw fit to hire?"

His English was excellent, and his dark eyes fiercely intelligent. And very angry. "She'd do better to hire a lawyer," he added, for my ears only.

"She has two," I said, just as softly.

His eyes glittered, and I wasn't sure if it was humor or outrage. Before he could respond, Jessup drew his attention back to her.

"His name is Arturo Benjamin," she said. "He is—or rather he was—on the board of Carli Fine Arts. What I don't understand is why is he is still lying there."

The walrus looked at her as if he was examining a small and unimportant bug. I wouldn't have wanted to be her. Though she had just, quite deliberately, I thought, drawn his ire away from me. I could do no less than return the favor.

Before I could do so, there was a commotion at the barricade the *surete* had set up, and the reason for the delay became evident. A slender man of medium height wearing a grey suit and wrapped in a long dark coat was making his way through the various officials, apologizing as he went. His pleasant expression and retiring demeanor suggested a man of little consequence, but the black bag he carried and the path that rapidly opened in front of him told another story.

This would be the coroner, then. The man everyone had been waiting for.

He said something quietly to the Inspector as he reached our little group, then walked back towards the body. A mild look of shock crossed his face, and he quickly crossed himself.

"Ah, M. Benjamin," he said sadly.

Bending down, he folded back the blanket until he could lift the dead man's wrist. Not surprisingly, he didn't appear to find a pulse, because he checked for one at the throat, as well, murmuring to himself as he did so.

It was nearly ten minutes later when the coroner straightened and made his way back to where the Inspector still stood a few feet away from the three of us. None of us had said a word in the interim, but the silence was chilly.

"I apologize for the delay," the coroner said formally in low tones. "He was found so?" And he half-turned and motioned back towards the body.

"As you see him. There was no pulse." The Inspector replied, staring over the coroner's head at the victim. "What can you tell me?"

From where I stood I could hear them clearly enough despite their low tones, and luckily my French skills were up to the challenge. Just.

"He was shot, and appears to have died instantly," the coroner said after a thoughtful pause.

That and the little blood I could see suggested a heart wound. Which required close proximity. Or an excellent marksman. Poor man. At least he hadn't suffered.

"Have you a time of death?" Inspector Gabriel asked. He seemed to feel no need to say more. Just waited.

"Nothing will be certain until the autopsy is completed, of course."

"Of course."

It struck me as an odd time and place for such a polite exchange. And left me wondering what lay behind it. There were undercurrents here that I couldn't read, even if I'd been sure I was translating the nuances accurately. I knew too little of the background. And the policies here. And what I did know wasn't helping.

I hoped Annegret hadn't made a mistake she'd come to regret by hiring an outsider like me. She, and her gallery, were in a ton of trouble. Which had just gotten exponentially worse. She couldn't afford a single misstep.

I had the nasty feeling I couldn't, either.

And I still didn't know enough to avoid them.

The coroner put the tips of his long, skinny fingers together and pursed his lips. The buildings behind us cast long shadows across the alley. The coroner looked suddenly macabre in the sudden glare of the lights.

"Unofficially, then. It is likely he died within the last few hours," he said.

"Can you be more precise?"

"I'm afraid not. Not yet, at least. You know I like to be sure of the details before I communicate anything."

"Yes, yes," the inspector said, waving it off. "Can you not give me an estimate to work with in the meantime?"

"I am afraid not," the coroner said. "You know my policies."

"I need whatever information this body can tell us. I have a killer to catch, and rapidly."

"That, I am afraid, is your job," the coroner said, even more quietly. "My job is simply to confirm how the poor man died. And when. Which the autopsy should tell us. And, from there, he is—how do they say it? Ah, yes,—all yours."

Did I imagine that small, smug curl to his lips as he said it?

"How long until the autopsy?" Gabriel asked. Through what sounded to me like gritted teeth.

"A day. Perhaps two."

"You're aware this is a sensitive case? And an urgent one."

"They all are," the coroner said with a slight sigh and a put-upon look.

He was baiting the inspector. If I'd been Gabriel, I'd have strangled him on the spot, consequences be damned. To his credit, Gabriel turned away without another word.

There was definitely history between these two. History I needed to know. And I was betting both Keller and Jessup knew what it was.

I'd have to ask her, though. Maybe she'd be straight with me on this one, since it wasn't related to her clients. I wasn't so sure about Keller. I hadn't missed the tension between him and the Inspector. What was going on there?

"We'll need lights here," Gabriel called out to his team.

There was a bustle and a pause while big lamps on tripods were brought out and set up. Then electrical cords were unravelled and strung. After a few minutes, the lamps blazed on and in the harsh light the dead man's face was painfully clear. He didn't look peaceful. Or as if he were sleeping. He looked sad, somehow.

But what had brought that look to his face?

And where did that leave my client?

I had no idea how her problems fit into any of this. Just a very bad feeling. However this victim was connected, it was going to make things worse.

CHAPTER TWENTY-NINE

We stood around for another hour, with little to see. The coroner bent to his work, but the precise measurements and photos seemed interminable. Still no information was forthcoming.

Twilight stretched into evening, the clouds overhead thickened until the air smelled of rain, scattering everyone who wasn't essential to the scene.

Once the coroner was finally satisfied and the body had been removed, there was no reason for me to stay. I invited both Jessup and Keller for drinks, but Keller declined. As I'd expected him to.

Jessup accepted, after giving me a thoughtful look. "We're not going to get much more here today, anyway," she said, as if agreeing with my unspoken thoughts. "Gabriel won't talk to us."

She turned to Keller. "But he'll have to share with you, given that you are colleagues and all. Even if he's still denying any connection to our case. And we'll expect you to share whatever goodies he lets fall. Do feel free to join us then. We'll be at the usual place."

Keller just nodded, his face expressionless, and she winked at me.

"I'd try my wiles on Gabriel," she said *sotto voce,* turning away. "But I've failed before, and this depressing case is already hard enough on my ego."

As we strode along narrow darkened streets towards the bistro, I wondered what she was up to. This 'we're all girls together' persona wasn't one I'd seen before. It didn't feel fake, though. Or not entirely.

It was possible it was genuine, or at least partly so. Maybe she was just fed up with running up against the wall of male privilege.

I'd been there often enough to recognize that one.

But Jessup was in the top tier of her very male-dominated business. She didn't get there by getting mad. I was willing to bet she kept track, and made sure she got even. I did the same.

So what was she up to now?

———

IT WAS STILL EARLY ENOUGH that the bistro was half empty. We snagged a corner table as the first big drops of rain streaked the glass. No-one was close enough to overhear us, though I suspected that wouldn't last.

Again, Jessup caught my quick assessing glance and read it correctly.

"This place will fill up quickly enough," she said. "Especially with this rain. It's usually very busy in here. And loud enough to drown any conversation, with the rain pounding off the roof and window."

We both glanced at the window. That wouldn't take long. Individual raindrops were fast being replacing by rivulets of water that would soon be sheets, to my experienced eye. Hey, I didn't grow up in a rainforest climate for nothing.

I gave her a nod of agreement, one professional to another. We were each here with our own agendas, and we both knew it. Now began the dance of exploration to see where our common ground —if any—might lie.

She started. "You must have questions after our last meeting," she said. "Especially if your team is as good as my sources tell me they are."

She had that right. I had to give her credit for just putting it out there. Was this yet another strategy? Or had she started to trust me?

It could be either. Or something else I hadn't considered yet. Time would tell.

I leaned forward. "Of course I have questions," I said. Matching honesty for honesty.

Sort of.

Before I could get into my first question, our server showed up. Jessup glanced at me. "Red wine?" she said.

I nodded, and she recommended a variety I'd never heard of. "Local specialty," she said, and we ended up ordering a half-liter between us, as well as a couple of small plates. Again, she suggested local specialties, and I agreed.

I already knew from the previous evening that I could trust her in this, at least. Her palate was excellent.

Once the server had departed, I matched bluntness with bluntness. "Let's start with the easy stuff. I gather you think tonight's victim is tied into my client's current problems?"

She nodded.

"And both our cases?"

"Yes, probably. Though the connection to yours is clear."

"How?" I asked. "You mentioned earlier that Arturo Benjamin was on the board of the gallery—thank you for that. But why would he be targeted? Or do you suspect he was involved, somehow?"

"That wouldn't match anything I knew about the man," she said slowly. "He'll be a major loss to the art community."

"Deep pockets?" I asked cynically.

"That, yes," she said. "But he knew everyone, and had a deep love and respect for great art. He'd spent a lifetime learning, and amassed a seemingly endless amount of information. Drawing on that, he could always see links and connections that no one else could."

"He lived here, then?"

"No," she said. "He was based in Paris for many years. Taught art history at the Sorbonne early in his career, then became a consultant and advisor to galleries all over Europe. He semi-retired to Aix-en-Provence a few years ago—told me he couldn't resist that light."

"You knew him?" I asked, surprised.

She nodded. "I hired him as a consultant on several cases in the past—he was a remarkable man. I was considering bringing him in on this case, once we had a little more to go on. I'll miss him."

She picked up her water glass, gave a silent toast, and drank deeply.

I wished I'd had the chance to meet M. Benjamin, and to discuss this case with him. I wondered what he'd have made of it. "You think he was killed because he uncovered something. Or suspected it."

She dipped her head. "I do. And it would be very like him to go straight to the source—the suspect—and give them a chance to explain. He was a gentleman of the old school. They don't make them like him any more."

No, they didn't.

"And he was killed outside the gallery," I said. "A second, very obvious connection."

"Indeed."

"But was he coming? Or going?"

One might mean he'd come to warn someone at the gallery. The other? More bad news for my case. And for my client.

"That is indeed the question," she said. "At the moment, there is no way of knowing."

"What was his connection with Carli Fine Arts? How did he come to be a director? And how long had he been involved with them?"

"I can't help you much there," Jessup said. "He'd been a director for a number of years, I believe. But he served on a number of gallery boards, because of his reputation and expertise. Beyond that, you'd need to ask your client."

I nodded, and shifted mental gears. "Who is Inspector Gabriel? How is he involved with this case? And what's the issue between him and the coroner? Not to mention him and Keller."

"Whoa!" she said, holding up a hand with a laugh. "Not so fast. After today, I need wine first."

She was sitting with her back to the wall, whereas I had my back to the door. Never my favorite seat. Too vulnerable.

This time, it just meant she'd seen our food approaching before I had. I waited with pretended patience until everything was set out, and she had a drink in her hand.

"And?" I prompted as she took a deep sip of wine.

"That's better," she said, setting down her glass. "Gabriel was formerly with Interpol. Where he was a colleague of Keller's."

"Colleague?" I repeated. After the interaction I'd witnessed between the two men, I doubted that was quite the word for it.

She raised her glass. "Observant of you. Rival, then."

That made more sense. "And now he's with the local force?"

"No, though he's working closely with them at the moment," she said. "He works for the investigative branch of the Federal Office of Police. And I gather he's been assigned to work with the *police cantonale* here in Geneva to investigate the murder of Mme. Duvant."

They were taking this death very seriously then. Good. "But I thought Keller..." I began.

She held up a hand. "The *police cantonale* of Geneva have not requested Interpol's assistance in what they see as a local case. Unfortunately, Keller and I are the only ones who see a connection between the two murders and the increase in art forgery cases."

Now we were getting somewhere. "Which explains the tension between Gabriel and Keller," I said.

"That was pre-existing," she said, but didn't explain further.

"Which has been unfortunate for Keller and myself. We can't get anyone to listen to our theory."

It also meant I was going to have to deal with Gabriel. Who had already judged and labeled me as being on the other side. This was going to be interesting.

"The theory you presented to me as fact," I said bluntly. "Why?"

She grinned. "It's a compliment, actually. Your reputation for solving impossible cases in improbable ways precedes you."

"And you have an impossible case plus an improbable theory," I said. "Or rather, you have half an impossible case. Since the other half now belongs to Inspector Gabriel. I see. And it never occurred to you that if I actually knew what was going on, I might stumble on that improbable solution a lot faster?"

Jessup lifted her glass in a half-toast, swallowed deeply. "Keller was all for that," she said. "But then he's worked with you before, seen first hand how you operate. I was more skeptical, I'm afraid."

Right.

"Which brings me to my next question," I said. "The one you no doubt anticipated. And if we're going to continue to work together, I'll need an answer. A real one."

"Go ahead," she said, watching me from behind the wineglass she was still holding.

"The more my team and I dig into the link between my client and our 'friends'," and here I paused for her reaction. Her slight nod said she knew we were discussing SaltonSecure. "The more I need to be sure exactly how your interests—or rather your clients' interests—match up with my clients' interests. Because whatever 'our friends' may be up to, right now my client's firm is the one in the spotlight."

I paused for a moment, but she didn't take advantage of it. "Your previous explanation seemed a bit," and I raised an eyebrow. "Vague, shall we say? Why did you begin to suspect that there might be a link between the forgeries and our 'friends'?"

"Bravo," she said. "That is exactly the question that I hoped you'd ask."

"That's nice," I said. "What's the answer?"

She made me wait while she took a slow sip of wine, then a moment to savor it. Strategy? Or was she deciding how much to tell me?

Probably both, I decided, watching her smooth face. No matter. Two could play at that game.

———

AROUND US THE restaurant was slowly filling up. Jessup had been right about the noise level. It rose far higher than the numbers of patrons seemed to justify. Some of that might have been due to the location—I could hear conversations in at least three different languages, and possibly an additional dialect or two. Voices tend to rise when multiple languages are spoken in a relatively small room.

While I out-waited her, I observed the crowd. It looked to me like a mix of locals and tourists—which meant the food would be good. The locals were well dressed, well-groomed, and arriving in small bunches. Work colleagues? After work destination? Probably both.

Jessup watched me watching everyone else, her head cocked a little to one side. Smiled. And dropped her bombshell.

"I began to suspect the connection between the cases the moment Annegret Carli hired you," she said.

Wait. What?

"I don't see the connection," I said. "And you haven't answered the why. Or told me why you were watching her in the first place."

"I know. There may be a few things I've left out of my story."

Just a few.

"So?" I said. Challenging her.

This one was up to her. If she wanted my help, that was.

"I'll have to go back to the beginning," she said.

Sure she did. We didn't have that kind of time. And she knew it.

I speared a cube of bread from the plate between us, swiped it through the rich wine and cheese mix simmering in the fondue pot and popped it in my mouth. And my eyes widened. It was the best fondue I'd ever tasted.

"Good choice on the food," I said, and picked up my wineglass. Waited.

Another smile. She was testing me.

I sipped my wine, savoring the rich body and complex flavor of what must have been a very good year.

She laughed, and capitulated. "Several of my firm's long term clients began to report—let's call them concerns—a year or so ago," she said then.

"Concerns," I repeated. "What kind of concerns?"

"These particular clients specialize in wealth management. And with little warning, they were losing big accounts. Individuals they'd advised for decades on investments—including investments in fine arts—who were suddenly doubting their advice. And looking elsewhere."

"I assume there was a similarity in these client accounts? Something that links to art fraud? And forgery?"

"There was. All of them had a substantial portion of their portfolio in masterpieces of world art, especially European art. And suddenly none of them were willing to even discuss investing in fine art. Our clients were losing too many of these accounts, for no apparent reason."

It was beginning to make sense. I'd been looking at it wrong. This wasn't about world famous masterpieces of art, items collectors would pay any sum to own. This was something else entirely.

Art as a medium of exchange. A different form of currency. A better widget for the criminal classes.

I'd seen it in a previous case, but not on a scale anything like this.

"Follow the money," I said, half to myself.

I'd known that from the beginning. So why did it feel like my missing piece? And maybe the reason I couldn't quite figure out Birgitte Jessup's stake in this game.

"Always," she said with a sly half-grin. "But to where?"

"Both Keller and I have been too focused on the forgeries them-selves," I said, thinking aloud now. "His specialty is international art theft. I was hired by an art gallery. For both of us, it's been all about the paintings themselves."

"So?" she said, an edge of impatience in her voice.

"You, on the other hand…" I swirled another piece of bread in the melted cheese, held it up to drip while I contemplated her, then ate it slowly.

I had her full attention now. I hid a grin, still thinking fast.

I knew I^2 served a wide variety of very large companies. Mostly what they had in common was their ability to make money. Vast quantities of it. From what Badger had dug up, Jessup didn't specialize any more than her firm did.

"You always had a different perspective. Because your clients did. They cared about the money, not the art. And that's why it seemed you knew something I didn't. The root of this case isn't about forged masterpieces. Not really."

She picked up her glass, toasted me with it. "And there's the reason for the reputation you're developing."

I ignored her, following my line of thought. "What have you found so far? When you dug into those deserting art collectors?"

"Forgeries. Good ones. But that was the only similarity—every-thing else was different. How they'd acquired them, where they'd acquired them…" She scowled, and drank some wine. "And most of them wouldn't talk about any of it."

Uh huh.

"They talked to you," I said. It wasn't a question.

"Eventually." She smiled. "I have my ways."

"What did you learn?"

"Most of them were legitimate transactions—at least on the surface—verified works with all the paperwork in place. The investors were furious. But they didn't want any disclosure of their involvement or their losses. Some were embarrassed to have been made victims. All of them wanted their extensive investments in art kept very private." Her eyes crinkled at the edges. "Though their reasons varied quite a bit."

I'd just bet they did. Some being far less legal than others.

Wait a minute. "If the transactions were legitimate, with verified works and all the provenance, then how did the fraud come to light?" I asked.

"The owners had the work tested."

"Why?"

She shrugged. "It varied. Reasons for those evaluations varied from estate planning purposes to selling or exchanging the piece to using it as collateral against something else. And the mess kept getting deeper as the news covered high-profile forgeries surfacing, and collectors started getting nervous."

"You've kept digging," I said, watching her. "And that's where the connection to 'our friends' came in."

"Yes." She picked up her glass and drank, using the opportunity to take a quick scan of the tables near her.

Apparently seeing nothing concerning, she resumed. "It was tenuous, and at first it seemed far-fetched. No two cases were the same. And the techniques involved? Those required some pretty specialized knowledge. But it was there. And the more we dug, the more connections we found."

I shook my head. "We're missing something."

Jessup grimaced. "I know. The question is what? I can't quite see it—not when the motive and the methods seem to shift from case to case."

I nodded, swallowed a little more wine. Still following that elusive trail. My mind ping-ponging from piece to piece. My excitement growing.

"It's our perspective that's off," I said. "How big is this thing, anyway? And how long has it been going on for?"

"I've been aware of it for just over a year," she said, her eyes fixed on me. "Keller's been seeing an impact in the markets for two. Now that we're aware of, it's clear that it has been growing fast, so the organization behind it has to have been building unnoticed for a while."

"They'd need deep roots, and a pretty broad base."

"Exactly."

"This isn't just our 'friends'," I said, suddenly sure. "There's another player somewhere. That's why we can't see it."

"See what?"

"I don't know," I said. "My own perspective has been skewed. Too limited. So most of the connections and conclusions I've been drawing..." I glanced up at her. "You and Keller too. We've all been wrong."

"I know. But wrong how?"

Hmmm. I forked up a mouthful of fondue as I considered that. The stuff was addictive.

"Try the *raclette*," Brigitte said, helping herself to a small serving of the potato, cheese and bacon version we'd ordered, as if trying to restore some semblance of normality to this conversation. "It's excellent here."

Of course she'd know that. And she was right. I sampled a perfectly seasoned, cheesy mouthful. Then another. Delicious. The hint of dill pickle was unexpected, but it worked.

And the thought I'd been fighting for slipped into place.

I shook my head. "It isn't enough."

"What do you mean?"

"'Our friends' are involved. No doubt about that. None of this would work without the role they're playing."

"I'd agree with that. But...?"

"They have the access, and expertise in preventing both theft and fraud. Plus experience in exposing forgeries. But they specialize in security."

She gave me an odd look. "So...?"

"So these cases are all about the money. Whoever is behind this plays in that world at your clients' level. And they know the art market. *Really* know it."

She stared at me. Reached for her wine. Drank. Then said slowly, "Okay, I can see that being the connection. But why?"

"Money. Obviously."

"Obviously." She gave me a tight smile, seemingly too caught up in the puzzle of it to appreciate the humor.

"Probably too obviously," I said. And watched that derail her thoughts.

"Excuse me. What?"

I grinned. "If this was just about money, you would have solved it already. Without either Keller or me."

She smiled back. "That's true. If it were just about money, our friends are the logical suspect."

"And they're still in it up to their necks."

She nodded. "I agree."

"But they aren't the ones driving it. It doesn't go high enough in the firm for that."

"How do you know?"

I didn't, yet. Not for sure. But it wouldn't help to tell her that. And I knew how to find out.

"My team has been digging," I said. "It's amazing how lax a security firm can be about their own security, sometimes."

She grinned. "I know. Arrogance." Then she sobered. "So, what is driving our master mind, then? There have to be easier ways for a mind like this to make money. Unless the scope of this is much, much bigger than I've been considering."

Given I^2's client list, and the kinds of money they must deal with on a regular basis, I couldn't even imagine how big that could be.

She could, though. Even in the subdued lighting, I watched the white lines of strain appear around her lips.

"I don't know," she said, the little lines around her mouth deepening. "Given everything we know so far, this scheme would have to have tentacles everywhere. If that kind of scope is even a possibility… We need to stop whoever this is. Now."

She was right about that last bit, anyway. We were already looking at two murders connected to this case. That we knew of.

Given her expression, I hoped she was wrong about the rest of it. Something that could scare a woman like her that badly?

Solving this one wasn't going to be easy. Or safe.

If we could pull it off at all.

CHAPTER THIRTY

As I'd anticipated, Jessup and I didn't stay for dinner. By the end of our conversation, both of us were eager to leave, no matter how good the food was. The more we talked, the more the increasingly upbeat mood of the place grated on both of us. And we had work to do.

With an increasing sense of urgency.

As soon as I got back to my hotel room, I sent off a text to Badger, another to Marie. I didn't call a team meeting, though. Not yet. First I needed to process everything I'd learned. And to rethink what I knew—and didn't know—about this case.

Then I'd work with my team to start turning over rocks.

Meanwhile, Jessup was going to call Keller and fill him in, then do some digging of her own. We both knew it was going to take every resource the three of us could throw at this thing to figure out what we were really dealing with. Let alone stop it.

But first, I needed fuel. A burger, or maybe a local dish. Those small plates had been good. And maybe another glass of that local wine.

I ORDERED FOOD, deciding against more wine, then pulled out my laptop and started throwing down thoughts and mental images that I'd need for the team briefing. I started with my conversation with Jessup, then worked backwards through the day. The latest murder. My conversation with Annegret. Every detail. Read it through. Then added, clarified, and tightened it into a report.

Then I turned to my last briefing notes, made a copy, and started updating that with everything I now knew. Some questions got answered, others were clearly misdirections. But the big questions remained. With a few new ones.

And one revelation that was going to make all the difference.

At its root, this case was all about the money.

Someone, somewhere, was looking to make easy money off the work of others. At any cost.

Hardly a new motive, unfortunately. But here? This was on a scale that I still couldn't get my head around.

If I was right, that is. I needed more answers before I was sure of that.

The big question on any case is where to focus. And the more complex this case grew, the harder it was to determine where to focus to begin uncovering those answers.

After my conversation with Jessup, the focus for this case was suddenly clear to me. This wasn't about a mad collector, or someone who was prepared to pay anything to own the painting they coveted. This was all—and only—about money. There was a simplicity in that.

We needed to 'follow the money'. See where it led.

Unravel that, and everything else—personal motive, traumas, secrets, revenge—all of the darker elements of the human drama? The money trail would lead us to the mind—or minds?—behind it all.

And hopefully keep my client out of jail.

I skimmed through what I'd done. Got up, stretched and put on a pot of coffee. Stared out at the night sky while it brewed.

Heavy clouds overhead, with the lights of the city sparkling against the dark expanse of the lake. It didn't lighten my mood. Nothing in me matched that sparkle.

Coffee in hand, I ran through my notes and updates again. And one question still niggled in the back of my mind.

Why art?

Yes, there's a lot of money there. If—and it's a big if—you know what you're doing. But without some connection to art, it isn't the first choice of any criminal I've ever heard of. Which could just be my own limitations. But still…

A second question occurred to me. Why Annegret's gallery? Why had forgery rumors about this particular gallery—Da Carli Fine Arts in Geneva, Switzerland—drawn the attention of Keller and Jessup?

If this case was all about money, why wasn't a gallery in Zurich, with its larger financial center being used in this scheme? Or London? Or Paris, with its myriad of galleries?

Was it something about Annegret's business practices—such as her practice of hanging copies instead of originals—that had drawn the attention of whoever was behind this conspiracy? Or was it something about where her gallery was located? About Geneva?

I made a note, then I skimmed through the briefing notes again, looking for something I suspected I'd not paid enough attention to. I'd know it when I saw it.

I stopped on murder.

It was Amara Duvant's murder that had pushed this investigation into overdrive. And had brought me to Switzerland. I'd been assuming I understood why she had been killed.

Either she knew too much. Or she'd refused to cooperate on whatever they'd wanted her to do next. Or her conscience had finally got the better of her. Or…I could probably come up with a dozen other possibilities.

Amara Duvant was part of this crime, an insider. Putting her automatically at risk. Murder was an extreme, but not unprecedented, outcome of that risk.

But this second murder. Arturo Benjamin. Why him? How did he fit in?

The little I knew about M. Benjamin raised more questions than it answered. How had he been involved?

And come to think of it, what was he doing in Geneva? What had called him here, away from the light in Aix-en-Provence?

Arturo Benjamin might have learned too much, and confronted the wrong person. But what had he known—or thought he knew? And more importantly, how had he learned it? How had he made the connection to Carli Fine Arts?

And who had he confronted?

If that's why he'd been murdered. Which was entirely an assumption on my part, with absolutely no basis in fact.

Other than the fact that I don't believe in coincidences. M. Benjamin and the first victim had died in the same alley. And the gallery was the common denominator between them.

Or was it?

And that question had me questioning my assumptions about Amara Duvant's death. We needed to dig deeper.

———

BADGER WOULD STILL BE FOCUSED on SaltonSecure. I sent Marie a text, asking her to dig into anything publicly available on Arturo Benjamin. I needed to know more about him than what Jessup had told me, especially about his connections in the art world.

With Duvant and her inside connections, it was probably a need for money that had lured her into the game. But how did this latest victim fit?

What had got Benjamin killed? Money? Or art?

Newly inspired, I reviewed the documents I'd just created. Made a few changes as new thoughts sparked. And sent the documents off to the team, with a note to Marie asking her to set up a team briefing as soon as possible.

I left the question of Cory's attendance up to the two of them. I needed all three of them focused on this case now. How they worked that was up to them. In the meantime, I'd start digging on this end.

And before this day was finally over, I promised myself, I was going to order an entire bottle of that wine. Maybe two.

Then my phone rang again.

Andrea.

Oh no. No, no, no.

———

I GLANCED AT THE CLOCK. It would be ten in the morning back home. Usually at this time Andrea was frantically busy putting out work fires. She seldom called me on a work morning even when I was home. She'd never done so while I was on a case.

"Andrea? What's wrong?" I said as soon as I picked up.

She laughed. She sounded happy. Not a disaster, then.

"Oh, Barb. Nothing. In fact, everything's gone right." She drew in a breath. "I'm engaged."

What? She'd barely told me about this guy last week. And she was only tentatively prepared to admit they were dating. Now, suddenly, they were engaged?

"Engaged? That's wonderful, Andrea," I said, and from somewhere found the part of me that really meant it.

This was my best friend, after all. She thought she'd found the man she wanted to spend her life with. And he thought the same.

Or said he did.

Which might only be true in some alternate universe—if you believed in such things—but right now that was Andrea's world. And in that world, he felt the same way she did.

And I was genuinely happy for her. Whatever followed it, in this moment, she was happy, in love, and loved in return.

And I'd never realized before how important I thought that was.

I shoved that thought away for later.

Along with all the fears I had for her, and the fact that I hated coincidences.

I hadn't even met this guy. How could I judge him, after all?

Wait… I. Hadn't. Even. Met. Him. That was huge, right? If he was connected to my case, he'd have made some effort to meet me, find out what I was up to, what I knew. If only through Andrea.

And he hadn't. I could share her joy with a clear conscience.

"I'm so happy for you," I said, meaning it. "What happens now?"

"Now we start planning a wedding!" she practically squealed. My competent, 'relationships-aren't-for-me' friend sounded like a giddy teenager. A euphoric one.

Okay, then.

"Have you set a date?" I asked. Trying to remember the stuff a best friend should care about.

"No. But he wants it soon. He says he's been waiting long enough for me to even see him. And he wants to be part of my life. To meet everyone."

"I should hope so," I said. "*I* haven't even met him yet. And if you're marrying the guy, he'll need my stamp of approval first."

She laughed, as I'd meant her to. It had been a joke between us for a long time. I hated that there was any part of me that wasn't joking.

"I know. And you're going to love him," she said. "Not as much as I do, of course. But Greg—he knows how much you mean to me. And now that we're engaged, he wants to meet you. Meet everyone, but he's impatient to meet you first of all. In fact, he's threatening to meet your plane and kidnap you the moment you set foot in Vancouver. Can you imagine?"

Only too well. But I really wanted to be wrong. "He sounds like quite the kidder. I can't wait to meet him."

"Oh, you'll love his sense of humor. He says the most outrageous things, totally straight faced and serious. And he looks the part of the dangerous security guy the whole time."

"What? He wears all black?"

She laughed again. "No, he likes color. Though he does look

great in a tux. Actually, he's got great taste. But there's this lethal security guy image he's got going—he's such a goofus when you get to know him."

At her words, the melty gooey happiness in her voice fought with the rising fear in my gut.

———

LUCKILY FOR ME, a minor office crisis erupted and Andrea had to go. After making me promise that the four of us—she and Greg, Nick and I—would have dinner together as soon as we could arrange it. I agreed, and said as many of the right things as I could manage. But I was done.

If I'd spent even one more minute on the phone with her, I don't think I could have kept the fear out of my voice. For her. And for Nick. As it was, she picked up on the exhaustion I was feeling. All I needed there was truth—this case was rapidly turning into one of the worst I'd ever faced.

"You know you always say that," she said with a laugh. "And then you solve it. You'll be fine."

I would. But only if she was too. And I couldn't tell her that part. Not without at least a fact or two that pointed to her Greg's involvement.

One she'd disconnected I drew in a deep breath. Exhaled slowly, and took another. Then I did a mental exercise that took the fear and everything else I was feeling, labeled it "later" and stuck it in a package, neatly tied with a rough string bow.

Badger was already looking into Younger. I could trust her to work faster and deeper than I ever could. And just the fact that she'd already made the connection to Andrea—and known to call me—reassured me that she'd take it seriously. If she found something, I'd know.

For now—my focus had to stay on solving this case. Gritting my teeth, I went back to it.

CHAPTER THIRTY-ONE

Less than an hour later, Marie had the meeting set. All three of them were online, and I could see the faces as clearly as if I'd been sitting across the table from them. Not that the experience of meeting like this was anything like actually being there. It wasn't. But it was better than a phone call. And miles better than email exchanges.

Unless our times were too far out of sync, anyway.

Marie didn't wait for me to open the meeting. "We've all read your briefing notes. Badger and I have had time to start the research. Cory hasn't yet."

"Later today," he said. I could hear the promise in his voice.

"That's good to hear," I said. "This case just got harder. And even less clear than it was before. I'm relying on all of you."

And I glanced from face to face, ending with Badger. "But before we start, are you sure this conversation is absolutely secure?"

She nodded. "The online part is. And I checked our office and your hotel room thoroughly for bugs just before we met."

"How… never mind," I said. "As long as you're sure?"

"I am."

"Okay. So, what have you got so far?"

"BladeSecure is definitely under our 'friends' umbrella," Badger said. "I've got enough of the structure to be sure now. Though I don't know—yet—if they're involved in this case. I still can't track how high up this forgery ring goes. I've sent you some stuff on the local guy, anyway."

I checked the vault on my laptop. Several files, one labeled 'Greg Younger'. "Got it. Thanks."

"Want me to keep digging on this?" she asked.

"Let me review these first," I said. "Stay on the bigger picture. But if anything else surfaces in connection with BladeSecure, let me know."

"Will do."

"I've been digging into Arturo Benjamin," Marie said, leaning forward a little, as if I was actually in the room with them. She was again sitting beside Badger, her expression intent. I wondered for a moment if I should read anything into that. And quickly decided not to go there. Some things I was better off not knowing.

"And?" I asked.

"I wish I'd met him," she said. "Or had a chance to study with him. He used to teach advanced classes in art history in Geneva and Paris. For a while."

I just nodded, knowing what she meant. Jessup's description of him had prepared me a bit for what I'd found when I started looking into the man. But not for the crushing sense of loss I'd felt as I found out more. His was the kind of mind that comes along once in a generation. His passion for art and his knowledge of it had been vast, his generosity in sharing what he knew seemingly endless.

I hadn't found any obvious connection between him and Amara Duvant, though. Except the gallery.

"Whoever did this, we have to get them. They have to pay," Marie said vehemently.

"We will," I promised. Even more than our client, this case for me was now about Arturo Benjamin's murder. "Did you find anything that might help?"

"No," she said. "Nothing but reasons why he should still be alive. Nothing about why he'd be dead. I can't even track who he might have been meeting with."

"I'm at least in the same city. I'll have a look," I said. "See if you can find out when he arrived in Geneva, and where he was staying."

Marie just nodded.

Which probably meant she'd get help with that one.

"What did you find out about his relationship with our client?" I asked her.

"He was an early supporter of her gallery, back when she first started," Marie said. "And she seems to have turned to him over the years. He'd retired from most everything, but he still accepted a spot on her board when she asked. I think he was a Director as a favor to her."

"He'd have known Amara Duvant through that. Did you find any other connection between the two of them?"

"No. And it was mostly Annegret who interacted with her board, from what I've found."

"When did M. Benjamin join her board?"

"A dozen years ago. Though it looks like he's been involved in different ways, off and on, from the beginning," Marie said.

"Interesting. I wonder how much he knew," I said as I made a note. I'd have to ask Annegret how much she'd told him about the rumors, and the trouble the gallery was in.

Technically, she should have made sure her Board knew all of it. From what I'd learned of her so far, I'd be amazed if she had. Though I suspected Arturo Benjamin might have been different.

I just hoped it hadn't got him killed. And I was very much afraid it had.

Which made me realize it was time to fill the team in on Annegret's habit of copying her most valuable works, and putting only the copy on display. Whether that came to light during the course of the investigation or not, it was seeming more and more important, especially in light of M. Benjamin's murder.

"There's just one other thing you need to know," I began, and filled them in.

"You didn't just learn this," Badger said. It wasn't a question.

"No," I said. "I've known since Monday."

"The day you arrived," Badger said with a little nod.

I wondered how much she'd suspected. Or if there were already rumors on the Dark Web. For the first time, I wondered just how discreet Annegret's copyist—her best friend—really was.

"Why are you only telling us now, two days later?" Cory demanded.

"It was in the client's best interests to keep her secret close," I said. "Given how dangerous any rumor of those copies could prove to be for Annegret's business and her career. Though technically, what she's been doing isn't illegal. She had no intent to sell the copies."

"Oh," he said.

I couldn't read his expression, but I could read Marie's. She was upset. "Then why bother telling us at all?" she said.

"Because given M. Benjamin's expertise in art history, it's very possible that those copies are relevant to his murder."

"You think he found out and she killed him?" Cory asked.

"No. I don't think our client is a murderer. But I think there's a possibility the victim found out about the copies, and it led to his death."

"And our client?" Cory asked.

"Our client is in denial," I said. "And about as much use as a wooden keyboard."

Cory laughed, and Marie looked even more upset. "But Annegret, with everything going for her. I can't believe she'd do this," she said.

"Think of it from her perspective for a moment," I said. "She made one bad decision, early in her career, to save a few dollars on insurance. And it's worked for her for decades, and she's been praised as building one of the leading, most innovative galleries out there. Now it's suddenly all coming crashing down around her ears, and she risks losing everything. What would you do?"

Marie glared at me. The screens and the distance between us couldn't diminish that look. "I'd face up to it," she said bluntly. "Of course."

I considered her for a moment. No, she wouldn't understand Annegret. Marie hadn't had it easy for the last dozen years. And she'd never give up. Or back away from a problem. Never had, never would.

Cory was nodding. Different reasons, same strength of character. I glanced at Badger. Even in small boxes on a computer screen, there it was. I hadn't consciously recognized what my team was made of, at the same time as I'd relied on them for exactly that reason.

I smiled at them. "I know you would," I said. "And Annegret will come around. She just needs a little time. She's not nearly as resilient as you lot."

Cory made a face, and the moment was gone. Good thing. I'd nearly felt weepy for a moment there. Can't have that.

"Now, let's sort out who's doing what," I said briskly. "We have a case to solve."

———

I HEARD BACK from Jessup later that evening, after she'd met with Adrien. He'd confirmed that the second death outside the gallery was now officially a homicide.

"Just one shot?" I asked. The coroner hadn't mentioned a second one at first look, but I'd learned the hard way it paid to verify.

"Yes. Both face to face, and close range," she confirmed. It appears to be the same calibre as the gun that killed Duvant."

I thought about that for a moment.

"So was the victim leaving the gallery? Or arriving? Did he say?" I asked her, trying to picture it. "Perhaps after an argument?"

I couldn't make that picture fit.

"Officially, no-one is saying much of anything at the moment," Jessup said. "But either situation is plausible. And from the evidence we're aware of, there's nothing to corroborate—or repudiate—either one."

"Neither is good news for my client," I observed. "Both suggest the killer is connected with the gallery, though the first one suggests the killer was a staff member. But neither one gets us a name."

"No."

"Where is the official investigation at, then?" I asked.

"They seem to be looking at your client pretty hard."

That wasn't much of a surprise. I hadn't had a chance to talk to Annegret after the murder. According to Jessup, Annegret and her lawyers—both of them—had been shepherded off to the police station before I even arrived at the scene. And I'd been getting nothing but her voicemail ever since.

"They didn't arrest her, though?" I asked Jessup.

"No. And they haven't declared her a person of interest, either."

Well, that was something.

"Not yet, at least," Jessup added, deflating my flicker of relief. "According to Keller, anyway."

And he would know. Despite the atmosphere between him and his former colleague, Adrien wouldn't be kept out of the facts of the investigation. He'd probably be aware of most of the strategy, too. As well as the theories.

I hoped he was sharing all of that with Jessup. And that she wasn't holding anything back from me.

Trust issues? Me? Well, I'm better than I used to be. But a healthy dose of skepticism is a fact of life in this business. Sometimes it can save your life.

And it's better than trusting the wrong person.

To mis-use the phrase that showed up on joke-gift Post-it notes for awhile—'If you're not paranoid when you get here, we can train you.'

They should try the P. I. business some time.

CHAPTER THIRTY-TWO

I woke the following morning tired and heavy-eyed. I'd worked late the night before, then polished off more of the bottle of rich red than I'd intended to. I'd gone through everything we had on SaltonSecure, including the files on Andrea's new beau. It still didn't give me the answers I needed.

We needed to know how high up the corruption in SaltonSecure went, and how far it had spread. And so far, we hadn't managed to track down where the money from the forgeries was going.

Or who was really behind this scheme.

It still felt like I was running in place. On the heels of that thought, a flash of image told me I'd been dreaming exactly that. No wonder it felt so real.

Coffee. I needed coffee. Then a shower. I had too much to accomplish today to be tired. Or discouraged.

Freshly showered, coffee in hand—I can't say I felt much better. But I could focus. That would do for now.

At five after nine, I strode into Annegret Carli Fine Arts. I'd walked over from the hotel and detoured by the back alley, which was still an active crime scene. From behind the crime scene tape at the end of the alley, I'd watched two techs meticulously scanning every inch of the cobblestones outside the gallery's back door, while two others were doing the same behind the jewelers. Where Duvant's body had been found.

I wondered what they were looking for so long after the first murder. And what piece of information had sent them back to look deeper.

I didn't recognize the equipment both teams were using to scan with, but clearly human vision wasn't going to find whatever they were hoping to find. I just hoped whatever they were searching for was better news for Annegret than what they'd found last night. Though I had a nasty feeling it wouldn't be.

It was a relief to find the front door of the gallery free of crime scene tape. It looked like a regular weekday morning for the gallery as weak sunlight filtered through the now leafless trees and bounced off their red awning. If you hadn't seen the activity in the alley.

As I stepped through the door, the soft tone gave its usual alert. Giselle's smile from behind the reception desk was decidedly wan, though, and the blue shadows under her eyes said she hadn't slept well.

"She's waiting for you," Giselle said. Her tone was flat, but today I couldn't tell if that reflected her boss's mood, or the miasma of violent death that seemed to hang in the silent air. What had been a calm and welcoming room now seemed cold and bleak. It felt as if the art itself was grieving.

'Snap out of it,' I told myself as I returned Giselle's smile.

"We'll solve this," I said to Giselle as I walked towards her. "Whoever is killing your colleagues—they won't get away with it."

She nodded, and swallowed hard.

"Are the lawyers here?"

"No. Annegret wanted to speak with you first," she said in a voice that cracked at the edges.

I nodded back, and moved past her.

Giselle's voice stopped me. "Ms. O'Grady? I mean, Barbara?"

I looked over my shoulder. "Yes?"

"Make them pay," she said in a voice that didn't shake at all. "For him. Make them pay."

"I will." And it was a promise. I'd done my own research, and I shared the sorrow she felt for Arturo Benjamin's loss. No matter that he'd been near the end of a spectacular life. He deserved to *live* every single day he had left. Not to have them stolen from him. And we, all of us, had desperately needed every day he had to give.

————

ANNEGRET CARLI SAT behind her pristine desk looking like she hadn't slept at all. Her eyes were bloodshot, and her usually upright posture sagged. She wore no makeup except for a slash of pale lipstick, and her hair hung lank around her narrow face.

She looked like a defeated ghost. One who had just been banished, and could feel herself being torn away from everything she cared about. I shed the macabre thought with a shiver, and gritted my teeth. Not if I could help it.

The only thing I could do for Arturo Benjamin and those who grieved him was to help solve this thing. And soon.

"I'm truly sorry for your loss," I said.

She just nodded.

"What are the police saying?"

"They're looking hard at me. As if I could ever…" Her lips tightened and she looked away. "They say he was shot face to face."

"So I heard."

She didn't ask from whom. "This has to stop."

"That's why you hired me," I said.

"I never imagined… I didn't expect to drag you into this."

"It's what I do," I said, surprising myself. Solving a double murder was a long way from my usual case. But it was certainly what I intended to do here. "I'll need your help."

"You have it."

"Why was Arturo Benjamin here last night?"

"The *surete* asked the same thing." Her neutral-toned lips twisted, looking nakedly vulnerable without her signature bright lipstick. "I didn't have an answer for them, either."

"Were you able to convince them of that?"

"What do you think?"

I was afraid of that. "But they didn't arrest you."

"No. Not yet. I'm expecting them to, though."

It was as if all the fight, all the personality had drained out of her. I wasn't sure if it was shock, grief, or the overload of emotions built from a combination of everything she'd been through.

But if the *surete* questioned her in this state of mind—I wondered if she'd even know what she was saying. With the guilt she was feeling, she'd convict herself so tightly I doubted she'd ever get out of it. Even if she was innocent. And no matter what I could dig up, or how good her lawyers were.

That had to change.

"Let me tell you my working theory," I said. "Then I'll need you to poke holes in it."

I couldn't even tell if she'd heard me.

No matter. I knew how to deal with shell-shocked clients. Even this one.

"Arturo Benjamin was the invisible man behind this gallery from the start, wasn't he?" I said sharply, leaning forward. "The one you relied on, the one you turned to when you faced a difficult situation. Or a difficult decision."

A minute inclination of her head was my only answer.

Good enough.

"But you didn't tell him about the rumors. Why not?" It was a guess, but an educated one.

I was beginning to understand my client. Finally.

She hadn't expected that, and as I'd hoped, it pulled an answer from her. "I… I…"

Well, sort of an answer.

"You couldn't," I continued, each word a carefully aimed missile. "You never told him about the copies you'd had done. And you were afraid there was a connection between that and the fraud rumors."

I'd been right. I could see it in her eyes. But I needed more from her now.

"Why didn't you tell me sooner?"

"How could I? I hadn't told anyone." It was nearly a whisper.

Meaning she hadn't told him. Her mentor. Which must feel to her now like a betrayal. Probably felt that way at the time, too.

"So why didn't you tell him?"

"I thought… I don't know what I thought. That the rumors were just jealousy, that they'd die away."

I looked at her. "Really?"

She looked away. "I was afraid someone had found out about the copies, and would twist what they knew to destroy me."

"And yet you'd done nothing wrong?"

"Not when I first started. But over time…" She hesitated. "More forgeries were being uncovered. It became a difficult issue. An uncomfortable one. Even rumors of fraud are enough to damage a gallery's reputation."

"So why not simply end your practice of copying your most valuable works?"

"And how would I explain my sudden need for a great deal more insurance?"

I just looked at her.

Her lips tightened. "I kept going around and around in my head. And never quite acting."

She'd dug herself in. It didn't seem like the Annegret Carli the world knew, but then, very few of us are only the image we present to the world. "I don't think you have a choice now."

She nodded. The brutal murder of her long-time mentor seemed to have knocked all the fight out of her.

"And if you had told M. Benjamin?" I hammered the words at her.

"He might still be alive."

The words fell into the silence, and spread like ripples. She looked devastated.

"You don't really believe that," I said gently.

She stared at me.

"If you'd gone to him about the rumors as soon as you heard them, what would have happened?"

"Nothing. He didn't live in that world. He cared about art, not business."

I didn't reply. She could hear the falseness in her words far more clearly than anything I could say.

After a moment, she looked away. "He'd have started digging. And he knew everyone. Plus he could put together snippets of information into a whole picture better than anyone I'd ever met."

I nodded. That matched what I'd learned elsewhere. "So?"

"He'd have figured it out. Without a doubt," she said heavily.

"And then?"

"It depended on who it was," she said. "If he had any connection to them at all, he'd have gone to that person. To give them a chance to explain."

She glanced at me. "As he must have done last night."

"You think that's what got him killed?"

"I do," she said.

So did I.

Now what did we do with that?

"Did you tell the *surete* your theory?" I asked.

"How could I?" she said. "Without knowing about the copies, the motive makes no sense. If I admitted to the copying now, they'd never look past that. I'd be in jail within the hour."

She tried to smile. "And they'd bury the key to my cell so deep in forensic analysis that they'd never look past me to find the real killer."

Unfortunately, she was probably right. We both knew it. And there was no humor to be found in her current situation.

I focused on the information I needed to help her.

"M. Benjamin seemed to be headed either to or from the gallery that night," I said. "Do you know which?"

"The *surete* asked that exact question," she said. "And I have no answer for you, either."

"Did you see him that day?"

"No. I didn't even know he was in town."

"Was he at the gallery?"

"No-one has told me if he was. And they would have."

There was that. I made a note to double check with Marie as well, to see what the gallery's security recordings from yesterday showed. Though she hadn't alerted me to anyone spotting M. Benjamin on it. And she would have.

BY THE TIME Annegret's legal team arrived at ten, we'd examined the evidence we had from a dozen different directions. And the conclusion was always the same. Annegret had no idea what the victim was doing in the alley that night. Or even why he was in town. He had known too many people to winnow it down to a few possible suspects.

After Annegret and I had spent an hour in a meeting with Dominic and Elise Marbach, I knew two things. One was that I couldn't stand another minute in their company. And the second was that these two lawyers were never going to help my client stay out of jail.

On his own, Dominic had seemed very competent, even impressive. But his sister? I couldn't tell if she thought our mutual client was guilty of both murders, or just one. Or if she simply didn't care.

Either way, her notion of a legal strategy seemed to be for Annegret to say nothing to the police. Or anyone else.

Which included me.

I could have lived with that. I'd pretty much got everything I was likely to get out of my client for the moment anyway. But Elise Marbach's entire focus seemed to be on minimizing Annegret's eventual sentence. The one both she and Annegret seemed to consider inevitable. At least Annegret considered it inevitable by the time Elise was done with her.

I made a few attempts to break Annegret out of the spell of hopelessness that Elise was only deepening, but got nowhere. Except with Elise, who seemed to have decided I was the enemy, and didn't belong there.

Dominic, on the other hand, seemed to consider Annegret a victim of someone who was out to frame her, and my investigation as her only hope of escape from it. But he did little to counteract—or even challenge—his sister. The few questions he did ask Elise either scoffed at or ignored, and each interaction seemed to send Annegret even deeper into her funk.

I finally couldn't stand it any longer and made an excuse to leave, telling Annegret I'd be in touch as soon as I had more information. As I closed her office door behind me, I could hear Elise counseling Annegret that she shouldn't be accepting my calls. Or talking to me any further. Which, according to her, would only "make the already strong case against her much, much worse."

I rolled my eyes and sent a text to Marie. "Need info on client's lawyers stat: Marbachs, Elise and Dominic."

It was mostly Elise that concerned me. Dominic I wasn't too worried about. Except he had recommended his sister to Annegret, knowing exactly how difficult her legal situation already was. He had to have known how Elise would operate.

Or was there something else at play?

I had the strong feeling there were more—and deadlier—players in this particular game than we'd managed to identify so far. And I kept running into dead ends trying to identify them.

While Annegret's credibility was seeping away. Taking her freedom and her future with it.

But this second murder had changed things. And I was beginning to think Arturo Benjamin's death was the key to all of it. Why was he even in town? And how had he ended up in the alley behind Carli Fine Arts?

Setting my jaw, I left the gallery. I had answers to find.

CHAPTER THIRTY-THREE

Marie came through with Arturo Benjamin's travel details, giving me my starting point. He had flown into Geneva at eight a.m. on Tuesday morning, and he'd been staying at L'Étoile, as I was. Which was more helpful than I'd anticipated, thanks to a very knowledgeable—and chatty—concierge at L'Étoile. I explained I was investigating an art case and needed to verify M. Benjamin's timetable. Clearly aware of his expertise in the field, she may have assumed I was working with, or for, him. My being a guest there too was a helpful detail. And that she was such a fan of his.

Since she was already being helpful, I was able to avoid telling her that he'd been killed. The police had managed to keep that information quiet, and I suspected they might not be best pleased if I leaked it now.

M. Benjamin, she told me, had been driven by chauffeured car from the airport straight to the hotel, where he sat down to one of their magnificent breakfasts in the formal dining room, while his case was taken up to his room.

He'd stayed with them often enough that the bell captain had personally unpacked his single suitcase and made sure his suits were properly hung the way he liked them, and his toiletries laid out on the bathroom counter.

"He is such a gentleman," she enthused. "All the staff take delight in doing these little chores for him. Though he has his favorites, of course, among those of us who have known him for more than twenty years. And since he is also one of our favorites, only in unusual circumstances is he assisted by a newer employee."

"And was that the case on Tuesday?" I asked.

"No, no. It was his old favorites," she said. "We hadn't seen him in a number of months, so all of us were most pleased to hear he was coming. And made a point of ensuring we were available to assist him should he need it."

"And how long… is he staying on this visit?" I asked. Hoping she hadn't noticed my slight stumble over the tense.

"He is booked for two more days," she said. "He made a point of stopping to chat with me first, even before he went in for breakfast, that first day. He often does so." She looked smug.

"Since he travels without a secretary, he trusts me to make certain bookings for him. Such a cultured man. He wanted tickets for the opera on Tuesday night. And then his favorites among the museums and galleries." Which she reeled off from memory, bless her. "Plus a gallery exhibit opening on Wednesday morning. He also has an appointment at the Carli Fine Arts gallery this afternoon. And he explained, in that gracious way of his, that the timing of each of these is important because he plans to leave Friday morning. Though business might keep him here until Saturday."

So when he arrived, had he planned to meet with Annegret this afternoon? Or just visit the gallery? The former was more likely, though Annegret seemingly hadn't known about it. And he hadn't intended to return home until tomorrow. My mind raced at the news.

I still didn't know why he'd made this particular visit, though the timing suggested he was investigating something, which he then intended to discuss with Annegret. And it had gotten him killed.

I hid my reaction as well as I could, and expressed my very genuine admiration that M. Benjamin was so esteemed here.

"Oh, he's a wonderful man," she said. "And despite who he is—he still has that impish sense of humor that he lets creep through now and again."

I hoped I wouldn't have to break the news of Benjamin's murder to her. I already felt badly enough.

"And were you able to arrange all those tickets as well as the appointment for today?"

"Of course," she said matter-of-factly. "It is all about knowing who to talk to. And having a certain reputation, of course."

"Oh?"

She nodded. "Yes. They know I won't waste their time. Or send guests who lack the heart to appreciate what they will see. If you respect their expertise, they will respect yours."

I found the idea of such a network fascinating, if snobbish. And briefly wondered what the staff here made of me.

"Did M. Benjamin have other appointments he needed you to make?"

"Oh, no, not this time," she said. "He was most apologetic and explained that it was such a flying visit, there was time for very little. And since he wasn't sure how long exactly some of the key components would take..."

I wondered why the apparently very astute Arturo Benjamin had told this friendly concierge so much about his trip. And where he'd be. Perhaps he was genuinely gregarious.

But it would be a simple way to throw someone looking to follow him off the scent, as it were. Or to leave a record of sorts of what he was planning. Just in case...

Especially when she was so very chatty.

But if it was the latter—how could he have known?

Everything I'd learned so far told me that this was a man who saw patterns, saw them across time and through the lens of art. He must have seen something, heard something. Somewhere. He knew what he was involving himself in. And how dangerous it could be.

And he did it anyway. For Annegret? Or for justice?

Perhaps it was both.

Now it was up to me to figure out what he had learned that made him suspicious. And where he'd gone, who he had talked to, in order to verify it.

Someone had killed him for that insight. And I was going to find them. Whatever it took.

I made mental notes of everything the concierge had told me, and thanked her for her time. As I left by one of the hotel's double doors, I spotted Inspector Gabriel and one of his officers coming in the other. I'd been just in time. He wouldn't be pleased to find out I'd been asking questions. I hoped he was tactful with that poor woman.

She was going to take the news of Benjamin's death hard.

And I needed to hurry and follow the trail he'd left with her. Before Inspector Gabriel had a chance to get ahead of me, and shut me down entirely.

———

I GRABBED a coffee and made quick notes of the information I'd just gathered from the chatty concierge. Then I called Annegret.

"Did you know Arturo Benjamin was planning to visit your gallery this afternoon?" I asked when she answered

Her shocked inhale told me everything I needed to know. "No. I didn't," she said.

"Was it usual for him to drop in there unannounced ?"

"No. He was very old world that way—courtly. He treated the gallery as if it was my home, and would never think of just appearing without an appointment."

I'd suspected as much. "Might he have made an appointment with someone else?"

"I doubt it. Normally they would have told me…" She hesitated. "But these are not normal times. I can check."

"Only if you can do so without bringing attention to yourself," I said. "Someone killed M. Benjamin, presumably because he asked the wrong question of the wrong person."

Silence. Then, "I'll be careful," she said.

"Thank you," I said, and rang off.

Then I visited each of the destinations Arturo Benjamin had booked. None of them were appointments with individuals—they were art galleries and museums. I showed his photo to receptionists and ticket takers. All of them recognized him, most with sadness—the news of his death had begun to leak out. It seemed he was known and loved in this city. At least on the artistic side of it.

All of them said he'd visited as he'd planned. If he'd met with anyone, or spent time on a particular exhibit, none of them could tell me. And I saw no benefit in drawing more attention to myself and my investigation by probing. Not yet, at least.

Instead I wandered through the paintings, paying particular attention to the old masters on display. What had he been looking for? And what had he noticed? Trying to see through a dead man's eyes.

It was a rather creepy feeling, but I persisted.

I had a murder to solve.

At the last museum I visited, a young woman with subtle makeup and dark, curly hair, wearing the uniform of one of their guides, came up to me as I left the reception desk.

"Pardon," she said as I made my way across the crowded space towards the elevator. "I couldn't help but hear. You had questions about M. Benjamin?"

I stopped and turned to face her. "I did. Did you know him?"

She nodded. "Yes. He came here often, to view his favorites among the old masters."

"And did he do so yesterday?"

"Yes. He spent half an hour with them."

At least I was on the right track. "Did you talk to him?"

"Very briefly," she said. "He asked after my studies. But he has so little time when he visits Geneva. I didn't keep him."

"I don't suppose he mentioned where he was going after he left here?" I said. Knowing it was a long shot.

"You are looking into his death?" she asked steadily, though her brown eyes were sad.

"Yes. Whoever did this needs to pay for it."

"Yes. They do," she said, giving a firm nod, agreement and decision in one. "I've never told anyone this before. He asked me to keep the confidence. But now..." The words trailed off and she wiped at a tear.

"You should talk to the people at XTC Tech," she continued, to my surprise. "They're out at the Freeport."

The Geneva Freeport has quite a reputation in the art world. The oldest freeport in the world, it has always specialized in the tax-free storage of art and other collectibles. Anything stored there is considered "in transit" under the local tax laws—meaning it is duty and tax free. Art worth billions of dollars is stored there while its value grows.

"XTC Tech has their offices inside the Freeport?" I asked, momentarily distracted by the information. How had I missed that?

"Sure," she said, looking at me a little strangely. "Where else? A lot of art gets stored there. Still."

She meant after the Swiss government changed the tax laws—especially tightening the rules on long term storage—in order to reduce tax avoidance and money laundering. Which could be relevant to this case. But I was more interested in XTC Tech's connection with M. Benjamin.

"Why XTC Tech?" I asked her.

"He does work for them, sometimes," she said. "Very quietly, so no-one ever knows. Only when they need his kind of expertise, which is—was—unique. It is why he was in town."

This was new. "How did you know?"

"I studied under him," she said with a blush. "Only a few courses, though, but one was on authentication. He...shared that information with several of us. In confidence."

She swallowed, hard. "He was an extraordinary teacher. He never hesitated to share his own knowledge, his skills. But he was always learning—took such joy in it. That was what inspired me the most. Inspired all of us, I think."

She must be very good as well. From what little I'd learned, he taught rarely, no more than one or two courses each year, and the competition was fierce, since he took only a few very select students for each course.

"Thank you. That information will make a difference," I told her. And I meant it.

She smiled. "I hope so. Because he made *such* a difference."

CHAPTER THIRTY-FOUR

After a harrowing trip on a very busy freeway, my taxi deposited me outside a huge, fairly nondescript warehouse complex that ran between the Voie Central Viaduct and the railway yards in the municipality of Lancy. This was the Geneva Freeport. Established in 1888, it remains a favorite tax haven with uber-wealthy art collectors around the globe.

Having XTC Tech so conveniently on-hand here to evaluate that very valuable art made good business sense, but the connection still bothered me, for some reason. I put the feeling aside, for the moment.

I was more interested in what Arturo Benjamin had uncovered here that sent him to the Carli gallery. And his death.

I nearly got lost twice, winding my way through the maze that was the freeport, but I eventually found the XTC Tech office. A plain wooden door with a small sign on it led me to a starkly minimalist reception space that gave little indication of the work they did here.

To my surprise, my name was recognized immediately and I was welcomed graciously. Annegret had obviously followed through on letting them know to expect a visit from me. Presumably because of that, my assigned guide was their technical supervisor, Babette Adjani. And she didn't hesitate to confirm that M. Benjamin had paid a visit to XTC Tech the previous day.

"He consults for us, on occasion. He is…," she paused, and I saw the awareness hit her in a wave of sorrow. "Or rather, he was, an expert in techniques. Specifically techniques and materials specific to various time periods. Especially for the old masters. Which canvases, which paints, which kinds of brushes were used in a particular timeframe. Which ones were used, and when, by which artists."

"Pardon my asking, but I'd have thought that would be basic knowledge for the kind of work you do," I said.

She nodded. "Of course. And there is nothing to pardon. It is basic. And we have access to databases of very specific information that we use in verifying these masterpieces."

Of course, they would have. "And yet you called in M. Benjamin?"

"We did," she said. "We are experts when it comes to the scientific analysis of these works. Not even the most minute details can escape our sophisticated sensors, our highly trained staff."

"But…?"

"But this is as much a science as an art. Because we are dealing with sublime works of art. And the great artists had students, and imitators, to say nothing of the forgers who have tried their hand at fooling the art world over the centuries…"

I said nothing. This was feeling more like a lecture than an answer.

She smiled. "You will have to forgive my enthusiasm. Working with some of the art we do, sometimes it is a little overwhelming. Even if most of the day we consider the chemical composition of a fleck of very dry paint. Or analyze the scan of an underpainting, or the angle of a brushstroke."

She still hadn't answered me. "Go on," I said, in the hopes it would lead to an actual answer.

"The masters—they were innovators. Take Leonardo's brushstrokes, his use of perspective. They evolved over time, yes. But genius isn't consistent. It is not enough to say—this is his style of painting, this is the palette—or even the brushstroke—he used in this particular year. For he might have gone back, to an earlier style. Or tried something that he would not use again for several years. You understand?"

Now I did. "You're saying that even with every technical tool and database at your disposal, sometimes authenticating an individual painting also requires an artistic evaluation that puts the work in the historic context of the artist's *oeuvre* as well as his or her timeline."

Now I felt like I was lecturing, but it was effective. She beamed at me. "Yes. That is it, exactly."

"And you brought in M. Benjamin for these types of examinations."

Again she nodded. "Sometimes we did. Sometimes the client did. M. Benjamin was one of the few evaluators that all could agree on. Always. And now he is gone. Murdered. It is… criminal."

It certainly was.

"The day he was last here…" I began.

"It was just yesterday. It seems impossible that now…" She broke off. Swiped at her eyes.

"You met with him?"

"I did."

"And did he evaluate a painting for you?"

"He certainly did. Or at least he started to."

"Started to? He didn't finish?"

"No. He spent his usual time with the work, reviewing our findings. And then he said he needed to do a little review of the historical sources. He made a booking for this morning, to come back and review the work again. At which point he would give us his answer. Though of course, he never returned."

She discreetly blinked away a hint of tears.

"And was this usual for him?"

"Yes. Though not with every painting, you understand. Usually he would spend an hour or two with the painting and our analyses. And then he would tell us. But occasionally he would take more time, usually overnight, though sometimes longer. It depended."

"On what?"

"On which sources he needed to consult with, or verify, I suppose," she said. "He never specified, and we never asked. His determinations were never successfully challenged, you see."

She blushed a little, and gave me a sideways look. "Personally, I always thought there was a little magic in his evaluations. As if the artist spoke directly to him over the centuries, and gave him the truth about the work."

Maybe she was right, at that. But M. Benjamin's magic wasn't why I was here.

"Which work was he evaluating?" I asked. Half anticipating, half dreading what I was sure I'd hear.

"A small Rembrandt," she said. "A beautiful thing."

Oh no. "A Rembrandt?" I said. "A portrait of an old woman?" And I described the painting I'd seen in Annegret's gallery the day I'd arrived in Geneva.

"Yes, that's the one," she said, looking perplexed. "However did you know?"

"I'm afraid that's confidential, for now," I said. "As I suspect is the name of the owner of that work?"

She nodded.

It would have to be. "Is that the only work that M. Benjamin evaluated for you while he was in town?"

"No, actually. It isn't. There was one other. Though that one he had no hesitation in declaring authentic."

"And that painting?"

"Another small Rembrandt," she said. "But I can say nothing more."

"Just one further question, and I promise I won't ask for details," I said.

"Go on."

"Were both Rembrandts brought in by the same client?" I asked.

"I'm not sure I should…" she began.

"That small detail gives nothing away," I said. Hoping it would be enough. "You've respected the confidentiality of your clients. And your answer could be the key in finding the person who killed M. Benjamin."

Something flared in her eyes, and she nodded. "Yes. It was the same."

And just like that, the pieces of the jigsaw puzzle rearranged themselves in my head.

"Do you have photos of those paintings?" I asked.

Wordlessly, she handed me her tablet in portrait mode. "Scroll right to see the other."

I did so, scrolling back and forth between the two paintings as the clues I'd missed slowly stacked up, one after another.

Half an hour later, I left XTC Tech with copies of both photos on my phone. And a sinking feeling that I now knew exactly what I was dealing with.

CHAPTER THIRTY-FIVE

Another harrowing taxi ride took me back to my hotel. I checked in with Marie, and updated my notes. The day had cleared, and the sunshine beckoned me, so I walked to the gallery. The air was still chilly, but the sunshine on beautiful old stone buildings gave the day a feeling of warmth. In contrast to the mellow beauty of Old Town, Geneva practically hums with activity, and that energy drove my thinking as I walked. My steps quickened as the picture in my head changed and came into a new, sharp focus.

I was almost there. The feeling energized me, and I strode out with purpose. As I reached the gallery, I was seeing it with new eyes. For me this case had started here, and I now suspected I knew how and maybe even why.

Now all I had to do was prove it.

I nodded at Giselle as I breezed past her. Barely pausing at Annegret's office door, I rapped twice, and strode in. She was behind her desk, with Dominic Marbach sitting across from her. He seemed to be trying to cheer her up. Elise was gone.

Good.

"Do you have anywhere you need to be after this?" I asked him.

He looked startled, and Annegret began dabbing at her reddened eyes. If she was hoping to pull herself together, she had a long way to go.

"No," Dominic said. "I cleared my schedule for today. Annegret…" He gestured towards her. "I'm here for as long as she needs me."

"I see. I need a few minutes with our client, if you don't mind?"

"Of course not," he said. "Let me know when you're ready for me."

"Thanks, I will," I said, and waited for him to leave the room before I sat down.

I turned to my client. Who was still a mess. Silently I took a tissue from the box that had somehow appeared on the desk since I left here earlier in the day, and passed it to her.

She sniffed, dabbed at her eyes, then gave up and blew her nose heartily.

"That's better," I said, and passed her another tissue.

She dumped both soggy tissues in the bin by her desk, gave me a searching look, and straightened her spine. "What did you find?" she asked me in a decent attempt at a brisk tone.

"You won't like it," I said.

"Probably not. Does it end with me in a jail cell?"

"No. Not if you have even a modicum of the courage I saw when you hired me."

"Then it has to be an improvement over the rest of this horrible day," she said, waving me to a chair opposite her. "Just tell me."

"I have two questions first," I said. "Have you ever handled a small Rembrandt, a portrait showing a young woman in her kitchen. A painting very similar to the one on display in your gallery, but with a subject a good twenty or thirty years younger? A daughter, perhaps?"

"No, I don't think so," she said, frowning a little. Then stood up and opened her hidden cabinet. "Wait…"

She pulled out a blue binder, flipped several pages, then ran a finger down the middle of the right-hand page, her eyes intent.

Closing it slowly, she stood up, put the ledger away, and looked at me. "No, never," she said definitely. "I've never even heard of one so similar. But let me check the *catalogue raisonné* for his works."

After a few minutes with the internet, she turned back to me. "They have no mention of such a work. It has to be a fraud," she said.

"I've just come from XTC Tech," I said. "They currently have both that painting, and one identical to yours at their labs for authentication. I've seen them," I added, to stave off the argument I could see forming.

"And?" she ground out, looking as if she'd been forced to eat the ground glass I heard in her voice.

"They have authenticated the portrait of the younger woman," I said, enunciating each word, so there could be no mistake. "And certified the painting similar to yours as a fake."

"But..." she began, then closed her lips tight around the rest of it as I handed her my phone, open to the first painting.

"Scroll left," I said. Then watched as she did exactly what I'd done, scrolling back and forth between the two portraits, the old woman and the younger one. Zooming in and out again and again.

"But they're nearly identical. How...?" she said at last, still staring at my phone. Looking up, meeting my eyes. "Where...?"

It was almost helpless, that word. Yet there was steel behind it. She'd seen exactly what I'd seen.

And Annegret Carli hadn't worked so long and so hard to have everything taken from her now. Not without a fight.

Good.

"I don't know," I said. "But Arturo Benjamin verified their findings. At least of the younger woman. He hadn't yet finalized his decision that the other was a forgery."

"When?"

"Yesterday."

She seemed to collapse in on herself. "And then he came here?"

"He did. And it gets worse."

She didn't answer, just turned and retrieved a bottle of

Hennessy XO cognac and two snifters from the cabinet behind her. Looked at me. I nodded.

"How?" she asked as she handed me a glass.

"Both paintings were sent to XTC Tech for authentication by the same client."

"Not this gallery?"

"They wouldn't tell me. But a copy of the painting of the old woman is still hanging in your gallery," I said. "I checked as I came in."

"The fragment of frame we saw in the video," she said. "They did copy it."

"I think so. I took a photo," I said, and handed her my phone with the photo I'd taken.

She stared at it for a moment, then zoomed in on several sections. Exactly as I'd done. Her face grew stonier with every detail she examined.

"I need to compare it to the one XTC Tech has," she said at last, and passed my phone back.

I pulled out my phone. "Check your email. The XTC Tech version is on the left, the one hanging in your gallery on the right."

She opened it, enlarged both to the maximum, then flipped back and forth between details on XTC Tech's version and hers. Finally she sat back, closed her eyes for a moment. Then she opened them and glared at me.

"They're both copies. They have to be. Extremely good ones."

I nodded. "You're sure the original of the older woman is still in secure storage?"

"Yes. I checked two days ago," she said, and leaned forward. "But this could be good, couldn't it? Could the copy that was stolen from here help us trace whoever is behind this?"

"There's a problem with that," I said.

"Just tell me," she said again, and the steel in her voice was harder and sharper now. "All of it."

I told her what I'd put together so far, and watched her use every smidgen of that courage I'd seen before to understand and accept the extent of the betrayal she faced.

Finally she looked up. "What do I need to do?"

I let out the breath I hadn't realized I was holding. There were so many ways this could have gone badly. Without her full cooperation, I had nothing.

So I told her everything.

She handled it better than I'd had any right to expect.

"Fine," was the only thing she said. "Set it up."

———

WE CALLED DOMINIC BACK IN. Once the three of us were sitting around the table, I told him, too.

Oh, not the whole thing. Not yet. Just my concerns about Arturo Benjamin's death, and how it might tie to the rumors of forged paintings. My fear that the police would arrest Annegret as their primary suspect before we could find the answers and gather the evidence we needed to convince them otherwise.

I didn't mention my recent explorations, or any of the work my team had been doing. I had some information to gather and a few facts to check first.

Dominic was remarkably patient with both of us, given that he'd gone through a very similar discussion with us in at least two previous meetings that same day. He wasn't quite a good as he thought he was at hiding the amused arrogance he felt at my lack of progress. 'Annegret's imported PI from Canada.' Clearly I'd become something of a joke.

I couldn't entirely blame him, since I had shared nothing of what I'd recently learned. Nor did I tell him about Adrien Keller from Interpol, much less about Birgitte Jessup and her 'clients'. That didn't stop me from resenting his attitude. No-one likes to be taken less than seriously. Much less be the butt of a joke.

No matter. He'd come to regret it, when I eventually laid my cards on the table.

More to the point, he finally agreed to do what we needed—to set up a meeting for the following afternoon, in his firm's conference room, with all the key players in attendance. Including Annegret and myself, both lawyers, Inspector Gabriel, a couple of key players from SaltonSecure and all of Annegret's staff.

There were only four staff left, after all. Two associate managers; Giselle Anton and Mai-lin Yee—who had been hired to replace Jana Bertrand. One of them would be promoted to fill Amara's vacant position as manager. Geoffrey Stern, who worked part-time as a framer. And of course Jacinta Roark, the restorer—and copyist—Annegret relied so heavily on.

The gallery would be closed for the day. Which oddly, had been the only point Annegret had argued with me on.

"If you want this nightmare to end, we need everyone," I'd said flatly, and she'd caved.

Dominic didn't like any of it, and argued at length, but finally Annegret reminded him that she was the client. He looked worried, muttered something about his sister under his breath.

"What was that?" Annegret asked.

"You need to know," he said clearly. "Your situation cannot be taken lightly. Elise may refuse to represent you if you will not accept her advice."

"That is her choice," Annegret said. "This is mine. There are other lawyers in Geneva. Good ones. But I will need an answer from her within the hour. And from you as well, if you are unable to work with me on this."

He stopped arguing at that point, and confirmed every detail with her. "Let me talk to Elise," he said.

"Why don't you call her now?" I suggested. No reason to make this easy for either of them. Not given the 'support' Elise had been giving Annegret.

Dominic texted his sister instead. His phone rang seconds later, and he read off Annegret's list of instructions. He listened for several minutes with no expression at all on his face. Then ended the call.

"She will represent you, as will I," he said. "However, we will draw up a document that spells out exactly what you've requested, and that we have informed you of the potential consequences. I'll need that signed and returned by this evening."

"You'll have it," Annegret said. He stood up, shook our hands, and left.

Annegret watched him close the door behind him with a little snick. Then turned to me. "Are you sure about this?" she asked, her voice a little shaky.

"Of course," I said. Letting no sign of the nerves I was feeling show. "As sure as I can be without the final pieces. Which my team is digging for now."

"And if you can't get those answers? Or they are not what you expected?"

"We needed to move fast," I reminded her. "You know we did. Yes, it's a risk. But that's why the meeting is tomorrow afternoon. You can always cancel it in the morning. Or reschedule."

"And what signal does that send to the *surete*, if I do so?"

"It can't be a worse one than the strategy half your legal team was advancing earlier—confessing to a lesser offense."

"Which I would not agree to. Ever. Since I did not commit the crime."

I was glad to hear it. And that she was still bristling over that one. I couldn't blame her.

There was no trace of the defeated woman I'd seen that morning. At least the news I'd had to share with her had done that much for her. Now we just needed to clear her name.

Just.

I gathered my own courage. "Let's see where we stand in the morning, shall we?" I said.

She grimaced, but didn't argue. I doubted either of us would get much sleep tonight. Though for different reasons.

———

BY THE TIME I left the gallery to walk back to my hotel it was already dark, and the streetlights glittered against the wet pavement. It must have rained while I was in the gallery, because it wasn't raining now. A wind had come up, though, straight off the mountains and gusting across the lake. I pulled my collar up, wishing I'd packed a warmer coat. Or at least a scarf.

I quickened my pace, my boot heels ringing on the sidewalk. My thoughts sped up to match as I tried to prioritize the questions I needed answered before tomorrow's meeting.

As I ran through the meetings I'd had that day, the pieces of the jigsaw puzzle rearranged themselves again in my head. It was discovering the location of the freeport that did it. Together with Arturo Benjamin's connection with XTC Tech. So conveniently located at the freeport.

Despite the best efforts of the Swiss government, too many of the transactions there remained anonymous. And the exact nature of art sales had always been obscured. "Privacy" the auction houses said. Combined with the tax-free status of any transactions occurring within the freeport? It was a license to print money for art dealers and criminals alike.

Now the fact that this case revolved around Geneva made sense. But I still didn't get why it was Annegret Carli Fine Arts that was at the center of it all. Unless somehow her practice of copying masterpieces and displaying only the copies had somehow triggered this?

I had more work to do. And my team would be starting their day in a few hours. But I could feel the pieces starting to fall into place. All we needed was proof.

A confession would be good, too.

I walked even faster, my heels ringing a crescendo against the sidewalk. It was time to end this.

CHAPTER THIRTY-SIX

I spent half the night and most of the morning working with my team, digging deeper, then reviewing everything we'd pulled together. By noon on Friday, I was ready.

And so was Dominic Marbach. Or at least, his conference room was.

I'd arrived more than an hour early—I wanted time to set up. And I wanted to be the first one there. Except for Dominic, of course, who had curtly shown me to his firm's conference room.

"I hope you know what you're doing, you and Annegret," he'd said as he unlocked the room. A glance at his watch. "You're early, so wait here—I'll send my assistant. She arranges these things. I'll see you at two."

Perfect.

I glanced around me. The conference room was spacious, with large windows giving a spectacular view of Lake Geneva. They'd even centered it on the fountain. After last night's windstorm, drifts of golden leaves lay like gilt along the water's edge and lapped against the fountain. Beyond the lake, trees burned crimson and gold against the mountains, hazy in the distance, and a deep blue sky. On the horizon, though, banks of dark clouds were gathering.

It was the second of November, and the air was sharp and heavy with the scent of a coming storm. You could feel change in the air as autumn surrendered to winter. If I were painting this, I'd call it *Waiting*.

Or maybe that was just my own mood.

Inside the room, dark-painted walls gave the illusion of warmth. A massive rectangular mahogany table was surrounded by enough deeply plush chairs to easily seat everyone. Even the guests I hadn't told Dominic we were expecting. I'd gambled he'd wouldn't be able to resist trying to intimidate Annegret into doing things their way with a setting that dwarfed her meeting. Looks like I'd been right.

Let's hope I was right about the rest of it.

Though I didn't really doubt it—not once I had a few key pieces, starting with what I'd learned from Benjamin's former student. Now it was time for the final act

And staging was going to be important.

I sauntered over to the windows, played for a moment with the window coverings. They had solar blinds—remote controlled ones —that would remove the distraction of that view at the touch of a button. Sweet.

Leaving the blinds fully up, I tested the remote. It also controlled a screen on the far wall, and the room's sound systems. Perfect. I pocketed it and surveyed the room, focusing on the seating.

The power seat would be facing the door. I wanted Annegret there. And I'd take the seat on her right, with my back to the view.

Dropping my bag and laptop on the table, I sat down and considered the strategic advantages of that spot. Yes, this would do. It clearly put me as Annegret's right hand, not either of her lawyers. It was the perfect spot to keep an eye on everyone's reactions. And to run the tech as we unveiled the surprises Annegret and I had planned.

As well as the ones I'd planned with my team. The ones Annegret knew nothing about. I was particularly looking forward to those.

Tucking my bag out of the way, I set up my laptop, connected to their tech and tested it. All good. I stood up and glanced around the room. I was ready.

My eyes went again to the clouds gathering on the horizon. I smiled to myself. Nothing like a really good storm to clear the air.

———

AS THE PARTICIPANTS gathered in the meeting room, I watched the interactions with interest. The first ten minutes were tense. Everyone helped themselves to coffee and small pastries from the narrow table at the far end of the room, then either formed small groups or immediately found a seat.

Inspector Gabriel arrived looking harried and impatient, and judging by the heaped plate he'd sat down with, without lunch. He'd glared at Keller the moment he arrived, and glared harder when he spotted Jessup. Both of whom looked inscrutable.

Annegret's two lawyers looked polished, the two mid-level executives from SaltonSecure looked confident.

Annegret looked momentarily surprised and then resigned to see her restorer take a seat amongst the gallery staff, though she quickly assumed the confident mask she'd worn when we first met. No-one seemed to react to the arrival of Babette Adjani from XTC Tech, which did surprise me.

Once people were seated and introductions made, I clicked a button and the blinds silently descended, taking away most of the distraction of the view. And Annegret took over.

"I have to thank you all for being here on such short notice," she said in a clear, carrying voice, looking around the table at each participant as she spoke. "I apologize for that, but these are unusual circumstances."

A low murmur ran around the table, recognition of just how unusual they were. I was watching Inspector Gabriel's reaction. He looked up, and something flashed across his face. Was that triumph?

If so, I'd been right that he'd zeroed in on Annegret as his prime suspect and intended to arrest her. We just had less time than I'd thought.

I glanced at Annegret, gave a tiny nod.

She gave me a flicker of a smile.

"As all of you are aware, two people I valued very much have been murdered outside my gallery," Annegret began.

In her clear tones, murder became an ugly sound. She uttered it like a curse.

And perhaps it was.

"A thorough police investigation is underway," she continued. "Which is why Inspector Gabriel has joined us. However, with the murder of Arturo Benjamin, my revered mentor, I can no longer dismiss the rumors of fraud and forgeries that have circled the gallery for a number of months now."

She glanced around the table. "Those rumors, and newer, darker ones following the murders, are linked to my name and my gallery. I am being accused, judged and convicted in the court of public opinion. And perhaps outside of it."

She paused, and let her gaze run around the table again, lingering here and there. I held my breath. So much depended on her now.

Could she pull it off?

A rustle across the table caught my attention. Elise Marbach made as if to speak. Uh oh.

But at a warning look from Annegret, Dominic put a hand on his sister's arm, and she subsided.

"I am telling you now. *I* am not guilty. Of any of it," Annegret said."And I intend to prove it.

With help from all of you in this room today. I believe that each of you holds a piece, which together creates the key to untangling this ugly conspiracy. A conspiracy that has resulted in at least two murders."

Again, the word was a curse.

"With your help, I believe we can solve it. Here. Now."

Before anyone could contradict her—and by my estimation, there were several who were itching to do so—she stepped back a little and turned to me.

"Barbara, if you will?"

———

I LOWERED the screen on the wall behind Annegret, and projected the first of the images I'd prepared. The two Rembrandt paintings, side by side. Taking up the entire screen.

Both images were of an old woman in her kitchen. One painting was from XTC Tech, the other was currently hanging in the Carli Fine Arts gallery.

They were identical.

Even shown at the highest resolution, enlarged multiple times on the screen, every detail, every brush stroke looked the same to the naked eye.

Silence fell, as everyone looked from the images on the screen to Annegret and back. Waiting for an explanation.

She said nothing, as I flashed a second image; the two Rembrandt paintings under review by XTC Tech. This time it was the old woman in her kitchen again, and the younger woman in hers. Seen side by side like that, it was clear they too were identical —in every detail but the age of the subject herself, and the color of her dress.

Every other detail—background, the way she sat, the knife she held, the onion she was slicing, the glimpse of the dark kitchen behind her, even the coarse fabric of her dress—was identical.

A murmur ran round the room, followed by a silence so thick you could touch it. Annegret let it hang there, looking around the table.

"So you see," she said after a precisely calculated moment, as I flashed on enlarged images comparing tiny details of the two paintings, side by side. Then the same enlarged details, but of all three paintings, shown lengthwise across the screen,

"There is no question we are dealing with forgeries," she said. "And fraud. This painting currently hangs in my gallery," she said as I flashed the image of the old woman on the screen. "I believe it to be a forgery."

There was several gasps around the table and Keller gave me a hard look. Jessup, however, looked amused.

"This one is being investigated for authenticity by an outside firm," Annegret said as I flashed up the matching image from XTC Tech.

"While this one," she continued while I showed the image of the younger woman in the blue dress. "Has been authenticated."

As I flashed up an image of the three paintings side by side— two of the old woman in the black dress, one of the younger woman in the dark blue dress—Annegret paused just long enough for people to take in the impact of seeing them like that.

"The painting on the far right, which depicts the younger woman, was authenticated by Arturo Benjamin," she said. "On the same day he was murdered."

I put up a studio portrait of M. Benjamin that Marie had found for me, looking like the scholar he had been. And watched it hit home around the room.

"I believe that in the process of evaluating this first painting for authenticity," she began, as I flashed the XTC Tech copy of the painting of the older woman up on the screen behind her. "M. Benjamin—Arturo—found details that made him suspicious. Knowing him as I did," she said, with a slight, and very private, quirk of her lips, as if at a fond memory. "I have no doubt he would immediately have gone to ask questions of whomever those details pointed towards."

"And he was found—dead—outside your gallery," Inspector Gabriel broke in, his voice heavily accusatory.

I love it when people are predictable. I flashed the image of the alley behind the gallery and M. Benjamin's body laying there only partially covered under the bright police lights. There was a harsh sound around the table, and Elise glared at me accusingly.

Between them, she and her brother had obviously worked out who was behind Annegret's new strategy. And clearly she thought it incriminated her client.

"He was," Annegret said. "And I believe someone in this room knows why. And that someone? Is. Not. Me."

CHAPTER THIRTY-SEVEN

There was a heavy silence in the meeting room after Annegret's words. No-one seemed to want to be the first to speak.

Perfect.

At Annegret's nod, I put up on the screen the video footage showing Mme. Duvant letting her unidentified and hooded visitor into the gallery via the alley door at midnight, and paused on the image of the two of them.

"The first murder? Was that of this woman. My trusted gallery manager and right hand Amara Duvant," Annegret said. "She was also killed in this same alley. Possibly by this person, who is shown visiting her. At the gallery. At midnight."

Annegret paused, let the silence stretch just that fraction longer than was comfortable. Reading the room. She was good at this.

There was no hint of the beaten woman I'd seen yesterday.

When she continued speaking, I could feel the tension level in the room ratcheting higher.

"Not. By. Me," she said again, emphasizing each word as she met the eyes of those around the table. Spending an extra fraction of a second on the Inspector, on her barracuda of a lawyer. "I was thousands of kilometers away at the time."

As she finished speaking, there was a little rustle around the room. People shifting uncomfortably, turning to exchange glances with colleagues. No one said a word.

I waited for two counts, giving people time to focus on the screen again, and note the date and time stamp. Then I let the video continue as Mme. Duvant and her mystery man, still concealed within his hood, disappeared into the cellar.

The video then cut to the point where they came out of the cellar, both of them carrying cylindrical parcels in plain brown wrapping, as this was the full version Badger had dug out somewhere in SaltonSecure's files.

As the video showed the two of them disappearing into the alley with their parcels, I watched the viewers. Especially the two conservatively dressed executives from SaltonSecure. The more senior of the two women, a VP, looked slightly bored. The other, the manager responsible for Annegret's account, showed a flicker of alarm, immediately hidden under a polished front.

Gotcha.

For an irrational second, I wondered what color her fingernails were.

I had no time for more, as Inspector Gabriel roared out of his seat. "Who is that in the hood? What are they carrying? And why have I not seen this footage before?" he demanded.

I clicked to a static image with the best angle on the hooded man. This was a blurred partial glimpse of his features, barely visible within the hood. I glanced at Keller, who was frowning a little as he jotted something down. That's what I'd thought.

Gabriel was glaring at my client. Who glared back.

"I have no idea," she said. "I was out of the country, remember?"

"It doesn't matter. This footage was shot at your gallery, and it is not the version that was shared with the *surete*. Why not?"

For a fleeting moment she looked confused, and I felt like

applauding. Annegret was a far better actress than I'd had any right to expect.

It was too bad I couldn't have used those skills more—but for this to work, I had to show how fully my client had been set-up by those she trusted.

"I thought the *surete* obtained copies of all of the gallery's security footage directly from our security company, SaltonSecure?" she was saying, and she indicated where their two representatives sat. "Perhaps you should ask them."

As the Inspector turned his glare on them, the two executives exchanged looks. "We will look into it immediately," the VP said smoothly. "And I can promise you an answer by the end of the day."

"And that is the best you can do on information that could help solve two murders?" Annegret asked. "Murders your very expensive security services did nothing to prevent."

She looked to Inspector Gabriel, who was clearly waiting for their response.

"I'm sure we can have an answer for you sooner," the gallery's account manager said quickly, white lines forming at the edges of her mouth.

Annegret gave a slight nod—seemingly to them—and I restarted the video showing Mme. Duvant's visitor's arrival, paused on the timestamp, then segued to the second hooded figure walking past the gallery and down the alley towards the murder site. The video paused on this time stamp, too, then jumped to Mme. Duvant and her midnight visitor exiting into the alley and disappearing out of camera range in the same direction. And paused again on the time stamp.

Then the action picked up with segments of video my team had dug out from shops on both sides of the alley between the gallery and the murder site. The images were jumpy, and fit together like a segment from the early days of cartooning. Not every shop had security on the alley, and many of the cameras were substandard. But my team had done an amazing job of piecing it together into a visual narrative.

The result was very shadowy, and jumped from image to image because of the motion-triggered cameras. But it was possible—just barely—to watch the players of that night. First the second hooded figure, walking past the gallery to the murder site, and disappearing behind the jewelry store. Then the victim and her midnight visitor, also hooded, leaving the gallery and walking towards the jewelry store.

Where they were met by the second hooded figure, who slipped out from behind the store and came up behind them where they stood waiting by the back door. Seeing them like this, it was clear that Mme. Duvant's midnight visitor was the taller of the two hooded figures.

Every eye in the place was riveted on the action unfolding on the screen. Mme. Duvant's midnight visitor turned, and appeared to greet the shorter figure. And I froze the recording.

There was absolute silence in the meeting room.

Until Inspector Gabriel spoke up. "This is all quite interesting, but essentially useless in a criminal investigation. The video quality is so poor, that while we can just see that several humans walked down a segment of the alley, there is nothing identifiable about any of them."

"True," Annegret said into the shocked silence that followed his words. "However, it seemed best to start with the original version of this footage. Which I am sure your officers also viewed at the various establishments along the alley."

Inspector Gabriel gave her a suspicious look and a sharp nod.

"Good. For the purposes of today, however, I asked my consultant," and she nodded towards me. "To have this footage cleaned up a bit, for clarity."

That was my cue.

———

I STARTED THE NEXT RECORDING, which showed the same three as they made the trek down the alley towards the murder scene.

Only this time, Marie and Cory had cleaned up the images and enhanced the color range and the focus. They did an unbelievable job. The resulting footage looked as if it had been filmed for an atmospheric noir film under a halfway competent director.

Only it was in full color. Which deepened the contrasts and highlighted details that had been lost in shadow.

Funny how digital changes everything, I thought as I watched it unfold. You aren't paying for the film—unless you're a Hitchcock aficionado who is determined to capture the entire look and feel of one of his masterpieces in your work. And full color video costs no more than black and white. In fact, scenes shot in color can be changed to black and white in editing with a single command.

You wouldn't think color would matter in scenes shot at night. It hadn't occurred to me that it would, when watching the various security videos for this case—my own bias, formed from a teenage love of noir films, was that night shots were always dark and brooding with little detail. Left to myself, I'd never have thought to push for more than cleaning up what video we had.

Good thing I had a team.

Individually, they're amazing, each in their own way. Put them together, and a kind of alchemy happens. I end up with tools that turn impossible cases into mostly impossible cases.

I was betting it would work again.

It did.

———

FROM WHERE I SAT, I could see the video reflecting off the glass covering a large watercolor on the far wall. The reflection wasn't particularly clear, but it was enough to show me what those gathered around the table were seeing. And I already knew every detail of every frame of that video. Including what was coming.

As the footage again stopped with the three figures standing together at the soon-to-be murder scene, Inspector Gabriel again surged to his feet. "What trickery is this?"

My client considered his flushed face for a moment, then turned to me. "Ms. O'Grady? If you will?"

I nodded to her. "Certainly."

And turned slightly so I was facing Inspector Gabriel directly.

"The original images haven't changed at all," I told him. "They've just been digitally enhanced for clarity."

He pounced, as I'd suspected he might. "Enhanced? You mean added to?"

"Not at all. Merely eliminating shadows and static where possible so the original image was cleaner."

"And why do the official investigators not have these images?" he demanded.

"It is my understanding that they do have them. I believe that your people canvased the shops along the alley the day after the murder, and obtained copies of all the footage available," I said.

Again he gave that sharp nod.

"However, this enhanced version was not finished until this morning. I would be pleased to provide your people with copies of all of it. Including the footage you're about to see, which has only just become available to my team," I added.

Even Annegret had not seen this footage. I wanted her reaction to it to be authentic. And unmistakable. There were sharp eyes in the room today—eyes that wouldn't miss a nuance.

Especially my client's reaction to this next footage—obtained from a small shop across from the murder site. A shop that had a well-hidden camera with a wide angle lens.

Apparently the store owner's teenage daughter was a videophile, with a fascination for new technology. She was using her indulgent father's store as a test site. Neither the camera nor the footage it recorded were part of his security system, and she hadn't checked the recordings since the murder.

No one had realized the video even existed. Until Badger made the connection. And got us copies late last night.

Given what was on that video, I would have expected a team led by the demanding Inspector Gabriel to have ferreted it out days ago. I couldn't help wondering if the official information gathering process had been deliberately sloppy. And if someone inside the investigation was in the pay of the forgers.

But I saw no point in suggesting that now. Especially not when Gabriel's jaw muscles set so hard they looked like they might crack.

"Perhaps you'd like to see the rest of it?" I asked before he could find his words.

Still wordless, he nodded.

I hit a key on my laptop, and the murder of Amara Duvant unfolded on the screen in front of us.

CHAPTER THIRTY-EIGHT

As the images began to play across the screen, I heard several harshly indrawn breaths and a small scream, quickly bitten off. Someone cursed. I couldn't tell if it was Inspector Gabriel or Aiden. Perhaps it was both of them.

The video was hard to watch when you knew the outcome, as everyone here did. Harder still for those who knew the victim. Even I found it hard, and I'd never known Amara Duvant as anything but a name—a murdered woman who had been involved in criminal activities at my client's gallery.

There was a creepy inevitability to the actions as they unrolled on the video. The first time I'd watched it, I'd shuddered, and repressed the impulse to stand up and turn on all the lights. Anything to banish the shadows.

The teenager's hidden camera wasn't quite good enough to record facial expressions, not in that lighting and at that distance, but it was plenty good enough to capture the nuances of their body language.

This was no impulsive action we were watching. This was a cold, deliberate plan. It was clear in the quick sure steps of the shorter hooded figure moving out from a waiting place in the shadows. Clearer still in the sudden hesitation of Duvant's midnight visitor, who hung back a little as Amara moved forward.

There was something that looked to me like shock in that hesitation, as if he'd seen something he hadn't expected. And suddenly realized he'd been leading Amara Duvant to her death.

Because that's what he'd done.

Mme. Duvant herself seemed oblivious to what was happening as she said something and handed the tube she was carrying to the waiting bad guy. Who accepted it with one hand, while raising the other in a smooth motion.

And shot Amara through the heart with the gun that had been concealed from her view.

The shock and horror of that abrupt action was indescribable.

Last night I had watched that moment again and again, forcing myself to take note of the sure movement and perfect aim. The killer was more than comfortable with a gun. Whoever was hiding behind that hood had killed before. I was sure of it.

As I ran the video for those gathered around the conference table, I wasn't watching the reflected screen this time. I was watching their faces. On some faces I saw the same shock and horror I'd felt. I saw others analyzing the crime being committed and reaching their own conclusions about the perpetrator. I didn't see a killer.

Which didn't mean the killer wasn't there.

I could feel the tension in the room spiraling higher and higher as the silent video unfolded. Somehow the silence made it worse. I knew what they were seeing—that moment of still shock after the bullet hit her. Before Amara Duvant fell.

I knew what was coming on the screen. I didn't know what was coming in the conference room. I only knew what I needed to happen. What I'd planned for.

Someone had to break.

On the screen, the two criminals faced each other over Amara Duvant's body, clearly arguing. Duvant's midnight visitor waved the mailing tube at the killer, then held it out of reach. The killer raised the gun again.

There was another frozen moment, then the visitor gave a half shrug, as if it didn't matter, and extended the mailing tube. Which the killer, already holding one mailing tube and the gun, didn't have a free hand to accept.

For a moment everyone watching the video was sure the visitor was a dead man, but instead the killer slid the first tube into a thigh pocket, and grabbed the second mailing tube from the visitor.

Who took a hurried step back, his hands held up in front of him, as if trying to ward off a bullet. Or talk himself out of a suddenly lethal situation.

You could feel the tension in the room as the video paused on the two of them facing each other.

Then the frames moved forward in super slow motion, and the images sharpened further, and bloomed into higher contrast. The true quality of the teenager's tech became apparent as the two images became clearer with every passing second. The shadows lightened to grays and the actual color of less shadowy areas became visible as the two stared at each other. Even skin tones.

Both of the bad guys were dressed all in black, their hoodies up. But for just a moment, as they focused on their confrontation, they had forgotten about keeping their faces hidden. And clearly, neither of them knew about the teenager's hidden camera. A fleeting glimpse of one face gave a suggestion of a light golden brown skin tone. Then the other—pale, almost colorless.

You couldn't hear a thing in the conference room. Not a rustle of movement. Not even breathing.

The tension grew as the video continued, inexorable.

There was another exchange of words, then the two bad guys turned away from each other, began walking towards opposite ends of the alley. With every painfully slow second, first one, then the other turned towards that hidden camera.

At that point, my team had edited the video so that it focused on and followed each one separately. It was cleverly done, and the effect was riveting.

First up was Duvant's midnight visitor, the taller of the two, as he moved farther down the alley, away from the camera. He'd been very careful to avoid the cameras in the gallery, and all we'd seen of him before was glimpses. In the earlier alley videos, the shadows gave us only a tall, lanky figure.

Now it was clear there was toned muscle on that long frame—he wore black athletic wear, and he moved like a runner. Then for a fraction of a second, we saw a partial side view. Light golden brown skin, darker brows and eyes. Not enough to identify, but there was something…

Then he was out of frame, and the other, shorter figure was the focus, moving up the alley. Angling towards that hidden camera.

Again, we saw matte black workout gear, loosely worn. A glimpse of pale, pale skin. A determined stride, hugging the far side of the alley, avoiding the various shop's security cameras. Moving closer and closer to our teenager's hidden camera.

With every step it was clearer. The second bad guy—the killer––was a woman. As fit as her colleague, judging by the way she moved, but even her looser clothing couldn't disguise the subtle curves. Not with the contrast my team had coaxed out of the original video.

They hadn't stopped there, either. As the killer continued to move towards the hidden camera across the alley, the team had zoomed in on her face. Fine white skin was visible, with a glimpse of a lighter eye, that might be pale blue or pale grey. And a wisp of red hair, flaming against the black of her hood.

There were several gasps, a harshly indrawn breath, and a flutter of movement, rapidly quelled. All eyes went to the far end of the table, where Annegret's 'expert copyist' sat statue still, her back erect and her face utterly blank. And her bright red hair cut in a stylish bob.

CHAPTER THIRTY-NINE

"Jacinta?" Annegret demanded in a voice that slid between accusing and broken, her eyes fixed on her restorer and friend. "All these years? I trusted you. And you… this… How could you?"

"Me? How could you even think such a thing?" Jacinta Roark threw back, her head thrust forward as if ready to leap across the table and attack. "All those years—all those *faithful* years of service I gave you? And from a partial glimpse in a badly doctored video, on this one's word"—and she sent an accusatory glare my way—"You're accusing me? You have decided I'm what? A killer? How could you think so little of me?"

For a moment I saw hope mingled with guilt on my client's face, then she swallowed hard and leaned forward. "Tell me that isn't you."

"It isn't me."

I saw the iron descend on Annegret. "All those years," she said. "And you think I can't hear a lie in your voice?"

Jacinta Roark didn't even flinch. Just looked angrier. "I don't care what you think you hear. Clearly you don't know me at all. Never have."

But Inspector Gabriel had heard enough. "Enough," he said, and looked at me.

"Is there more?" he asked as the room fell silent.

I nodded.

"Play it then," he said. And standing, he strode to the door. Where he planted himself firmly. A formidable barrier, as well as a warning to anyone who might consider leaving before we were done.

I let the video run.

As the killer on the screen angled even closer to the hidden camera, she looked back at where her victim's body lay. A small smile crossed her face. Then she increased her pace until she vanished from the camera's view.

But for a fraction of a second the killer had faced the camera directly. I wasn't sure if anyone here had caught that moment. But the camera had.

So had my team.

The screen went blank and I paused the video. For a long moment, no one said a word. Or even moved.

It was Aiden who broke the silence, not Inspector Gabriel, which surprised me. "Is there a better angle on those two?" he asked.

I glanced at Annegret, who wasn't paying attention. To anything, it seemed.

Then at the Inspector, who pulled out his handcuffs and nodded impatiently. I noted him exchanging glances with Aiden as I turned back to my laptop and hit play.

The screen filled with the full-face image of the killer, caught with the beginnings of that smile and a satisfied gleam in her eyes. This time, there could be no question. It was Jacinta Roark.

The collective gasp in the room nearly covered the noise of a chair sliding back as the killer half-stood. Then she took in the Inspector's firm stance blocking the door, handcuffs at the ready. And Aidan, between her and the window, eyes alert. Jacinta sank back down, a feral expression on her face.

She wasn't done yet.

That was fine. I wasn't either.

Jacinta was probably wishing she had her gun. But she'd never have got it through the building's security. Which was *not* handled by SaltonSecure. Another reason I'd chosen to hold this meeting here.

I considered the other faces around the table. Most looked stunned. A few looked relieved. The only one who looked worried was Annegret. I wondered what she was thinking.

I glanced from Aiden to Jessup. Received nods from both. We were good to go.

I hoped they really were ready for this next bit. I hadn't told them everything, either.

At my command, the image of the killer dissolved from the screen, to be replaced by that of the second bad guy. There was no helpful full-face image here. Nothing but that partial image of not quite familiar features. Which often meant only that many people shared the same characteristics.

Slowly the image sharpened, the contrast increased, then paused. It still wasn't enough for recognition, let alone identification.

I scanned the room. Annegret had joined us again from wherever she'd been, and was squinting at the screen as if she almost recognized him. Jacinta was glaring at the screen, her lips pressed tightly together. Nothing else.

On the screen, the image dissolved, to be replaced with a montage from the various cameras. We'd seen all of this before, but this time, instead of trying to make out distinguishing features, someone on my team—and I was guessing Marie—had focused on the man's athleticism, and capturing how his body moved through space. The various pieces of video had been recombined with that focus, and the images sharpened so we saw him in motion. Quick moments of a distinct figure in black moving against a softly blurred background. Then again in slow motion.

This time someone gasped. I was surprised to note it was

Jessup. Whose eyes had locked onto Dominic Marbach's face for a telling moment. Now she was carefully not looking at anyone in particular, and her face was a harsh mask.

Interesting. I hadn't expected that connection. Perhaps I should have.

Aiden's eyes flicked from Jessup to Dominic, and there was a split second expression on his face. There and gone again. Shocked comprehension. I could almost hear the click of that connection.

My eyes swept the table. There were no other reactions, though Gabriel was eyeing Aiden and Jessup thoughtfully.

Dominic's face was bland and he sat relaxed in his chair. He had himself well in hand. For now.

I glanced at Jacinta. Who didn't. She looked about to explode.

Good. The next move was mine.

———

I TAPPED a few keys on my laptop. The moving image of Duvant's midnight visitor froze, then dissolved. To be replaced by his partial-face image on the left side, and the full-face image of the killer on the right. Below them ran smaller images of the three Rembrandt—or fake Rembrandt—paintings we'd seen earlier.

All eyes were now fixed on the screen. Waiting.

As the seconds clicked away and the images didn't move, the feeling in the room changed from expectation to nervousness. The silence grew around me until it felt sticky. A nervous throat clearing from someone, more than a few sideways glances, and more silence.

I was watching the faces, weighing and discarding strategy. Just as it became clear that Inspector Gabriel's impatience was going to get the better of him, a voice from beside me surprised me. Annegret.

"It is not enough for me to say that none of this was my doing," she said slowly. "Not when there have been two murders—and who knows how many forgeries—connected to my gallery."

It was so unexpected I nearly panicked and tried to stop her.

Where was she going with this? It wasn't part of any strategy we'd discussed. And it didn't sound like anything I'd even considered.

Please tell me she wasn't going to confess to something that would destroy everything.

I should have had more faith.

Annegret met my gaze and gave me a tiny nod. Then she smiled like the shark she was.

"This is much bigger than my gallery," Annegret said. "This is about a criminal organization that has been eating our art community alive. World-wide."

Oh, she was good. She'd taken the strategy we'd developed together to clear her name, and used it as a springboard.

Gone from "I couldn't have done this" to recognizing the killer. Then used the shock and betrayal of realizing who that killer was to her as fuel. To challenge her accusers to admit the truth and solve it with her.

Annegret paused, and glanced around the table. Ignoring both of her lawyers. Her gaze lingered on Jacinta Roark. Who stared defiantly back. Looking far too pleased with herself, given the situation she was in.

I wondered exactly what Jacinta had planned. She must have anticipated at least the possibility of a trap? It was why I'd asked Inspector Gabriel to have men in plain clothes covering the entrances. And why I'd mentioned that conversation to Adrien when I invited him to this meeting.

Of course, I intended to net more than one bad guy here today. No matter what the others might have in mind.

So far it wasn't exactly working as I'd expected. I glanced around the table and my shoulder muscles tightened.

It wasn't going to work. We needed more.

Annegret must have thought so as well, because she played a card I hadn't expected her to realize she held.

She looked round the table, meeting each person's eyes as she spoke. "Each one of you is here because you are connected to this thing, in one way or another. And we need to take the whole mess apart, piece by piece. Player by player.

Thanks to the unrelenting efforts of Barbara O'Grady and her team, we have the evidence to arrest a killer. But that isn't enough. Really, Jacinta Roark is just a small player," she said, with a dismissive glance at her restorer. "Arresting her won't stop this thing."

I watched the killer bristle at Annegret's words, and tensed.

Ready for what came next.

"What do you mean?" snapped out the account manager from SaltonSecure. "Are you saying that somehow this is *our* fault? Our responsibility?"

"Isn't it?" Annegret shot back, her chin raised. "I was betrayed by a woman who'd worked for me for years. On my own property. I didn't see it. And your very expensive security apparently didn't see it either."

"That is surely not our fault," the woman said. "You hired the woman."

"I hired your firm, too," Annegret snapped back. "And yet, the surveillance cameras your firm recommended and installed sent me footage that had been doctored just enough so they didn't show what was going on."

"If the killer you hired managed to corrupt the cameras Salton-Secure installed, that is surely not our failing…"

"Oh, but it is," the VP said. "We charge the fees we do because we guarantee the level of security we provide. If we have failed here—as what I have heard so far suggests—then we will make it right. Whatever that takes."

"But our reputation…" the first woman bleated.

"Is being questioned in other areas, for issues very similar to this one," Jessup said, apparently having had enough of her.

Both of the executives from SaltonSecure froze and stared at her. Apparently Jessup's reputation—and the influence of the companies she represented—was well known here.

Annegret nodded. "Exactly. There is a bigger issue here. And uncovering Amara's killer, and whatever is going on at your firm, is just one tiny part of it."

The SaltonSecure account manager looked ready to argue with her again, but Inspector Gabriel beat her to it. "You cannot dismiss murder so easily. Convicting a ruthless killer is what matters here."

His words fell like anvils. Heavy. Final. Breaking apart every argument.

And he was wrong.

I caught Aiden and Jessup exchanging a speaking glance, but neither of them spoke.

I didn't either. Not yet.

Turns out I didn't need to. Annegret had the bit well and truly between her teeth. And she was running with it. Hard.

CHAPTER FORTY

"Killers are easy to hire," Annegret said in a clear voice. Keeping her attention on Inspector Gabriel.

Not even looking at Jacinta.

"And security companies come and go."

Annegret flicked a glance from one SaltonSecure executive to the other, then away as if they didn't matter either.

"We haven't even talked about the most crucial player in all of this," she said. "The brains behind it—their CEO, if you will. The one whose ideas and planning are behind this explosion of forgeries. That is who you should be focusing on. And searching for."

You go, Annegret, I cheered silently. She'd figured out who the players were, and she was baiting them. Regardless of what it cost her personally to do so. It could be our best chance to expose that CEO.

Or it could backfire on her.

I braced myself, ready to respond to either outcome. If she needed me.

And she might not, I realized, looking at Jacinta Roark. And the white lines forming around her mouth. Fury? Or fear, I decided.

Either could work.

I glanced back at Annegret. Who was now staring at Inspector Gabriel.

"This isn't some brilliant serial killer who is outsmarting everyone. She's a killer for hire. No more," she told him. Digging at Jacinta again.

Who glared at her, having lost all pretense of calm.

"You keep focusing on the obvious," Annegret said, still staring at the Inspector. And pointedly ignoring Jacinta. "First me. And now that my investigator has uncovered the real killer, you want to make it all about her."

Oh, this was good.

"This isn't about some serial killer you need to stop before she kills again," Annegret said again. Still digging. "She's a hireling. Following orders. And completely replaceable. It's the one behind it all who matters."

Gabriel's luxuriant mustache quivered, and he scowled at her. "I have yet to see a shred of proof that this CEO of yours even exists," he began.

Only to be cut off by a howl of protest from Jacinta.

"A hireling? Replaceable?" she spat out, rising from her chair and glaring at Annegret. "Who do you think you are dealing with? None of this would be possible without me."

Annegret sat back and gave her a cynical little smile. "I know exactly who I'm dealing with. I worked with you for decades, remember? So you can aim a gun and pull a trigger on command. Good for you. A trained monkey could do as much."

"A monkey? This is what you think of me?" Jacinta stretched herself taller, her voice rising even higher. "Me, I am an artist. A great one. Which you know. You have used my talents to build your business. But did you ever recognize me? My talents? No! You couldn't stand to see me know success as a brilliant artist."

Annegret stared at Jacinta. "I gave you a chance to work in the world you love. And paid you very, very well for the work you did."

"You did not pay me well enough. Not for the quality of those works. The knowledge. The skill. The *love* I poured into them."

"You are a talented restorer," Annegret said. "And an exceptional copyist. But an artist? No."

The slow shake of her head with which Annegret delivered these words was genius. It ignited what was clearly a long held resentment in Jacinta.

Who leaned forward and hissed at Annegret, "Those three paintings shown on the screen? Those masterpieces? I painted every stroke of those. All three of them. Including the one that your beloved Arturo authenticated."

At Jacinta's words, the woman from XTC Tech drew in a harsh breath.

The two former colleagues ignored it, eyes locked together.

"As I stated earlier," Annegret said calmly. "You are an exceptional copyist. But you lack originality. This CEO of yours has shown far more creativity in the criminal enterprise he has built than you have in any painting you've ever done."

Jacinta let out a little shriek, and clutched her heart, as if she'd been stabbed. She was playing a role on a screen of her own. But her eyes never left Annegret's.

"He is not my CEO. He is my partner. And he has not the slightest hint of creativity in him. Only those stupid spreadsheets and legal papers."

At her words, Inspector Gabriel and Aiden exchanged glances across the table, but Jacinta was too caught up in her drama to notice.

"*I* am the genius," she said. "*He...*" and she waved a dismissive hand at Dominic Marback. Who was sitting very still, his face a mask. "He is useful, no more. And so, so boring. All he cares about is the money."

Other eyes were shifting to Dominic now. I saw shock, disbelief and incomprehension, but only one face showed fear. The account manager from SaltonSecure

A quick glance told me Aidan and Annegret had both caught that fleeting expression, though I thought Gabriel had missed it from where he stood by the door.

Annegret looked pissed, so I was pretty sure I could rely on her to push that one harder. If it was needed. If Jacinta didn't manage to implicate everyone involved first.

The killer wasn't even looking at the others in the room. Still standing, she was too wound up in her list of grievances to realize the impact of her words. And seemingly too determined to bring Annegret down.

"I, on the other hand? I care only about art. Art must be recognized," Jacinta proclaimed, and flung her arms wide. "Genius cannot be squashed by uncaring avarice day after day, not without consequences. As you see."

Her eyes narrowed, drilling into Annegret. "And you have to know—this is all your fault. You refused to recognize a true artist. At least Dominic acknowledges my genius for what it is."

He was probably acknowledging a few other things about her at the moment, too, I thought. The lawyer's face still showed nothing —nor, for that matter, did his sister's—but I watched in glee as Gabriel's head swung to focus on the two of them.

The Inspector hadn't missed that one.

By now, Annegret's lawyer was probably regretting that he'd ever involved Jacinta Roark in anything.

From numerous watchings of the teenager's video clip, I'd been pretty certain the taller bad guy had been Dominic. I was even more certain he hadn't expected Jacinta to shoot Amara Duvant. That had not been part of his plan.

I wondered if the same held true for Arturo Benjamin's murder. Had M. Benjamin recognized something in the paintings, made the connection to Jacinta? Then confronted her with the fraud?

I didn't see how. But when the likely answers are eliminated, all that's left is the truth.

And she'd shot him for it.

Looking at her now, that wasn't hard to believe. After that first kill, I suspected anyone who challenged Jacinta's view of her own art became a target.

In the end, Dominic's reasons for being involved in this scheme might prove more interesting.

Though I did wonder where—and why—Jacinta had learned to shoot so accurately. She hadn't even hesitated to pull the trigger on Amara Duvant. Whom had she killed before now?

Annegret wasn't done with Jacinta yet, either. "You call yourself an artist? Say you care about art? " she said in a tone that had her one-time friend's eyes locking on her face. "Yet you're proud of killing M. Benjamin? Someone so far above you in talent…" She stopped. "There is no point."

"I never said I was proud of it," Jacinta fired back. "I loved him too. But he gave me no choice. He knew. He knew it all, from one look at those paintings you showed us. And instead of acknowledging my art, my *genius,* he was all sorrowful, all 'I hate to expose you, but this cannot continue'. He had to die. He would have tried to stop me—us—and that could not be. Even Dominic admitted I had no choice."

And there was Dominic, neatly trapped. Thank you, Annegret.

Any chance Jacinta would go for a trifecta? She'd left rational thought behind a while ago. I decided it was worth the gamble.

"And yet there was nothing on the security video," I said. "You must have planned his murder, if you knew to shut off those cameras ahead of time."

Jacinta's head whipped around so that she faced me. I'd been concerned that it was her fury with Annegret that was fueling her outburst, and that distracting her would break the spell. I needn't have worried.

Jacinta's outrage simply spread like a pool to encompass me. She was so angry, her eyes seemed to glow with it. "A second rate artist like you would think so, wouldn't you? Jealousy of my talent, that's all. The lies you've spun for her? Annegret's little lap dog. All jealousy. You'd never believe that talent such as mine attracts others, those who will help. They wiped the video for me, of course."

"You're the one who is lying," I said.

Jacinta tried to incinerate me with those eyes, then swung her attention to the pair from SaltonSecure.

"Tell her, Beatrice," she said to Annegret's account manager, as the VP looked between the two of them with horrified eyes. "Tell her how you erased that video after I shot him."

———

THINGS HAPPENED FAST AFTER THAT. Aidan moved to stand shoulder to shoulder with the Inspector, while Jessup took his place by the window. Judging by her fierce expression, she'd reached the same conclusion I had—on this floor, the only way out would involve narrow window ledges, uneven roof lines, and a death defying leap or two. And of everyone in the room, Dominic Marbach was the only one with both the height and the athleticism to successfully make that escape. Clearly, Jessup intended to make sure that no one—no matter who they were—was getting out that way.

The account manager from SaltonSecure, Beatrice Jenson, looked too cowed to make a move, but I kept an eye on her all the same.

Before we knew it, the room was full of cantonal police, and Inspector Gabriel was arresting all three of the conspirators.

Dominic hadn't said a word, and his sister was equally stony faced. I'd have liked to see her arrested, too, just on principle, but being obnoxious isn't exactly grounds. I wondered what she was thinking, and if she'd known what he was up to.

Jacinta was still throwing out insults and naming names, even after they read her what I assume were her rights. My French isn't good enough to follow the legalese in the midst of all the commotion, but her expression told me all I needed to know.

CHAPTER FORTY-ONE

Hours later I was back in my hotel room, standing looking out at the storm tossed waters of the lake. The clouds overhead were nearly black and the wind had risen. We were in for the storm that had been threatening all day.

The weather matched my mood. I should be on top of the world, but I was too drained to feel much other than a driving need for solitude.

I was just glad I had nowhere else to be, nothing I needed to investigate. The case was finally over.

Except for the inevitable legal proceedings, which would undoubtedly grind slowly through the system. I didn't care. I could fly in if needed, but for now, I had nothing I had to do. Nowhere I had to be.

The aftermath of that afternoon's meeting had entailed hours at the police station, then Aiden and Jessup had invited me for dinner. Annegret had overheard and had insisted on joining us and paying for everything, including several bottles of a vintage champagne that sparkled and bit at the same time. It was the best I'd ever tasted, and the meal they'd ordered between them? Well.

Despite my exhaustion, my taste buds were still doing a happy dance.The rest of me wanted to crawl into bed and pull the covers over my head.

The memory that stuck with me, though, was when Annegret confirmed that Arturo Benjamin had indeed met her restorer several times over the years, had actually purchased one of Jacinta's own paintings many years before.

"He must have recognized something in it," she said, looking baffled and deeply sad.

Somewhere in the chaos I'd texted Marie, who had booked my flight for the following afternoon. I was going home.

But first, I needed sleep.

Then my phone warbled. I grimaced. Answering that phone was the last thing I felt like doing. But habit is a funny thing, especially in concert with a sense of duty. I walked back to the desk and dug it out of my purse.

Glancing at the number, I was glad I had.

"Nick," I said as I sank into the comfy chair by the window. "Where are you?"

"Not home yet," he said.

I could tell he was trying for levity, but he sounded more dispirited than I'd ever heard him. Despite that, it was so good to hear his voice.

It was only four days since I'd last talked to him, but it felt so much longer. Too much had happened. For both of us, from the sound of it.

"How did it go?" I asked, trying to kept the concern out of my voice.

"I'm looking forward to being home," was all he said.

"Me too." I said, meaning it. "When do you get in?'

"Tomorrow evening. You?"

I checked the itinerary Marie had sent. "Same. Around eight p.m. How about you?"

"Close enough. How about I buy you a drink in the Footloose Lounge? You can tell me how your case went."

"Only if you order for me. I'll probably get stuck in customs forever."

"Done. Red wine?"

"Make it Scotch. A double."

"Great minds," was all he said. Meaning whatever he'd been involved with had been as bad, or worse, than my case. Which his tone had already told me.

"I'll see you there," I said. "We can share a cab, if you want to stay over." The thought made me smile.

"Now you're talking," he said, a touch of his usual humor in his voice. "I might just survive the flight, with that to look forward to."

"Sweet talker," I said, playing to it. "It's the Scotch that's going to get me through."

He laughed then, and wished me good night. Then I was left with empty air space and an emptier hotel room.

Thinking how good it would feel to be able to just say "then we can go home together." I'm not sure how it happened, but tonight, this whole living together thing sounded like a really good idea.

Apparently it was growing on me.

———

WHEN MY FLIGHT finally touched down in Vancouver, I felt relieved, but also disconnected. As though having left Geneva and crossed so many time zones, I no longer belonged anywhere. The abrupt end of a case—no matter how successful—that had absorbed all my attention for such an intense period, only fed that feeling.

The whole process of deplaning, being herded off the plane then making my way as part of a crowd winding through the long corridors and immense spaces of the international terminal only increased that feeling. It was nice to be greeted by carved totem poles and the sound of flowing water, but no matter how well-designed their niches, these elements of my homeland seemed lost in the vastness of the airport. Or maybe that was me.

When I finally made it through customs and more escalators and corridors to the lounge where Nick waited, all I could think of was that Scotch. I didn't even feel up to talking to him right now, not with all we'd left unsaid between us the last time I'd seen him.

Then I rounded a pillar. And there he was. Sitting half-slouched at a table on the far side, two glasses in front of him. One half-empty, the other, glinting gold, full. For me?

He didn't see me. Half turned away, his gaze seemed fixed on something that wasn't there. Yet there was no mistaking that wave of dark hair, those broad shoulders. Nick.

He looked the way I felt. Only more so. Some cases will do that to you.

The incessant din of the busy airport fell away, and all I saw was him. My eyes on him, my steps sped up. My concerns about seeing him fell away, and I reconnected with a snap I could almost hear.

The first part of our meeting was intense, and we both said some things that had needed saying for a long time. Both of us were too wrung out from our respective cases to hold back. It wasn't until we were on our second Scotches that we even mentioned those cases.

He still didn't say much about his. "It's over. Let it rest," he said briefly with a dark look and I knew it had been a bad one.

"But tell me about your case," he said, shaking off that darkness. "I take it that it went well?"

"I'm not sure well is the word," I said, and summarized what I'd been dealing with for the last few days. In trying to lighten the telling a little for him—focusing on the various people I'd interacted with—I found closure for myself. It had been an ugly case, but it, too, was done.

"And Dominic's reasons?" Nick asked when I was done. "Were they more interesting than Jacinta's?"

I shook my head, drank a little more Scotch. The subtle burn warmed me. "Not in the least. Sadly, his reasons for the criminal empire he'd been building were as banal—and as ugly—as his co-conspirator's."

If colder. But I didn't need to say those last words. Nick understood.

He nodded once. "Greed."

"That's the one," I said. "Coupled with few, if any, morals. He had the access, he knew about art as investment, knew the players. He saw a way to make money, and he took it."

"So why target Annegret's gallery?" he asked.

"That was simple," I said. "She was a client, so he had inside knowledge. He found Annegret's gallery to be a very convenient source. And Jacinta—who was useful to him—was pleased to betray Annegret. So why not?"

"A well-positioned sociopath," was Nick's summary. "And Jacinta?"

I made a face and slugged back some whiskey. Which is an insult to good whiskey, but the smooth, slightly peaty depth was the only thing that could scrub away the taste of this case.

"Dominic underestimated just how deep Jacinta's need for revenge ran. She didn't care about his fraud scheme, or that he and his team were unknowingly stealing her copied works from Carli Fine Arts, and replacing them with identical copies," I said.

"She was copying her own frauds? How did that work?" he asked with a small frown, as if he was trying to picture it.

I grinned, despite everything. "Dominic would identify which "masterpiece" he wanted from the Da Carli gallery—which was actually a copy Jacinta had done for Annegret before the painting was ever hung there. Then Amara and Jana would sneak that painting down to the cellar after hours, carefully photographing every detail of the painting, front and back using a high resolution digital camera."

"Why the back?"

"Because there are unique markings on the edges of old canvases which are normally hidden under the frame. Insurance companies keep records of those markings, and use them to verify an original from a copy."

"Except that good forgers copy those, too?"

"Exactly," I said wryly. "Especially when they are officially restorers."

He nodded. "Okay. Then what?"

"Then Amara and Jana would reframe the painting, take it back upstairs and rehang it in the gallery. Once Jacinta had completed her copy, Amara or Jana again took the gallery copy of the painting down to the cellar, painstakingly removed it from its frame, and substituted the fresh copy Jacinta had made for Dominic in its place. That supposed masterpiece—which was actually the copy Jacinta originally made for Annegret to display—was carried out in those plastic tubes that Amara was sneaking out of the gallery."

Nick just shook his head at it. "What did Jacinta make of this process?"

"I gather she was highly amused by it all. Her mission was to prove her own artistic genius, and to embarrass and discredit Annegret. All that mattered to her was that her paintings—her copies of the great masters—be accepted everywhere as genuine."

"Which they were?" Nick looked less exhausted now, and his eyes sparked with the genuine interest of a good detective recognizing a hot lead.

"Oh yeah. At first, anyway. Some of them were challenged on a deeper evaluation, but Dominic's schemes had blurred the provenance so well that the immediate history didn't help the investigators."

"Until Jacinta?" he asked with grin that looked almost natural.

"Until Jacinta," I said.

I couldn't manage a smile that wouldn't look like a grimace, so I didn't bother. "Jacinta didn't care. If her actions ended up exposing Dominic's schemes, or getting him killed by some of those less-than-honest customers—so be it. He was motivated by greed. She wasn't. Though I have no doubt she talked a good game to him when they teamed up."

Nick drank a slow swallow of his whiskey, clearly picturing this. "Dominic thought he was running things, building a forgery ring using a number of very talented copyists that even Interpol couldn't find or take down," he said. "And she was pursuing her own ends."

"You got it," I said. "And Jacinta's ends didn't exactly align with Dominic's, whatever she might have convinced him of."

"She's the reason for all the rumors about your client's gallery?"

"Oh, yeah. Jacinta wanted to punish Annegret. No matter what."

"Annegret is probably lucky you figured it all out when you did," he said. "She would likely have been next."

I nodded. "Probably."

"And the sister? Was she involved?"

"Elise Marback? No, surprisingly. Dominic seems to have found her useful in distracting attention from his schemes, but she was his dupe. She may have been aware something was wrong on some level, but never admitted it even to herself. Which I suspect made her nastier than she might otherwise have been. She really loves him."

Nick frowned, slugged back some whisky. "Those kind of illogical patterns make one hell of a tough case to solve."

"Tell me about it," I said.

Just hearing him say that made something inside me start to unwind. He was right. It had been one hell of a case. And it was over. Finally.

I couldn't tell him, but Nick understood. I could see it in his eyes.

Just like I understood that he wasn't yet ready to tell me even that much about his own case.

"Jacinta Roark was definitely not operating in the realms of logic anymore," was all I said. "If she ever had."

"Poor woman," Nick said.

Something in his tone made me wonder who in his recent case had been struggling with mental health issues. But I didn't ask. He'd talk when he was ready.

I nodded. Now that it was over, and Jacinta was likely to spend the rest of her life behind locked doors, unable to kill again, I could find it in me to feel compassion for a woman whose passion for art had fed her delusions until she no longer recognized any kind of limit.

And the truly sad thing was, she had the skills and the eye of a true artist—if something in her life had been different, she might have been a major talent.

For a moment I wondered if they'd let her paint in prison. And whether, in that circumstance, she'd find the originality that, together with her technical skills, might even result in a true masterpiece. Or at least some stunning paintings.

CHAPTER FORTY-TWO

Nick and I spent the weekend together, and the following Monday morning I dragged myself into the office. Sunshine and driving down Granville with that spectacular view of snow dusting the North Shore mountains had me feeling at least awake by the time I arrived.

To be greeted by Marie's smiling face.

And I was happy to see her.

Badger was in, too—early for her. And Cory. I didn't even ask what my nephew was doing in the office on a school morning. Probably that would cost me later. But it was a price I was willing to pay.

The pastries I'd picked up at a little Swiss place on Burrard that Giselle had recommended—some cousin of a friend of a friend had raved about their baking—were a hit. Cory made the coffee, and we spread everything out in the meeting room, while I debriefed them on that final meeting in Geneva.

They all knew the outcome, but it seemed we all—me included —needed to revisit the details, and discuss exactly how the denouement had unfolded, and what the triggers had been.

"Until that teenager's video, we didn't have enough to save

Annegret, never mind see the key players arrested," I said with a nod to Badger. "Good find, that one."

She grinned, and shrugged at me, as if to say 'all in a day's work'. And for her, it probably was.

"Annegret has already paid us," Marie said. "The money's in the checking account, at least for now."

"Good to know, thanks," I told her. I'd been amazed to discover that Marie, of all people, was both comfortable with and capable of handling our finances so efficiently. But it sure made my life easier.

"Good, since Badger has probably spent most of it on her new toys," I quipped, and got a wider grin in return.

Marie shook her head at both of us. "Annegret called to pass on her thanks, and she sounded good. Despite everything."

'Everything' probably included some hits our client had taken from the police at all levels over her borderline illegal "security system" for her most valuable works. Given how instrumental she'd been in exposing Dominic's fraud ring, they were prepared to overlook it, though. As long as she implemented a new, much higher level security system. Immediately. One that didn't include copying masterpieces.

Which Annegret was now more than happy to do. She told me before I left that she'd already fired SaltonSecure and hired a firm Interpol had recommended to set her systems up right.

"And Badger and I finished looking into the local affiliate of SaltonSecure," Marie continued. "And they're not involved."

"Squeaky clean," Cory added with a grin that said he'd figured out a few things. Including who Andrea was dating.

That was probably inevitable. But I was too relieved not to have to tell Andrea she was dating a crook to care.

"Thanks," I said, and raised my coffee cup in a toast to all three of them.

"You should know that they're still tracking down the fraud ring," Badger said. "Your Inspector Gabriel…"

"He's hardly mine," I interjected—and she grinned and ignored me.

"...he's working with Aiden at Interpol, finally, and the arrests continue, in an ever-widening circle," she finished. "His latest report's on your desk, along with a translation."

I nearly asked how she'd managed that, but what was the point? The answer would either be illegal or beyond me. Or both. "Thanks," I said.

"And your new laptop is there, too," she added. "Cory will..."

"I get to show you," he broke in. "It's got all these great features. And wait 'til you see how fast this thing is!"

Badger gave him a look, and he subsided.

"Thank you both, but I'm sure it can wait until tomorrow," I began. Only to find myself the recipient of Badger's look.

"This case has proven how inadequate our security is against some of what's out there now," she said. "We're all using the new laptops. You need to, as well. Before our next case walks in that door and proves even more dangerous."

I couldn't exactly argue with that. Much as I wanted to. Instead I changed the subject. "Our security may have needed an upgrade," I said. "But our teamwork sure didn't."

I looked around the table. "In fact, we worked pretty well together, despite the distance and the time pressure we were under. I'm very grateful for the work all of you did," I said. Then broke the moment with a wave towards the pastries. "Have another pastry. You deserve it."

Marie, nearly as elegant as Justine these days, grinned at me. Cory made a face. Badger just shook her head. But all of them reached for a pastry.

Seems the cousin of Giselle's friend's friend had been right—the Swiss pastries were authentic. And exceptional. I'd brought more than enough for everyone, but by the time we'd finished, there were only crumbs left.

AUTHOR'S NOTE

It's hard to believe that this is the seventh book in Barbara's series, and that it has been so long since the last one was published. Other stories, and well, life—complete with a worldwide pandemic—got in the way. Welcome back to all of you who hung in for Barbara's latest adventure.

You may notice a different cover style on this book. We're rebranding the series, and I've added an extra personal touch. Since I know Vancouver well, the covers are based on some of my own photos.

Many thanks go to Linda Roggeveen for her talented copy edit. Any errors or omissions are, of course, mine.